The New War

The face of the enemy has changed. His weapon is terror; his target is the innocent. The first strike could come at any time—and the deadliest, most undetectable weapon that ever prowled the oceans' depths is going back to war . . . and the battleground is the Middle East.

The *U.S.S. Ohio* has new weapons and astonishing new capabilities—and her officers and crew are being dispatched, along with a SEAL team, to destroy a poisonous viper in its lair. A fanatic hardliner has risen to the top of Iran's ruling mullahs—and he and his terrorist allies now possess the nuclear capability to deal the U.S. a devastating blow.

Now the *Ohio* has to end the threat while sailing dangerously narrow and shallow waters in the Straits of Hormuz. The time to strike is now . . . or never.

D1115179

The Silent Service
by H. Jay Riker

OHIO CLASS
VIRGINIA CLASS
SEAWOLF CLASS
LOS ANGELES CLASS
GRAYBACK CLASS

THE SILENT SERVICE

OHIO CLASS

H. JAY RIKER

AVON BOOKS

An Imprint of HarperCollinsPublishers

AVON BOOKS
An Imprint of HarperCollins*Publishers*
10 East 53rd Street
New York, New York 10022-5299

Copyright © 2006 by Bill Fawcett and Associates
ISBN-13: 978-0-06-052439-5
ISBN-10: 0-06-052439-1
www.avonbooks.com

First Avon Books paperback printing: August 2006

Avon Trademark Reg. U.S. Pat. Off. and in Other Countries, Marca Registrada, Hecho en U.S.A.
HarperCollins® is a registered trademark of HarperCollins Publishers Inc.

Printed in the U.S.A.

10 9 8 7 6 5 4 3 2 1

For Brea,
who believed in me

THE
SILENT
SERVICE

OHIO CLASS

PROLOGUE

Tuesday, 27 May 2008

Delta Pier
Naval Intermediate Maintenance Facility
Puget Sound Naval Shipyard
Bangor, Washington
1925 hours PST

Once, she had been the most powerful, the most terrifying weapon on Earth.

She rested at her berth at the Puget Sound Naval Yard, quiescent now, but still conveying a somewhat ominous, even sinister feeling through her dark-gray hull plating, her sheer size, and the knowledge of what she once had been.

Commander Keith H. Stewart approached the head of the pier. A Marine sentry snapped to port arms in front of him. "Halt! Who goes there?"

"Captain Stewart, son," he replied. He nodded toward

the bulk of the huge vessel, silhouetted against a glorious orange sunset. "I'm her skipper."

"Sir! Advance and be recognized."

Stewart stepped closer.

"Sir! May I see your papers, sir!"

It was not a question, but a demand. Stewart studied the Marine as he handed over his ID and the authorization that permitted him to be on this highly sensitive and restricted bit of boardwalk. Since 9/11, over six years before, security at all U.S. military installations had been tight . . . and the security for nukes was tighter still.

The Marine—he couldn't be more than twenty, Stewart thought—completed his inspection of ID and pass, returned them, brought his rifle to a crisp right-shoulder arms, and delivered a rifle salute so sharp Stewart could have sworn he heard the air snap. "Sir! I recognize you, sir! You may pass, sir!"

"Thank you, son." Slowly, he walked past the sentry post, moving closer to the looming bulk of the vessel moored to the pier. Other Marine sentries stood farther down the pier, and on the deck of the vessel herself. Farther out in the harbor, a patrol boat maintained her watch.

On the *Ohio*'s deck, a working party was loading supplies down the forward logistics hatch. At the moment, a dockside crane was lowering a supply pallet gently toward the upstretched hands of half a dozen dungaree-clad sailors, who together swayed the pallet inboard and down the open hatch at their feet.

He looked up at her sail, towering above the steady lap of wavelets at the waterline. Magnetic numerals adhered to the side beneath the weather bridge: 726.

My command . . .

Familiarly known as a "boomer," slang for any ballistic missile submarine, the USS *Ohio*, SSBN-726, had once carried twenty-four Trident II D-5 ICBMs, each delivering fourteen MIRVed nuclear warheads across a range of up to six thousand nautical miles with astonishing accuracy, able to place them to within four hundred feet of any designated target. Packing 150 kilotons of destructive capability apiece, those 336 individual warheads together amounted to a total of almost four megatons—over 2,500 Hiroshimas packed into a single vessel 560 feet in length and forty-two feet wide at the beam.

The *Ohio,* the lead ship of her class, had been launched on 7 April 1979, and commissioned on Veteran's Day of 1981, under the command of Captain A. K. Thompson. For over two decades the *Ohio,* joined year by year by the sister ships of the class, had fought a singular and vital campaign of the Cold War. Those eighteen Ohio-class boomers saw to it that at any given moment enough sheer megatonnage to annihilate the Soviet Union or any other potential nuclear enemy was patrolling *somewhere* out in the dark depths of the world ocean, utterly silent, undetected by the enemy's attack subs and ASW forces. Even an overwhelming nuclear strike against the United States and all of her forces worldwide could not hope to kill all of those hidden boomers, which carried half of the total U.S. deterrent strike force.

The strategy was known as MAD—the singularly apt acronym for Mutual Assured Destruction—and the Ohio boats played their part in assuring that the nukes never flew, mushroom clouds never blossomed above the world's cities, and civilization—indeed, humankind—survived the forty-four years of the Cold War, until the collapse of the Soviet Empire in 1989. Somehow, and against all expectations, nuclear deterrence had worked. *Ohio* had deployed on sixty-one deterrent patrols.

But with the reduction of the Russian nuclear threat had come new treaties, and a general trend toward disarmament, part of the promise of the so-called "peace dividend." America's boomer fleet would be reduced to fourteen boats.

Ohio and three of her sisters—the *Michigan,* the *Florida,* and the *Georgia*—would not be decommissioned, however. *Ohio* had recently emerged from a year-long overhaul at Puget Sound, with extensive upgrades to her sonar, fire control, and navigation systems. The original plans had called for her to be retired in 2002, but the rise of terrorism worldwide had suggested a new strategy.

In November 2002 the *Ohio* had entered drydock to begin a long refueling and conversion overhaul. Early in 2008 her conversion from SSBN to SSGN had been completed, and she'd rejoined the Pacific Submarine Force as a conventional missile submarine.

Instead of multikiloton nukes, she now carried vertical launch systems for up to 154 BGM-109 Tomahawk cruise missiles, and various other specialized payload packages. Two of her twenty-four launch tubes had been converted to swimmer lockout and equipment tubes. The refitted boat was superbly equipped and outfitted to conduct Special Warfare operations anywhere in the world.

The old girl was still a force to be reckoned with.

Stewart passed inspection with another Marine sentry at the bow, then started up the bunting-draped gangway toward the temporary in-port quarterdeck abaft the sail. As he strode toward his command, a boatswain's pipe shrilled, and he heard a voice announce from a loudspeaker, "Now hear this, now hear this. *Ohio,* arriving."

It was the time-honored formula announcing the arrival of a captain on board his ship.

They'd said the fall of the old Soviet Union would

make the world a safer place. "They," as usual, had been wrong. Stewart certainly didn't mourn the Soviets' passing, but without the superpower balance, the situation throughout the world had gone rapidly from bad to worse. The danger of all-out nuclear holocaust might have lessened somewhat, but there were still plenty of weapons out there in the hands of rogue states and power-hungry dictators, and the possibility of mischance had been magnified enormously.

The real wild cards, though, were al-Qaeda and the other terror groups constantly seeking power and recognition, seeking confrontation with the hated United States, seeking revenge for Afghanistan and Iraq, ever seeking a means of successfully waging war against the world's only remaining superpower. They were destabilizing, they were deadly, and the threat of nuclear force didn't work with them. By going underground in cities all over the world, al-Qaeda and the others could carry on their clandestine operations secure in the knowledge that the United States would never incinerate a city filled with innocent bystanders in order to take them down.

But in the *Ohio*, phoenix-risen in her new configuration, America possessed a new and potent weapon in her arsenal against the terrorists and the rogue states.

Stewart saluted the ensign hanging from the flagstaff aft, then returned the waiting salute of the Officer of the Deck. "Welcome aboard, Captain," Lieutenant James Piper, the boat's weapons officer, said.

"Thank you, Weps," Stewart replied. "It's good to be aboard."

The world, he thought, was shortly going to become a more dangerous place . . . for the terrorists.

Tuesday, 27 May 2008

SEAL Team Detachment Echo
Near Bandar-e Charak, Iran
2204 hours Zulu

Lieutenant Christopher Wolfe dropped behind the illusory shelter of a boulder outcropping, scanning the ridge crest above and behind them, his H&K MP5SD at his shoulder. Through his night vision goggles the sky appeared as a pale, luminous green backdrop, the hillside as a black and rugged silhouette. No sign yet of—

Movement! A figure, dark green against the sky, emerged from behind the ridge, wearing a short-billed service cap and carrying an AK-47. Wolfe shifted the aim on his H&K; his NVGs revealed the otherwise invisible spot of red light marking his aim point, which he planted squarely on the target's center of mass. He tapped the trigger, and his sound-suppressed weapon gave a stuttering hiss, sending a quick-spaced three rounds into the target just as it emerged fully from the cover of the hilltop.

The target flopped backward, the AK flying end over end through the night.

"Echo One-one," Wolfe said, identifying himself over the Motorola strapped to his combat harness. The needle mike secured just in front of his lips transmitted every word to the other members of his squad, and to his far larger audience elsewhere. "Contact! North ridge, bearing zero-zero-five. Tango down."

In Wolfe's specialized lexicon, tango could mean either *terrorist* or *target*. Usually, in his line of work, the two were synonymous; this time, though, he wasn't facing terrorists, but an enemy far more dangerous to him, his men, and his mission.

"Echo One-five," a voice said over the speaker in Wolfe's ear. One-five was Machinist's Mate First Class Danny French. "Multiple contacts, at two-eight-zero. Tango down! Correction, two tangos down!"

Tangos to the north, tangos to the west. The bastards were moving to cut the team off from the sea.

"Echo One! Fall back! Fall back!" Another target appeared on the north ridge, and Wolfe tapped him down. "On the double! *Move!*"

Chris Wolfe was a SEAL, a member of the elite naval commando unit deriving its acronymic name from the words Sea, Air, and Land, the elements within which the Teams routinely operated. From their first day of Basic Underwater Demolition School—BUD/S—SEALs were hammered with a particular piece of life-saving indoctrination: *The water is your friend. When you're in trouble, get to the water.*

SEAL Team Detachment Echo One was in very bad trouble now, but the sea was less than a mile away.

The question was whether they would be able to reach it in time.

Special Operations Watch Center
Pentagon Basement
Arlington, Virginia
1704 hours EST

"Thank you for coming down, Captain," the intelligence analyst said. "We appear to be watching the proverbial shit hit the fan. Thought you would want to see. . . ."

Captain Thomas Garrett sized up the speaker in a glance—a small and wiry individual with a bushy mustache just barely regulation in its exuberance. The three gold stripes above the cuff of each sleeve identified him as a naval commander, a rank not usually given access to the deliberations held within such deep and clandestine electronic fortresses as this. The bulky eagle and trident pin on the breast of his uniform, however—his "Budweiser"—marked him as a Navy SEAL. His name was Carl Berkowitz, and he was one of the Navy's premier spooks in the ONI—the Office of Naval Intelligence.

"I do indeed, Commander," Garrett replied. "Thank you."

A dozen men and women sat at as many work stations around the basement communications center, with a dozen more high-ranking officers—admirals and captains, generals and colonels, most of them—watching over their shoulders. Several civilians were present as well, some in suits, some in shirtsleeves. Most of the audience's attention was focused on a single large display screen on the wall, a green-lit monochrome image of several men running down a steep hillside, viewed from high overhead.

"So what's going on?" Garrett asked. He'd known the op was going down tonight, but no details.

Berkowitz pointed at the monitor. "We're aborting. Two hours, seventeen minutes into the op. Damn it."

"What happened?"

"Echo One ran into some unexpected opposition. We think it's Pasdaran. A Guards unit that moved into the area without our seeing it. Our people have been engaged in a fighting withdrawal back to the beach."

"Shit."

"Exactly."

Garrett watched the scene unfold on the screen. The detail, even with infrared imaging, was startling. He could see the individual members of the SEAL unit designated Echo One working their way rapidly down the hillside, two men moving from one position of cover to the next while two more held their ground and covered their retreat, then switching off in a deadly game of leapfrog. But another four weren't playing. Garrett could see two men, each hauling another in a fireman's carry across their shoulders.

Two casualties. It could have been worse, he thought. Then he added to himself, *But it might get a hell of a lot worse, too.*

Voices crackled from speakers overhead, voices ragged with exhaustion and edged with stress.

"Okay! We're set! Move! Move! Move!"

"Echo One-one, Echo One-seven! Shooters! Shooters on the north ridge, more shooters on the crest to the west! We're taking fire!"

"One-seven, One-one! Never mind the shooters! Just keep moving!"

One of the technicians made an adjustment, and the image zoomed in on one of the SEALs. Though grainy and taken from an awkward angle overhead, the image clearly showed a man in combat vest and balaclava, wearing a night vision headset and carrying an H&K MP5SD submachine gun, the heavy length of its integral sound suppressor unmistakable. The man was crouched behind a boulder, loosing short, precisely controlled bursts of fire at an off-screen enemy. Garrett could see empty cartridges, aglow with heat, spinning clear of the weapon's receiver three at a time. The picture drifted, zoomed in and out, then pulled back to show a broader view once more.

"Good detail," Garrett observed. "Satellite?"

"Hell no," Berkowitz replied with a shake of the head. "UAVs. Better than satellites. They stay put. We have three of 'em up, off the *Sirocco*."

"Ah." Yeah, he should have known. Spy satellites were good, but they couldn't resolve an individual expended 9mm cartridge, even by infrared. Garrett turned his attention to the words appearing on-screen along the bottom of the picture—date, time, GPS positioning data, altitude . . . right. That was a UAV feed, real-time data from an Unmanned Aerial Vehicle orbiting eight hundred feet above the battle area—a Navy Fire Scout, to be exact. Since Afghanistan, UAVs of various types— all-but-invisible aerial recon platforms—had become more vital in the observation and control of the modern battlefield.

"Take cover!" A new, frenzied shouting erupted from the overhead speakers. *"RPG! RPG!"*

On the screen, a brilliant white point of light streaked in from the upper right, then detonated in a silent, blossoming flare. One of the SEALs carrying a wounded buddy fell, knocked forward by the blast, which sent the two tumbling down the slope. Two more SEALs rushed to their aid, as others turned their weapons toward this latest threat.

Garrett saw Berkowitz leaning forward, his lips moving in some unvoiced command . . . or prayer. Fellow SEALS, Garrett thought. Those are his brothers out there.

"Let's see number three," one of the other watchers, a lean and weathered-looking civilian, said in a dry voice with a touch of New England to it. The scene on the display screen switched to another aerial view, this one of a large number of armed troops advancing along the crest of a ridge. They were accompanied by several vehicles, trucks and Russian-built BMP-2 armored fighting vehicles, the heat from their engines showing white against the cooler green backdrop. Two of the figures on the ground carried the unmistakable sewer-pipe bulk of a loaded RPG-7.

"Damn it!" a Marine general growled from nearby. "Can't we take those things out?"

"Negative, sir," the technician replied. "All three platforms are dry."

Fire Scout UAVs could and often did mount a pair of detachable munitions pods, each carrying four 2.75-inch Hydra 70 rockets. This battle evidently had been going on for some time, now, and apparently all of the munitions had already been expended.

"How long until help gets there?" a heavyset man in an admiral's uniform demanded. He was Vincent Forsythe of Naval Special Warfare Command, the man ultimately in command of this operation.

"Sierra Foxtrot Four-one is en route, sir," a woman's voice replied. "ETA fifty-three minutes."

The exchange was cool and professional, but Garrett could hear, could *feel,* the tension growing. American combat personnel, Navy SEALs, were ashore on the southwestern coast of Iran just west of the Straits of Hormuz, near the port of Bandar-e Charak. Operation Black Stallion had been planned and under preparation for months now, rehearsed and rehearsed again until each move unfolded with the precise choreography of a ballet.

But something had gone wrong, *terribly* wrong, and the dancers were falling.

"Tell Echo Two to get their asses in gear," Admiral Forsythe said. "Echo One is getting cut to pieces."

A moment later they heard the curt reply from the speaker. *"Echo Two. We're moving."*

Black Stallion consisted of three elements. Two Cyclone-class coastal patrol craft, the *Sirocco,* PC-6, and the *Firebolt,* PC-10, lay just offshore, waiting to retrieve the SEALs. The eight men of Echo One had swum ashore from the *Sirocco* over three hours ago and made their way to the objective, but now were falling back to the beach. Echo Two was a second eight-man SEAL squad deployed off the *Firebolt* as a rear security element. They were redeploying now to reinforce the hard-pressed Echo One, but it would be minutes more before they could enter the fight.

And even when they did, how would it help? Sixteen men, three of them wounded, against what looked like a battalion-strength force—six or eight hundred men at least. SEALs were the world's premier special operations force, but they were *not* frontline troops to be thrown away in a pitched, stand-up battle. An old maxim of special ops declared that any covert mission ending in gunfire was a failure; the idea was to get in, do the deed, and get out undetected.

"What else do we have in the AO?" Garrett asked Berkowitz, whispering. "What backup?"

"Nothing at the beach but the PBCs," Berkowitz admitted. "The *Kitty Hawk* is outside the Straits of Hormuz . . . five hundred miles away. And the *Pittsburgh* is transiting the straits now. About forty miles."

Garrett's mouth twitched in a sudden grin. The *Pittsburgh,* SSN-720, had been his first command ten years ago. She was a Los Angeles–class attack boat, swift, silent, and deadly, currently assigned to the *Kitty Hawk*'s battle group.

"Whose skippering the *'Burgh*?"

"Jack Creighton, sir."

"Good. A good man."

One of the civilians, a young man with thick-framed glasses, appeared to notice Garrett for the first time. "What is *he* doing here?"

"This is Captain Garrett," Berkowitz said. "NAV-LITWAR."

The man glanced at the gold dolphins on Garrett's breast, pinned just above the ranks of brightly colored ribbons—his "fruit salad."

"Sub driver?"

"Used to be, sir," Garrett replied evenly. "Now I drive a desk."

"Uh. Welcome to the club." The man returned his attention to the screen.

"Echo Two, Echo Two! We are engaging the enemy!"

"That's Paul Myers," Berkowitz told Garrett. "National Security Advisor."

Garrett was impressed. The National Security Council, or NSC, was the advisory body within the executive branch of government responsible for assessing all risks, objectives, and commitments related to the U.S. military. Its day-to-day activities were run by the Assistant to the President for National Security Affairs—better known as the National Security Advisor—*this* man, though he didn't appear old enough to have the ear of the President himself. If Paul Myers was here, watching Black Stallion unfold on these monitors in real-time, this was a very important operation indeed.

It also meant that some of the civilians in the room, at least, were security personnel—possibly Secret Service, possibly CIA. One or two, likely, were with Central Intelligence, which had a hand in staffing the NSC.

Garrett was beginning to realize just how hot Black Stallion actually was.

**SEAL Team Detachment Echo
Near Bandar-e Charak, Iran
2212 hours Zulu**

Wolfe raised himself to a half crouch, knocking down two more Pasdaran guardsmen with tight-grouped bursts from his H&K. "Echo Two, One-one!" he called. "Hold your position on the ridge and give us cover!"

"One-one, Two-one, copy," Chief Hadley replied. "Get your asses out of there."

At the moment, Wolf and EM1 Brown were providing cover for Jordan, Creston, and Dole as they carried Johnson, Applebee, and Miller to the beach. Two men against hundreds; they wouldn't be able to hold on much longer.

Especially, Wolfe thought as he dropped an empty 9mm magazine and snapped a fresh one home, with ammo running low. The team had gone in with a light load-out, just eight mags—240 rounds—per man. Reconnaissance operations weren't supposed to end in prolonged firefights. After this one, he had one loaded magazine left.

Gunfire cracked and rattled from the ridge to the west, echoing off the boulders and steep-sided gullies. All of the SEALs carried sound-suppressed weapons, so the racket was all from the hostiles—AK-47s, to judge from the distinctive flat crack they made when they fired. The bad guys were pressing hard. At least they hadn't launched any more rocket-propelled grenades at the retreating SEALs, though that respite, he was sure, would not last for much longer.

"Hey, Wheel," EM1 Brown called from a few feet to his left, using SEAL slang for the platoon CO. "I'm almost dry."

"Same here. Move upslope to the left. We'll try to join with Echo Two, give the others a chance to reach the beach."

"Roger that."

The mission was screwed, a cluster-fuck from minute one. Right now, Wolfe had just two tactical priorities to worry about—getting his unit as a whole out of this trap, and getting the three wounded men back to the boats. The situation was fast developing into a SEAL unit commander's worst nightmare. The Team could break contact with the enemy and E&E back to the beach rendezvous, could even split up, every man for himself, to better slip through the closing Pasdaran trap and get to the sea.

But the three wounded men were slowing them down. Jordan, Creston, and Dole could only move so fast carrying their injured teammates, and they couldn't defend themselves while they moved. Either what was left of Det Echo had to provide cover for them until they reached the beach, providing a rough defensive perimeter along the ridge to the west, or they had to leave the wounded behind and run for it.

And, damn it, SEALs *never* left their own behind. *Never!*

Special Operations Watch Center
Pentagon Basement
Arlington, Virginia
1714 hours EST

"They're not going to leave the wounded behind," Garrett said quietly. "You know that, right?"

"I know," Berkowitz replied.

Of course he knew. Berkowitz was a SEAL himself.

"So how are we going to get them out of there?"

"We're open to suggestions, sir."

For most of his naval career Tom Garrett had been a sub driver. He'd skippered the *Pittsburgh* ten years ago. After that, he'd been captain of the SSN *Seawolf,* and later of the newly commissioned SSN *Virginia,* the two most recent and magically high-tech additions to America's submarine fleet.

Six months ago, when he'd rotated ashore after his deployment with the *Virginia,* his experience had dropped him here in the Pentagon, as advisory staff for the newly formed NAVLITWARCOM—Naval Littoral Warfare Command.

It was, he knew, a choice assignment, one offering him the fast track to flag rank. "Littoral Warfare" was the hot new catch phrase for the Navy. With the demise of the Soviet Union, there'd been much less emphasis on deep-water naval deployments. The wars of the foreseeable future would be fought against enemies who lacked anything like America's sophisticated and high-tech fleet, and they would be fought close inshore, along hostile coasts within the world's littoral regions.

Operation Black Stallion had been *his* idea, originally, though the plan that eventually emerged bore few similarities to his original proposal. Two months ago images from a high-orbiting spy satellite had revealed some major construction going on among the rugged coastal foothills of the Shib Kuh mountain range within Iran's Darya-ye region, at the mouth of a valley in a mountain called Kuh-e Gab. Analyses suggested that the Darya-ye complex might include a battery of intermediate-range ballistic missiles, as well as structures that might be related to NBC warfare—manufacturing nuclear, biological, or chemical weapons.

Ever since the intelligence debacle of Iraq's presumed weapons of mass destruction, and the resulting public and media fallout, Washington was playing it *very* cautious when it came to identifying WMDs elsewhere in the world. Garrett had advanced the idea of Black Stallion in a proposal forwarded to the Joint Chiefs—a SEAL four-man recon detachment inserted by submarine along the Darya-ye coast, slipping undetected close to the suspected weapons site five miles inland, and getting close-up photographs, radiation readings, and eyeball observations from inside the complex itself.

It was a reasonable idea, and one eminently suitable to the SEAL Teams and their mission capabilities. Based on his career experience, Garrett had suggested that the deployment be made off of the USS *Texas,* the second of the four Virginia-class submarines now in service.

That had been two months ago. Plans unfolded remarkably quickly after that, with concept approval and mission training beginning almost at once. Unfortunately, the dreaded "committee effect" had descended almost at once. A full, sixteen-man SEAL platoon would deploy, not a four-man recon team.

And, perhaps most important, it wouldn't be the *Texas* delivering them.

The SSN *Virginia* had been sold as the submarine that would command the world's littorals for the U.S. Navy, an ultraquiet and high-tech vessel that could creep undetected into enemy harbors, or covertly put commandos ashore anywhere in the world.

Unfortunately, the *Virginia* and her sister boats were fouled in budgetary draw-downs, bureaucratic turf wars, and departmental politics, just as the *Seawolf* had been. The Virginias did what they did well, but they were also seen as the replacement for the Navy's aging fleet of Los Angeles–class attack boats. Thirty were planned; only four were in service so far, and the others now rested uncertainly beneath the budgetary ax. There simply weren't enough either in the water or planned to do everything expected of them, from battle group deployments to coastal reconnaissance missions, from special ops to escort duty, from showing the flag in foreign ports to electronic signals intelligence to ASW patrols to fulfilling the swiftly growing demands of Homeland Security.

Someone higher up the mission planning totem pole had decided that the SEALs should deploy from a pair of Cyclones instead.

PC-6, the USS *Sirocco,* and PC-10, the USS *Firebolt,* were two of thirteen coastal patrol craft designed originally to operate as deployment platforms for the U.S. Navy SEALs. Measuring 170 feet in length, with a beam of twenty-five feet and a displacement of 328.5 tons, the Cyclone-class PCs were the first genuine oceangoing ships in the Navy's Special Warfare community. Although their primary mission was coastal patrol work,

SEAL support remained an important, dedicated assignment.

They'd also been controversial from the very first, from the moment in 1990 the contract had been awarded to the Bollinger Machine Shop and Shipyard. Big enough to venture into blue water and endure up to sea state five, their range was still limited—about three thousand nautical miles. That meant they had to be based in their operational region, along with full maintenance, repair, and supply facilities, and support personnel. They carried a crew of four officers and twenty-four enlisted men—conventional black-shoe sailors, not SPECWAR personnel, and that decision had caused an interdepartmental firestorm all by itself.

Worse, they only had space aboard for nine SPEC-WAR operators—a single SEAL squad and one or two tech specialists, plus their equipment. True, few SEAL ops required or were best served by large contingents, but the small payload limited the craft's mission scope.

And, worst of all, the PBCs weren't really *covert*. Too small to carry a sizable SEAL force, they were too large to sneak in under an enemy's radar for the sort of sneak-and-peak op at which the Teams traditionally excelled.

The Special Boat Squadrons operating the PBCs—Patrol Boat, Coastal—had been repeatedly encouraged from further up the chain of command to find a mission for the expensive craft. PC-6 and PC-10 were currently stationed in Oman, escorting tankers and patrolling the sensitive Straits of Hormuz.

It had seemed logical—to someone, at any rate—to use them to deploy Det Echo. ECM aircraft off the *Kitty Hawk* could jam local Iranian radar, and strike fighters from the Carrier Battle Group and out of U.S. bases in Iraq could fly combat support, if that proved necessary.

What no one had anticipated was that the enemy would have such a heavy presence in the AO . . . or that he would react this quickly and this decisively.

And Garrett was feeling a strong sense of responsibility for those boys out there.

SEAL Team Detachment Echo
Near Bandar-e Charak, Iran
2251 hours Zulu

"One-one, this is One-four!" TM2 Dole called over the Motorola. "We're on the beach! Our guys are in RIB-2 and we're moving out!"

"Copy that, One-four." Wolfe laser-targeted another Pasdaran trooper and fired, a single shot only. He'd switched to single-shot from burst fire when he'd reached his last magazine. He saw the soldier pitch backward and collapse. "Okay, Echoes," he called. "Time to get the hell out of Dodge!"

An instant later, however, a savage explosion rocked the hillside, throwing Wolfe against the ground.

"Mortar fire!" Echo Two's Chief Hadley yelled. *"Incoming!"*

And then the machine gun opened up.

Just fucking great! Wolfe thought as another blast from a mortar round hammered at his senses, showering him with gravel and sand, and an Iranian machine gun sent a stream of bright green tracers snapping overhead.

The ten Det Echo SEALs remaining ashore were trapped, pinned down by heavy fire and very nearly surrounded.

"Backstop, Backstop!" Wolfe called, using the call

sign for the mission's Pentagon controllers. "Echo is pinned down and cannot move! Request air support fucking *now*!"

Special Operations Watch Center
Pentagon Basement
Arlington, Virginia
1752 hours EST

"Backstop, Backstop! Echo is pinned down and cannot move! Request air support fucking now!"

"Where the hell is Sierra Foxtrot Four-one?" Forsythe demanded.

"ETA four minutes," a technician replied.

"Too long! Our people are out of time! What about fire support from the Cyclones?"

The two PBCs each mounted a pair of Mk 38 Bushmasters, 25mm chain guns capable of firing a blistering two hundred rounds per minute.

"Sirocco reports they are still out of effective range, sir." Bushmasters had a range of 2,500 yards—about two and a third miles. Though they were now en route to the rendezvous point, they were still a good two miles offshore.

"Damn it to hell!"

Garrett watched the green-monochrome image for a moment. The last of the SEALs on shore were scattered in a ragged defensive perimeter across the southern slope of the ridge, perhaps half a mile from the beach. The view was partially obscured by drifting clouds of smoke, but he could see the sharp pulse and flash of exploding mortar rounds, the drifting streams of tracer fire, and the flicker of muzzle flashes from enemy positions. The

Iranian troops must have suffered heavy casualties already, but they'd pushed up close and pressed hard; they were on three sides of Det Echo now, and reinforcements—in the form of a convoy of BMPs racing down the coast road from the west—would be there in moments.

SEAL Detachment Echo was doomed.

Unless . . .

Tuesday, 27 May 2008

Special Operations Watch Center
Pentagon Basement
Arlington, Virginia
1752 hours EST

It might work. It offered a chance, at least.

"What about using the UAVs?" Garrett asked.

"They're empty, Captain," Myers said. "Or haven't you been listening?"

"No . . . I mean what about using the UAVs themselves as weapons? Fly them into enemy positions . . . or send them in low enough to scare the enemy and make him duck. All the SEALs need is a few minutes to break contact, and then the cavalry will arrive."

For a second a startled silence gripped the basement communications center. "Well? How about it?" Forsythe asked.

There was a flurry of activity, and calls to the patrol

boats off shore. The three Unmanned Aerial Vehicles were being controlled by technicians on board the *Sirocco*, though the audience watching from the bowels of the Pentagon could control camera angles, within limits, as well as image magnification through a remote satellite hookup.

"Okay!" a technician said, pointing. "They're going to try it with UAV-3!"

On the screen, the green-hued landscape tilted suddenly as the operator on board *Sirocco* put the Fire Scout UAV into a steep left bank. A targeting reticule floated across the screen, centering on a small cluster of figures behind the Iranian lines. The cluster grew larger on the screen . . . and larger . . . until Garrett could see the mustached faces of several Iranian soldiers and the glowing hot tube of an 81mm mortar in front of them.

At the last moment possible those faces turned suddenly toward the Predator's camera, eyes widening, mouths gaping . . . and then the soldiers were scattering in every direction.

An RQ-8B Fire Scout looked exactly like a small, smooth-skinned, torpedo-nosed helicopter with no cockpit. The aircraft had a takeoff weight of a ton and a half, and its four-blade rotors spanned just twenty-seven and a half feet. Garrett could only imagine the feelings of a soldier suddenly confronted by that apparition stooping on his position out of the night sky.

The mortar position blurred as the Fire Scout streaked past at 125 knots. "*Yee-ha!*" a voice cried over the speaker system. "*Video games rock!*"

"Who said that?" a Marine general, Thomas Schaler, demanded.

"Someone on the *Sirocco,* sir," the technician reported. "I think they're having fun out there."

Garrett suppressed a grin. For years, now, there'd been

speculation within the military as to whether a generation of kids raised on joysticks and video games would amount to anything. Evidently, the answer was yes.

A secondary monitor showed another group of Iranian troops diving for cover—the machine gun nest that had been pinning the SEALs in place.

"Echo, Echo, this is Backstop," Admiral Forsythe called, using a telephone handset patched into the satcom link. "We're keeping the bad guys occupied for a moment. Now's your chance to break contact!"

"Copy that, Backstop. Thanks."

UAV-2 continued to relay the overall tactical view from an altitude of several hundred feet. Garrett could see the SEALs rising from cover now and beginning to hurry on down the slope toward the beach. It was less an orderly withdrawal than a headlong plunge, but there was no time for finesse. Those Iranian BMPs would be along in minutes.

For several gut-twisting minutes UAV-1 and UAV-3 buzzed the Iranian lines. UAV-2 revealed the confusion in their ranks, as tracer streams crisscrossed through the air, trying to knock down the wildly swooping teleoperated aircraft.

"Shortstop, Shortstop, this is Night Rider," a new voice called. *"We have a delivery for you. Where do you want it?"*

The watching officers and technicians broke into a chorused cheer. Night Rider was the call sign for Sierra Foxtrot Four-one, a pair of Air Force F-117 stealth fighters flying out of an American air base in southern Iraq.

Help for the beleaguered SEALs had arrived at last.

"We have seven light armored vehicles on the coast road," the combat controller on board the *Sirocco* was heard to reply. *"Wait one and we'll illuminate the lead target."*

Besides unguided rockets and its regular sensor suite of cameras and radar, the Fire Scout also mounted a laser target designation system, allowing a remote operator to laser a target for incoming smart munitions. Garrett saw the square targeting cursor drift across the screen as the aircraft swung toward the west. He could make out the road now, and the darker, colder surge of the waters of the Gulf. And there, traveling in close-spaced line-ahead, the white-hot engine signatures of several vehicles. The UAV operator on board the distant *Sirocco* selected the lead vehicle, the cursor positioned itself over the target, and the words TARGET LOCK and LASER ACTIVE appeared alongside.

"Night Rider. I have the target. Weapon release . . ."
Long seconds dragged past. The people in the communications center held their collective breath.

Then the lead vehicle, an armored BMP-2, exploded in a silent flare of white light, and the men and women in the room cheered again. On the screen, the Fire Scout was already selecting a second target. The rest of the Iranian convoy, however, had pulled to a halt behind the burning armored vehicle, and now appeared to be trying to turn around.

At the very least, the SEALs had just won a desperately needed respite.

SEAL Team Detachment Echo
Near Bandar-e Charak, Iran
2254 hours Zulu

Lieutenant Wolfe raised his head above the boulder, checking right. Flames danced and flared in the night a few hundred yards up the road, and by the uncertain light he could see the other Iranian armored vehicles beating a hasty retreat.

At his signal, the ten SEALs emerged from the shadows at the base of the hill, crossed the gravel road, and jogged south across the narrow beach. Their remaining two CRRCs were waiting for them in the shadow of an outcropping of boulders.

The Combat Rubber Raiding Craft was the SEALs' legendary rubber duck—a Zodiac-style inflatable boat fifteen feet long and six feet wide, weighing in at 256 pounds. Each Cyclone-class patrol boat possessed ramps at the stern for hauling them onto the fantail. All they needed to do now was reach the *Sirocco*.

Together, the SEALs shoved and manhandled the two rubber ducks off the sand and into the surf, then crowded on board. In seconds the men at the sterns had fired up the fifty-five-horsepower outboards and put their helms over. In moments more they were motoring clear of the beach, headed for open water.

A CRRC had a total mission range of about sixty-five miles, but that kind of endurance wouldn't be necessary tonight. The two PBCs were only a couple of miles out, and closing. At a full throttle they would reach their rendezvous in another six minutes.

Wolfe allowed himself a last look back at the beach, where flames continued to leap from the stricken BMP. He could see the shadowy forms of soldiers reaching the beach now. They'd only just escaped.

But he wouldn't allow himself to relax . . . not yet.

Special Operations Watch Center
Pentagon Basement
Arlington, Virginia
1759 hours EST

"Sir!" a technician yelled, the word cutting through the sibilant and self-congratulatory cheers.

That, Garrett thought, sounds like more bad news. . . .

It was. "Missiles! Missiles incoming!" A beat passed in shocked silence. "*Sirocco* reports two Exocets inbound! They're targeting the Cyclones!"

"Jesus Christ!" Admiral Forsythe snapped.

Abruptly, the atmosphere inside the Pentagon basement communications center chilled. Radar reports coming back from both the *Firebolt* and the *Sirocco* showed a pair of sea-skimming missiles hurtling toward the PCBs at 700 miles per hour. Evidently, these were the MM40 variant—fired from a ship or a coastal defense battery rather than an aircraft.

Exocets were antiship missiles, French-built but exported to dozens of nations, including Iran. Each was eighteen feet long, carried a seventy-five-pound high-explosive warhead, and had a range of just over forty miles.

"*Sirocco* is firing chaff," a technician reported. "*Firebolt* firing chaff. Missiles now fifteen seconds out . . . twelve seconds . . ."

Among their other weapons, the PCBs mounted M52 decoy systems that fired chaff canisters designed to fool the active homing radar of cruise missiles such as the Exocet.

One of the Fire Scouts, heading out to sea and climbing fast, revealed the scene. The two patrol boats, their propulsion plants glowing white on the infrared image, were turning sharply to starboard, away from the coast. A pair of bright white stars appeared from the upper right corner of the screen, streaking low across the water with the speed of a bullet. One, apparently, had been successfully decoyed by the chaff, swinging wide and flashing off the left-hand side of the monitor.

Chaff decoys could not promise a hundred percent protection, however. They merely lengthened the odds of a hit. The second Exocet ignored the decoy and slammed into the right-hand patrol boat, engulfing the craft in a searing flare of light.

"Oh, my God!" someone in the room said softly.

For a long time after that no one spoke.

SEAL Team Detachment Echo
Near Bandar-e Charak, Iran
2259 hours Zulu

Wolfe saw the flash on the southern horizon, heard the sharp *bang* of the missile's detonation long seconds later. Swinging their tillers over, the two CRRCs motored rapidly across the choppy water toward the pillar of flame shooting up into the night.

This had always been a possibility—a worst-case scenario discussed and rehashed during the training phase of this op. The Cyclones were not stealthy, and *would* be seen by hostile shore defenses. The only question was how long their discovery could be delayed by Navy Electronic Countermeasures, or ECM, and the elements of surprise and shock.

Minutes later the two CRRCs approached the scene of the disaster. *Sirocco* had been hit. She was dead in the water now, heeled far over to port and down by the stern. Flame and orange-shot clouds of greasy smoke continued to boil from her afterdeck, and from the sea itself as fuel oil on the surface caught fire. Wolfe could see several men in the water, swimming to get clear, while others still on deck wrestled a pair of lifeboats similar to the CRRCs into the oily sea.

Despite the possibility that the Iranians would loose another volley—or that ammunition stores on the burning craft might explode—*Firebolt* was laying alongside, upwind of the sinking vessel. Wolfe could see wounded men being handed across from the stricken boat's deck to the second patrol boat.

"There," he said, pointing. Two sailors were struggling in the oily water fifty yards away. "Get us over there."

EM1 Brown adjusted the tiller, and the CRRC swung onto its new heading, bumping a little with the swell. Moments later they pulled alongside the two life-jacketed sailors and hauled them up onto the CRRC's gunnel.

Sirocco continued settling into the sea, her list increasing until at last her superstructure hit the water and she lay fully on her port side. As *Firebolt* and the rubber boats pulled back, the stricken vessel continued to roll, exposing her keel above the oily swell.

Within another five minutes she was gone.

With the last of the swimmers rescued, the two SEAL CRRCs were quickly hauled onto *Firebolt*'s fantail, and the remaining PBC got under way once more.

On board, Wolfe and the other SEALs sat anywhere there was a clear bit of deck. With double her normal complement on board, *Firebolt* was heavily laden, and there wasn't much free space.

Wolfe pulled back the Velcro strap hiding the luminous dial of his dive watch and frowned. Mission time was 2315 hours Zulu, but Iran's time zone was three and a half hours ahead of GMT, which meant it was 0245 local. Local sunrise at this latitude wouldn't be for another two hours, but the eastern sky was already showing a touch of predawn glow. With the Iranians aware of their presence, and the time to daylight fast running out, Wolfe was beginning to feel like a particularly large and vulnerable target.

Thunder rolled in the sky, and the SEALs looked up. A pair of aircraft howled low overhead. For a moment Wolfe's thoughts froze, trapped by the certainty that those must be Iranian F-4s.

But Iranian aircraft would be coming out of the north, not from the southeast. Unless these two had circled far around and out of their way, they must be U.S. strike fighters off the *Kitty Hawk,* arriving at last. And Night Rider was still out there, too, somewhere, flying CAP to keep the bad guys off the surviving PCB's tail.

The border threading through the Straits of Hormuz, separating Iranian waters from those controlled by Oman and the United Arab Emirates, lay perhaps ninety miles to the southeast, a three-hour run for the *Firebolt.* Technically, they already were in international waters, or would be in a very few minutes, but there were numerous islands in this area belonging to Iran, and many had a naval or coastal defense presence.

Threading that gauntlet was going to take a lot of skill on the part of *Firebolt*'s skipper, and a very great deal of luck.

Special Operations Watch Center
Pentagon Basement
Arlington, Virginia
1835 hours EST

"It looks like they might make it," Captain Grimes, one of Forsythe's aides, observed.

"Unless the bastards pop a Silkworm at them, or another flight of Exocets," Forsythe said.

"The worst is still to come, Admiral," Grimes pointed out. "We've just lost a Navy ship inside Iranian territorial waters. The media firestorm when this gets out . . ."

"Jesus. Is there any way to put a lid on it?" one of the other civilians asked.

"You're kidding, Dan," Myers said. "Right?"

"What we have here is a genu-wine international incident," General Schaler said. He chuckled. "Let the ass-covering being!"

"It's not funny, General," Myers said. "The President is going to want to know who screwed up on this one. *He's* going to be the one taking flak from the press, and he's the one the Iranians are going to be burning in effigy tomorrow morning in the streets of Tehran, along with the American flag. Believe me, some heads are going to roll after this—this disaster."

"I imagine they'll round up the usual suspects," Forsythe said. His voice was grim. "Sacrificial lambs, on the altar of public opinion?"

Schaler chuckled. "Just be glad, gentlemen, that this isn't England. Over there, they hold the government accountable for its screw-ups with a vote of no-confidence. In Washington it's stonewalling as usual. Say nothing, and it'll all blow over."

"Somehow, I don't think this one *will* blow over," Forsythe said. "It's Operation Eagle's Claw all over again."

Eagle's Claw had been the aborted 1980 rescue mission of American hostages held by the revolutionary government of Iran. The attempt to sneak in, grab the hostages, and get out again had ended at the refueling base tagged Desert One when a Navy helicopter had collided on takeoff with a grounded C-130 transport. They never got close to Tehran, and the Iranians had made the most of the propaganda victory handed to them. The next day the entire world had seen the films of triumphant Iranian soldiers among the burned-out hulks of helicopters left behind at Desert One.

There was no burned-out wreckage to show on the evening news this time around—not with *Sirocco* at the bottom of the Gulf—but the Iranian mullahs could be trusted to point out America's transgression to the world in lovingly histrionic detail, especially to an Islamic world that already felt threatened by American global policy.

"Eagle's Claw had the advantage of the sympathy vote," Myers said. "We were seen as trying to rescue our own people, as having a right to at least try. We know the Iranians hate us already. This time around we're going to get crucified by American voters as well."

"Possibly," Forsythe said, "there will be some confusion as to just where our ships were when they were attacked. After all, they were less than a mile inside the three-mile limit. . . ."

"Iran," Myers pointed out, "claims a *twelve*-mile limit.

The civilian, Dan, shrugged. "That's for the lawyers to argue," he said. "We will need to consider means for media damage control."

"Who the hell is that?" Garrett asked Berkowitz, whispering.

"Daniel Hardy," was the low-voiced reply. "Assistant SecDef, Public Affairs."

Garrett blinked, startled. The Secretary of Defense was charged with acting as the principle advisor to the President on defense policy, as the civilian leadership of the Department of Defense. Having the SecDef's head of Public Affairs present brought a surreal touch to this gathering, something akin to having a public relations front man present at a lynching.

But then, if Garrett had learned anything since taking command of his new Pentagon desk, it was that Washington ran by its own rules and its own logic.

And that at times that logic appeared to be anything but.

Forsythe was looking at Garrett. He cleared his throat. "Ah . . . that was sharp thinking, Captain, using the UAVs to distract the Pasdaran gunners and mortar crew."

"Thank you, Admiral."

"Bought them the time they needed to get clear and get down to the beach. I gather this op was your brainchild to begin with?"

Garrett hesitated. Within Pentagon circles, it was never a good career move to pass the blame for failure back up the chain of command, and in any case, that was not Garrett's style. Still, the talk about heads rolling and sacrificial lambs made him less than eager to admit any connection with Black Stallion whatsoever.

"I wrote the original paper, yes, sir."

"The original plan called for a submarine insertion, sir," Berkowitz added. "Not those damned PCBs. Who the hell's idea was that?"

"Gentlemen!" General Schaler put in. "Now is *not* the time for recriminations!"

"Submarine insertion?" Myers said, raising an eyebrow. "In those confined waters? Surely that would be suicide."

"It's been done before, sir," Garrett said with a shrug. "And the *Pittsburgh*'s transiting the straits now. A sub's certainly not as high-profile as a coastal patrol boat."

"Captain Garrett," Myers said, sounding thoughtful. "You were in on the Ohio conversion project, weren't you?"

"Yes, sir. Still am."

"I think I understand why you suggested using submarines for this op."

"The PBCs are still expensive toys looking for a mission," Berkowitz put in. "Remember, their primary mission remains coastal patrol duty. *Not* sneaking into enemy harbors."

"Captain Garrett," Myers said, "would an Ohio boat have better served the infil-exfil needs for this mission?"

"Absolutely, sir. This sort of sneak-and-peek was what the Ohio conversion was all about."

The Pentagon group continued to monitor the mission as, half a world away, the *Firebolt* continued to race for the safety of Omani waters. The two Stealth fighters engaged the battery that had fired the Exocet missiles, while F/A-18 Hornets of VFA-17 off the *Kitty Hawk* wheeled and circled above the straits. An hour after Det Echo had escaped the trap ashore, the USS *Pittsburgh* surfaced alongside the *Firebolt* and began taking off some of the SEALs. Medevac Sea Stallions were on the way to pick up the most seriously wounded.

The final butcher's bill was not nearly as bad as it might have been. Two SEALs had been killed and six wounded altogether, while three sailors off the *Sirocco* were dead, nine wounded, with two more missing and presumed dead.

"At least casualties were light," Hardy, the Public Affairs man, said brightly.

Garrett considered strangling the man. "Casualties were light" would be of little comfort to the families and friends of those Navy men who'd died tonight.

Disgusted, Garrett glanced at his watch. "Oh, Christ."

"What's the matter?" Berkowitz asked.

"It's almost 2000 hours, is what's the matter. Brenda is going to shoot me. No. First she's going to hang, draw, and quarter me. *Then* she's going to shoot me."

"Damn. You had a date?"

Garrett nodded. "Just dinner at her place." He reached for the cell phone in his pocket, then remembered that the electronic shielding in the Pentagon basement wouldn't let him get a signal.

"Sorry, Captain," Berkowitz said. "But I thought it important that you be here."

"Absolutely! I wouldn't have missed it. I just should have called the lady first."

Garrett thought fast. His usual workday was over at five or five-thirty—1730 hours in Navy parlance. Beltway construction and its effect on rush hour traffic being what they were, it would have taken him an hour and a half to get out to Silver Spring, on the Beltway north of Washington. Now, though, the traffic would have cleared a bit. If he hurried, he wouldn't be more than forty minutes late.

The assembled admirals, generals, civilians, and lesser-ranking officials were gathering up briefcases and calling it a night, so there might yet be time.

"There will be a postmission analysis," Myers told them all. "Concord Briefing Room, 0900 hours." He cocked an eye at Garrett. "I'd like you to be there as well, Captain Garrett. Captain Berkowitz? See that he has the necessary clearances."

"Aye aye, sir."

Garrett was pulling out of the Pentagon complex onto the 395 entrance ramp when the incongruity of the evening hit him. Minutes ago, satellite communications networks and high-speed computers had let him literally look over the shoulders of SEAL operators in coastal Iran. He'd watched an Exocet hit the *Sirocco*, watched the subsequent fight for survival in the warm waters of the Arabian Gulf.

And now he was worried about what he would tell his girlfriend when he met her for dinner.

It was, he thought, a hell of a way to fight a war.

And war it was. America's fight against terrorism had begun long before al-Qaeda's attacks on the World Trade Center and the Pentagon on September 11, 2001. So far as the public at large was concerned, however, that date was to the War on Terror the same as December 7, 1941, was to America's entry into World War II.

Whatever the starting date, however, it remained a war with few front lines against an enemy as insubstantially ghostlike as he was determined. Over the years, the United States had taken on a number of countries known to support the terrorists and their goals—Libya, Afghanistan, Iraq—but the terrorists themselves remained devilishly elusive.

For some time now Iran had been the nation most visibly in America's sights. Not that an invasion was being planned, necessarily, though there was considerable scuttlebutt to that effect. But reports coming out of Central Intelligence continued to stress possible Iranian support of terror groups like al-Qaeda, the virtual certainty that they were working on nuclear and biological weapons, and their destabilizing actions in an already notoriously unstable part of the world. With the governments of the nations to either side of her—Iraq and Afghanistan—taken down by U.S. invasions and replaced by fledgling democracies, the mullahs of Tehran were beginning to feel isolated . . . and threatened.

And they were reacting in a predictable way, with bluster and bombast and threats against their neighbors. That mysterious facility near Bandar-e Charak might well hold the key to Tehran's intentions. Operation Black Stallion had been intended to reveal that key.

Unfortunately, the attempt had almost certainly made things worse.

Much worse.

He thought about the terrorists.

America's single advantage over such an enemy remained her technology, from UAVs to satcom links that let senior leaders in Washington look in on what passed for the front lines in real-time.

Of course, Garrett reflected as he merged with the Beltway traffic heading north, that could also be America's single greatest *dis*advantage in this war. The bane of every commander in the field was micromanagement by the rear-echelon brass. It was said that on the night of the debacle at Desert One, Colonel Beckwith, the Delta Force commander, had suddenly developed "communications difficulties" so that he could conveniently ignore orders coming from the basement of the White House to press on with a mission already obviously doomed.

Orders from then–President Carter himself.

It felt strange being part of the rear-echelon command now instead of where he felt he really belonged—on the sharp point of the spear. He was a sub driver, damn it. He belonged out there: the eyes, ears, and—at times—the fist of American military policy.

Not *here,* as part of the American military policy's fat ass.

Come to think of it, Jimmy Carter had been a sub

driver before he'd become President. Garrett wondered if Carter had had similar thoughts . . . especially during that night of flame and death in a remote desert refueling site deep inside of Iran.

Flame and death.

He thought about Kazuko.

Damn it. He'd not thought of her for some time, now, but the realities of the terror war always brought her memory back. She'd been his lover, his fiancée . . . and a flight attendant on board a passenger plane shot down by terrorists over the South China Sea.

Again he wished he were still a sub skipper. He felt so . . . *helpless.*

And useless.

But Garrett knew his sub-driving days were over. His experience in the boats had brought him here, to a job conning a damned desk, writing reports suggesting novel uses of submarines in the fast-paced and deadly war America was now fighting.

He hoped Brenda would understand when he showed up late.

He pulled his cell phone out of his uniform's jacket pocket to give her a call.

Wednesday, 28 May 2008

Concord Briefing Room
Pentagon, C Ring
Arlington, Virginia
0915 hours EST

"Our target remains the same," the briefing officer said. He clicked the remote control in his hand, and a satellite photo came up on the screen behind him. "Objective White Scimitar, ten kilometers north of the port of Bandar-e Charak. Satellite reconnaissance over the past three months has indicated heavy ongoing construction in this area. In addition, the port facilities themselves are being expanded, and a new road is being cut down out of the mountains, from White Scimitar to Bandar-e Charak.

"And we don't know what the hell they're building over there."

The briefing officer was Gerald Markham, a civilian

on the staff of the DNI. The Director of National Intelligence was the relatively new cabinet-level position created by President Bush in the wake of 9/11, a post that had superceded the Director of Central Intelligence in many of his critical functions, including that of giving the President his daily briefing on intelligence matters. The DNI ostensibly ran and coordinated all fifteen of America's spook agencies, a task formerly assigned to the Director of Central Intelligence.

Garrett wondered if the high-echelon shake-up within the intelligence community had made a difference in the efficiency and timeliness of America's spy efforts . . . or if the change was cosmetic only. So far it didn't look like the office of the DNI knew any more about what was going on in the world than the DCI had.

Markham paused and looked around the room. About twenty people were gathered around the long, hardwood conference table—most in uniform, but a few suits in evidence as well. Garrett recognized the men who'd been in the Pentagon basement room last night—in particular Paul Myers, who'd taken his seat at the head of the table. Most, though, were unknown to him.

"A number of you are new to this working group," Markham continued. "So before looking at White Scimitar in detail, a brief overview of Iran's recent history is in order. You all know the basic outlines, at least. Called Persia until 1935, Iran became an Islamic republic in 1979 with the overthrow of the Shah. Highly conservative clerical forces created a theocracy with the ultimate political authority residing in a religious scholar—the Ayatollah—and a Guardian Council of twelve clerics."

Markham had a slow and measured way of speaking that bordered on the pedantic, even the tedious. Garrett wished he would get on with it.

"Of course," Markham said, "U.S. relations with

Tehran have been strained since Iranian students under the guidance of the Ayatollah Khomeini seized the U.S. Embassy in Tehran on 4 November 1979, and took the American citizens working there hostage. They held over fifty hostages for 444 days, until 20 January 1981.

"From 1980 to 1988, Iran fought an extraordinarily bloody war with Iraq. During that conflict, tanker traffic in the Gulf was threatened by Iranian forces, and that led to several armed clashes between the U.S. Navy and the Iranians.

"Due to its activities in Lebanon and elsewhere, Iran has been designated as a sponsor of global terrorism, and for that reason economic sanctions and export controls remain in effect. During President Bush's 2002 State of the Union address—his famous 'Axis of Evil' speech, he included Iran with the regimes of Iraq and North Korea as nations dedicated to supporting terrorist activities worldwide."

Garrett felt a pang of irritation at that—not at the briefing officer himself, but at the domestic political situation behind his words. Fallout from the war in Iraq continued to sift down on news broadcasts and newspaper editorials across the country. America and Great Britain had invaded Iraq and deposed its leader, Saddam Hussein, in 2003. Though few people either at home or abroad had supported the bloodthirsty Saddam, few thought the war justified, especially when Coalition forces were unable to find WMDs—the weapons of mass destruction Saddam was supposed to be building and hiding.

And as Washington's saber-rattling rhetoric against Iran had grown louder, so too had the voices of protest against a possible war against Iran. Editorialists and activists across America continued to make fun of the

President's emotionally charged comment about an "Axis of Evil."

"The Islamic Republic of Iran continues to seek to be the dominant power in the Arab Gulf region," Markham continued. "They are actively seeking to become a nuclear power, though they insist that they are interested only in the peaceful uses of nuclear power. Of particular concern to U.S. intelligence is their program of cooperation with the government of North Korea, in which they have shared their nuclear research with Pyongyang in exchange for PDRK long-range missiles and missile guidance technology.

"There is a growing body of evidence that Iran has supported al-Qaeda in numerous ways. Ominously, an Iranian defector gave detailed information to American authorities in Azerbaijan about an upcoming al-Qaeda and Iranian terror attack on New York City just prior to September 11. The report was not confirmed, and Iran was not indicted in the attack, primarily for political reasons. There are also well-attested reports that Iran sheltered Osama bin Laden after his escape from Afghanistan in 2002 or 2003.

"This potential cooperation between al-Qaeda and the Tehran regime has been downplayed in the past, principally because the revolutionary government of Iran is Shi'ite, whereas Osama bin Laden, the former Taliban government of Afghanistan, and most of al-Qaeda's leadership are all Sunni. These two branches of Islamic belief view one another as heretical, and traditionally there has been little cooperation between the two. We believe, however, that increased pressure from the West is forcing a greater degree of cooperation between them, especially in terms of logistical support, transport, supplies, weapons, and ammunition. 'The enemy of my enemy is my friend' appears to be the new order of the day when it comes to cooperation between disparate Islamic groups.

"The possibility of increased cooperation between the extremist elements of both the Sunnis and the Shi'ites is a matter of considerable concern to us.

"Publicly," Markham went on, "Iran has been pushing for a reduction of tensions with the U.S. for a long time. The government in Tehran claims to want full normalization of relations. More than anything else, they want Washington to lift the freeze on some eleven billion in assets that we slapped on them in 1979, at the beginning of the hostage crisis.

"Privately, however, Iran seems unalterably set on a policy of military buildup, territorial gain, the acquisition of nuclear weapons, and general religious and social destabilization within the Gulf region. This policy keeps them at odds with the United States, and seems destined to lead Iran and the U.S. into head-to-head conflict."

The satellite photograph was replaced by a head shot of a bearded man in a turban.

"This man," Markham said, indicating the face on the screen, "is a real sweetheart. The Ayatollah Karim Amir Moaveni. He's only recently emerged as the supreme leader of the Iranian Guardian Council. Ultrahardliner, ultraconservative. He's something of a living saint to Shi'ites in both Iran and in Afghanistan. And he won out in the power struggle within the twelve-man council that makes all important decisions in Iran.

"It's a little hard for Americans to understand just how powerful this Guardian Council of Twelve really is. They must approve *all* political decisions, and they approve who may and may not run for office in Iran's elections. In recent years Iran's president has made much of being a reformer . . . but, believe me, he cannot get into office and he will not stay in office without the express approval of the Guardian Council.

"Back in 2000 the president of Iran was Mohammed Khatami. At the UN, Khatami actually refused to shake hands with President Clinton until he'd checked in with the then-supreme leader, the Ayatollah Khamenei, and asked for permission. That permission, by the way, was refused.

"Ayatollah Moaveni has been of particular interest to National Intelligence lately, because he is a staunch militarist . . . and a hardcore fanatic. In the 1980s he pioneered the use of civilians—including children—to move ahead of advancing Iranian troops to find Iraqi minefields. When Iranian forces recaptured the port of Abadan after the Iraqi invasion, he was one of the clerics who insisted that the war continue, and *kept* it going for eight bloody years. He was also directly responsible for ordering the assassination of some hundreds of Iranian nationals worldwide: people considered to be enemies of the regime.

"In recent years there's been some loosening of the mullahs' control, some indications that they might be trying to pursue a more liberal policy, both toward the West and toward their own people. The younger segment of the population—teens and twenty-somethings—have been disaffected and restless. They've been protesting by boycotting elections. The mullahs have arranged for what amount to government subsidies for everything from buying a house to getting married, and lifted some of the government controls on dress and public behavior, apparently to defuse that discontent, or at least to keep the younger crowd apathetic.

"Currently, Iran stands at a difficult juncture. The people want greater freedom, especially in the economic sector. The mullahs want to maintain strong control over all aspects of Iranian life . . . not unlike the late lamented Taliban in Afghanistan, though they haven't been as bloody or as ham-handed as that. The clerical forces have tried to engage civilian support by loosening economic controls somewhat, but their control is backed by the Revolutionary Army; by Savama, the successor to the Shah's Savak secret police; and by gangs of thugs known as the 'Ansar-e Hezbollah.' Those last are gangs of thugs, usually aligned with one or another of the clerics. Their name means 'Helpers of the Party of God,' and they're used to intimidate and physically threaten demonstrators, journalists, and anyone engaged in what the regime considers to be immoral or counterrevolutionary activities.

"The big question in Iran today is whether the ordinary people are going to get sick enough of the human rights abuses to get rid of the clerics.

"So much for the historical background," Markham said. He clicked the remote, and another aerial photo came up, showing a large-scale construction site. "We're now interested in what we're seeing here in the Bandar-e Charak region—at White Scimitar. The DNI has been keeping the President apprised of the construction of the White Scimitar site. Given the current political situation in Iran, and between Tehran and Washington just now, the President has assigned the highest priority to intelligence gathering efforts in this region."

Turning, Markham used a laser pointer to place a bright red dot on the screen. "Some of what we can see here is pretty obvious." The dot swiftly orbited several objects. "We can see bulldozers . . . new road construction . . . a rail bed . . . and what look like concrete bunkers. Over here . . . these appear to be new barracks, storehouses, and POL storage tanks. If it was just this, we'd assume the facility was a new army base and let it go at that.

"But here are the things that have us concerned." The satellite photo clicked to another shot, closer in, centered on a line of blurry patches at the base of a mountain. Two large dump trucks and a bulldozer were clearly visible in the harsh sunlight. The red dot of the laser pointer circled the dark patches on the hillside.

"These are tunnel entrances, eight of them. Fifteen feet tall, twelve wide . . . big enough to receive a fair-sized truck or other vehicle. Our satellite recons have shown them moving hundreds of thousands of cubic meters of rock and earth out of that mountainside. Whatever they're building here, most of it is underground, where our spy sats can't see it.

"What is particularly alarming is some ancillary intelligence we received from our Azerbaijani station three months ago. CIA officers in Iran made contact with an Iranian citizen identified as a member of the MKO. That stands for Mujahedin-e-Khalq, a group originally formed to oppose the Shah and his pro-West policies back in the 1960s. Now, the MKO is currently on the U.S. State Department's list of terrorist organizations, because of their past use of bombings and assassinations to advance their political agenda. However, they currently oppose the Tehran regime, and have provided us with substantial information about Iran's nuclear, chemical, and biological warfare programs. According to our MKO informant, the White Scimitar site is planned as a storage area for Iranian WMDs."

A ripple of emotion ran down the table, a mingling of suspicion, denial, and a sense of "Oh, no, not *that* again."

The powerfully negative reaction, Garrett thought,

was certainly justified. Rumors of weapons of mass destruction had been the principle public justification for the 2003 invasion of Iraq, and careers had been ruined by the political flak when those WMDs could not be found.

That, of course, didn't mean the weapons hadn't existed. But to the public mind, the government had either lied to the people or been lied to by its own intelligence services, and neither possibility sat well with the voters.

"And that brings us to the failed op yesterday," Markham said, "to Black Stallion. As most of you know, a sixteen-man SEAL platoon was inserted off the coast by PBC. Eight of them moved inland in order to have a close covert look at the White Scimitar site, but encountered a heavy Iranian force—almost certainly a unit of the Sepah-e Pasdaran-e Enqelab-e Eslam, the Islamic Revolutionary Guard Corps. The SEALs successfully fought their way back to the beach. However, one of the PBCs was hit by an Iranian antiship missile and sunk. We lost two SEALs and five other Navy personnel. The rest of them made it back to our base in Oman this morning.

"The mission was a complete failure. They ran into the Pasdaran patrol while still more than a mile from their objective. We're not sure yet, but the Iranian defenses may have been higher tech than expected. The enemy may have been equipped with starlight night vision devices or sophisticated perimeter defense sensors.

"Needless to say, we expect some serious political fallout from this . . . incident, both at home and abroad. The Iranians will most likely use it to fan anti-American sentiment throughout the Islamic world . . . and to try to present themselves as *the* defenders of Islam against American aggression. Our Middle East desk analysts predict that the Shi'ite populations of both

Iraq and Syria could explode in anti-American riots and demonstrations. Israel is afraid that this could provide a major impetus for their ongoing Palestinian insurrection.

"Despite this, the President is still *most* insistent that we identify the nature of the White Scimitar site, and, in particular, find out what those tunnel entrances are for. To that end, he has authorized a second attempt at the covert infiltration and reconnaissance of Objective White Scimitar. The new mission has been code-named 'Operation Sea Hammer.'

"Obviously, such an attempt must be highly secret. The proposal has been made that a sizable SEAL or Special Forces unit could be put ashore by submarine . . . specifically by the newly recommissioned SSGN *Ohio*. To address that possibility, we have Captain Tom Garrett here this morning, of Naval Littoral Warfare. Captain Garrett?"

Garrett pushed back from the table and walked past its length to the front of the room, working to quell the butterfly flutter in his stomach. Commanding a submarine in combat was one thing; addressing a roomful of admirals, generals, and National Security types was something quite else.

Berkowitz had told him what to prepare for, and even quizzed him a bit last night, but the moment was on him now and he found himself nervous as hell.

"Gentlemen," he said as he stepped behind the podium. "Mr. Myers. I think by now most of you have at least seen the stat sheets on the *Ohio*. Here she is."

He picked up the remote control Markham had left at the podium and clicked it. A color photograph came up on the screen behind him—the *Ohio* under way, returning from her shakedown cruise six weeks before. The camera had caught her just exiting the Admiralty Inlet as she passed the Twin Spits and Port Ludlow, slipping gently into the quiet waters of the Hood Canal.

"Under the terms of the Start II arms limitations treaty, four of our SSBN boomers were scheduled to be stricken from the fleet. The *Ohio,* which was our very first Trident sub, was the first launched—back in 1979—and was originally scheduled for decommissioning.

"However, in the early 1990s, Congress directed that *Ohio* and three of her sister vessels be converted into conventional war-fighting platforms." He clicked the remote, and a schematic came up on the screen, a cutaway showing the submarine's interior. Most of the space aft of the sub's sail appeared to be taken up by a single compartment, the long and cavernous missile room, containing twelve pairs of forty-foot launch tubes down its length.

"As an SSBN, an Ohio-class boat mounts twenty-four launch tubes for Trident ICBMs. In the Ohio conversion to SSGN, each of twenty-two of her launch tubes now mounts seven VLS tubes—that's Vertical Launch System—firing TLAMs. A single converted Ohio-class submarine can carry 154 vertical launch TLAM Tomahawk missiles, the equivalent in cruise-missile firepower of an entire surface battle group.

"In addition, the *Ohio* now has facilities to carry a sizable special operations force—up to four platoons, or sixty-six men. The remaining two missile launch tubes have been redesigned as airlock compartments, allowing SEALs or other commandos to lock out of the sub while she remains submerged.

"*Ohio* currently is serving as a test bed for two miniature special-warfare submarines, the Advanced SEAL Delivery System, or ASDS, which has recently been deployed on the new Virginia-class boats, and the experimental prototype Manta SF/NB. Both of these will be useful in conducting covert reconnaissance of hostile coastlines, in advance of a commando insertion, or a full-blown invasion. An ASDS will be operated off the *Ohio*'s aft deck using a Dry Deck Shelter, with access through the lockout tubes. The SF/NB will operate out of one of the missile tubes, which has been temporarily coopted for the test series.

"We envision the *Ohio* and her sister SSGN conversions giving us a very special capability in Littoral Warfare . . . the ability to put a sizable covert special-ops unit ashore anywhere in the world, and to support that op from the submarine for the duration of the mission. In other words, *Ohio* could put a large SEAL team ashore, monitor the progress of the op, provide logistical support and resupply, and handle the extraction and withdrawal at the mission's end. If the situation called for it, the *Ohio* could lay down a devastating barrage of cruise missiles, either in support of forces ashore or as a means of eliminating the target after the completion of the initial reconnaissance. . . ."

Garrett was beginning to get into the flow of things, describing the redesigned *Ohio* boat and how she might be used in Operation Sea Hammer, to an attentive audience. He noticed several in the room were scribbling in notepads as he spoke. Myers, at the head of the table, leaned back in his swivel chair, elbow on the edge of the table, his head propped up on two fingers as he listened with an unreadable expression.

As he completed his presentation, he could feel an almost electric excitement throughout the room.

". . . and so it is my considered opinion," he concluded, "that the best platform for this operation by far is the SSGN *Ohio*. She has just completed her postconversion sea trials out of the Bangor Trident base. She is scheduled for deployment to Pearl Harbor to take part in a training exercise—Freeboard '08—with a sailing date set for two weeks from yesterday. However, her skipper informs me that she could be ready for departure as early as this coming Saturday, three days from now. She would need to take on board a SEAL unit plus the experimental Manta at Pearl, but allowing for a two-day layover there, she could be in the Gulf of Oman and ready to commence operations by Wednesday, June 25. All that is needed is for me to give the order." He looked at the oval of attentive faces. "Questions?"

"Captain Garrett," a Navy admiral said. His name tag read SCOFIELD, and he was CONAVSPECWAR— the commanding officer of all Naval Special Warfare units, including the Navy SEALs.

"Yes, sir."

"Just how close can this submarine get to the coast in that region?" Scofield asked with a pronounced midwestern twang. "The water is damned shallow in there, and you have Bandar Abbas right up the coast. Iranian waters will be mined, and the Straits of Hormuz have a nasty reputation for shoals and tight corners."

"As close as we need to, Admiral. The final decision will be up to the SEAL Team leader, and the captain of the *Ohio,* of course."

"That's my point, Captain. Sub drivers always want the SEALs to go in over the horizon. SEALs want the sub to put them on the beach."

Garrett nodded. This was an old and familiar tactical discussion within both the SF and submarine communities. "That's one reason for the *Ohio* conversion, Admiral. The *Ohio is* big, and won't be able to enter waters much shallower than a hundred feet and still stay submerged, but she *can* carry a lot of special equipment—including a couple of ASDVs. Those have an operational range of over one hundred nautical miles, and can carry eight SEALs apiece. The idea is to give the striking force as much flexibility—as many options—as possible."

"Well, now, correct me if I'm wrong . . . but an Ohio-class boomer is about as maneuverable as an eighteen-wheeler on the Beltway at rush hour. We've already lost a PBC in there; why the hell should we risk a nuclear sub?"

"Fair question, sir." Garrett didn't add that no naval officer of his acquaintance would consider it a career-positive move to correct an admiral . . . even if he *was* wrong. "I think the best answer I can give you is that submarines are designed to be sneaky. An Ohio-class boat is *quiet.* Even with the ASDS on her afterdeck, she's damned tough to pick up on sonar, and shallow waters make sonar detection even more challenging. Her skipper might take a couple of days to maneuver in as close as he needs to go, but she won't make a sound and the enemy will never know she's there. Patrol boats *are* surface craft, they *are* noisy, and they *are* easy to spot, visually and by radar." He hesitated, then took a deep breath. "Admiral, in my considered opinion, it was a serious tactical error sending Black Stallion in on board PCBs. That's what submarines are for."

"Captain Garrett," Myers said. "Why not deploy off of a Los Angeles boat? Or the *Seawolf*? We've used them for Special Forces missions in the past."

"Yes, sir, we have. And they've done well in that capacity. However, SSNs are attack boats. With SEALs on board, they're damned crowded, and they can't haul as much equipment along. The Ohio conversion is designed to serve as an advance operational base, remember. Attack boats are not.

"There's also the difference in firepower to consider. A Los Angeles Flight III boat has twelve vertical launch tubes for TLAMs. In addition, she can carry up to twenty-six tube-launched weapons . . . so, theoretically, she could carry thirty-eight Tomahawk missiles, though in practice, of course, some of her tube-launched weapons will be torpedoes or Harpoon antiship missiles.

"Even shy a couple of tubes for the ASDV and a Manta experimental fighter, as she is now, the *Ohio* can carry 140 Tomahawk missiles. That, sir, is one hell of a punch."

Myers nodded. "You've made your point, Captain. Thank you for your presentation."

Garrett took his seat.

But *had* he made his point? Decisions at the Pentagon, so often, seemed to be made by committee. Concepts went in through one door, but what came out was rarely recognizable even to their creators.

It would have been humorous if men's lives weren't so often riding on the outcome.

Wednesday, 28 May 2008

BJ's
Ninth Street,
Bremerton, Washington
2120 hours PST

Sonar technician second class Roger Caswell wasn't entirely sure what he was getting into. His buddies had told him they were just going out on the town, and asked if he would like to come along. But after a few drinks at the Torpedo Tube outside the main gate, they'd brought him here—to "round out the evening," as Doc Kettering had put it.

He'd never been inside a strip club.

Technically, EM1 Rodriguez had told him, it was a pasty club, but apparently in this neighborhood "pasty" meant tiny flecks of metallic glitter artfully enhancing—rather than concealing—the nipple. Besides the glitter, the dancers wore dental floss G-strings and the most ungainly shoes he'd ever seen: great, clunky plastic things with nine-inch heels that the girls wielded like deadly weapons when they lay on their backs and swung their legs about in something approximating time to the music.

The music. *God*, the music! It pounded and hammered, the beat so heavy Caswell wasn't even sure there was a tune to it. As a Navy sonar man, he was proud of his hearing, of the keen *discernment* of his hearing, and he much preferred classical music and light jazz to this . . . this *noise*.

"Oww . . . *dig* it!" Moone cried as they walked inside. "Now that's what I mean! They got *music* here, not that elevator mu-zak you can't even feel!"

"You mean the stuff that's all beat and no harmony?" Caswell replied. He had to raise his voice, and even then he doubted that Moone had heard him over the racket.

BJ's was a popular watering hole and ogling spot for enlisted men stationed in the Bremerton area. Half of the room was taken up by the bar, which featured a large-screen TV hanging from the ceiling, while the other half was devoted to a big, kidney-shaped stage on which the girls did their routines, complete with pole and trapeze. The big game between the Dodgers and the Angels was playing on the TV.

On weekend evenings the place could be packed. Wednesday nights, though, were slower, and the five of them had gathered on chairs along the edge of the stage—Caswell, Rodriguez, and the Doc, plus TM1 Moone and MM2 Jakowiac. House rules said they had to have a drink in front of them at all times. Jak was driving and had ordered a Diet Coke, but the rest were nursing overpriced beers, making them last as the dancers performed one after another.

"Hi, there," a big-breasted redhead said, crouching at the edge of the stage with her head close enough to Caswell's that her breathy voice carried above the background thumping. "Welcome to BJ's! What's your name?"

"Rog— Roger," he managed to say. He was finding it tough to pull his eyes away from her breasts. Her nipples must have been a good inch long apiece and sported very little in the way of glitter that Caswell could see.

"Hey, Roger! I'm Crystal!" She lowered herself onto her back, spread her legs with her crotch a couple of feet from Caswell's face, and began writhing on the stage with urgent, copulatory movements of her pelvis.

"Man, oh, man!" Moone said from Caswell's side. "Lookit them Mark one mod-zero detonators on *her* torpedoes!"

"I'll give her a torpedo, man," Rodriguez said, gripping his crotch suggestively. "I'll give her *my* torpedo right up her number one tube!"

"Whatcha think, Cas?" Moone asked, clapping him on the shoulder. "Howdja like a little I-and-I with *that*?"

Kettering hoisted his half-empty bottle. "Intercourse and intoxication! Damn the torpedoes and full speed ahead! Aye aye!"

"I'm not sure Nina would understand," Caswell said.

"Aw, Nina doesn't *have* to understand!" Moone said. He downed a swig from his bottle.

"What do you think, Roger?" the dancer asked him. It was a bit disconcerting; Caswell hadn't realized the dancers in places like this actually *talked* to the customers.

"Uh . . . very nice," he said. He held up his hands, palms out. "I'm being good. I'm not touching."

"He's *drooling*," Kettering added. "But he's not touching!"

"Drooling is okay," Crystal said, rubbing her breasts slowly. "You're allowed." Deftly, she moved her hand down to her crotch and tugged the black triangle of her G-string just far enough to the side to reveal a bit of clean-shaven pubic mound. As Caswell gaped, Crystal abruptly scissored her legs, sending her heavy right shoe inches above his head and past his right shoulder before rolling to the side and saucily sticking her tongue out at him.

"Awright!" Rodriguez called, clapping his hands. "Awright, baby!"

Crystal sat up, her right foot hovering a few inches in front of Caswell's face. A wad of folding money—mostly ones, but a few fives and tens—were tucked into the strap of her oversized shoe.

Caswell reached for his wallet, but Moone stopped him. "Uh-uh," he said. "The party's on us tonight. This boy is getting married on Saturday!" Moone snapped a dollar bill taut, then slipped it under the strap.

"Hey, congratulations!" Crystal said brightly.

"Thanks!" Caswell said. "Hey, can I ask you a question?"

"Sure." She looked as though she were bracing herself. Caswell imagined the girls in joints like this must get all kinds of propositions from the customers.

"How the hell do you walk in those damned shoes?"

Crystal rolled her eyes. "Carefully!" She scooted over and began writhing anew, this time in front of Rodriguez.

"Hey, Ohios!" someone yelled at them from the bar a few minutes later. "Listen up! It's hot poop!"

"Put the TV up, BJ!" someone else added.

Men around the stage began drifting away toward the bar, craning their necks to see the big-screen TV hanging overhead. A special news bulletin was coming over the channel that a few moments ago had been showing a baseball game. A TV news reporter faced the camera at his desk, his words lost beneath the boom of the dance music. The larger-than-life face of a bearded man in a turban making a televised address glared down over his right shoulder.

The words IRAN CRISIS were prominently displayed across the bottom of the screen.

Her audience gone, Crystal shrugged, stood up, and walked—carefully—to the steps leading down to the back room, as the man at the DJ control board lowered the music's volume.

". . . and Iranian authorities claim the U.S. Navy vessel was well inside their territorial waters when the incident occurred. Iran's President Rafsanjani said from his office earlier today that the attack was deliberate and calculated, and a clear violation of international law . . ."

"What's going down?" Caswell asked.

"Navy ship got sunk in the Gulf yesterday," a burly sailor at the bar told him. "We sent in an air strike and took out a missile launcher and some radar sites."

"Which ship?"

"They haven't said. Shut your hole and let me hear this."

". . . Secretary of Defense Donald Rumsfeld held a press conference at the Pentagon today," the announcer continued. "He said that America 'remains committed to maintaining free passage through the international waters within the Straits of Hormuz, and to the security of our many allies in the region . . . ' "

"Meanin' fuckin' raghead oil!" someone in the audience yelled. He sounded drunk. "Get back to the fuckin' game!"

"Shaddap, Lou! Gulf championships're more important, know what I mean?"

There were several brief sound-bite interviews with various talking heads, but Caswell was no longer listening. Another crisis in the Gulf, so what else was new? There'd been saber-rattling over Iran since the invasion of Iraq, and a number of cries and confrontations that had made it to CNN. Actually, and for the most part, things had been pretty quiet out there for several years now, so maybe it was time for another one.

The chances were, it wouldn't affect him. The U.S. Fifth Fleet was in the Gulf, based at Qatar. Caswell and his buddies were crew members of the USGN *Ohio*, and therefore part of the Third Fleet and based in the eastern Pacific. Scuttlebutt had it that the *Ohio* would be spending the next year or so conducting training missions with the froggies—the Navy SEALs—in Hawaii and in San Diego.

As for him, well, he was getting married in another week and a half—Saturday, June 7. He already had it figured how he could take some leave time while *Ohio* was at Pearl. Nina would fly out to meet him, and they'd have a few days of honeymoon together on exotic and romantic Maui.

The news report ended with the inevitable promise of more to come at eleven. The music came back up . . . but something special was happening. There were five dancers on tonight, and all five were on the stage now.

"We have a soon-to-be ex-bachelor in the audience," the DJ announced over the sound system. "Let's get him up here and let him say farewell to the bachelor life! Roger Caswell? Get your tail up here, Roger! Someone get the man a chair!"

A chair was produced and put in the middle of the stage, just in front of the vertical pole, and a couple of lovely, mostly naked young women took him by the hands and led him up the steps. The others were waiting for him there. They sat him in the chair with his back to the pole, and as the music thumped and pounded, they began their energetic gyrations around him.

The whole routine was pretty much a blur for Caswell . . . very pleasant, but hard to take in. At one point he had a woman perched on each knee, another at his back reaching down and pinching his nipples through his shirt, and two more pressed up close, one to either side. One of them produced a pair of white panties, which she pulled down over his head, arranging it so it covered his mouth but left his eyes free.

The audience was cheering, catcalling, and clapping in time to the brutal rhythm.

Caswell was a quiet guy who hated being the center of attention, and right now he felt miserably foolish. The worst part about it was not knowing what to do with his hands. All of that naked female flesh so temptingly close, but he knew he wasn't allowed to touch. He was afraid he was going to get called for groping one of them by accident. . . .

Turning his head, he looked past a bare breast and locked eyes with Moone. "I'm going to get you for this, Moonie!" he called, but he didn't know if he'd been heard.

The torture ended with Crystal doing a lap dance, squatting over him with her arms reaching past his head and her hands on the pole, those magnificent naked breasts bobbing up and down just inches from his face. The other girls huddled close around, swaying to the music, stroking his arms, chest, and the back of his head.

And then, mercifully, the ordeal was over. The girls, grinning and patting his shoulders, walked off the stage.

Well, perhaps the ordeal wasn't *quite* over. He still

had to stand up and leave the stage himself, and the past several minutes had been somewhat . . . arousing. He managed to pick up the chair and hold it in front of him as he carried it off the stage, the best cover he could arrange on short notice. He stumbled a bit on the steps, but recovered his balance. Damn, he was having trouble walking! Somehow, he made it back to his seat, still wearing the panties around his neck.

"Which one of you clowns put them up to that?" he demanded, pulling the underwear off over his head. "You, Moonie? Doc?"

"Well," Kettering said with an evil grin, "I might have had a word or three with the DJ. It's their traditional bachelor's send-off, y'know?"

"Howdja like it, Cas?" Jakowiac asked him. "Man, they were all *over* you!"

He stuck a finger in his right ear and dug at it, as though trying to clear his hearing. "Didn't care for the music. . . ."

"Aw, you and that freakin' highbrow intellectual shit of yours!" Moone said, shaking his head with mock sadness. "We gotta educate you, newbie!"

"Tell you what, Moonie. You can teach me about that rap-crap you like if you let me teach you about Bach and Mozart!"

"And I will *see* you your Mozart, m'man, and raise you some Eminem!"

They got up and made their way toward the exit not long after. Crystal, modestly clad for the moment in a dressing gown, came up to him while Moone and Doc were in the head. "Aw, you guys aren't leaving already, are you?"

" 'Fraid so, honey," Rodriguez said with a pleasant leer. "When you get off, anyway?"

She pointedly ignored him as she turned to Caswell. "You seem really nice," she told him. "Good luck with getting married and everything!"

"Thanks, Crystal," he said.

Jakowiac exploded with a guffaw as she walked away, buttocks shifting delightfully beneath her sheer gown. "Hey, Cas! You've got a friend! She was really comin' on to ya!"

"Ah," Rodriguez said with a dismissive wave of his hand. "Fuckin' bitch just liked how much money we dropped on 'em!"

But Caswell didn't think it was like that at all. Some of the girls dancing up there tonight had seemed, well, a bit fake, somehow. Posturing. Pasting on a smile along with the sparkles, to make the customers happy. Crystal, though, had seemed like the most genuine of the lot.

Nina, he thought, definitely wouldn't understand.

Officers' Housing
Bremerton, Washington
2340 hours PST

The phone shrilled on the nightstand, as insistent as a bucket of cold water. Commander Keith H. Stewart groaned and pulled away from his wife. Their lovemaking an hour ago had been passionate and intense, leaving him deep in a pleasant, sex-induced coma.

Sixteen years as a naval officer, however, the last two of them as XO of the SSBN *Maine,* and two more before that as exec of the SSN *Pittsburgh,* had instilled in him the singular ability to come wide-awake in an instant, whatever the physical circumstances. "Stewart."

"Sorry to call so late, Commander," the voice on the other end of the line said. "This is Tom Garrett."

That name brought him even wider awake. He sat up in bed, swinging his legs over the side. "Sir."

Captain Garrett had been his skipper on the *Pittsburgh*. More recently, the man had been working on the *Ohio* project for months; had been, more than anyone else, the driving force behind the SSGN conversion program as it reached its final stages. There were still those in Congress and in the Pentagon who would kill the *Ohio* conversion if they could, despite the fact that four billion dollars had already been spent on the program and the physical conversion was complete.

The fact that Garrett was calling *now* . . .

Stewart fumbled for his watch on the nightstand. God . . . 2340 hours? That meant 0240 Eastern Time. Didn't the guy ever sleep?

"It looks like your op eval is getting moved up a bit, Bob," Garrett said. "We're deploying you."

An active-duty patrol? *Ohio* had been scheduled for a year-long operational evaluation, which meant lots of tests, drills, and exercises designed to see just what she could do. If LitWar was bypassing that crucial phase . . ."Sounds like the big time."

"You could say that. Straits of Hormuz."

"Ah. I was wondering. I've been watching the reports on CNN. What's going down?"

"Your orders will be arriving aboard sometime later this morning," Garrett told him. "The details are still being chewed on at this end. All I can tell you at the moment is that we're going to try to get you out of port ASAP. Think you can have *Ohio* ready in all respects for sea by Saturday?"

Saturday! Hell and damnation! "Yes, sir. She will be ready."

"Good man."

"Are we going out solo, sir? Or being assigned to a task force?"

"As I said, the details are being worked out. Likeliest scenario is you'll head straight for Oahu, pick up your subs and a SEAL component, and then make for the Gulf. Meanwhile, we'll have a submarine already on-station checking out the lay of the land ahead of your arrival. You'll remember her. . . ."

"The *Pittsburgh*?"

"The same. She's at Qatar now, offloading the SEALs she picked up after the *Sirocco* went down. We're going to have her off Bandar Abbas just as quick as we can turn her around. She'll reconnoiter the AO, and you'll coordinate your intel gathering with her."

"That's good news, sir. The *'Burgh* is a good boat."

"That she is. Oh, and one more thing."

"Yes, sir?"

"You're going to have a VIP on board tomorrow."

"Sir?"

"Marine General Andrew Vintner."

"A jarhead? Are we going to be working with the Marines?"

"General Vintner is retired, Bob. *Forcibly* retired. I want you to listen to what he has to say."

"Certainly, sir." Inwardly, Stewart groaned. Retired leatherneck generals didn't pay social calls on submarine skippers. If Garrett wanted him to talk to the man, there was a damned heavy reason for it. Garrett's emphasis on the word *forcibly,* and his unwillingness to discuss the topic openly over the phone, together suggested politics. *Nasty* politics.

But . . . a retired Marine general serving as a briefing officer? *That* didn't sound likely. Things definitely were out of kilter somehow.

Not a pleasant thought when the boat you skippered was about to be the pointy end of the stick.

"I'll look forward to meeting him, Captain."

"Don't. You won't like what he has to say."

"Yes, sir." Stewart hesitated. "Captain?"

"Yes?"

"Why the hell are you still at your desk at zero-dark-thirty hours? You're not pulling night duty at the Pentagon information desk, are you?"

Garrett chuckled. "Not yet, Keith. Suffice to say that the *Sirocco* incident has a lot of people in Washington very unhappy right now. And nervous. There is a . . . perception that we may be coming down to a final showdown with Tehran."

"Meaning?"

There was a long hesitation. "Spear-to-spear."

"My God."

"There is that possibility," Garrett told him. "Just listen to what General Vintner has to say. He'll bring you up to speed."

"Yes, sir."

"Again . . . sorry to call you so late. I hope you hadn't already turned in."

"No, sir. Not a problem."

"Good. I'll talk to you later today. I just wanted to give you a heads-up on General Vintner's visit. Good night, Keith."

"Good night, sir."

He stared at the telephone in his hand for a long moment before quietly hanging it up. *Spear-to-spear.* The phrase, he knew, had been floating around the Pentagon and in various Navy headquarters for some time now as a deliberately misleading and unexciting euphemism. "Broken spear" had long been the code phrase for an incident involving a nuclear weapon or warhead that could lead to a nuclear accident. That phrase had led to the use of the more colorful "spear-to-spear" as a term for a nuclear showdown, a confrontation between two nuke-armed adversaries, each expecting the other to blink.

Nuclear confrontation. Washington's number one nightmare scenario.

He lifted his legs and rolled back into bed, trying to gently reestablish the warm spoon-embrace from which he'd been awakened. Kathy—somehow she'd slept through the phone's ring—stirred and mumbled something, but didn't wake up all the way.

Iran had nuclear warheads. There was little enough doubt about that. Tehran hadn't publicly announced the fact, or conducted a test, but they'd been spreading the word across the Middle East on an unofficial basis for at least the past two years, and getting a fair amount of political leverage for their effort throughout the region. North Korea had been selling them the equipment, the raw materials, and the know-how for ten years at least. Possibly they'd finally sold them a bomb as well . . . or possibly their own home-grown nuclear research had finally paid off.

Either way, Tehran had a long history of working closely with Islamic terrorists, as well as an even longer history of seeking military, political, and religious dominance throughout the Gulf. They might easily decide that nuclear confrontation with America would make them *the* heroes of the Muslim world.

And North Korea had also been giving them a lot of help with their ballistic missile program lately. There were intelligence estimates floating around inside the Washington Beltway now to the effect that Iran might be capable of hitting the continental U.S. with a nuclear ICBM within another five to seven years.

Scary, scary stuff.

And there wasn't a lot that could be done about it, either. Ever since the invasion of Iraq had failed to turn up the WMDs that were the purported excuse for the invasion, the news media, Hollywood, and the more liberal segments of the U.S. population had been particularly outspoken in their stand against what they called American militarism. In his opinion, if those jokers could be believed, Iran had a perfect right to develop its own nuke weaponry.

Stewart wondered sometimes if the United States was going to have to lose a city or two before she woke up to the realities of a very dangerous modern world. He'd thought the loss of a couple of Manhattan skyscrapers had awakened the nation seven years ago. Evidently, it was going to take something more.

New York City, perhaps? Or Washington, D.C.?

As a U.S. naval officer and as the CO of a Navy warship, Stewart was oath-bound to stand between America and any enemy who sought to inflict that kind of harm on her. Unfortunately, there was only so much he could do, only so much *any* man could do.

But, by God, if there was a way the refurbished *Ohio* could make a difference out there in the narrow shallows of the Straits of Hormuz, then he would see to it that she made that difference.

Perhaps an hour later he knew he was not going to get back to sleep. Carefully easing his way out of the bed, he got up, dressed, wrote a note for Kathy on the computer for her to find when she got up, and left the house.

There was a hell of a lot of work to be done if the *Ohio* was to be ready for departure by Saturday.

Thursday, 29 May, 2008

Captain's Office, SSGN *Ohio*
Puget Sound Naval Shipyard
Bangor, Washington
1015 hours PST

A knock sounded on the door. Stewart looked up from the maintenance log he was reviewing. "Come."

The door swung open and the Marine sentry leaned inside. "Sir. General Vintner to see you, sir."

"Send him in!"

A submarine, even a vessel as relatively spacious as the *Ohio,* was a bit cramped for formalities, and even the captain's office—a small compartment adjoining his stateroom, which, with desk, chairs, and other essentials, was almost claustrophobic—was little more than a glorified walk-in closet.

Still, Stewart stood as the general entered. Vintner wore a civilian jacket and tie. He was gray-haired, in his late fifties or early sixties, Stewart guessed, but steel-hard in both his bearing and the expression in his eye. "Captain Stewart?" he said, extending a hand. "Thank you for seeing me."

"Captain Garrett strongly suggested that I see you, sir. But it *is* a pleasure, believe me." He gestured to the only chair other than his own in the room.

Vintner chuckled as he took a seat. "Captain Garrett can have strong opinions. He's a real hard-charger. As well as a good friend."

Stewart sat down again behind the desk. "Yes, sir. Uh . . . coffee?"

"Thank you, no. I don't want to take up too much of your time, Captain. I understand you're making ready for sea."

"That's what they tell me. I . . . gather you have something to talk to me about that may have a bearing on this deployment?"

"Possibly," Vintner said. His jaw hardened. "Possibly. If you will indulge me, I'd like to tell you a little story."

"Of course."

"Operation Millennium Challenge. Have you read anything about it? Summer of '02."

Stewart searched his memory. "Um . . . something in *Naval Proceedings*? The war games in the Gulf just before we invaded Iraq?"

"That's the one. What do you know about it?"

Stewart shrugged. "It was a large-scale exercise. We needed to know we could deploy our fleet elements efficiently. A preparatory exercise for the real thing."

"Exactly." Vintner leaned back in his chair. "As it happens, I was part of the OPFOR staff."

OPFOR. Opposing Force. In military war games, OPFOR was the U.S. force serving as the enemy against which U.S. units could be deployed, trained, and tested.

"Millennium Challenge," Vintner went on, "was the most elaborate and expensive war game we've ever put together—two years in the planning, and costing something like $250 million. Altogether, it involved all of the service branches, with almost fourteen thousand U.S. troops at seventeen locations and nine life-force training sites, and using a small army of computers to run the simulations. It wasn't aimed at Iraq, exactly, but it *was* set in the Arabian Gulf, and it simulated a conflict with a hypothetical rogue nation. The good guys were 'Force Blue,' of course. The bad guys, OPFOR, were 'Force Red.' The war was set to last for three weeks, and to end with the overthrow of Force Red's tyrannical dictator on August fifteenth."

"Nice to know things like that in advance."

"Tell me about it." He made a sour face. "It's important that you understand something here. This wasn't just posturing or saber-rattling—trying to be the big, tough kid on the block—and it wasn't intended to send a message to the Iraqi regime . . . at least, not solely. The commanding officer of the Joint Forces Command—under whose auspices the games were held—announced to the press before things got under way that the war games would test a whole series of new war-fighting techniques and concepts."

Stewart cocked his head to the side. "Like what? Nathan Bedford Forrest was supposed to have said the important thing in war was to get there 'fustest with the mostest,' or something of the sort. That's still pretty much what warfare comes down to."

"This is modern warfare, Captain Stewart. We're dealing with really key concepts here . . . like 'rapid decisive operations,' 'effects-based operations,' 'operational net assessments,' crap like that."

"Uh. Is this war-fighting, sir? Or marketing department buzz words like some major corporation?"

"Sometimes, Captain, it's damned hard to tell. In any case, at the conclusion of the operation, JOINT-FOR drafted a set of recommendations to the Joint Chiefs of Staff, insisting that all points and concepts had been demonstrated successfully.

"That, Captain, is on the public record. Millennium Challenge was a huge success. We proved what we wanted to prove, and we've implemented key changes in our training, procurement, and war-fighting strategy based on that success."

"Uh-huh. Sounds good. What's the catch?"

"The catch is that it didn't happen the way we told the reporters, or the Joint Chiefs."

"Go on."

"The commander of Force Red was Lieutenant General Paul Van Riper, an old-school Marine. They actually brought him out of retirement to play the role of the shrewd but crazy Middle Eastern dictator who headed up OPFOR's hypothetical country. Most of the details still aren't public. Some of the story, though, was leaked to the *Army Times*. Millennium Challenge was described as 'free play,' meaning both sides were unrestrained in their tactics, free to implement any strategy they pleased to secure victory. The emphasis, remember, was on a realistic analysis of a potential war in the Gulf. Force Blue was built around a standard U.S. naval carrier battle group. Force Red was much weaker, clearly inferior in strength and technology, with smaller vessels, including numerous civilian small craft and air assets. The sort of thing you'd be likely to find with a typical third world power in the region.

"General Van Riper protested the official assessment of the games. He called the new war-fighting techniques—the 'effects-based operations' and all the rest of that bullshit—'empty sloganeering.' And he should know. In the first three days of the 'war,' in simulation, General Van Riper and his vastly inferior Force Red managed to send most of the U.S. fleet—including one of our supercarriers—to the bottom."

"Jesus Christ! . . ."

Vintner chuckled. "It's been called 'the worst U.S. naval disaster since Pearl Harbor.' General Van Riper was brilliant, absolutely *brilliant*! Perhaps his best stroke was in not using any radio communications at all. You know, of course, that we scored some of our best intelligence coups in Afghanistan by listening in on al-Qaeda's cell phone conversations. Well, Van Riper didn't use cell phones, and he didn't use radios. Nothing to give Force Blue's SIGINT boys anything to work with. The man employed *couriers* to get orders to his field commanders . . . and he also employed coded messages delivered from the minarets of local mosques."

"God. Like Paul Revere and his lanterns in the Old North Church."

"Exactly. Low-tech all the way. The important thing was, he never tried to confront the U.S. armada directly. He armed his small craft and pleasure boats, maneuvered them in close, and waited. When Force Blue gave him an ultimatum to surrender, he delivered a coded signal . . . and the entire carrier battle group found itself under attack by swarms of pleasure boats and prop-driven civilian light aircraft. Some of the boats and light planes made suicide attacks, kamikaze style. Other pleasure boats were carrying Silkworm antiship missiles. One of those sank the supercarrier. Got it at damned near point-blank range, before its Phalanx defensive batteries could be powered up. Two more sank a couple of helicopter carriers with several thousand sailors and Marines on board. In fact, most of the U.S. ship losses were to cruise missiles that had been jury-rigged to fire off of yachts, barges, fishing boats, and that sort of thing.

"The really scary part was, as brilliant as the attack was, there was *nothing* in Van Riper's tactics that was new or startling. It was essentially just a larger scale repeat of al-Qaeda's attack on the USS *Cole* in Yemen back in 2000. Remember that? A small civilian barge comes alongside while the ship is in port, and . . . bam! One of our destroyers crippled, seventeen American sailors dead, and thirty more injured.

"This time around, though, in simulation, sixteen U.S. warships had been sunk, and I don't know how many thousands of sailors, Marines, and soldiers were 'dead.' The rest of the American fleet was scattered and in complete disarray."

"You said, though, that the operation was a success."

"Uh-huh. It was. JOINTFOR Command simply resumed the game. The sunken ships were brought back to the surface, the dead sailors brought back to life, and the invasion continued as originally scheduled. Force Red continued to harass the U.S. fleet, but then General Van Riper discovered that his orders to his field commanders were actually being countermanded." Vintner shrugged. "At that point he quit. Resigned in disgust. In his after-action report, he charged that the whole exercise had been scripted so it would turn out the way it was supposed to. With a resounding Force Blue victory."

"Sounds like that's exactly what happened."

"Actually, no. Millennium Challenge started off as a genuine free-play exercise. I'm convinced of that. Only after day three, when Force Blue realized it didn't have a fleet any longer, did JOINTFOR step in and begin rewriting things."

"I don't get it! How could they justify a thing like that?"

"Easy. By backpedaling and by throwing out smoke screens. When the press questioned the JOINTFOR commander, he admitted the fleet had been 'sunk' . . . but said that the nature of the war game was such that we were operating in a heavily traveled international shipping lane—true—and that we were constrained by that in what defenses we could employ. *Partly* true . . . but misleading. He said we had to deploy our ships close to shore, and that in a real war, they would have been over the horizon and safe from that type of attack.

"What he didn't add, though, was that the Gulf is essentially a large lake. It's shallow, it's narrow, there's only one way in or out, and there's no room for maneuver. And there *is* no over-the-horizon where the fleet could be safe. Our potential enemies over there have very good radar coverage—and that means missile coverage—of the entire Gulf. Most of the sinkings in our little war-game exercise were carried out by cruise missiles launched at close range.

"Basically, what Millennium Challenge proved was that the U.S. Fifth Fleet is in a very tiny, very narrow trap . . . kind of like the box canyons that figured so large in the TV westerns we watched as kids. Perfect place for an ambush, and damned hard to get out of if things turn sour."

"And so what the hell did it all prove, anyway?" Just hearing Vintner's description made Stewart angry. It was the protect-your-turf ass-covering that had been prominent during Vietnam, and forty years later it clearly was still business-as-fucking-usual.

Vintner shrugged. "JOINTFOR got its victory. The rest was pretty much covered up, except for the bit that got leaked."

"What happened to General Van Riper?" Stewart asked.

A shrug. "He went back into retirement."

"And you? Where were you in all of this?"

"I was a colonel then, serving on General Van Riper's staff. During the hearings afterward, I came across . . . well, a little shrill, I'm afraid. I was the one who first said things were rigged to guarantee a Force Blue win. Some of that was attributed to the general. Eventually, I was . . . *encouraged* to take an early retirement. They sweetened the deal by letting me retire as a general." Vintner looked away, his fist clenched on the arm of his chair. "Maybe I shouldn't have taken it. But there wasn't any other option open to me. If I'd refused, I would have spent my last six years in as a colonel, probably in charge of the penguin census in Antarctica."

"I see."

"At the time, I thought that was just the way things were. That I should be a team player, shut up, and let them do it their way."

"Well, the invasion of Iraq went off without a hitch. The Fifth Fleet wasn't sunk."

"Iraq wasn't being led by Saddam Van Riper, either. But you'll notice that the enemy's tactics over there have pretty much followed those employed by Van Riper. The insurgency in Iraq . . . that was mostly carried out by suicide bombers and IEDs"—Improvised Explosive Devices—"basically, home-made bombs and other low-tech tactics. Never try matching the U.S. forces strength for strength. Always try for the unexpected."

"Are you saying they're following Van Riper's lead?"

"No." He sighed. "Fortunately for our side, al-Qaeda and most of the military leaders in Iran right now are not anywhere close to being in Van Riper's league. Most of them are idiots . . . or at least completely uneducated in the science of modern warfare.

"But you don't have to be a freaking military genius to figure out that it's a bad idea to take on a U.S. carrier battle group with a small surface navy . . . but that ambushing that CBG with cruise missiles and suicide boats might give you a good chance of scoring at least a kill or two. And, God help me, I have to wonder how long public support for a war would last—no, worse, how long *congressional* support for the war would last—if we lost an LPD with a thousand Marines on board in there, or maybe the *Kitty Hawk* or *Abraham Lincoln*."

"You're saying we might win the war militarily, but lose it politically," Stewart said. "Just like in Vietnam."

"Bingo." Vintner shifted in his chair, folding his hands. "In modern war-fighting parlance, it's called 'asymmetric advantage,' meaning the little guy finds a way to yank the rug out from under the big guy.

"Mostly, though, I'm saying that exercises like Millennium Challenge perform a serious disservice to our young men and women in uniform. That kind of self-serving ass-covering bullshit puts their lives in danger. I don't care how many generals' and admirals' careers are saved—it's not worth the life of a single one of our people."

"I agree. But why . . ."

"Why am I coming to you with this?" Vintner grinned. "Actually, I went to Tom Garrett first. He's in Littoral Warfare, and in a position to put the word where it'll do the most good. And, like I said earlier, he's a hard-charger.

"And he suggested I come talk to you because you are going to be the sharp end of the spear pretty soon. I don't know what the *Ohio* is going to be doing out there. I'm not in the service anymore, and that's not my responsibility. But I do know that the people who ought to know better, the people in charge, didn't learn a damned thing from Millennium Challenge. For them, it's all cosmetic. A game to play, to win, and then they get to congratulate themselves on how great everything was, and maybe pass around some medals and citations.

"Captain Stewart, I am convinced that the Fifth Fleet is in serious danger over there. If Iran can find a way to launch a crippling strike on the fleet, or on the base at Qatar, it would make them the overnight heroes of the whole damned Muslim world. They know damned well they wouldn't win a stand-up fight. But they might think they could hurt us enough that we would apologize and leave. At the very least, they would have a shot at rallying the Islamic militants around their banner.

"And if that ever happens, the United States will find herself in a very precarious position."

"I'm not sure the *Ohio* could do much about it if it did."

"Maybe not. But Captain Garrett felt it was important that you know what's going on at the top of the brass pyramid. We have good people at every level of our military hierarchy, but we also have sycophants, blame-passers, and assholes, too, just like in any big organization. If enough people at high command levels have the same head-in-the-sand attitude as the JOINTFOR people running Millennium Challenge, it could seriously hamper us, even cripple us, if we found ourselves up against an adversary worthy of the name in the Gulf. The more people at an operational level who know the score, the better. At least, that's my feeling. And Tom Garrett's, too, evidently."

"And mine."

Vintner stood up. "Well, I've said my piece. Like I say, I don't want to take up any more of your time."

Stewart stood as well, and they shook hands. "I appreciate your coming in to talk to me. Did you have a long drive?"

"Nah. I live in Oregon. A few hours' drive. No biggie."

"Well, thank you, just the same. Believe me, I'll keep in mind what you said."

"Thank you, sir. That's all I ask."

The retired Marine came to rigid attention for a moment, just as though he were centering on the hatch in front of a superior officer. Then he turned, opened the door, and was gone. Stewart heard the Marine outside the office door snap to attention, heard Vintner's easy "As you were, son."

And then he was gone.

Was it Josephus, the First-century Jewish historian who'd written of the Roman army, who said that the Romans' battles were bloody exercises, while their exercises were bloodless wars? His point had been that Rome had conquered the known world because they had a superb army, one that trained constantly and in the most realistic ways possible.

The U.S. Navy submarine service had a similar philosophy. Drills and training exercises were as realistic as possible, in order to give the men a taste of what the real thing was like, whether it was a torpedo attack, an emergency surfacing, or a fire or flooding "casualty," as an accident on board a sub was known.

But realistic training exercises weren't just to help the crew prepare for the real thing. They were designed to help the officers overseeing the evolution learn where the crew was weak, what needed attention or more work, where a problem might arise if the real thing arose, even to pinpoint individual sailors who might be having a problem in some area, where they might be given some extra help or incentive.

If problems were noted, then ignored because they made a department look bad, that was a deadly threat to the entire boat. Within the brotherhood of the submariner service, there was no room for that kind of deliberate blindness.

And that, Stewart reflected, could as easily be applied to the whole world of international relations and the U.S. Navy's role both as peacekeepers and as guardians of the sea lanes.

A U.S. Navy submariner was used to being the sharp point of the weapon—out in front where the action was hottest. It always helped to know, though, that your own people were there to support you, to provide the backup and support you needed to survive.

He did *not* like what Vintner's indictment implied.

Control Room, SSN *Pittsburgh*
Off Bandar Abbas, Iran
2220 hours Zulu

Commander Jack Creighton stepped up to the periscope dais.

He surveyed his domain. *Pittsburgh*'s control room was surprisingly spacious, though crowded at the moment with officers and men at their duty stations. Popular myth insisted that submarines were claustrophobic sewer pipes crowded to the point of madness. In fact, Creighton felt a certain fondness for the close quarters. It was reassuring to know that over a hundred shipmates shared this sealed space, which had been designed with astonishing precision and efficiency.

Along the starboard bulkhead were the fire control stations, including the BSY-1—pronounced "Busy-one"—combat system, the heart of *Pittsburgh*'s death-dealing power. To port were the ship controls, including the ballast controls, ship status board, and navigational consoles. In the port-forward corner were the side-by-side bucket seats—complete with seat belts—for the helmsman and planesman, with the diving officer between and behind them, literally watching over their shoulders. At the moment, the control room was red-lit, standard procedure when it was night "on the roof" and the crew needed to keep their eyes dark-adjusted.

Satisfied that all was running nominally, Creighton walked the few feet aft to the Mark 18 periscope. There were two periscope mountings, set side by side on the raised platform. The Type 2 scope, to port, was a basic optical attack scope—one little changed from its WWI antecedents. The Mk. 18, however, was the most advanced optical periscope in the Navy's inventory, though it had been superceded in terms of bells and whistles by the more advanced photonics mast system employed on board the new Virginia-class attack boat . . . or on the Ohio-class refit. The Mk. 18 could see in low-light conditions, and the view could be projected to a number of large-screen monitors elsewhere on the boat. It also included a 70mm camera for recording the scenes for later analyses.

"Up scope."

As the periscope slid silently up out of its deck housing, Creighton draped his arms over the snap-down handles, "hanging on the scope" as he pressed his eye against the eyepiece, and walked it in a complete circle, checking the horizon for a full three-sixty to make sure they hadn't come up close aboard an unheard and un-suspected surface vessel.

The surface upstairs was brightly if unevenly lit. The waters were moonlit, and the light from the city cast a wavering glow that shifted and broke with the movement of the waves. The immediate area was clear, though there were a number of vessels visible. Most serious was a light patrol frigate less than a thousand yards off *Pittsburgh*'s starboard beam. She was close, and she was in approach . . . though not dead-on.

He centered the frigate in the periscope's crosshairs. "Target, bearing zero-zero-five . . . mark."

"Sonar contact Sierra Niner-five," the sonar officer called back, identifying the target. "Twin screw, military screw. Library IDs her as a Vosper Mark 5. Speed fifteen knots."

"Hull number seventy-two," Creighton said. "What do you have on her, Dick?"

Lieutenant Commander Dwayne Tracy—with the inevitable nickname "Dick"—was *Pittsburgh*'s executive officer. He was already looking up the warbook information on the contact, which was stored in *Pittsburgh*'s extensive computer memory.

"Iranian Navy Alvand class," he said. "Former Vosper Mark 5 class. Hull 72 is the *Alborz* . . . formerly the *Zaal*. Displacement of 1,540 tons, full load. Two shafts. Two cruise diesels, 3,800 bhp, top speed seventeen knots . . . but with two TM-3A boost gas turbines at 46,000 shp, top sprint speed of 39 knots. Sonar, Type 174, hull-mounted. Armament . . . five-cell Sea Killer SSM, one 114mm DP, one dual 35mm AA, four 20mm mounts, two 12.7mm MGs, one Limbo ASW mortar. Crew of 135."

The frigate was probably primarily employed for

harbor patrol off Bandar Abbas. She could sprint and she could hit, though ASW mortars, like the hedgehogs of WWII, were not notoriously accurate. At a speed of fifteen knots, she was *not* going to pick up anything on sonar. The roar of water rushing past her hull would drown out any trace of the lurking American sub.

On her current heading, the *Alborz* would miss the *Pittsburgh* by a generous margin, passing off her starboard side, coming no closer than eight hundred yards.

"Control Room, Sonar!"

"Go ahead, Sonar."

"Captain . . . new contact, designated Sierra One-one-eight, bearing zero-zero-zero. Single shaft, military screw . . . and she's *quiet*. On the surface, but I think it's a diesel boat, sir."

Creighton panned the periscope slightly counter-clockwise, checking astern of the passing *Alborz*. He didn't see anything. . . .

No! Wait! A low, black shadow momentarily blotted out the lights of the port.

"Helloooo . . . target!" he said softly. "Sonar! You think it's a Kilo?"

"Negative, Con. Not a Kilo. I don't know what the hell it is. But it's damned quiet. My guess is it's trying to slip out in the Vosper's wake."

Over the past decade or so, Iran had acquired a number of Kilo-class diesel attack submarines from the former Soviet Union. The boat was the CIS's premier military export sub, deadly and stealthy in the extreme. Some sources said Iran now possessed ten Kilos.

But the new target wasn't a Kilo . . .

Creighton took his time examining the low silhouette. Under starlight enhancement he could make some details of the other boat's sail. She was rising low, her deck completely submerged, but the sail wasn't as long as a Kilo's, and the periscope mast arrangement was different.

He couldn't be certain, but he thought he just might be looking at an Iranian Ghadir-class submarine.

The *Ghadir* had been launched three years ago, in May 2005. Precious little was known about them, though, because the Iranians had been careful about deploying them. All that was known was that they were ultraquiet, the design based on the Russian Kilos.

The frigate's speed suddenly made some sense. By creating a churned-up wake of white noise, the frigate's captain was creating a kind of shield within which the Iranian boat could travel almost undetected. It was sheer chance—as well as a tribute to U.S. sonar technology and the sonar watch's talent—that they'd picked that target out of the hash.

Creighton considered the situation a moment. *Pittsburgh* had been deployed to the waters off Bandar Abbas for several reasons: to scout out the harbor approaches, determine the nature and strength of the local defenses, and to pay close attention to military vessels in-port.

The Ghadir-class boats were definitely of serious military concern to the United States, and this was a God-given opportunity to get a closer look at one.

"Helm!" he said. "Come right to zero-zero-zero. Maneuvering, ahead slow."

"Helm coming right to zero-zero-zero, aye aye, sir," the enlisted man at the helm announced.

"Con, Maneuvering. Ahead slow."

They would come about in a half circle and drop onto the Iranian submarine's tail. The frigate could provide a sound screen for both submarines.

Efficiency. Creighton liked that.

"Down scope!" He didn't want to give *Pittsburgh*'s presence away with either a periscope wake or the telltale rush of surface water on the tube.

Silently, a black shadow in the black waters, the *Pittsburgh* turned to pursue her prey.

Thursday, 29 May 2008

Enlisted Mess, SSGN *Ohio*
Puget Sound Naval Shipyard
Bangor, Washington
1225 hours PST

"Damn it, COB!" ST2 Roger Caswell wailed. "You can't do this to me! I'm getting *married* this Saturday!"

"I've got news for you, son," Master Chief Earnest O'Day said with an easy smile. "The Navy *can* do it to you . . . and, in fact, the Navy has *done* it to you. Saturday morning you're going to be saying farewell to the fleshpots of Bremerton and be on your way to Hawaii."

"Fare-well to all these joys," Moonie sang happily from the seat beside Caswell, "We sail at break of day-*hey!-hey!-hey!*" Several of the other men at the mess table joined in to the ragged rendition of "Anchors

Aweigh," shouting the final chorus of *heys!* loud enough to ring off the bulkhead.

"Shaddup, you screwballs," O'Day said, still grinning.

"But COB, it's not fair!"

"*Fair,*" *Ohio*'s Chief of the Boat said, "was not mentioned in your enlistment contract. That I guar-an-tee!"

Caswell looked down at the remnants of dinner—ham steak, mashed potatoes and gravy, pineapple, and green beans. He didn't feel much like eating anymore.

"Damn, isn't there something I can do, COB?" he asked. "Donny was telling me I might get special leave or something."

"Sick leave if you're sick, son. Compassionate leave if someone in your family died. Other than your soon-to-be-dead bachelor status, I don't see anyone dead here, do you?"

"No . . ."

"Well, then, there you are! Anyway, you know what they say. If the Navy wanted you to have a wife, they'd've issued you one with your sea bag!"

"The man's right, Cas," Rodriguez told him. "You got everything you need right here! You've got *us!*"

"You gonna climb into his rack with the kid, Rodriguez?" Moonie asked. "It'll be a fuckin' tight fit!" The others laughed.

"What do you expect?" Doc Kettering said. "Roddy has a big cock, and Cas has a tight ass!"

"How would you know?"

"I'm a Navy corpsman," Kettering said serenely. "Corpsmen *know* these things."

"I'm gonna sell tickets!" TM3 Dobrowski said. "Or take pictures!"

"Nah, the MAA'd just fuckin' confiscate 'em, man,"

Moonie said. "They don't want none of that homo-porno shit on the boat!"

"Aw, shut up, guys!" Caswell said. He looked at O'Day, his eyes damn close to tears. "COB, you gotta help me. I don't think Nina's going to understand!"

"If Nina has what it takes to be a good Navy wife," O'Day replied, "she'll understand. Or she'll learn to understand. Or you'll talk to her and *make* her understand. But you gotta realize, son . . . the needs of the Navy come first. *Always*."

Caswell was still feeling stunned—and completely blindsided. There'd been some scuttlebutt over the past couple of days about their sailing orders being moved up, that *Ohio* might be sent out on her deployment early, but he'd dismissed it as wild rumors, or as deliberate attempts by his shipmates to yank his chain. When the official word had come down from the exec this morning, however—that all leave and liberty would be cancelled as of 2400 hours Friday, and that the *Ohio* would be putting to sea by 0700 hours Saturday morning—it had felt like the end of the world.

At 1100 hours Saturday morning he was *supposed* to be at Our Lady of the Sea Catholic Church saying "I do," not standing sonar watch as the *Ohio* entered the Pacific Ocean.

Nina Dumont was the only daughter of a guy who'd made his fortune in Redmond's computer empire, and whose wife considered herself to be *the* rising star of Washington state's social elite. Mama and Papa Dumont were less than thrilled to begin with that their daughter was marrying a *sailor,* of all things . . . and an enlisted man at that, rather than an officer. Unthinkable!

Once they'd accepted the idea, though, they hijacked the wedding plans. Correction, Alice Dumont had hijacked the wedding; George had remained in his upstairs office, writing checks. Half of Redmond was supposed to be there this Saturday, and at the reception that afternoon. The cake, the flowers, the reception hall, the dinner—everything had already been ordered and at least partly paid for. Those damned, fancy engraved invitations had gone out a month ago.

Jesus!

Nina's folks had been adamantly opposed to her marrying a sailor. Part of that had been due to the stereotypical sailor's image—a girl in every port, drunken carousing at topless bars on liberty, and all the rest—but part, too, had been aimed at the fact that a Navy wife faced long stretches, months at a time, when her husband was at sea and she was left home alone. *No daughter of mine is going to be put through that!* George Dumont had declared during one fiery encounter.

He'd won them over at last, though . . . or maybe what had won them over was Nina's announcement that she would elope with him if she had to. In any case, they'd accepted him, and now he called them "Mom" and "Dad."

When they found out the wedding was off, he was dead meat. He wouldn't mind so much if it was just the elder Dumonts who cut him off. What was Nina going to say? Would she, *could* she, even understand?

Well, he had liberty tonight, and he was supposed to go over to the Dumonts' house for dinner with the three of them.

He would know the worst then.

Experimental Prototype XSSF-1 *Manta*
Off Kalaeloa, Hawaii
Depth 810 meters
1350 hours CPT

Lieutenant Commander Gary Hawking pulled back gently—very gently—on the control yoke, bringing the *Manta* into level flight. He still considered it "flying," even though he was currently piloting the Navy's newest deep-diving submersible at a depth of over 2,700 feet.

Once a naval aviator, he thought, always a naval aviator.

Hawking had joined the Navy twelve years ago, and had two tours of flight duty under his belt. Upon completion of his last deployment, though, he'd had the offer to volunteer for something that sounded really interesting—research work on the XSSF-1 *Manta*. He'd volunteered, been accepted, and in short order was transferred to Pearl Harbor where the final tests on the *Manta* were being conducted.

His move to Hawaii, however, had been by way of Connecticut, and a training tour at the Navy's submarine school at New London.

Technically, now, he was both a Navy aviator *and* a submariner. He didn't have his dolphins yet, though. A submariner's coveted dolphins were awarded after six months in the boats, and after he'd passed his quals—his qualifying tests—covering every system on the submarine. Hawking's last six months had been spent shuttling between Pearl and the Naval Research and Development lab—NRaD—in San Diego. Technically a creature of both worlds now, of air and of deep water, he wasn't yet wholly comfortable with the latter, nor had he been completely accepted by the submarine community.

But that, he was convinced, would come, given time

and patience. The *Manta,* this weird little SciFi hybrid, was going to prove her worth . . . and so was he.

The *Manta,* in fact, was more like a traditional aircraft than a submarine. The XSSF stood for "Experimental Submarine Fighter," and not, as some wags had it, for "X-Files Super-Science Fiction."

She *looked* like something out of a science fiction movie, though. Just over ten meters in length and two meters thick, the *Manta* looked like a squat and slightly flattened torpedo in prelaunch mode, its overall dimensions dictated by those of the Trident II D5 ICBM. With waterfoils folded, the *Manta* fit neatly if snugly into one of the launch tubes on board an Ohio-class boomer. Once ejected from the launch tube by a burst of compressed air, the *Manta's* aft section unfolded to create a downward-angled delta with a gaping forward intake.

Water entered the intake, was heated by power from an array of fuel cells, and squirted astern like the exhaust of a ramjet, which in effect the *Manta* was. The engineers were still tinkering with the craft's dynamics. Top speed was believed to be in excess of 100 knots, however. They hadn't pushed that particular design envelope very hard yet in the testing program. Hawking had only had the tough little delta-foil up to eighty knots.

The real advance, though, was in the use of negative buoyancy. Traditional submarines used ballast tanks to adjust their buoyancy, surfacing when the tanks were blown empty. The *Manta* did not have ballast tanks, however, and, like an aircraft, was heavier than the medium through which it "flew," remaining aloft by creating a difference in pressure between its upper and lower body surfaces. So long as it was moving at a speed of at least fifteen knots, the *Manta* flew; if it lost power or fell below that critical speed, it would sink . . . and somewhere in the dark and crushing depths below, it would be destroyed.

Hawking took some comfort from the knowledge that in an emergency his cockpit module could be ejected from the *Manta,* and that *did* possess the buoyancy necessary to take him to the surface.

How deep was the *Manta*'s crush depth? That was still an unknown, though numbers cranked through NRaD's computers suggested that the hull—a fantastically tough composite of titanium and carbon weave—would withstand the pressures of depths down to a thousand meters. This afternoon, Hawking was deliberately testing those numbers. The bottom here off the southern coast of Oahu was about 820 meters down. He'd taken the *Manta* into a deep dive, allowing sensors planted along the hull to register the stresses they encountered.

At 810 meters—2,700 feet—the water pressure exceeded 1,200 psi—a full three-fifths of a *ton* squeezing down on each and every square inch of the *Manta*'s hull.

Well, so far, so good. The hull was designed with a certain amount of give, actually becoming stronger as pressure increased. There was stress, yes . . . but it was nowhere near the red line yet. Affectionately, Hawking reached up and patted the curved surface of the canopy, inches above his head. *Good girl.* She was a sweet craft.

Outside the canopy it was the blackest of black nights. It might be mid-afternoon on the surface, but sunlight could not penetrate more than about a hundred feet through even the most crystalline of tropical ocean waters. Here, in the Abyss, it was night absolute. He had the forward light on, but there was nothing to illuminate here save flecks of muck like drifting stars, tumbling past the canopy.

It was an eerie and somewhat unsettling feeling. It felt like he was flying at night, with the drifting debris serving as a poor substitute for stars. And yet, inches above his head, over half a ton of water for every square inch of his body lay waiting, held back by the high-tech plastic of the low, bubble canopy. If the bubble gave way, he would be dead before his nerve endings had time to react to the blast of infalling water.

He checked his sonar. A transponder signal was giving him a steady, pulsing beat, three hundred meters away and slightly to the left. He pulled the yoke again, nudging it to port.

The *Manta* had been envisioned as the world's first fighter submarine—a one-man, maneuverable craft that could "fly" far and fast from the parent boat, reconnoiter approaches to ports or shallow waters, identify potentially hostile targets such as mines, undersea sensor arrays, or enemy submarines, and even kill those targets with the high-speed microtorpedoes she carried in her bow. Someday, such fighters might provide an aircraft carrier with ASW defense, or protect conventional submarines from enemy subs. For now, the program was testing the feasibility of deploying them out of the missile launch tubes on board a converted Ohio-class boomer . . . in a sense turning the *Ohio* into a submarine carrier.

Science fiction indeed.

The target was less than a hundred meters ahead. He still couldn't see a thing through the murk. All his light revealed was a gray and shapeless emptiness alive with dancing motes of crud.

The bottom warning sounded, and he pulled the

fighter's nose up slightly, slowing her. He thought he could see a thicker texture to the gray now, ahead and below . . . but it was still almost impossible to make out what he was actually seeing.

And then, out of nowhere, a shadow emerged from the gray, a cliff towering above his tiny craft, to his left.

His jaw dropped. *That's it! Incredible!*

Slowing now to just below the speed necessary to stay level, he let the *Manta* drift along the cliff's side. Almost as an afterthought, he tapped the touch-screen controls, switching on his port lateral lights.

Details sprang into sharply shadowed relief . . . black metal coated in slime . . . antiaircraft guns pointed skyward from clumsy looking, antique mounts . . . stanchions and railings and even deck cleats clearly visible. Ahead and just above him, he could make out faded white letters and numerals painted five feet tall . . . the legend *I-401*.

He'd found her.

Hawking touched another point on the control screen, which set the portside automatic cameras running. He'd promised Dr. Henson he'd record the site if he found it.

Correction. *When* he found it. He was the best there was, and the *Manta* was pure magic. There'd never been the slightest doubt.

Well, the dive transponder had helped.

The *Manta* was drifting down past the hull of a true leviathan, a Japanese submarine sunk off the coast of Hawaii sixty-three years before.

And what a submarine! The I-400 class, designated *Sensuikan Toku* by the Imperial Japanese Navy, had been a monster in her day . . . four hundred feet long and forty high, with a displacement of 3,530 tons and a crew of 144. She was the largest submarine ever to sail the world's seas until the advent of the ballistic missile submarines of the 1960s. There'd been four of the monsters all together—the I-400 and I-401, plus two slightly smaller vessels, I-13 and I-14. Launched in 1944, they'd been incorporated into Submarine Squadron One, under the command of Captain Tatsunosuke Ariizumi.

Hawking had studied up on his target before making the dive. The I-401 was of special interest to him because she was, in fact, a submersible aircraft carrier, a radical concept that had, fortunately, entered the war too late to affect its outcome. I-400 and I-401 had each carried three disassembled M6A1 torpedo bombers, while the smaller I-13 and I-14 each had carried two.

The Japanese had called the Aichi floatplanes Seiran. Various authoritative sources Hawking had consulted translated the name as "Mountain Haze." Equally authoritative sources translated the name as "Storm from a Clear Sky."

His money was on Storm from a Clear Sky, an apt enough name for the sleek little aircraft, given the manner in which it was to have been used. The I-400 subs had fuel tanks capacious enough to give them a range of 37,500 miles—one and a half times around the world without refueling, and this ten years before the advent of the nuclear-powered *Nautilus*. The Imperial Japanese Navy strategic planners had considered using the *Sensuikan Toku*—the name simply meant "Special Submarine"—to stage air raids against San Francisco, New York, or Washington, D.C.

That would have been a nasty surprise in the final year of the war. "Air Raid, Pentagon . . . This is no drill. . . ."

Eventually, though, Vice Admiral Jisaburo Ozawa, Vice Chief of the IJN General Staff, had settled on a truly chilling concept, designated Operation PX. SubRon

One's ten-plane armada would be employed to launch a biological warfare attack against U.S. population centers along the Pacific Coast, delivering "payloads" of rats and insects infected with bubonic plague, cholera, dengue fever, typhus, and other germ warfare agents developed and tested at the infamous General Ishi's medical laboratory at Harbin, in Manchuria.

On March 26, 1945, however, Operation PX had been cancelled on the orders of General Yoshijiro Umezu, Chief of the Army General Staff. "Germ warfare against the United States," Umezu had declared, "will escalate into war against all humanity."

And so the IJN's planning staff had shifted their sights to another possibility—a sneak air attack against the Panama Canal. If the Gatun Locks could be destroyed, Gatun Lake would be emptied, blocking the canal for months and seriously delaying the redeployment of elements of the U.S. Atlantic Fleet to the Pacific, where they would be employed in the inevitable invasion of the Japanese home islands.

Hawking added a bit of forward throttle and gained altitude, skimming past the conning tower and banking to port in front of the forward end of her 115-foot hangar. He could see something fallen on deck along the port side forward . . . probably the boat's enormous hydraulic crane . . . or possibly it had been lowered and stored that way. The I-401 had an eighty-five-foot pneumatic catapult extending from the hangar door to the bow. Reportedly, the submarine aircraft carrier could surface and all three torpedo bombers could be assembled, armed, fueled, and launched within forty-five minutes. Those floatplanes could land alongside after their mission was complete and be hauled aboard by that crane; likely, though, their raid against the Panama Canal would have been a one-way flight. *Kamikaze.*

But, of course, the raid against the canal had never come off. During the summer months of 1945, some three thousand ships of the United States Navy began closing in on the Japanese home islands in preparation for Operation Olympic, the invasion of Japan. The Panama Canal raid had been cancelled, and the four submarines of SubRon One were redeployed for an operation closer to home—Operation Arashi, or "Mountain Storm." I-13 was sunk en route, but the remaining three rendezvoused at the embattled Japanese base at Truk and prepared for a raid against the U.S. fleet at Ulithi, scheduled for August 17. The eight Aichi aircraft were painted with fake American markings, to let them get in close.

History caught up with the I-401, however, when the atomic bombs were dropped on Hiroshima and Nagasaki, and, on August 15, the Emperor broadcast his order to surrender. By the end of August, the I-401 and her consorts were under American command.

Under skeleton American and Japanese crews, all three had been conned across the Pacific to Hawaii, where they'd arrived in January 1946 to a spectacular welcoming celebration. In March, however, it was decided to dispose of the captured supersubs . . . reportedly because the Russians were demanding access to them. I-401 had been scuttled, sent to the bottom here off Kalaeloa Harbor, and here she had rested for over six decades, until the slowly corroding hulk had been discovered by accident by a deep-sea research team in 2005. On subsequent dives, they'd attached the sonar locator transponder, and several research teams had visited her since in deep submersibles or with robotic underwater vehicles.

Hawking completed his circuit of the I-401's upper works, noting how the conning tower was offset some seven feet to port off the centerline, while the long hangar was offset two feet to starboard to compensate. That monster, he decided, must have been a bitch to maneuver, with a sharper turning radius to starboard than to port.

The I-401 was decades ahead of her time, anticipating, in some ways, the Ohio-class conversion and the use of on-board submersible fighters like the *Manta*. *Ohio*'s new mission, as he understood it, was similar in many respects to that of the I-401—to take the war to the enemy's coast.

A series of sharp chirps sounded from his console—a message alert. Radio didn't work across more than a few meters of water, and the various new phone systems using sound transmitted through the water were still unreliable at great depth. The chirping signal was unambiguous, however. *Surface at once.*

Pity. He'd hoped to make several circuits of the sunken behemoth, but if he didn't take the *Manta* to the surface at once, he could expect a real ass-chewing from Captain Hargreave and the submersible test bed facility brass at Pearl Harbor. Maneuvering well clear of the I-401, he took a last look at her vast and shadowed bulk receding into the night once more, then cut in full power to the *Manta*'s thrusters and pulled back on the yoke. Nosing high, he began to angle up toward daylight, just over half a mile overhead.

Piloting the *Manta*, he reflected, involved one important difference from traditional flight. With an airplane, as his flight instructor at Pensacola had always said, "Whether or not you take off is optional; landing is mandatory." In other words, if you got off the ground, you *would* be coming back down again, one way or another.

With the *Manta*, though, it was just the opposite.

Negative buoyancy meant that the fighter sub was guaranteed to sink when it entered the water; getting back to the surface at the end of the mission was the worrisome part. If the engine or power plant gave out on him, the *Manta* would nose over and begin a one-way descent to the bottom once more . . . and he would get to test the ejection/surface escape system. That system, he was all too aware, had never been tested in an operational XSSF-1; there were only two test bed models available, and they were too damned expensive to lose in a test of the ejector system.

Minutes passed, however, and all of his readouts stayed green. He kept a particularly sharp eye on the hull stress sensors; as the outside pressure was relieved, the hull tended to flex and expand slightly—"unpacking" was what the engineers called it. If there was going to be a problem, this would be the time.

But as more minutes passed and the waters above began to show a faint tinge of luminous blue, it became clear that, once again, the *Manta* had passed her quals with flying colors. At thirty meters he could see the surface as a dancing pattern of blue and green. At ten meters he could see the hull of the *Dolores Chouest,* his mother ship, off to starboard.

Moments later he brought the sub level and rode the canopy through the surface, breaching in a burst of white spray, and he felt the craft's heavy roll with the ocean's surface swell. *Dolores Chouest* rode just ahead, already positioning herself to take him aboard up her docking well aft.

The *Dolores Chouest* was an ungainly looking vessel, with bright red hull and buff-painted superstructure, her bridge mounted far forward, above her bow, and with side-by-side stacks amidships. Aft, her stern was split in a deep U, with a lift designed to raise small submersibles out of the water. The *Dolores Chouest*, a civilian vessel under long-term charter to the Navy, had originally been configured to serve as a support vessel for DSRV rescue submersibles, but was now serving as the mobile home base and mother ship for the XSSF-1 as she completed her sea trials.

"*Manta, Dolores,*" crackled over his radio headset. "We have you in sight. Welcome home."

"Copy that, *Dolores*. Spread your legs, I'm coming in!"

"Roger that, big boy. Please be gentle."

Docking the *Manta* wasn't as simple as cutting the engine and drifting up to a dock, with sailors ready to toss him a line. As soon as he cut power, he would begin to sink, so he had to carefully gauge his approach, coming in under power just barely fast enough to stay afloat. To help him maintain his critical speed, the *Dolores* was motoring away from him at ten knots. As he made his docking approach at fifteen knots, his actual closing speed was only five. At the last moment he touched the screen control to fold the fighter's waterfoils and increased speed slightly to compensate.

The docking maneuver was almost blatantly phallic, with the torpedo-shaped *Manta* sliding in between *Dolores*'s open "legs."

It wasn't quite the same as a trap on a carrier deck, but it would do. A landing on board an aircraft carrier required touching down and trying to snag, or "trap," one of the arrestor cables stretched across the deck, while simultaneously giving the aircraft full throttle just in case the arrestor hook missed and the aviator needed to fly off the deck again to make a second pass.

A signal light flashed on, indicating he'd crossed the threshold and was over the platform. He cut power then and drifted forward another few feet, before striking the thickly padded fender and coming to rest.

Sailors waiting to either side jumped down onto the platform, making the *Manta* fast with lines secured to her recessed hull cleats. In another few moments, as Hawking continued powering down the submersible's systems, the lift began hauling the *Manta* completely out of the water.

A chief boatswain's mate cracked the canopy, sliding it back, as Hawking unstrapped his harness and climbed—a bit unsteadily—out of the cockpit. After over two hours in the ocean's depths, the tropical mid-afternoon sun was dazzling.

Someone handed him a pair of aviator's sunglasses.

"Thanks," he said, donning them. "Why the early recall?"

"We're headed back to Pearl, Commander," the chief said with a lopsided grin. "Looks like you're deploying early."

"Early? Where?"

"Yup. Word just got passed down. The *Ohio* is putting to sea Saturday morning. The brass wants a final top-to-bottom check of the *Manta* before she gets here on the seventh."

"Jesus! So the boomer gets here in one week instead of three! Is that any reason to haul me off the bottom? I wasn't done yet!"

"You know the Navy, sir," the chief said. "Hurry up and wait!"

Typical. Probably some junior officer back at headquarters had seen the orders and assumed the recall meant now.

It wasn't really a problem. He'd have time for sightseeing on the I-401 hulk another day. In the meantime *Dolores Chouest* had throttled up to twelve knots and was making her way back toward Oahu with a rolling gait. They should put in back at Pearl sometime late tonight . . . and that might mean a chance to call Kathy. He hadn't been expecting to see her before the weekend. Sweet.

He patted the *Manta*'s dripping hull with a grin, before starting forward toward his quarters. If he was lucky, he might be able to enjoy the docking maneuver for *real* tonight.

Saturday, 31 May 2008

Sonar Room
SSGN *Ohio*
Straits of San Juan de Fuca
0915 hours PST

"So fuck her, man," Sonar Technician Chief Sommersby said with a broad shrug. "No one needs that kind of hassle."

"Actually, Chief," ST1 Dobbs said, leering, "Cassie's problem is he *can't* fuck her! He ain't getting none now, right, Cas?"

"And there's all that money to consider, too," the COB said from the open door leading to the bridge. "Didn't you say her folks were loaded?"

"I don't care about the damned money, COB!" Caswell said. "It's Nina I want. And now I've lost her!"

He was seated at his station in front of one of *Ohio*'s four sonar displays, Dobbs to his left, Sommersby to his right. In front of him was his waterfall, a display, so called, because vertical green lines of light cascaded slowly down the screen, each one a readout for a particular direction. The screen was divided into horizontal thirds, with the older information at the bottom. At the moment, his display was configured to show broadband contacts from *Ohio*'s spherical bow sonar array.

Intermittent white lines were sonar contacts. There were now five of them at various bearings . . . already designated as Sierras One through Five, then redesignated as Mikes, because they'd been identified by radar—Romeo—and by visual observation from the fair-water—Victor. Vertical white lines indicated that the target was stationary with respect to the *Ohio*; moving targets drifted at a slant across the display. Four of the five Mikes were slanting in various directions at various angles as *Ohio*, cruising now at eight knots, passed them, or they passed her. Mike One was a Coast Guard cutter on harbor security patrol, escorting the *Ohio* through the straits, and so she was represented by a perfectly vertical line, dead abeam to starboard.

"You shouldn't let it get ya, kid," Dobbs said. "No dame is worth it, see?"

"What'd she say, anyway?" Master Chief O'Day asked, taking a sip from the big coffee mug that was a near-permanent fixture in his right hand. "Did she dump you?"

"Not exactly. But her parents sure were unhappy about the wedding and everything. They were telling her to reconsider marrying me . . . and she told me we would have to—"

Another white contact line appeared, this one forward and to port.

"Shit. Chief? New contact, bearing two-zero-three. Designate as Sierra Six."

"I've got it too, Chief," Dobbs said. "Sounds like a pleasure boat . . . maybe a cabin cruiser. Single screw, high-speed."

"Right," Chief Sommersby said. He picked up a handset. "Bridge, Sonar. New target, designated Sierra Six, bearing two-zero-three. Probable civilian pleasure craft." He listened for a moment to the reply, then said, "Aye aye, sir."

He hung up the handset. "Skipper says he's got it—looks like a weekend party boat. Redesignate the target as Mike Six."

Caswell typed the new characters into the display from his keyboard. "Mike Six it is."

"So finish the story," Dobbs said. "What did your girl say she was going to have to do?"

"Not see me for a while. At least until things blew over."

"Well, that's reasonable enough," O'Day said.

"Sure," Sommersby added. "Ain't like you're going to be around to see her for the next couple of months or so, right?"

"Right." But he felt miserable as he agreed. To his mind, it had seemed as though Nina was seriously considering her parents' demand—that she drop him and never see him again. As with her family's money, he didn't care so much about them or what they thought, but he very much cared about Nina.

God, he hated the Navy right now. That crack about the Navy issuing a wife with your sea bag. It was an ancient line, but it emerged from a nasty truth. Life in the service took you away from your loved ones, often for months at a time.

It wasn't fair.

But he'd also chosen this life. He'd volunteered, first for the Navy, and then for the submarine service. And now he was stuck with the consequences of those choices.

Weather Bridge
SSGN *Ohio*
Straits of San Juan de Fuca
0921 hours PST

Captain Stewart leaned against the fair-water, taking another long look through his binoculars at the new contact ahead and to starboard. It looked like a typical pleasure boat . . . nothing out of the ordinary. She'd popped out from behind Ediz Hook a moment ago, just west of Port Angeles, swung hard to starboard, and was now roughly paralleling *Ohio*'s course.

Ohio was cruising slowly on the surface, on a heading of WNW, making for the middle of the channel. The sky was typical for Washington . . . overcast, but there was a hint of blue sky beyond the clouds and open sea to the west. South lay the state of Washington, beneath the dramatic loom of Mount Olympus; north, across the line into Canada, was the port of Victoria and the eastern tip of Vancouver Island. The straits were twelve miles across at this point—a ninety-minute ferry ride—and *Ohio* was currently three to four miles from the U.S. coastline.

Traffic was surprisingly light today for this busy, international waterway. The Island-class Coast Guard cutter *Edisto* was cruising two hundred yards to port. An oil tanker . . . a Japanese *maru* . . . two other pleasure boats . . .

Still, Stewart was wary of pleasure craft while entering or leaving port. He remembered an incident while he was exec on the *Pittsburgh,* when a boatload of Greenpeace protestors had made a run on them while they were navigating through the waters of San Francisco Bay. And Garrett had regaled him once with some pretty wild stories . . . including the time a bright red cigarette boat had tried to make a high-speed run close across the bow of the brand new SSN *Virginia,* just outside of New London.

The Greenpeace activists could be particularly annoying. They meant well—saving the whales and the environment and all of that—but trying to come close astern a U.S. Navy nuclear submarine was just plain freaking stupid. What did they think . . . that the skipper was going to suddenly have a change of heart and put back into port?

Ohio, though, might be a particularly tempting target for the antinuke protestors. She was nuclear-powered, and—at least before her conversion—she'd packed the sizable payload of four megatons, total, in her twenty-four missile tubes. The fact that *Ohio* was now armed solely with conventional warheads meant nothing; the protestors couldn't be expected to know that *Ohio* was now an SSGN. Besides, they could equally well just be protesting the various skirmishes being fought around the planet in the name of the War on Terror, or the government's buildup toward war with Iran.

In any case, the lookouts had been cautioned to pay particular attention to civilian pleasure boats during *Ohio*'s transit of the Straits of San Juan de Fuca.

"My *God,* it stinks!" his exec, Lieutenant Commander Wayne Shea, said. "Even over here."

"It can be pretty bad sometimes," Stewart agreed.

"I don't really care for the Canadians using the straits as their toilet, y'know?"

Stewart lowered his binoculars and shifted his attention back forward. *Ohio*'s bow wake rippled and flowed smoothly up over the forward deck. He could see some garbage in the water, though . . . an empty two-liter soda-pop bottle, and a nasty-looking clump of plastic netting, Styrofoam, and God-knew-what.

"Maybe," Stewart replied, "we should dock at Victoria and issue them a citation."

Canada and the United States tended to be pretty good neighbors . . . but the issue of environmental pollution was ongoing and stubborn. Canada could be downright snooty at times over U.S. environmental policies—such as the celebrated rejection of the Kyoto Treaty a few years back—and over such genuinely problematical issues as acid rain from the U.S. Northeast.

But Canada was far from blameless when it came to international environmental issues. One of the worst problems was the fact that Victoria and several other cities on Vancouver and in British Columbia continued to dump raw, untreated sewage or lightly treated sewage into the Straits of San Juan de Fuca. The joke was that Ottawa would still be planning feasibility studies on B.C. sewage treatment plants when the entire strait had been filled in with solids, and the stench had made the region uninhabitable as far south as Portland.

Boomer crews joked that the passage through the sewage-laden straits was necessary to grease up the submarine's hull, so she could slip more quietly through the ocean depths.

They also joked that the pollution had been started by the Russians back during the Cold War as an attempt to seal off the straits and isolate America's Pacific boomer fleet, trapped in the Hood Canal behind a solid wall of shit.

He glanced again at the pleasure boat to port. It was

closer than he liked, three miles off now, and on a slightly converging course that was bringing it slowly nearer to the *Ohio*. The idiot might be trying to pass across their bow.

Weekend boaters. Drunk, probably, and here it wasn't even 1000 hours yet. He found the stupidity of people amazing sometimes.

All things considered, it would be good to reach the open ocean. Submariners didn't like being on the surface, especially in such tight quarters, with no room to maneuver. Back during the Cold War, boomer skippers had submerged as soon as possible after transiting the Hood Canal, knowing that Russian attack subs were lurking just beyond the mouth of the strait. They would wait there, submerged, listening for the whisper of a boomer coming into the Pacific in order to try to tail them.

Some of the wild sea stories of those days were pretty incredible. Ohio-class boats were very quiet, and their skippers well-trained in being cunning. One common trick was to come through submerged with several surface ships making as hellacious a racket as possible. That was almost guaranteed to confuse the Soviet sonar operators, and allow the boomer to slip into the quiet depths undetected.

Nowadays, of course, they still took precautions, just in case. But chances were, no one was out there waiting for them this time. . . .

"Missile launch! Missile launch!"

The port lookout in his manhole-sized opening in the sail aft of the weather bridge was pointing past Stewart's shoulder, screaming the warning. Stewart looked . . . and saw the white-star pinpoint of a missile exhaust streaking across the water.

"Where, damn it?" Shea demanded.

"There," Stewart said, pointing. It looked like a small,

shoulder-launched missile—probably a Stinger—fired from that pleasure boat that had just emerged from behind Ediz Hook.

"Son of a bitch!"

Stewart's mind flashed ahead through several blocks of information. If it was a Stinger, it was an infrared homing missile . . . and most likely one of the older models, not one of the reprogrammable upgrades.

There was no time to submerge. A Stinger had a range of . . . what was it? About 4,800 meters for the older models—make it three miles. Speed Mach 2.2—say half a mile a second . . . or less than six seconds' total flight time.

Almost without thinking, he reached past Shea and grabbed the Very pistol mounted on a rack on the inside of the weather bridge, checked to see that it was loaded, and took aim . . . not directly at the missile, but slightly off to the right and well ahead of the swell of *Ohio*'s bow wake, angled high, at about forty-five degrees.

He fired, and the Very pistol thumped in his hand. The flare streaked through the morning sky, a bright point of light dragging its white contrail behind.

Everything depended on how late-model the Stinger missile was. The more recent designs had a focal plane array imaging IR sensor, which let them more effectively lock onto low-signature targets, and could be programmed to ignore many common countermeasures . . . including flares.

If that missile had been launched by al-Qaeda operatives—just a wild guess, of course—then chances were their toy was one of the old, early-model Stingers, one of the ones provided to the various Mujahideen guerrillas fighting the Soviets in Afghanistan during the 1980s by the American CIA.

The flare burst well ahead of the *Ohio,* and began

drifting toward the water on its parachute. The oncoming missile, weaving its zigzag course toward the sub just above the surface of the water, seemed to hesitate . . . then swung hard to the right, climbing to track the flare, not the submarine. The *Ohio* made a far larger target, of course . . . but the flare was much, *much* hotter, a far more inviting target to the infrared sensor mounted in the missile's nose.

Stewart, Shea, and the two enlisted lookouts watched the Stinger climb sharply, miss the descending flare, and arc high up over the center of the waterway. The engine burned out while it was still climbing, and the missile, now invisible, plunged harmlessly into the middle of the strait. Stewart thought he saw the splash in the dark water a mile or more off to port.

"Bridge, Comm!" a voice said over the speaker. "Sir, the Coasties say we're under attack, and want to give chase!"

"Tell 'em to go get the bastards," Stewart replied. A moment later the *Edisto* lunged ahead, throttling up to an all-ahead 28 knots. Stewart could see *Edisto*'s CO on the bridge. He tossed the man a salute, and thought he saw a salute in reply.

The cabin cruiser had already put his helm over and was running for shore. He wouldn't have much luck there; the coastline west of Port Angeles was flat and straight, offering no hiding places. Maybe the guy was going to try running his boat ashore so the crew could leap out and escape across the beach on foot.

They probably wouldn't get far. The skipper of the cutter was probably on the horn to everyone from local law enforcement agencies to the U.S. Marine Corps right now, letting them know what was going down.

A military attack on a U.S. nuclear sub—inside American waters, no less—was very serious business.

At the same time, Stewart thought, the attack was abysmally *stupid*. He was pretty sure it was a Stinger that the bad guys had popped at the *Ohio*. A Stinger mounted a four-kilogram warhead of high explosives, nowhere near enough to sink or even cripple a target as big as the *Ohio*. Her hull was three-inch steel; an explosion that size might have breached her sail, where the steel was thinner, but the operative word was *might*. Or a lucky shot could have hit the sail and killed or injured her captain and exec . . . but luck rarely came gift-wrapped in such a large package.

And the sub was *cold* . . . barely warmer than the chilly waters around her. Definitely a low-signature target.

Still . . . it was conceivable that if the missile had hit them, the sub might have been damaged. Maybe all the attackers had been hoping for was to hurt the *Ohio* enough to make her put about and head back for port.

Was that enough, though, to warrant sacrificing a boat and crew?

The attackers, whoever they were, were not sophisticated and they weren't well-trained. They'd fired the Stinger from pretty much the maximum possible range— three miles or so. They would have been better off arranging to surprise the *Ohio* at a narrow chokepoint—like the exit from the Hood Canal—and pop several missiles from close range.

The *Edisto* passed across *Ohio*'s bow, sounding a blast from its horn. Stewart touched the intercom button. "Maneuvering, Bridge!" he called. "Come right ten degrees, and increase speed to fifteen knots."

"Bridge, Maneuvering. Come right ten degrees, aye. Increase speed to one-five knots, aye aye!"

"Diving Officer, this is the captain. What's our bottom look like?"

"Twelve fathoms beneath the keel, Skipper. Dropping . . . thirteen fathoms now."

"Let me know when we have twenty fathoms under us, Lieutenant. I want to go where the sun don't shine!"

"Aye aye, Captain."

Shea was looking at Stewart with just a touch of awe. "That was mighty fast thinking, Skipper," he said, nodding at the empty Very pistol still gripped in Stewart's right hand.

He looked down at the pistol, surprised. He'd forgotten he was still holding the thing. He leaned over and clipped it back in its mount, snapping down the cover and locking it.

"Aircraft use flares to decoy IR-homing missiles," he said with a shrug. "Why not a submarine?"

"You saved us. . . ."

"At worst, I saved us a return trip to NIMF," he said. "That thing wouldn't have delivered more than a pinprick."

But it *would* have aborted the mission.

That raised several ugly thoughts in Stewart's mind. Had the attack been simply carried out against a target of opportunity? By terrorists waiting in a boat along the Washington coast for the first likely U.S. Navy target to present itself? Maybe even by domestic terrorists . . . Greenpeace activists gone bad, or something of the sort?

Or had the attack been a part of a deliberate military attack? One carried out by a foreign enemy?

Iran was known to have Savam agents in the United States. There was supposed to be a fairly well-organized al-Qaeda intelligence ring as well. The FBI issued regular reports on their known or suspected activities.

For that matter, Stewart had read a report lately about Stinger missiles in the hands of terrorist groups.

At the end of the Soviet-Afghan War, the CIA had tried to buy back the Stinger missiles they'd given to the Mujahideen; the effort had been a complete failure, and hundreds of the shoulder-launched missiles had passed into terrorist hands.

MANPADS—Man-Portable Air Defense Systems— were a major worry for commercial airline companies the world over. One classified Department of Defense report suggested that MANPADS of various types, including Stingers, had been the leading cause of loss of life in commercial aviation over the past several decades, with over thirty aircraft downed worldwide. There'd been no known Stinger attacks recently; it was believed that the batteries necessary to fire the things had all gone dead by now.

But that wasn't the whole story. A CIA report indicated that no fewer than sixteen Stingers had been delivered by Mujahideen guerrillas to Iran, and Iran had successfully duplicated the design.

Had the *Ohio* just been attacked by Iranian commandos while still in U.S. waters?

And, again . . . had the missile been launched at a target of opportunity? Or did Iranian military intelligence know about *Ohio*'s mission, and had the attack been an attempt to stop that mission before it was even properly under way?

A very unpleasant thought indeed. . . .

Sonar Room
SSGN *Ohio*
Straits of San Juan de Fuca
0928 hours PST

"What the hell's going on, man?" Dobbs wanted to know.

Caswell couldn't give him an answer. The white line on his waterfall marking Mike One—the Coastie escorting *Ohio* out to sea—had suddenly taken a sharp dogleg to the left and cut almost straight across the screen horizontally, as the cutter crossed *Ohio*'s bows. "Hey, COB!" someone called from the bridge. "Sparks says we're under fire!"

"How the hell does he know?" Abruptly, O'Day turned and left the sonar room, taking his coffee with him.

"Aw, nobody ever tells us shit," Dobbs said.

"So much for being the eyes and the ears of the sub," Caswell said with grim humor. Back in sonar school, that litany had been recited almost daily; so vital was the work of the sonar department that the ST supervisor could, at any time, request a course change from the Officer of the Deck, so the sonar techs could get a better angle on a contact. "Look at that! Mike Six is really lighting out."

"And Mike One is chasing him," Chief Sommersby noted. "Maybe Greenpeace is putting in an appearance."

A sharp sound cracked in Caswell's headphones, followed by a grinding, scraping noise. "Ow! What was that?"

"Mike Six just ran aground." Sommersby had heard the same broadband noise over his headset. The white line indicating Mike-six stopped growing, indicating that the boat's screw had stopped, but now there were rapid-fire popping sounds. "That," Sommersby said, "is gunfire. *Someone* is in damn bad trouble over there."

Weather Bridge
SSGN *Ohio*
Straits of San Juan de Fuca
0930 hours PST

Captain Stewart studied the scene through his binoculars. The *Edisto* had just swung parallel to the coast and several hundred yards out, unwilling to follow the cabin cruiser onto the beach. A small storm of white geysers suddenly erupted from the water around the cabin cruiser, which was now visibly heeled over to port close to the rocky beach. Several seconds later he heard the insistent rattle of chain-gun fire; *Edisto* was firing a long burst from her 25mm Bushmaster cannon.

Seconds later another player entered the scene—a police helicopter, swooping in low above the shoreline, then coming to an ominous hover. Smoke was rising from the cabin cruiser now.

"Bridge, this is the diving officer," a voice called over the intercom. "Depth-below-keel is twenty fathoms."

"Very well. Prepare to dive."

"Prepare to dive, aye aye."

Stewart looked around. "Clear the bridge!"

The two lookouts ducked down their holes, the pressure doors slamming tight above them. "Our last look at daylight for a while, Skipper," Shea said. "After you, sir?"

Stewart took a last look at the shore, then nodded and climbed down into the sail well. Above him, Shea secured the cockpit, pulling in the Plexiglas windshield and securing it, then dogging tight the pressure hatch.

Stewart scrambled down the long ladder and emerged in the control room, just abaft the periscopes. Lieutenant Myers, who was Officer of the Deck this watch, looked up from the chart table. "Captain on deck!"

"As you were," he said. "Diving Officer! Take us down, periscope depth."

"Take us down, periscope depth, aye aye, sir!"

The water was shallow yet. At periscope depth they'd damned near be scraping barnacles—if there'd been any barnacles to scrape on *Ohio*'s newly scraped, cleaned, and painted keel. But Stewart wanted to get her down into her real element . . . the silent darkness below the surface. That pleasure boat up there might have been the only attacker, but it was also possible the attacker had been the first of several, possibly set up in layers. That way, just when the *Ohio*'s crew thought they were in the clear, just when her escort had been pulled out of position, another ambush would be sprung. A Stinger missile might not have made much of an impression on *Ohio*'s tough skin, but what if there was someone up there with a military surplus Exocet?

Good sub drivers didn't take that kind of chance.

"Flood main ballast," the D.O. ordered. "Five degrees down plane."

The deck tilted beneath Stewart's feet, and the *Ohio* slid gently into the depths.

Saturday, 7 June 2008

Experimental Prototype XSSF-1 *Manta*
Off Kalaeloa, Hawaii
Depth 58 meters
1425 hours CPT

This is nuts, Hawking told himself. *Submarines don't want to be found!*

During his tenure as a naval aviator, he'd joked often enough about "postage stamp landings" . . . about what it was like dropping out of rain clouds or darkness in an F/A-18 to trap on a carrier deck, and about how tiny that deck looked from the air. A super carrier was a floating colossus, over a thousand feet long and displacing in the neighborhood of eighty thousand tons, but it looked like a freaking postage stamp from the air, and a *moving* postage stamp at that.

But the aviator had access to a whole array of navigational data—radio beacons and radar and GPS fixes beamed to him by satellite. He might not be able to see the carrier until the last moment before he came in over the fantail, but he knew exactly where it was.

Not so with submarines. Even something as large as an Ohio SSGN was a tiny, tiny sliver in a very large and opaque emptiness. No radio beacons. No satellite signals unless you had an antenna extended above the surface. Blue-green lasers penetrated seawater to a degree, allowing communications over limited distances, but you pretty much had to be on top of the other guy before that became practical.

As always, as it had been for decades, sound was the best way to spot a target. The trouble was, submarines went out of their way to eliminate sound so the enemy couldn't track them. Both *Ohio* and the *Manta* had sonar, of course, and by going active, either vessel could pinpoint the other in a matter of seconds.

This was an exercise, however, intended to simulate possible submerged operations in potentially hostile waters. *Ohio* wasn't broadcasting. She was *listening*.

And so Hawking was doing the broadcasting, and he was doing it on a very narrow frequency, at very low power. It was, he'd been told, the same sort of low-power sonar pulse used by *Ohio*'s diving officer to determine the depth beneath the keel, a signal so weak that other submarines wouldn't pick it up unless they were quite close—within a few thousand yards, say.

To Hawking, who was used to a distant horizon in a fighter—CAVU, or Ceiling Absolute, Visibility Unlimited—this felt like a blind man feeling his way through a dark cellar at night, using a stick to try to identify that one postage stamp that had to be in here *somewhere*. . . .

At eighty-five meters the water was as dark as it had been at ten times that depth, without even a trace of illumination from the surface. The one difference was that this far from the bottom there was less particulate matter, no drifting flecks of muck imitating stars.

And no fish, either. Hawking had wondered about that during his various training dives and test runs with the *Manta*. Only rarely had he actually seen signs of sea life, and then only in the upper few tens of meters of sea. The ocean—out here away from the shoreline, at any rate—appeared to be a barren and empty desert.

A warning light flickered on his control screen, accompanied by a tone over his headset. Contact! Weak as his sonar emanations were, they'd reflected off something large somewhere up ahead. He banked the *Manta* to the right, bringing his heading onto a direct line with the contact, and increased his speed.

If it was the *Ohio,* they would hear him coming, of course. Unlike conventional submarines, the *Manta* was not specifically designed as a quiet submersible. It wasn't that noisy, either, but at speeds of more than about twenty knots, he'd been told the Manta sounded like one of those bicycle noisemakers he'd employed as a kid, a piece of cardboard attached to the wheel in such a way that it made a motorcyclelike clacking as it turned. This was due to the *Manta*'s aquafoil design, which, like an aircraft wing, was shaped to create greater pressure below the vessel than above it, providing lift. When the two unequal streams of water met and mixed aft of his wing, they created turbulence, and that announced his presence as clearly as if he'd come in with horns blaring. The water jet used for propulsion was noisy as well. There were no moving parts, but the rush of water through the aft venturi created a kind of freight-train rumble in the headphones of submarine sonar techs in the area.

So at the moment, not only was the *Ohio* pinpointing

his position by sonar, but every other submarine and undersea sound sensor from here to Midway Island must be picking him up as well. The trick was for him to pick up the echoes from the very quiet submarine somewhere up ahead.

Since he was using active sonar, sending out pulses of sound like a bat or a dolphin, rather than simply listening for the noise the *Ohio* wasn't making, he could employ Doppler ranging to pick up an accurate distance to the target. *Manta*'s on-board computer was quite sophisticated, and could give him range readouts to the meter . . . if the target's relative bearing and velocity were known. Since he didn't know how fast the *Ohio* was traveling, or what her aspect was relative to his approach—bow-on, stern-to, or somewhere in between—her motion relative to his caused some uncertainty in the ranging data. According to the console readout, however, the target was now between nine hundred and eleven hundred meters away—less than half a mile.

His lights were on. There was nothing to see, however, save for a greenish haze about his vessel, backscatter from the external lamps. Nothing . . . nothing . . .

And then there she was, looming out of the night, a vast and dark shadow imperfectly illuminated by the *Manta*'s forward light. She'd already turned away from him, stern-to, and was moving ahead through the depths at ten knots. Between the shrouded screw and cruciform tail, and the erect rectangle of the sail, he could see the long double row of hatches down her afterdeck. The two hatches closest to the sail were covered by the blunt, stubby cylinder of the ASDS—the dry-deck shelter used by the sub's complement of SEALs or other Special Forces. Halfway down the row, however, the twelfth hatch to port had been opened and the capture gantry deployed.

The gantry, actually, was little more than a single, slender pole, deployed straight up out of the missile launch tube, then lowered forward on a hydraulically operated hinge until it rested flat on the deck. Magnetic grapples extended to either side, and a red strobe light pulsed in the water, marking the top end of the gantry.

A contact light went on at the top of the *Manta*'s touch-screen console. He was close enough now that he could communicate directly with *Ohio*'s command center, either via high frequency sonar pulses or through blue-green laser.

"*Ohio*, this is XSSF-1 on capture approach, coming up on your six, range two-two-five meters, speed one-five knots."

"XSSF-1, *Ohio*. We heard you coming a mile away. You are clear for final approach and lockdown. The fishing pole is deployed."

"Fishing pole" was slang for the capture gantry. In early days of prototype testing, capture had actually involved firing a powerful magnetic grapple connected to a tow line to the fighter, hooking on, and dragging the craft in. Operational techniques had improved a lot during the past year, however.

"Roger that, *Ohio*. XSSF-1 on final."

Hawking accelerated the *Manta* slightly, pushing through the turbulence of the *Ohio*'s wake. As soon as the slight buffeting subsided and he emerged above *Ohio*'s stern, he cut back on the throttle and brought the fighter's nose up, matching speed with the much larger submarine beneath him and settling in toward the gantry. This part took a delicate touch and skillful coordination between fighter pilot and sub driver; during the last few seconds of the approach, he couldn't see the gantry directly, but had to rely on a small monitor on his console that relayed the view from a camera mounted on the keel. Although a flashing green light assured him his approach was nominal, it didn't have the same feel as judging the final few meters by eye.

The flashing green light went yellow as he drifted a bit too far to port. "XSSF-1, Control. Adjust right one meter."

"Yeah, yeah . . ."

It was much like calling the ball on a carrier deck approach, but in slow motion compared with the high-speed slam-down onto a carrier's fantail. He adjusted his course slightly, and the flashing green light came back . . . then switched to steady green as the magnetic grapples caught him. There was a gentle thump, a jar transmitted through the cockpit's deck.

"XSSF-1, we have capture. Kill your power and enjoy the ride."

"Roger that, *Ohio*." He switched off the *Manta*'s power systems. "All systems powered down."

His external lights switched off; all was blackness again save for the intermittent red flare of the docking light. After a moment he felt another jerk, and the sensation of being tipped back in his seat. The fishing pole was being elevated once more, brought back into its upright position. In a few more moments Hawking was on his back, his head lower than the rest of his body due to the angle of his seat. Gently, the fishing pole and its catch were lowered down into the launch tube.

Another solid thump, a long pause, and the clank and thud of the external tube hatch closing and locking above him. Hawking waited there, head-down in the darkness, feeling more than a little claustrophobic. In a way, the darkness helped, since he couldn't see the walls of the missile tube just outside the cockpit. He didn't like admitting it—and he for *damn* sure hadn't admitted it to the headshrinkers during his selection process for this gig—but he was slightly claustrophobic, had never cared for being cooped up in a coffin-sized box.

Give me the wide open sky anytime, he thought. A cockpit was tight-fitting, but with the sky around him, he'd never felt cooped up. Even when "flying" the *Manta*, the view of the surrounding ocean held the unpleasant twist in his stomach at bay.

It was just when he was locked up inside the missile tube, at the start or at the conclusion of a run, that he began to want to scream. . . .

He heard the hiss and roar of water being forced out of the missile tube, and a moment later light came on. When the pressures equalized, a hatch cracked open opposite the *Manta*'s canopy, the canopy slid back and out of the way, and hands reached in to help him.

"Welcome aboard, sir," a Navy chief said. Two other enlisted men crowded in close, helping him remove and secure his headset. "Let's get you out of that harness. . . ."

With the harness released, he slid down and back into the sailors' waiting arms, a decidedly undignified way to come on board.

He was a bit unsteady as he rose to his feet. The compartment he was standing in was huge, dominated by the massive paired pillars of the launch tubes extending into the distance in both directions.

The chief seemed to guess what he was staring at. "Yeah, it's something, all right," he said. "Welcome to Sherwood Forest, Commander. I'm Chief Connolly, and I've been assigned to the *Manta* as crew chief."

"Sherwood Forest?"

A shrug. "Sorta like the deep woods in here, with the giant trees, y'know? C'mon, sir. The skipper'll want to see you."

Bemused, Hawking followed the chief forward, past

the ranks of enormous, green-painted "trees," while the other enlisted men continued to work on the *Manta*, securing it from operational status, rendering the weapons safe, and removing the swim recorder and other instrumentation.

The deck, he noted, was actually a metal grating that surrounded the ranks of launch tubes. It was difficult to see through to the next level below . . . but it looked as though a number of dark, head-sized shapes were hanging there, just beneath his feet.

Connolly noticed his curious stare and grinned. "Fresh produce," he said. "When a submarine puts out to sea, every available space is pretty much crammed with food—enough for a hundred forty–some men for anywhere from two to six months, depending on the mission. Down there, in the keel below Sherwood Forest, that's the coolest part of the boat, and there's a lot of air circulation, too. The galley crew stores string bags full of heads of lettuce and potatoes there, hanging up from the deck grating."

Hawking looked around. "Doesn't look to me like every available space is packed with food."

"Not this time, sir. We got caught short at Bremerton, with only three days to load supplies. Normally takes a good six days to get all of the food stowed on board before a long mission.

"But Ohio boats are big. Lots more room to store stuff than on an L.A. SSN. And, well, this probably won't be a long deployment."

"How long?"

"Do I look like the skipper?" He shrugged. "They're saying six weeks at most. In any case, we'll have a big, well-stocked friendly port close by our patrol area— Bahrain. We'll be able to resupply there any time we need to."

"Well, I've heard that submarine chow is the best in the Navy."

Connolly grinned. "Oh, it's better than best, sir! Surf and turf once a week? Of course, on a long patrol the fresh fruit and produce goes pretty fast, and things can be a bit monotonous on the homeward leg."

As they kept walking, a sharp voice cried out, "Gangway!" Hawking turned, startled, to see a line of sailors wearing shorts and sweat-stained T-shirts jogging up the narrow passageway behind them. He and the chief stepped aside as the party ran past; one of them must have glimpsed the rank insignia on the collar of Hawking's poopie suit, for he called out "By your leave, sir!" as he passed them.

"This compartment is the biggest on the boat," Connolly explained. "Twenty or so times around equals one mile. These boomers are the only submarines large enough to really let a man get any exercise."

"I'll remember that." Hawking tended to go with the minimum exercise required. He was young and in good shape, with little interest in renewing the physical regimen he'd endured at flight school in Pensacola.

Exercise on a submarine? They had to be kidding.

Shaking his head, he followed Connolly forward and out of the compartment.

MCAS Kaneohe Bay
Oahu, Hawaii
1720 hours CPT

The Navy C-130 Hercules thundered down out of the tropical sky, its tires hitting the tarmac once with a squeal, bouncing, then hitting again and taking hold.

The big turboprops began braking hard, and the transport slowed with a long, stomach-jolting shudder.

Hospitalman Chief David Tangretti turned in his narrow, cargo deck seat to peer through the round porthole at his side. He could see palm trees and endless blue ocean. "Welcome to Hawaii, gents," he said, to no one in particular.

"You see any hula girls out there, Doc?" BM1 Olivetti asked, shouting to be heard above the roar of the CH-130's four big turboprops. "I don't get off this here Herky Bird less'n there's hula girls out there to put flowers around my neck and give me a big kiss."

"Shee-it, Olive," EM1 Hutchinson shouted back, sneering. "Who the hell would kiss *you*?"

"Twenty says I get laid tonight, asshole."

"You're on!"

"I'll take a piece of that," Tangretti said, grinning. "Twenty says you *don't* get laid tonight."

"Done!" Olivetti laughed. "Ha! Easy money! Happens I know this little girl, works in a bar on Ala Moana Boulevard. She's gonna be so glad to see me and my six-inch gun, I'll be pounding her in the rack ten minutes after liberty call!"

"Haven't you heard, Olive?" EM2 Richardson laughed. "The Navy's gone metric! That's a six *millimeter* gun!"

"Fuck you, asshole!"

The Hercules thundered to a stop, and the ramp at the rear of the cargo bay began opening with a shrill whine.

"On your feet!" Commander Drake called, standing. "Muster on the tarmac with your gear!"

Tangretti hauled his sea bag out of the pile of olive-green strapped bags stored down the center of the aisle, shouldered it, and followed Richardson aft and down the ramp. Warm, humid air assaulted them, heavy with the smell of sea salt and avgas. The men, SEALs from SEAL Team Three, fell into ranks next to the ramp, in the shade of the Hercules's massive tail: four blocks of sixteen men each.

Detachment Delta was unusual in its design and makeup. SEAL units were built up in relatively small units—two eight-man squads to a sixteen-man platoon, four platoons to a sixty-four man SEAL company. The usual field deployment of a SEAL element was at platoon strength, with a lieutenant as CO or "Wheel," and a lieutenant j.g. as his XO. Detachment Delta, however, was an entire company, deployed under the command of Commander Charles G. Drake, and with Lieutenant Richard Mayhew as executive officer.

Tangretti wondered if he would ever get used to the larger formation, and to the additional problems of supply, logistics, and tactics it created. SEALs—the *old* SEALs he'd grown up with—were masters of small-unit operations, usually deploying teams of eight or sixteen, and often as few as two or four. Sixty-four men were a freaking army, and a guarantee of confusion once things went hot.

The last time JSOC had tried to put this large a unit of SEALs into action had been during Operation Just Cause, in Panama. There, forty-eight SEALs in Task Unit Papa had been tasked with moving into Paitilla Airfield and disabling President Noriega's private jet to prevent his escape.

The operation had been a cluster fuck from the git-go . . . not because of any lack on the part of the Navy SEALs on the op, but because of poor planning and mismanagement all the way up the chain of command. Those forty-eight SEALs had been employed as assault troops, for God's sake, and walked into a deadly cross fire on a brightly lit and exposed tarmac. Four SEALs had been killed, and eight seriously wounded, the highest casualty rate ever suffered by a SEAL unit. Task Unit Papa *had* carried out the mission. They'd also been stranded on that airfield surrounded by hostile forces for twenty-four hours before they could be relieved; the original op had called for a five-hour mission.

The story of what had happened at Paitilla was well-known within the Naval Special Warfare community, a kind of cautionary tale against poor or overambitious planning. Lately, though, it seemed that more and more of the higher-ranking planners—the ones in JSOC and at the Pentagon—were coming up with SEAL deployment concepts involving large numbers of operators. The *Seawolf* SSN was supposed to carry up to sixty Special Forces.

What the hell did you use that many SEALs for, anyway? Tangretti wondered.

Perhaps, with this upcoming op in Iran, he thought, they would find out.

The last of the SEALs filed down the Hercules's ramp, dropped into ranks, and set their sea bags at their feet. There was a little chatter among them, but the company was disciplined and restrained. Several pulled chewing gum out of their mouths and deposited it on the tarmac—or, in one case, on the outside bottom of the lowered ramp on the aircraft.

SEALs could be a casual lot when it came to military formalities. Their officers went through the same BUD/S training as the enlisted men, and camaraderie, experience, and professionalism were far more important in the measure of a man than mere rank. Drake was unusual, though, for being something of a stickler for the formal details. He stood off to one side, aloof, as Lieutenant Mayhew took his position in front of the waiting ranks. With clipboard in hand, he bellowed,

"Atten . . . hut!" The SEALs came to attention, and he began calling the roll. "Alloway!"

"Here!"

"Anderson!"

"Yo!"

"Avery!"

"Present."

The roll call went down the list of names until Mayhew checked off the last name—as if any of the men had somehow escaped from the C-130 during the flight from San Diego—then he turned to face Drake.

"All personnel present or accounted for, *sir!*"

"Very well, Lieutenant." Drake waited as Mayhew took his place with First Platoon. "Welcome to Hawaii," he told them. "Do *not* get comfortable, however. Transportation has been provided to Pearl Harbor, where the *Ohio* is docking as we speak. We will be boarding *Ohio* and getting squared away this evening. Needless to say, there will be no liberty on this stop."

A chorus of groans sounded from the ranks. Drake glared at the men, and Tangretti barked a sharp, "As you were!"

Out of the corner of his eye he saw Olivetti's start of surprise, followed by a scowl. Collecting on that bet would be amusing. One of the small perks of senior rank was occasionally having a bit of extra insight into what the hell was going on. The night before, back at Coronado, Mayhew had informed the detachment's senior NCOs that there would be no liberty when they got to Hawaii. The schedule was going to be way too tight.

"Tonight," Drake continued, as if nothing had happened, "we will load our munitions and supplies on board the *Ohio* and get settled in to our quarters. The *Ohio* will depart Pearl at zero-six-hundred hours tomorrow morning. We do not expect to see daylight until we reach our final destination, off the coast of Iran in the Straits of Hormuz."

Drake ran through a few more formalities, then turned the formation over to Mayhew. At his command, they shouldered their sea bags and walked across the tarmac to a line of waiting trucks.

At least Drake didn't order them to *march* to the trucks in formation.

Jesus, Tangretti thought. Next thing you know, the Teams are going to be wearing black shoes, just like the regular Navy.

But when you'd been in the Navy long enough to make chief, you'd learned to adopt a philosophical attitude. Commanding officers came and commanding officers went, some of them good, some bad. It was a fact of Navy life.

"You *knew* about liberty being cancelled tonight, Chief," Olivetti growled as they clambered onto the back of the truck. "Didn't you?"

"Oh, I might have heard something in a briefing last night," Tangretti admitted with a grin. "And you should know better than to count on liberty. Liberty is a—"

"Yeah, yeah, yeah. 'Liberty is a right, not a privilege.'" He had his wallet out and was peeling off a couple of twenties, one for Hutchinson, one for Tangretti. "Been there. Done that. Caught the clap."

"There's shots for that."

"Yeah, you pecker checkers are all alike. Got a shot for everything."

"If you don't go on liberty, you won't need the shots, right?"

"So what's the word, Chief?" Hutchinson asked, leaning forward on the hard bench they were riding on. "What'd they tell you at the briefing about this op?"

Tangretti thought about the meeting, an informal

session in Captain Jacobson's office. Was it all classified? Or just the bit about their target, and the operational aspects of the mission?

"Not a whole lot," he said, truthfully enough. "It's Iran."

"Shit, everyone knows that," Olivetti said.

"Let's hope 'everyone' doesn't include the Iranians," Tangretti said. "I'd like this to be a picture-perfect op, right out of the textbook, know what I mean?"

Hutchinson nodded. "In, get the job done, and out, with no one even aware we were there."

"Fuckin' A," Olivetti agreed.

"Exactly." Tangretti leaned back against the railing, eyes closed. "The only trick is to get the bad guys to go along with the script. . . ."

Saturday, 7 June 2008

Weather Bridge, SSGN *Ohio*
Pearl Harbor
Oahu, Hawaii
2032 hours CPT

"Ship's comp'ny . . . attention to port!"

Long, low, black, and sleek, the SSGN *Ohio* slipped
through the waters of Pearl Harbor, slowly making the
broad turn to starboard that would take them into
Merry Loch and the submarine base. North, beyond
the gray loom of the USS *Missouri*, lay the monument
dedicated to the USS *Arizona*, whose skeletal remains
still lay in the waters along the eastern shore of Ford
Island. Sixty-seven years before, that stretch of shoreline had been Battleship Row, and early on a certain
December morning, sky and sea had burned as Japanese aircraft launched their surprise attack.

Now, sky and sea burned again, but in the more

peaceful, silent glow of a dazzling red-orange tropical sunset.

Ohio's deck party stood in a silent row, facing the memorial as the submarine completed her turn.

"Salute!"

The men in ranks did not salute, but the chief in charge of the deck party did. High atop *Ohio*'s weather bridge, Stewart and his XO both faced the memorial and rendered crisp, tight salutes. As *Ohio* entered the submarine loch and the memorial was lost to view, Stewart dropped his hand.

"I guess some things don't change, Captain," Shea said.

"What's that?"

"Oh . . . well, it's just the Japanese launched their sneak attack against us, and then sixty years later al-Qaeda launched theirs. Both strikes started a war. And submarines took a major part in World War Two in the Pacific, and, if we're lucky, they'll play a major part in the war against terror."

"Ah." Stewart nodded. Wayne Shea, he was learning, was something of an armchair historian, and at times had an interesting perspective on current events. Sometimes, though, his thinking was a bit obscure and hard to follow. "Subs have already played their part in this war. Lots of long-range deployment of commando forces. And some of the cruise-missile attacks launched by SSNs on Iraq and on Afghanistan, of course."

"Yes, sir. But the *Ohio,* now . . . she's something special. We could make a real difference out there."

Stewart nodded. "We could. If we can find the right target. That's the problem with the War on Terror. It's tough to sort the bad guys out from the good guys, and there's always that unpleasant possibility of collateral damage."

The dock that had been designated for *Ohio* was just ahead, inside the submarine facility. The light was fast failing, but there appeared to be a welcoming committee . . . Marine guards and a tight little coterie of high-ranking brass waiting on the dock.

Stewart picked up the intercom handset. "Helm, Bridge. Come right five degrees."

"Helm, come right five degrees, aye aye."

"Maneuvering, Bridge. All back one-third."

"Maneuvering, engines all back one-third, aye aye."

He felt the tug as *Ohio* slowed, her single screw reversing against her forward drift. Her bow swung gently away from the pier. The deck party that had been rendering honors to the *Arizona* was dividing now into three line-handling parties, one moving past the sail forward to the bow, one moving astern, and one spreading out amidships near the ASDS canister aft of the sail.

"Whatcha think, XO?" he asked. "How many points if we take out the brass gallery?"

Shea shot him a nervous look, and Stewart cracked a grin and winked at him. It was pure showmanship, to hide his nervousness. He'd had the *Ohio* out for trials earlier, out of Bremerton, and knew he had a good crew . . . but it always made you a bit nervous when someone was watching.

And from the look of things, *this* someone watching was a rear admiral, complete with entourage. A miscalculation in docking at this point, especially one that damaged either submarine or dock, would *not* be a career-enhancing move.

"Helm, Bridge. Come right two degrees."

"Helm, come right, two degrees."

Docking an Ohio-class took a light touch and a good sense of balance. *Ohio* was *long*—unwieldy and precariously balanced on the revolutions of her single screw mounted all the way at the aft end of her 560-foot length. Her surfaced displacement of over seventeen thousand metric tons did not stop on the proverbial dime, either.

He had to time this just right. . . .

"Maneuvering, Bridge! All back full."

"Maneuvering, all back full, aye aye, sir!"

The fresh surge of power rumbled through the deck plating at his feet. *Ohio* had been barely making way before. Going all back brought her nearly to a dead stop, while putting the rudder over helped swing the boat's stern gently toward the pier.

"*Handsomely* there!" Boatswain's Chief Griswold yelled from the forward deck, as a monkey's fist came sailing across from the pier—a thick, heavy knot of two-inch hawser connected to a light line, which in turn was connected to the forward mooring line. "Now *haul!*"

The line handling party hauled in on the line, dragging the heavier cable across and above the water. They secured the eye to the bowline cleat, which had been exposed within its recessed chamber on the forward deck.

"Maneuvering, Bridge," Stewart called. "All stop."

"Maneuvering, all stop, aye aye!"

Another line came across the stern, and the aft line handlers grabbed it and made the cable fast. Sailors ashore were taking up the strain, gently easing the behemoth in snug against the pier. Another detail stood ready with the brow—a gangplank extended from pier to quarterdeck, which by submariner tradition was just aft of the sail.

"Let's get below and welcome our guest," Stewart said.

Any time a flag officer paid a call on a mere ship captain, he reflected, it almost certainly meant trouble.

As required by protocol and ancient tradition, Stewart

met the admiral on the quarterdeck as he came aboard. There'd been no time—or advance warning—to prepare a formal reception, with sideboys and dress uniforms, but Chief Griswold let loose a skirling, wavering blast from his boson's pipe and gave the formal announcement: "Central Command, Fifth Fleet, arriving!"

Rear Admiral Chester R. Brady gave the customary salute to the ensign—raised moments before on the fantail—then turned to face Stewart. "Permission to come aboard, Captain."

"Granted, Admiral," Stewart said, saluting. "Welcome aboard."

"Captain Stewart? We need to talk."

"I figured as much, sir. If you'll follow me?"

Though he'd been announced as Central Command, Fifth Fleet, Brady was in fact the *Deputy* Commander, U.S. Naval Forces, Central Command, which made him the number-two man in the hierarchy of naval forces in the Middle East. As the senior officer in the Fifth Fleet present at Pearl, however, he rated the reception as the Fifth Fleet's CO.

The question was what the man wanted. Fifth Fleet was currently deployed out of Dhahran, in the Gulf, naval linchpin of U.S. Central Command. As such, *Ohio* would be transferring to Fifth Fleet operational command . . . and taking orders from Admiral Brady's boss.

Ohio's wardroom would serve as a briefing room. There wasn't space in Stewart's office to accommodate the entourage Brady had brought on board: a captain and three commanders. Several more officers remained on the pier, where Marine sentries had set up a perimeter cordon in depth.

What Stewart was most concerned about was why an *admiral* would be sent out here to talk with him.

This definitely was *not* business as usual.

Enlisted Mess, SSGN *Ohio*
Pearl Harbor
Oahu, Hawaii
2115 hours CPT

"What's the word, Cassie?" Sommersby asked. "You look like you just got torpedoed clean out of the water."

"I dunno," Caswell said, slipping into his seat. "I think I did."

"She wouldn't talk to you?"

Caswell sighed, slumping forward and folding his arms on the table. Moone was at his side with a mug of coffee.

"Drink this, man," Moone said. "Perk ya right up."

"Keep him up all night, is what you mean," Jak said.

"S'all right," Caswell told them. "I got the ten-to-two watch."

"So what *happened*?" Sommersby demanded. "Did they patch you through?"

Sommersby and the COB had arranged for Caswell to get priority on the ship-to-shore telephone line, as soon as it was patched in. Caswell had been increasingly frantic with worry ever since they'd left Bremerton and he was forced to miss his own wedding. He'd transmitted a familygram to Nina while en route, a brief message saying only that he was sorry and that he loved her, but *Ohio* had been out of telephone contact for the entire week. Tonight, when they hooked up at the pier in Oahu, was the first chance he'd had to call her.

"Yeah, they patched me through," Caswell said. "But it was her *mother* who answered."

"Shit."

"Yeah. She didn't much like me before, I think. Now she hates me. The fact that her mom was at Nina's place, though, tells me Nina was there, too. Her mom said she didn't want to talk to me."

"Well, you don't know the old bag was telling the truth, do you?" Jak said. "I mean, your mother-in-law-elect might have just picked up the phone and told you that, without asking Nina. Right?"

"Maybe. Maybe. Damn it, I don't know." He looked at Sommersby. "Chief? What's the straight dope, anyway? They're saying this cruise could be two months long. Is there any chance we'll be home sooner than that?"

"That, my friend," Sommersby said, "depends on what the brass is telling the Old Man right now." He glanced up at the overhead, indicating the conference still going on in the officers' wardroom one deck up. "Your first duty is to this boat, her mission, and your shipmates. You know that, right?"

"Yeah. I know. Damn it, it doesn't make it easy. It *sucks*. . . ."

"I know, son. But it's like our SEAL friends always like to say, 'The only easy day was *yesterday*.'"

Officers' Wardroom, SSGN *Ohio*
Pearl Harbor
Oahu, Hawaii
2140 hours CPT

"Your orders, Captain," Brady said, as one of the officers opened a briefcase and handed him a string-tied manila envelope.

"Thank you, sir. Isn't this . . . a little unusual?"

"What . . . having a rear admiral as messenger boy?"

"I guess so, sir."

"CENTCOM wanted me to talk with you in person, before you enter the AO. They want to be sure you understand the, ah, sensitivity of this operation."

"I see."

"These orders," Brady said, tapping the envelope, "put you under the command of Fifth Fleet. Admiral Costigan."

"Yes, sir . . ."

"However, the situation is, shall we say . . . politically deadly."

Stewart folded his arms and remained silent. He was picking up some unpleasant undercurrents here. *Politics . . .*

"I gather you've heard about JOINTFOR and Millennium Challenge."

Stewart nodded. "Yes, sir. Unofficially."

"That was six years ago. Ought to be old news. But the issue resurfaced recently. The *Washington Post* dredged up the story and ran with it. An article highly critical of the President and his foreign policy.

"Admiral Costigan duly trotted out the reports on Millennium Challenge, shined them up to put Fifth Fleet in the best possible light, and essentially told the press to shove it. Fifth Fleet is ready for *any* attempt by *any* aggressor to control the Straits of Hormuz."

"I . . . see." Stewart kept his voice carefully neutral. An enlisted rating appeared, carrying a tray with mugs of coffee, sugar, and creamer. He took one of the mugs—emblazoned with *Ohio*'s logo—and waited for the admiral to continue.

"Inevitably, Admiral Costigan started taking some heat. CENTCOM is furious right now, as are the Joint Chiefs. JOINTFOR's decision to override the outcome of the war games puts the U.S. military in a bad light.

However . . . the White House and SecDef both are supporting the admiral in announcing the success of Millennium Challenge."

"Wait a second, sir," Stewart said, alarmed. "You're saying there's some sort of power struggle going on with the Joint Chiefs on one side and the President on the other?"

"Well . . . no. I wouldn't call it a 'power struggle,' exactly. But there's some nasty political infighting going on between the various departments concerned. General Taylor wanted to sack Admiral Costigan . . . but SecDef intervened and reversed the decision."

"Sir, just how does this involve the *Ohio*?" He didn't add that, as a naval officer, his oath was to the Constitution, and his loyalty to the President, as Commander-in-Chief of the Armed Forces.

"*Ohio* is sailing into a trap, Captain."

"Come again?"

"The Iranians know what *really* happened during Millennium Challenge. They know about the controversy right now between CENTCOM, the Joint Chiefs, and the White House. And they know Admiral Costigan's career is on the line right now. They may think we're in enough disarray that we'll back down if we're confronted."

"Are we?"

"No. But this, ah, disagreement at high levels makes us look pretty bad. It could lead to a . . . miscalculation. You're going to have to watch your step over there."

"I'm not about to issue any press releases, if that's what you mean."

"That's not what we're concerned about. Captain Stewart, this is off the record . . . but right now the United States and Iran are *very* close to open war. Technically, the first shots have already been fired."

"The SEAL op near Bandar Abbas."

"Yes . . . and also the attack on the *Ohio*."

Stewart was raising his mug to his lips, but that stopped him. Careful, he set the mug down again. "I had assumed," he said carefully, "that that attack was carried out by al-Qaeda, or by a domestic group supporting them."

"That's what the FBI report says. Have you seen it?"

Stewart shook his head. "No, sir."

"There's a copy in with your orders. Classified 'secret.' There were five men on that boat that attacked you. Four were KIA. The Coasties were . . . a bit zealous, let's say.

"The fifth man was wounded, but we took him alive. Under questioning, he admitted to being Savama."

"Iranian Intelligence?"

"Yes. We've known for a long time that there're a number of Iranian sleeper agents in the United States. There's no way we can deport them all."

"Of course not." It was the single major disadvantage the United States faced in domestic terrorism. Attempts to identify possible terrorists on the basis of nationality or ethnicity constituted profiling, and were both illegal and futile. Most Iranians living in the United States were peaceful, law-abiding, and—insofar as many had fled the theocracy of their homeland—even enthusiastically pro-American.

All U.S. law enforcement could do was watch . . . and wait for the next attack.

"Three of the men on that boat were al-Qaeda fighters," Brady went on, "two Saudis and a Pakistani. The other two, including the prisoner, were Iranian. Entered the U.S. six months ago, seeking asylum. We think they're part of a cell operating out of Seattle. We also think that Tehran may know *Ohio*'s mission, which is why they targeted her. If they don't know, they've taken a damned good guess."

A disturbing, dangerous thought. "That's why all the security on the pier outside?"

"Security levels on all military bases worldwide have been elevated," Brady said, "but, yes. In part."

"I also find it interesting that there were Iranians, Saudis, and Pakistanis all working together."

Brady nodded. "We've been seeing a lot of that in al-Qaeda. The common fight against America overrides the factionalism, Shi'ite versus Sunni. That's what Tehran is counting on, of course."

Iran was predominantly Shi'ite Muslim. Both Saudi Arabia—the birthplace of bin Laden and al-Qaeda—and, to a lesser extent, Pakistan, were Sunni, a particularly vicious and fundamentalist brand of Wahabi Sunni belief. Since Shi'ite and Sunni tended to consider one another heretics, getting them to work together could be a problem.

But al-Qaeda appeared to be pulling it off.

"Now, we're not going to go to war because these creeps took a shot at you, Captain," Brady went on. "For one thing, we don't want Tehran to know we captured one of their people. For another, Tehran would just deny the connection, and the media—especially Al Jazeera and the rest of the Islamic news media—would accuse us of using or even *staging* a minor terrorist incident as an excuse to invade Iran.

"And so we want you to use *extreme* caution when you enter the Gulf, Captain. Tehran is going to be looking for an excuse to provoke an incident . . . something like the *Sirocco* sinking, but bigger."

"Why, sir? What's it going to buy them?"

"A victory. A propaganda victory if they can't beat

us in a face-to-face showdown. They're trying to maneuver themselves into a win-win situation. If they
provoke a confrontation, and we back down because
we can't get our own act together, they look like heroes to the whole damned Islamic world. If they provoke us into attacking them, into an overt act of war,
they don't *have* to win. Not if the whole Islamic world
turns against us because we were clearly the aggressors."

Stewart shook his head. "Admiral, this is way outside
my area of expertise. I'm a ship captain, a submariner.
I do *not* set policy."

"Of course not. But you'll still be the sharp end of the
stick out there, Captain. The sinking of the *Sirocco* has
people dancing in the streets in Tehran right now, burning American flags and daring us to fight them. So far
as they're concerned, they just won their biggest victory
since Desert One."

"Okay . . . I follow that, sir. They want to provoke us
into hitting them first, so they look like the good guys
to the rest of the world." Stewart shrugged. "So . . . why
should we give them the ammunition? Why not just sit
back and let them stew? We don't *have* to give them
what they want."

"Because we don't know what those excavations outside of Bandar Abbas are. We don't know if it's some
sort of NBC facility . . . or a long-range missile battery
that would command the straits. We think they're about
to try something big, but we don't have a clue what that
might be.

"And so *Ohio* is going to do what she was designed
to do. She's going to slip inside Iranian territorial waters without being detected and put a SEAL team
ashore. And if you get caught, Captain Stewart, you

could be providing them with the excuse they're looking for. *Ohio* could be the trigger for the world's next big war."

Stewart made a face. "Pleasant thought."

"Indeed. And here's another one. Our best intelligence analysis of Iranian intentions suggests two possible options for them. One . . . they arrange a confrontation, we back down, and the Fifth Fleet leaves the Gulf voluntarily. If that happens, Iran becomes *the* naval power in the region, and would immediately gain control over the oil shipment routes through the straits."

"I can't see us giving that to them. And their other option?"

"They move to close the Straits of Hormuz, and trap the Fifth Fleet at Dhahran. If they can isolate Admiral Costigan, Millennium Challenge might become something other than a war-game simulation. The Fifth Fleet could be wiped out for real."

"Jesus! And they think they can actually pull that off?"

"After they smeared mud in our faces—running off the SEALs in Operation Black Stallion and sinking the *Sirocco*? Yeah, they think they can do it. And it's even possible they could."

"Sir . . . the Iranians don't have much of a navy. They couldn't hope to win against us, not in the long run."

"Here's a hot news flash, Captain. If they try to shut down the Straits of Hormuz, we *will* go to war. Our strategic imperative is to keep the international shipping lanes in and out of the Gulf open.

"But—and this is a very important 'but'—while they can't win a long war, they *can* hurt us, and badly. General Van Riper proved it could be done by sinking the Fifth Fleet—at least in simulation. The U.S. public has been ambivalent about our presence in the Gulf since Iraqi War Two. They don't like to hear about high casualties on the evening news. What do you think the reaction of the American people would be if we lost a supercarrier in there? Or even if we just lose the *Ohio*?"

"Well, I would *like* to believe that the American public would roll up their sleeves, pitch in, and do what has to be done."

Brady sighed. "Maybe they would. Maybe they'd be willing to try, at least. But their representatives in Washington may think differently."

Stewart considered this. Most Americans he knew were behind the War on Terror one hundred percent, but for many recent operations—Iraq and Afghanistan were two excellent examples—the emphasis had become tangled up with the idea of not losing lives. The notorious Rumsfeld Doctrine, applied in Afghanistan, had emphasized the need to keep American casualties to an absolute minimum by relying on high technology—smart bombs and UAVs—and on the efforts of local forces.

And yet, in war, lives were lost. *Always.* And in Afghanistan, it was more than possible that the reliance on unreliable local militias had let many in the al-Qaeda leadership, including bin Laden himself, escape.

One reason the second Iraqi war had become so unpopular at home was the high rate of casualties—not so much the losses suffered during the actual invasion, which were remarkably low, but in the insurrections and suicide bombings that followed.

Maybe Brady had a point. Maybe American will *would* fold in the face of a really nasty butcher's bill . . . especially if it came all at once. Part of the horror of 9/11 had been the deaths of three thousand people in the space of a handful of minutes. There were close to twice that many sailors on board a single supercarrier. . . .

He also clearly heard Brady's warning.

The *Ohio* would be in truly tight straits, both in terms of physical geography and politics. The Straits of Hormuz were dangerously narrow and dangerously shallow, especially for a leviathan like the *Ohio*.

But worse than that were the political shoal waters. If *Ohio* was discovered, she might be sunk or run aground, and the propaganda triumph Tehran would enjoy in trumpeting the news—an American nuclear submarine destroyed or, worse, captured—might well unite the fractured Islamic world. Even if the *Ohio* wasn't sunk or captured, even if she were simply spotted and shown to be invading Iranian territory, Tehran might still get a political win out of it, and attack the Fifth Fleet under the guise of self-defense.

There weren't a lot of good options. The only one that worked would be to carry out the assigned mission in complete secrecy, without being discovered. That was the textbook outcome his superiors were expecting of him and his command, of course.

But Stewart knew just how likely it was that *any* mission of this size and scope could be carried out perfectly according to plan.

No plan of battle ever survives contact with the enemy. Who'd said that? The Prussian strategist van Moltke, he thought . . . or was it Napoleon? Shea would know. He'd ask the XO about it later.

"One more thing, Captain."

There's more? But he didn't voice the thought. "Yes, Admiral."

Brady extended a hand, and one of the aides produced another envelope from the briefcase. Brady opened it and handed the contents to Stewart.

Photographs. Several of them, all with digital imprints, and cropped in a fuzzy, dark circle, which indicated they'd been shot through a submarine's periscope. He recognized the legend—the SSN *Pittsburgh*. These had been shot ten days ago, on May 28.

Most of the shots were of the low, dark conning tower of a submarine. Two were underwater shots, looking up at a sub's keel from beneath, and so close you could see the individual hull plates, and see how clean the bottom was.

"Those were taken of the new Iranian diesel boat," Brady explained. "Jack Creighton's been tracking her in and out of Bandar Abbas. We think they're getting her ready for a long patrol."

"What would a 'long patrol' be for one of these?"

"Several weeks at least. What we're concerned about is the fact that the Iranians know *Ohio* is coming, and have guessed her mission."

"In other words, they're laying an ambush."

"It's a possibility. We think, we *think*, that they may try to intercept you while you're still in the Indian Ocean. Not to attack you. They'd rather catch you inside their territorial waters. But if they can pick you up with a sonar sweep coming in, they might trail you into the straits, then put a couple of torpedoes up your ass the moment you enter Iranian waters."

Brady seemed to be following his thoughts, watching his face. "If the job was going to be *easy*," he said, grinning, "we wouldn't be paying you the big bucks, right?"

"It's not the paycheck," Stewart replied absently. "It's the benefits and the retirement package."

An old joke, with just enough truth to it that Brady gave him a quizzical look, as though trying to decide whether he was serious.

He sighed. "Consider me duly warned, Admiral. We'll watch our ass."

He just wished he could promise that *Ohio* wouldn't get caught. Stewart, however, never made promises that he wasn't absolutely certain he could carry out.

Saturday, 7 June 2008

Pier One, SSGN *Ohio*
Pearl Harbor
Oahu, Hawaii
2316 hours CPT

It was starting to rain, a thin, warm, tropical mist that
floated on the air more than fell, and turned the glare
of high-intensity floodlights into soft blurs of white.
Marine guards, in camo utilities and carrying M-16s,
stood stoically in the drizzle, watching the night.

Lieutenant Christopher Wolfe stood on the concrete
dock near the pier, watching the line of powerfully mus-
cled, hard young men filing past him and onto the pier.
The SEALs, as ever, bore an aura of quiet and deadly
competence. They were very, very good at what they did,
and that expertise carried over into their silent manner.

Outwardly, they ignored Wolfe as they passed him.
A number had formed up a working party and were

shifting ammunition containers and other equipment from a pile on the pier up onto the *Ohio*'s afterdeck, helped by dungaree-clad sailors off the sub. Others, each with a heavy sea bag over his shoulder, were filing onto the pier and up a specially rigged brow leading to the forward deck, then taking a sharp right to the weapons loading hatch just ahead of *Ohio*'s sail.

He felt their notice of him, and their curiosity, even if they didn't voice it.

Weapons, Lieutenant Christopher Wolfe thought, and his mouth pulled back in a wry but humorless grin. That's what we are. They might as well load us through the weapons hatch.

"Lieutenant Wolfe?"

He turned to face two men. The speaker was a lean, hard individual who might have been as old as thirty-five, with sandy hair matted against his forehead by the rain. Like the others, he was wearing a dark blue Navy work jacket, with no indication of rank.

"Yes?"

"I'm Commander Drake, Detachment Delta." He indicated the man next to him, dark-skinned, dark-eyed. "This is my exec, Lieutenant Mayhew. You're the Detachment Echo guy . . . from Black Stallion?"

"Yes, sir."

"And you want to go *back* there?" Mayhew asked with a sudden grin.

"I don't *want* to, no," Wolfe said. "But I guess someone decided you boys needed a friendly native guide."

"It would help to have someone who'd seen the ground before," Drake said. "And maybe someone who can tell us what to avoid this time around."

Wolfe nodded, tired. "I can tell you where we went wrong before, Commander. You'll have to make your own mistakes for yourself. New ones, all your own."

He'd intended the words as a joke, but he caught the flash of irritation in Drake's eye. The man seemed a humorless sort, not the kind of officer who would allow himself to become familiar with those under his command.

"We will *not* be making any mistakes this time around, Lieutenant," Drake said.

"I'm very glad to hear that, sir."

He lifted his wrist, peering at his diving watch. "It's late . . . but I'd like to go over your debriefing, if you don't mind."

How many times had he been through it already? The grilling? The memories?

"Very well, sir."

"Let's get on board, and get the hell out of this rain."

His first job, though, was to check in with *Ohio*'s OOD, who assigned an enlisted man to take him to the compartment set aside as bunking quarters for the SEALs.

Ohio-class boats might be roomy compared to an SSN, but space was still precious. Sixty-six SEALs could not simply insert themselves into a boat already occupied by over 140 enlisted men and officers without crowding. Sleeping space for the SEALs consisted of racks stacked five high, with room to lie down but not to sit up—with about eighteen inches of headroom between one rack and the next rack above.

Ohio's enlisted crewmen had the same facilities.

Submariners might be used to such cramped sleeping arrangements, Wolfe thought, but living in a sardine can took some getting used to. SEALs learned to sleep in the mud—or go forty-eight hours at a stretch with no sleep at all—but when they had a rack, they expected it to be a real bed, not a coffin with a mattress in it. Nor did the officers usually barrack with enlisted men; Commander

Drake and Captain Martin were sharing a cabin, Wolfe understood, but the lieutenants were racking out with the enlisted SEALs.

Rank might have its privileges on a submarine, but not when those privileges took up space.

Sunday, 8 June 2008

Office of the Ministry of Defense
Tehran, Iran
1425 hours local time

"I assure you, General, that your country has *nothing* to fear in this matter." Admiral Mehdi Baba-Janzadeh, Iran's Minister of Defense, folded his hands on the desk. "We have a clear division of our mutual areas of interest, your people and mine. Your nation's help, both in terms of military assistance and in the more, ah, technical matters at Arak and Natanz, will assure our hegemony over the Persian Gulf, and your security at home, for many years to come."

General Igor Sergeyev studied the man across the desk for a long moment before replying. Outside, the sun beat down hard on the gray streets of Tehran, and he could hear the rumble and clatter of traffic on Mozhdeh Street. "We recognize that, Admiral," he said slowly, in his somewhat halting Farsi. "But my superiors at home are . . . concerned. A major war in the Gulf could easily grow to something larger. Things could get out of hand."

"General, I promise you that there is no need for concern. We do not intend to actually fight the Americans. Not in an all-out, protracted war."

"Neither," Sergeyev said with a bland lack of expression, "did the Taliban."

"Ah. Point taken. But I assure you that it will not come to that."

"How can you be so certain? The Americans have been . . . insatiable since the terrorist attacks on New York and Washington. Their invasions of Afghanistan and Iraq—"

"I am sure," Baba-Janzadeh said, interrupting, "that the Americans lack the *will* to fight, in particular when they are confronted with high casualties. Look at the record! Their leaders are terrified of an engagement that will, in their words, become another Vietnam. They take every opportunity to avoid direct combat, preferring to use stand-off weapons or intermediaries simply in order to preserve American lives. In Afghanistan, they relied for the most part on anti-Taliban rebels, on locals, and upon the use of massive air power when the Taliban had almost nothing in the way of antiair defenses."

"Iraq had a sizable army, and formidable defenses."

Baba-Janzadeh shrugged. "That, General, is a matter of opinion. Their army had been largely destroyed during their *first* war with the Americans, and had not been substantially rebuilt."

"And the American invasion of Iraq was not carried out by surrogates."

"No . . . though you will notice that their propaganda machine stressed that it was an allied *coalition* that was attacking Iraq, not solely the Americans. We also know that they originally planned to carry out much of the campaign using Kurdish surrogates in the North. That idea was rendered ineffective when the Turks refused to allow American operations from their soil.

"And the outcome of that invasion only proves my point. American forces suffered relatively few casualties in the actual invasion. Subsequent combat losses were incurred over the next several years, in guerrilla warfare against Iraqi insurgents and al-Qaeda fighters. Meanwhile the western press—especially the American press—agonized over mounting casualties and castigated the Bush administration for the 'Iraq quagmire,' as they liked to call it.

"The nation of Iran, my dear general, is far better able to defend itself, far more capable and deadly than the Iraqi military ever was. Faced with the certainty of high casualties if they invade our country, the Americans will back down."

Sergeyev raised an eyebrow, but refrained from the obvious rejoinder. In eight years of insanely bitter warfare, Iran had been unable to overcome Iraq. The two had, in essence, fought one another to a bloody and mutually exhausted standstill between 1980 and 1988. If Iran had recovered in some measure in the two decades since, it hadn't been to the point where they could last for long against an all-out invasion by the United States.

In any case, Baba-Janzadeh was right about the will and the determination of the American public, or, rather, of the American government. They remained mesmerized by the specter of their long struggle in Vietnam, by the fear of finding themselves again mired in a war they could neither win nor from which they could extricate themselves.

"It is not my place, Admiral," Sergeyev said after a moment, "to criticize your government, or even to offer military advice. My government only wishes certain . . . assurances that the balance of power in this region not be upset by Iranian adventurism."

"Adventurism? We seek to claim our rightful place as leaders of Islam! Of Shi'a Islam! To achieve this, we challenge the American Satan, which has invaded our neighbors and which now threatens us! It is they who threaten the balance of power in the region, my dear Sergeyev, not us!"

Sergeyev made a placating gesture. "Please, Admiral, I meant no offense," he said. "And I assure you that it is not Moscow's wish to intervene in your internal *or* regional affairs. Certainly not! But . . . do you see our concern? If you provoke an American attack, and if you are conquered, the United States will be the only power in the region! Iraq's government follows America's dictates. They must, because the Americans put them in power, and keep them there! The Saudi princes remain committed only to themselves, but have been increasingly pressured by Washington lately. Again, support from the United States is all that keeps them in power. The same with the Emirates and lesser Gulf states. Even Syria has become . . . tractable of late. With Iraq's conquest, they feared they would be next.

"Iran remains the only truly independent power in the region. If you fall, Russia will find itself with an American hegemony in the Gulf."

Baba-Janzadeh gave a grim smile. "I thought you and the Americans were such great friends now. Your old enemies, become allies."

He shrugged. "Alliances come and go. The Commonwealth of Independent States still has strategic interests in the Gulf region, best served by a strong and independent Iran. It wouldn't do to let the Americans win the upper hand here."

"No . . . what you fear, General, is that the Shi'ite populations within your own borders will one day rise up and destroy you. You know that so long as you have us as an active trading partner, so long as we are willing to pay you hard currency for weapons, we have a certain amount of influence over those Islamic populations. Is that not true?"

"I . . . cannot address that issue, Admiral."

"Indeed. Your bosses in Moscow, no doubt, ordered you not to discuss religious matters with me. It is of no importance. I simply want you to know that we know the true picture. You fear having an American hegemony in the region, because without our guidance, your Shi'a population will become restive. You hope that their focus will be on the Americans—on driving the Americans out of our lands once and for all—but are afraid that without our leadership, they will act independently and chaotically.

"And to that, General, all I can say is that your best hope is that we win in our confrontation with the Americans. Continue to supply us with arms and military equipment, with supplies, and with technology . . . especially with the technology for the new uranium enrichment plants. Tell your superiors that the Americans *will* back down, because they know they cannot beat us without suffering intolerable casualties. If we win, we will be grateful to those of our allies who helped us, and you will have a powerful friend here on the shores of the Gulf." He smiled, a dangerous showing of teeth with no humor behind it. "Can I make this any clearer?"

"No, Admiral. I understand you perfectly."

"Good."

"Just so long as you understand, Admiral, that a miscalculation could have devastating consequences for you. As you say, in you we have a useful and active trading partner. We have no wish to lose you as such."

The audience, unsatisfactory as it was, ended moments

later. General Sergeyev thanked his host for his time and, following the Pasdaran officer who was both his guide and guard in the building, made his way out of the warren of offices and passageways that was Tehran's Ministry of Defense.

His destination now was the Russian embassy. He had much to discuss with his superiors in Moscow—a cable, first, but then, he thought, a flight back home. He needed to speak with the Defense minister, *his* Defense minister, and with others, in person.

Did the Iranians know the deadliness of the game they were playing?

He'd seen the outlines of their plan, and he had to admit that it had been carefully and meticulously worked out. Baba-Janzadeh hadn't told him everything, of course, but he'd also seen details from secret documents acquired by the SVR, the Sluzhba Vneshney Razvedki—Russia's foreign intelligence service, operating out of the local Russian embassy. According to the military operation the Iranians were calling "Azar Bahadur," they intended to use a virtual armada of small craft of various types armed with antiship missiles, as well as their fleet of submarines, all backed up by missile batteries along the Hormuz coast. Their goal was nothing less than the destruction of the American Fifth Fleet, currently headquartered across the Gulf from the Iranian west coast, while at the same time closing the Straits of Hormuz to all shipping.

Sergeyev was forced to admit that if the Iranians pulled off even a partial success—if they could sink three or four capital ships, and especially if they could sink an American aircraft carrier—the Americans might well decide they had no stomach for further losses and withdraw. Further, world opinion would swiftly gravitate to support for Iran, if *they* controlled the keys to the world's oil supply, and not the Americans.

But Sergeyev had been an officer in the Red Army before the collapse of the Communist state. As a young lieutenant, he'd served in the GRU, the Soviet Army's bureau of intelligence. He'd been stationed in America—in New York City and in Washington—for a total of three years, and he felt that he knew them as well as any Russian could. During those years he'd dealt with the Americans as enemies—as enemies in all but fact, at any rate—on an almost daily basis, getting to know them, how they thought, how they reacted to threats.

He believed that their chief weakness as a foe lay in their government, which surrendered focus, order, and will in order to entertain their curious interpretation of what a "democracy" truly was.

Oddly, paradoxically, their military's greatest strength, in his opinion, lay in that same interpretation of democracy, which gave it tremendous flexibility. American field commanders, ship captains, even regimental commanders exercised far greater freedom in interpreting and carrying out their orders than their Russian counterparts had ever known. Had things ever come to an actual war between the United States and the old Soviet Union, Sergeyev feared the Americans would have won. By the time a developing situation on the battlefield could be identified, the proper request for orders routed up the chain of command, and a reply be routed back down and received, an American field commander would have recognized the problem and taken action.

In many ways, Iran's military enjoyed the same shackles as had the Red Army. Instead of political control, the mullahs exerted religious control, but the result was much the same. A Russian colonel who made a fatal strategic mistake would have found himself replaced; a Pasdaran colonel who blundered might well find himself dead.

The effect, in terms of squelching any real initiative among field officers, was very much the same.

The imbalance in forces didn't concern Sergeyev much. America's conflict in Vietnam had demonstrated to the world that a nation did not need to match the Americans tank for tank, ship for ship, man for man in order to win. What was necessary was will. Mehdi Baba-Janzadeh was absolutely right. Faced with high casualty rates and falling numbers in the polls, the American Congress lacked will.

But the American people . . . ah, that was another thing entirely. America's citizens were much like ordinary Russians—strong, proud, resilient, determined, and willing to sacrifice for the greater good.

Would the loss of a nuclear aircraft carrier or a few thousand of their Marines convince Washington to withdraw from the Gulf? Or would the American people roll up their sleeves and settle in for a long and brutal war, determined to carry it through to the end? Sergeyev honestly didn't know the answer to that, so finely balanced was it on the sword's edge of history. During the Great Patriotic War, the Americans had fought through to final and decisive victory both in Europe and in the Pacific. In Vietnam, the American public had been weakened and divided by dissent; their military had won the victories, but their politicians had lost the war.

Baba-Janzadeh's problem was that he assumed that the majority of the American public, because they were not devotees of Islam, were weak and dissolute, lacking in will and determination. During the Cold War, Moscow had underestimated them in a similar way because they were capitalists rather than Communists. Sergeyev's deployment in the United States with the GRU had convinced him that ordinary Americans should *never* be underestimated.

Even so, he did believe the Iranian plan had a fair chance of success. Back home in Moscow his superiors were still bickering over whether to warn the Americans of their peril. Their decision, he knew, depended in large part on his assessment of the situation in Tehran. If the Iranians had no chance of success, it was in Moscow's best interests to throw in their lot with the Americans. However, a successful American invasion of Iran would bring certain documents to light—most especially those regarding Moscow's covert assistance with Iran's military nuclear program—that were best left in darkness. By distancing themselves from Iran, by actively providing accurate intelligence to Washington, Moscow might be able to take advantage of the situation, and even provide military assistance that would create and guarantee a Russian presence in the Gulf. And those embarrassing papers would remain out of sight.

But if Tehran had even a fair chance of winning, Russia would benefit to a far greater degree by covertly remaining friends with the current regime. Control of Russia's native Islamic population *was* part of it, yes, as was the cash flow generated by Iran's purchase of military and nuclear technology.

Of far greater importance, however, was the possibility of a major strategic shift. As the United States pulled out of the Gulf, they would leave behind a power vacuum only partially replaced by the tiny Iranian navy. Russia could capitalize on that, could step in with sales of Russian aircraft, tanks, ships, and submarines that would make all previous sales pale in comparison. Russian influence would grow in the region as well.

It was a long-established if unspoken fact of global realpolitik that he who controlled the waters of the Persian Gulf could dictate to the rest of the world. The United States was very close to achieving that enviable position.

But soon, with luck, Moscow could replace the Americans as lords of the oil-rich Middle East.

It was definitely a goal worth the tremendous risk, and Sergeyev intended to present his view on the matter to his superiors in the most forcible manner possible.

Office of the Ministry of Defense
Tehran, Iran
1455 hours local time

Admiral Mehdi Baba-Janzadeh remained motionless behind his desk for a long time after Sergeyev's departure. The fool. The poor, deluded, godless fool. He had no idea what was in store for his country once Iran emerged triumphant in the coming struggle.

Risk? Of course there was risk! What great endeavor, what heroic effort, lacked all risk, all danger? And what great victory for the cause of Allah, the merciful, the munificent, was won without sacrifice, even martyrdom? The West—and Baba-Janzadeh included Russia within that category—simply did not, simply could not, understand.

And the planners of Operation Azar Bahadur—the Farsi meant "Bold Fire"—had honed the plan to the diamond-keen edge of a scimitar. Even if the Americans won, they would lose.

During the War of the Cities, the eight-year struggle

with Iraq, Iran had been forced to accept devastating, inconceivable losses in order to prevail over Saddam Hussein's invasion. Women and children had been recruited to walk ahead of advancing troops in order to clear the approach of land mines, and assaulting Pasdaran units had been forced to scramble over the thickly stacked walls of their own dead to reach the enemy. Iranians knew what sacrifice truly was.

Before the first American war with Iraq, Saddam Hussein had boasted that the coming conflict would be the "Mother of All Battles," and confidently predicted hundreds of thousands of American dead. And indeed, that might have been the outcome had Saddam been a better general. He'd failed, however, by relying on the mass-army tactics he'd employed with less than complete success against Iran, by completely underestimating the superiority of American technology, and by waiting for the Americans to come to him, rather than striking the first blow.

Oh, he'd launched an attack—the abortive attempt at al Khafji that had been handily beaten back at the Saudi border—but that had been more of a probing attack, a tentative feeling-out of American and Saudi defenses.

Baba-Janzadeh had studied the first Iraqi war exhaustively, and he'd made his senior field commanders study its lessons as well. Except for that limited exploration-in-force at al Khafji, Saddam had waited for the Americans to come to him, waited behind his earth berms and fields of land mines and dug-in tanks and static fortifications, assuming that the Americans, when they came, would come that way. Their flanking attack around the western Iraqi defenses and their near-complete encirclement of the Revolutionary Guard had caught Saddam and his generals totally and fatally by surprise.

Iran's military council had no intention of making the same mistakes as had the unlamented Saddam Hussein. Preparations were all but complete, and the first stages were already in motion. At the moment, according to Iranian Intelligence, there were some thirty-four American warships based at Dhahran—the vessels of their Fifth Fleet. At any given time, perhaps a third of these were on patrol—escorting international shipping in and out of the Gulf, suppressing piracy, and operating in support of the Iraqi government.

Against that flotilla—impressive in firepower as it might be—was a true armada, numbering in the hundreds . . . most of them small craft, light patrol boats, even fishing boats, but all equipped with deadly anti-ship missiles, including the deadly new C-802 missiles acquired from the Chinese.

Iran also now possessed six diesel-electric submarines, three Kilo-class subs purchased from the Russians over the past two decades, and three of the newer Ghadir-class boats, designed and built entirely in Iran.

And finally there were the new Iranian missile forces. The new Faateh A-110 medium-range surface-to-surface missile and the highly accurate updated Shahab-3 together would enable Iran to utterly dominate the entire Gulf. The better-than-1,300-kilometer range of the Shahab-3, in fact, would let Iran strike Israel. Indeed, at recent military parades through Tehran, six of the big solid-fuel rockets had been on prominent display, each with a banner declaring, "We will wipe Israel from the map."

The attacks would be coordinated, with the first strike coming from small craft sneaking in close, and follow-on strikes by surface-to-surface missiles fired from Iranian territory. At the same time, Iranian commandos—the Qods Special Forces—and the Iranian-based arm of al-Qaeda, together would launch simultaneous attacks of sabotage and suicide bombings.

The U.S. Fifth Fleet would find itself under sudden and ferocious attack from all quarters, many of the ships destroyed as they rested in port. Still other attacks would be aimed at the American military base at Dhahar, killing the sailors, soldiers, and Marines of the fleet before they knew what had happened. Missiles and submarines would be used to simultaneously close the Straits of Hormuz; the surviving American warships would be unable to escape, and reinforcements would not be able to enter.

America would be presented with a disaster as potent as the one they'd suffered at Pearl Harbor: their fleet crippled at best, with thousands of casualties at the very least. And this time, Washington would not have the will or the determination they'd found in the aftermath of the Japanese attack.

But the plan's real strength lay in what it would do to rally Islamic support throughout the world. Even if the initial strike were less than completely successful, even if the American fleet escaped the trap at the straits, the mere fact that Iran had struck such a blow would be hailed as an astonishing victory throughout the Islamic world. There would be risings, such risings, risings that would sweep secular governments from power from Ankara and Cairo to Kuala Lumpur, and that might well topple the governments of non-Islamic states as well. Indonesia, the Philippines, the former Soviet states of Uzbekistan and Kazakhstan. Russia herself would be engulfed in the flames of religious jihad.

That fool Sergeyev didn't have an inkling of what was to come. He thought to use Iran for his nation's interests; in fact, Iran would use him.

Iran would use his nation's greed and manipulative instincts to advance the cause of Allah and His Prophet.

And, truly, the world would never again be the same.

Friday, 20 June 2008

Sonar Room, SSGN *Ohio*
Indian Ocean
0745 hours local time

ST2 Roger Caswell entered the sonar room, still groggy.
He laid his hand on ST1 Penrod's shoulder. "I relieve
you," he said.

"You're welcome to it," Penrod said. Dobbs walked
in behind him, relieving another watch-stander. Chief
Sommersby was already there, a fresh mug of coffee in
hand as he leafed through the sonar log.

"Anything interesting?" Caswell asked.

"Whales humping," Sommersby said, replacing the
log. "And the usual commercial targets."

He chuckled as he took his seat. So far as submariners
were concerned, there were two and only two types of
seagoing vessels: other submarines and *targets*, meaning
all surface traffic. A peculiar view of the outside world,

he thought, but one that certainly reflected the submariner's unique perspective.

"We've got one noisy broadband contact," Penrod said, pointing at a bright line slanting across the waterfall, "but that one's ours."

"Our pet zoomie," Sommersby said. "He took the *Manta* out for another test run an hour ago. He's been out ahead of us since."

"What," Caswell said, "he couldn't sleep?"

"I think he just misses all of that sun and sky shit," Dobbs said.

"Sun?" Sommersby asked. "What is this 'sun' thing of which you speak?"

"Big ball of flaming gas up in the sky," Caswell said. "I read about it once."

"Ah! Sounds like Chief Griswold's been at it again," Sommersby replied, nodding. "At least he's letting them rip out in the open now, instead of in the goat's locker."

"How's he getting up to the roof?" Penrod asked.

"Damfino. Maybe he pays the zoomie to take him topside when he needs to fart. In which case, the guy's doing the rest of us a real service!"

Caswell took Penrod's place at the console while the good-natured bantering went on. He yawned.

Day and night meant nothing on board a submarine. Standard orders dictated four-hour watches, standing one in three, which meant that when he was working 0800 to 1200 one day, like today, his *next* watch would begin at 2000 tonight and last to 2400 tomorrow morning.

Technically, that left eight hours of free time between watches . . . but besides sleep, he needed to perform other incidentals, including eating, taking care of personal needs, and—above all—continuing to study for his quals.

Together with perhaps a quarter of *Ohio*'s crew, Caswell was a nonqual—or, in the more usual shipboard terminology, a fucking nonqual. During his first six months or so on board a submarine, a newbie was expected to rotate through every one of the ship's departments, primarily learning damage control and emergency procedures, and passing a test administered by each department head. Only when he'd demonstrated proficiency in every area of the boat was a new submariner accepted as fully qualified; a trusted member of the team.

After three weeks at sea, Caswell's body had begun adjusting to this new way of dividing the waking and sleeping periods of his day, but he still felt like he was running short on sleep. Since there was no actual night on board the *Ohio,* at any given time roughly a third of the crew would be at their duty stations, while another third or more would be in their racks.

His rack in the enlisted berthing area was a box smaller than a coffin, with a two-inch-thick mattress resting on a hinged lid that, when opened, gave him access to his small personal storage locker. The fluorescent lighting in the compartment was always on. Darkness—and his only bid for privacy—was provided by the curtains he could draw shut between his rack and the passageway. And there was *always* noise . . . men talking, men getting up or racking out, and all the thumps and bangs that accompanied men going about their duties in a closely confined space.

You learned to live with it.

Tougher to live with, though, was the hazing. All nonquals got the treatment, to one degree or another. In a way, it was a mark of belonging—at least until he earned his final qualifications and received the coveted silver dolphins of the *true* submariner.

So far, Caswell hadn't been hit too badly—the dead,

wet fish in his rack and the usual round of being sent to find a skyhook or a left-handed blivet was about the worst of it. In fact, he'd heard tales of much worse—sailors who'd had their shampoo replaced with Nair, for instance . . . and were then regaled by their shipmates with stories of the dangers of living and working on board a nuclear submarine.

In fact, the crossing-the-line ceremony last week had been a lot rougher. When *Ohio* had crossed the equator east of the Philippines, all pollywogs—personnel who'd never before crossed the equator—had been brought up on charges before King Neptune, and forced to do various unmentionable things with various unspeakable substances from the galley and elsewhere.

And now Caswell was a pollywog no longer, but a true son of Neptune, and he had the certificate to prove it. He just wished some uninterrupted sleep came with the package.

He relaxed at his console, eyes on his waterfall, and slipped on the headphones that let him listen to the ocean depths around him. On the broadband channel he could hear the gentle susurration of the water as *Ohio* slipped along at almost twenty-five knots. At that speed, sonar was largely useless unless the target was very noisy or very close.

The *Manta* matched both criteria; he could hear it plainly—a kind of high-pitched whine with a deeper throb to it, coupled with the hiss of its wake.

Eyes closed now, as though in deep meditation, Caswell listened. . . .

Experimental Prototype XSSF-1 *Manta*
Indian Ocean
0752 hours local time

Lieutenant Commander Hawking opened up the *Manta*'s throttle, putting the nimble little craft into a high-speed banking turn. Ninety knots! Not quite like putting an F/A-18 Hornet through its paces, but it would do.

At one hundred meters, the water was clear but utterly dark. Switching on his headlights, he seemed to be moving alone in a vast, empty bubble of deep and hazy blue.

His fuel cells were draining fast. It was time to go home.

He opened the sound channel to *Ohio*.

"*Ohio, Ohio,* this is *Manta.* Do you copy?"

"Copy, *Manta,*" came the reply over his headset. "Go ahead."

"Open the barn doors, folks. I'm bringing this baby in."

"*Manta,* you are clear for approach."

"Thank you, *Ohio.* Open wide and say 'ah. . . .'"

The sound channel gave him the direction to *Ohio,* while Doppler ranging gave him an estimated distance—half a mile, more or less.

The run this morning had let him complete the last few items on his predeployment checklist. His superiors back on Oahu might have some quibbles, but so far as Hawking was concerned, the *Manta* was tight, hot, and ready to take on the real world.

What he didn't understand was why his shipmates on board the *Ohio* weren't more excited. The *Manta*'s technology was damned impressive. Her fuel cells alone represented a major leap forward in power generation for small underwater craft. In the future, they might well allow the deployment of whole fleets of microsub-marines, robots raging independently across the world's oceans or deploying from manned submarine mother-ships. Manned fighters like the *Manta,* operating from undersea carriers like the *Ohio* conversions, might make hunter-killer boats like the new Virginia class obsolete.

Somehow, though, neither *Ohio*'s officers nor her crew seemed that interested in the *Manta.* Or maybe, Hawking thought, it was simply that he himself had yet to be fully accepted by the rest. He'd tried being his usual open, friendly self, even with the enlisted men, and if he'd not been rebuffed directly, then at the least they'd maintained a cool distance.

No matter. He'd made a breakthrough yesterday af-ternoon, while going over the checklist for the *Manta.* A young first-class torpedo man who called himself Moonie had been assigned to the work detail loading the *Manta*'s kinetic-kill torps, and Hawking had managed to strike up a friendly conversation. He had an idea he wanted to try, and the guy had loaned him a music CD so he could pull it off. The CD was already loaded and cued. All he needed to do was switch it on and patch it through the deep sound channel.

Ohio materialized out of the gloom dead ahead, vast and dark. He was approaching her bow-on. A slight adjustment of the controls would send him down the sub's starboard side.

"*Manta,* this is *Ohio.* Reduce speed and alter course to maintain safe clearance."

"*Ohio,* this is *Manta.* I've got it covered."

At just under ninety knots, the *Manta* began rolling as it shrieked past the huge vessel. Hawking switched on the CD and patched it through. . . .

Sonar Room, SSGN *Ohio*
Indian Ocean
0806 hours local time

Caswell could hear the approaching *Manta*. In fact, the high-pitched flutter of its wake was pretty near all he *could* hear. "What the hell?"

"What is it, kid?" Sommersby asked.

"Sounds like the zoomie's coming straight for us."

"He's coming down the starboard side," Dobbs said. "Sounds like a high-speed torpedo, doesn't he?"

Reaching out, Caswell switched to the broadband deep sound channel. . . .

"*Can't touch this!*
Can't touch this!
Oh-oh oh oh oh-oh-oh . . ."

Caswell jumped in his chair as he yanked the headphones off his ears. "*What the fuck?*"

"What's the matter, Cass?" Sommersby demanded.

Caswell pointed shakily at the headphones on the console. He could still hear a harsh, hip-hop beat rattling from the earpieces.

"*Thank you for blessing me with a mind to rhyme.* . . ."

"That son of a bitch just tried to deafen me!" The racket, in fact, was loud enough that every man on board the *Ohio* could hear it, muffled and distorted by the water and the boat's hull, and overlaid by the fluttering whine of the passing fighter sub. The heavy, thumping beat, however, was insistent, and as intrusive within the submarine's normally silent world as a blaring, too-loud stereo in the car next to yours at a traffic light.

"What is that?" Dobbs asked. "Rap?"

Sommersby picked up the headset and held it to his ear. He smiled. "M.C. Hammer. Our zoomie likes puns."

"Puns?" Dobbs asked.

"M.C. Hammer. Operation *Sea* Hammer. Cute. Real cute. I just hope for his sake the skipper shares his sense of humor."

Captain's Office, SSGN *Ohio*
Indian Ocean
1545 hours local time

"Mr. Hawking," Stewart said above steepled fingers. "Do you have any idea what the very first order in my order book reads?"

Hawking was standing on the other side of the desk, at rigid attention. He'd come to attention when he reported to Stewart moments ago, and Stewart had not yet told him to stand at ease. "No, sir."

"It's the same as the first order in *every* sub captain's book. No guesses?"

"No, sir."

"It's *remain undetected*. Do you have any idea how deadly your little stunt out there this morning could have been?"

"Sir, there wasn't another vessel for five hundred miles in any direction."

"Really? How do you know this?"

Hawking opened his mouth as though to reply, then clamped it shut again.

"For your information, mister, sound travels well under water. *Very* well. It can reflect off the bottom and off of the thermocline and travel hundreds of miles; a phenomenon we call convergence. If there was an enemy submarine out there, even a thousand miles away, he heard us. Or, rather, he heard *you*."

"Sir, I didn't think there was any harm."

Stewart leafed through the papers in Hawking's personnel folder, which he'd had delivered to his desk an hour before. "You *did* go to submarine school, didn't you? It says you did . . . New London, right here."

"Yes, sir."

He leafed through more pages in the service record, then stopped, reading one of the sheets more closely. He'd noticed this one when he reviewed Hawking's record upon being assigned to the *Ohio*, but hadn't actually read it carefully. "My God."

"Sir?"

"This is a letter of reprimand. It says that while you were stationed on board the *Eisenhower,* you performed a low-altitude high-speed maneuver without proper authorization, passing 'level with the flight deck' and just a few meters to port—"

"I buzzed pri-fly, yessir."

"I should have known. You're a hot dog."

"Uh . . . I had a bet with—"

"I don't care if you had communion with the Pope!" Stewart studied the man at attention before him a moment. "You have jeopardized the security of this mission and the safety of this vessel. I don't know what they expected of you when you were flying Hornets off the *Ike,* but that kind of behavior is something I *will* not stand for!"

He read through several more pages. "In fact, it seems you were given an offer you couldn't refuse. They were going to pull your flight status. You got out of it by volunteering for the *Manta* project. *Mm.* Did the people at the submarine research facility know they were getting a hot dog from the fleet?"

"Uh, I believe it was deemed best not to worry them, sir."

"Uh-huh. I'll believe that."

"Sir . . . I am sorry, and it won't happen again."

"You're damned right it won't!" The words were a growl.

"I just . . ."

"Go on."

"Sir, I just didn't think it would do any harm! It's not like we're up against the Soviets or anything like a world-class twenty-first-century navy! We're still a couple of thousand miles from the Gulf, and the Iranians don't have shit to track us! Hell, I figure the *Manta* puts more noise into the ocean than that CD did."

"Mister," Stewart said, his voice very low, and very dangerous. "Don't you *dare* lecture me on my assets or my strategic imperatives on my own boat! What the Iranians have or don't have is beside the point!

"As for making noise . . . I'm well aware of how noisy that toy of yours is. I was under orders to take it and you on board, but I have yet to determine whether it or you will be of any use on this operation. Frankly, I doubt it, because a submarine's mission *always* involves laying low and remaining undetected."

"I'm aware of that, sir."

"Your head is aware of it, maybe. But not your heart. Are you aware, Commander, that this vessel has already come under attack, just after we left port and while we were still within American territorial waters?"

"Uh, yes, sir. I was briefed."

"We might be a couple of thousand miles from our AO, and we might be fighting a third-world enemy who has technology we consider primitive . . . but I absolutely will *not* jeopardize this mission or this ship by underestimating him. Is that clear?"

"Clear, sir."

"Another point. I wonder if you understand how sensitive some of our sonar equipment is. Your little impromptu concert out there could have damaged some of the Busy-one gear. It could also have injured the hearing of my sonar technicians, and, let me tell you something, Commander—on this boat, on this mission, my lowest-ranking sonar tech is worth twenty of you. No, I take that back. There's no comparison, because you are a fucking nonqual who doesn't know how to conduct himself, is of no use to the boat or the mission, and who doesn't know how to exercise good judgment or self-discipline! Do you have anything to add?"

Hawking looked pale, although that might have been the effect of the fluorescent lighting in the overhead. "Sir, it *was* a joke. Maybe . . . well, I guess I went too far, and I apologize. But sir, the *Manta* is a valuable asset, and I would like an opportunity to prove that to you, and to the Navy."

"A combat mission may not be the best venue for offering that proof. Until further notice, Commander, the *Manta* is off-line. You will report to the XO, Commander Shea. I believe we can find some admin duties to keep you out of our hair. Dismissed."

"Sir, I—"

"Dismissed!"

"Aye aye, sir!" Glowering, Hawking turned, opened the door, and walked out.

Stewart stared at the door a moment before closing the personnel folder and setting it aside on his desk. Lieutenant Commander Hawking was something of an anomaly on board a submarine. The SEALs were also "guests," supernumeraries with no specific duties who could hinder the smooth operation of the boat, but they kept to themselves in the area set aside for them and didn't try to mix. Hawking, on the other hand, having gone through sub school, was convinced that he was part of the crew, but hadn't yet figured out that a newbie wasn't a submariner until he'd completed his qualifications.

In fact, there was no room on a submarine for anyone who couldn't pull his own weight. Back in WWII, sub personnel had to actually know all aspects of all departments—not just emergency procedures—so that any man could fill in anywhere on board where he was needed. That level of broadband competence wasn't possible today, so specialized was the training and knowledge required for each station. But it was still a goal to shoot for.

Maybe, Stewart thought, if he required Hawking to go through the quals program . . . That hadn't been in the man's orders, but a sub skipper had broad powers in so far as what he required of personnel stationed on board his vessel. He'd talk to Shea and the COB about it later.

At least it might keep that young hot dog out of trouble.

Wardroom, SSGN *Ohio*
Indian Ocean
1610 hours local time

Hawking entered the officer's wardroom and made straight for the coffee mess. *Damn the man! Admin duty! Admin duty!* He was an *aviator,* damn it, Hawking thought, *and* a submariner; *not* a pencil-pusher!

Oh, he knew the others on board didn't accept him as such. *Ohio*'s crew was a close-knit and cliquish bunch, and they kept tight and quiet around people they considered to be outsiders. Same with the SEALs, or worse. *That* lot didn't talk to *anybody*!

Angrily, he poured coffee into one of the mugs painted with *Ohio*'s logo, then added sugar and creamer. He now had the strong feeling that Moonie had set him up by giving him that CD and suggesting that he play it while "flying" past the *Ohio*. Well, there would be a reckoning. Indeed there would!

Returning to the wardroom table, he sat down and indulged in a sulk. At least *Ohio*'s crew *did* talk. But they kept their distance—a superior distance—and as a member of a naval elite, he wasn't used to that kind of treatment. They were so freaking snide. Just yesterday he'd said something to Lieutenant Commander Carter, the engineering officer, about being a submariner. He'd pronounced the word as he'd always heard it pronounced—"sub-MAR-i-ner." Carter had looked at him as though he'd just crawled out of the bilge, and said "Commander Hawking, a sub-MAR-i-ner is the brand of wristwatch the Captain wears. The officers and crew of the *Ohio* are 'sub-muh-REE-ners.'"

Carter had been careful not to include him in that definition, Hawking had noticed.

Well, he would show them. Somehow.

He took a sip of coffee, blinked, and set the mug down again. Hawking was not, by nature, introspective. He was damned good at what he did, and he tended not to indulge in soul-searching or angst. However, it was beginning to occur to him that this time around *he* was the one with the problem, not everyone else around him.

Oh, it was still everyone else on the goddamned boat who was acting like assholes. There was no question about *that*. But Hawking was self-aware enough to know that he was overreacting to the treatment he was getting, and he wanted to know why.

The answer, he thought, lay in the fact that he *was* a member of an elite group within the Navy. Aviators—they *never* called themselves "pilots"—were the modern knights-errant of the service, very much in the public eye, very much used to the glory and the headlines that came with their position.

There was a paradox there. Hollywood tended to portray aviators as glory hounds and loose cannons. In fact, although there were a few hot dogs, most aviators were cool and calm to the point of being dispassionate, professional, competent—and very much team players, as opposed to their lone-wolf rep on the silver screen.

At the same time, though, most aviators grandly accepted the acclaim and the notoriety. Hawking, for instance, never had any trouble picking up willing women ashore. He considered it one of the perks that came with the job. And now he was an outsider, tolerated but not accepted as a member of the community.

And that thought *rankled*.

Saturday, 21 June 2008

Sonar Room, SSGN *Ohio*
Indian Ocean
0245 hours local time

"Hey, Cassie?" The COB stood in the doorway to the sonar room. "I need to see you a moment."

"S-Sure, Master Chief." He looked at the other sonar watch-standers, as if to say, *What'd I do?* Dobbs shrugged and Sommersby shook his head. No hints there.

"We've got your station covered, kid," Sommersby told him. "Go on."

Caswell followed O'Day forward and down one deck, then aft to the mess hall. At least, he thought, if the Chief of the Boat was about to give him an ass-chewing, it wasn't bad enough to warrant being hauled up to the ship's office. But he couldn't imagine what it was he'd done.

Caswell took a seat at the COB's gestured invitation. "Sorry to interrupt," he said, "but a familygram just came through for you. I thought you'd want to see it in private."

Caswell instantly felt a cold fist clench in his stomach. Familygrams—instituted by the legendary Admiral Zumwalt thirty years before—were intended as morale boosters: short, often maddeningly cryptic messages sent to and from a sub with the regular radio traffic, which helped keep the crew in touch with their families.

Normally, this was a *good* thing . . . a twenty-five-word announcement of the birth of a daughter, a first tooth or a first step, or even of the need to get a plumber to fix the frozen pipes at home. Familygrams from home helped keep the men going, helped remind them of what was really important. But when the Chief of the Boat delivered one personally, and in private, the damned thing was more like the traditional telegram, almost certainly bearing unpleasant, even disastrous news. *We regret to inform you . . .*

He took the flimsy from O'Day's hand and opened it.

PARENTS RIGHT. RELATIONSHIP NOT WORKING OUT, TIME TO END IT. LUCK WITH THE LIFE YOU'VE CHOSEN. DON'T CALL ME. DON'T WANT MY MIND CHANGED. FAREWELL.

SIGNED: NINA

The words blurred for a moment. Damn . . . damn . . . *damn*! He'd been more than half expecting this to happen, but the reality . . .

"You okay, son?" O'Day asked.

Caswell nodded, not trusting himself to speak. He wadded up the message flimsy, looked around for a waste receptacle, and seeing none, stuffed the ball into a pocket of his blue poopie suit.

"Life sucks," O'Day said. "You need some time to yourself? I'll square it with your division chief."

"N-No, Master Chief," he said. "I think I'd better get back to my watch."

"Suit yourself. If you need to talk, though, my office door is open."

"Yeah . . ."

Somehow, thoughts reeling, he made his way back up to the sonar room.

Tuesday, 24 June 2008

Sonar Room, SSGN *Ohio*
Arabian Sea
1340 hours local time

Roger Caswell had never known such pain.

Four long days had dragged by since he'd gotten that familygram, and each day he'd settled a bit deeper into depression. It was the *helplessness* more than anything else that hurt. *Ohio*'s early sailing date had been beyond his control, and now Nina had arbitrarily decided to call off their marriage without giving him a chance to discuss things, to talk, to negotiate in any way. If her parents had argued her into changing her mind, he hadn't been given the chance to answer.

He *really* didn't understand her refusal to listen to anything he had to say. *Don't call me. Don't want my mind changed*. What did that mean . . . that she was afraid that if they talked again, he would convince her to give him another chance? That if her parents had convinced her he was wrong for her, he might be able to make her change her mind again?

That was crazy. Caswell was a rational sort, the kind of man who thought things through carefully and wanted to know the whole story. If he was wrong, if he'd made a mistake, he wanted to know so he could correct it. To deliberately refuse to listen to someone else because to do so might lead you to change your mind . . . that was just fucking nuts.

Somehow, *somehow,* he had to get through to her. . . .

"Cassie!"

"Huh?"

Dobbs had placed a hand on his shoulder and was shaking him. Caswell realized, belatedly, that the other sonar tech had been trying to get his attention for several seconds.

"Watch your screen, man!" Dobbs said, pointing. "You got a contact!"

"Uh, yeah. Thanks." A thread of white light had just begun slanting across the cascade of green up at the top. It was a weak contact, a distant one, but loud enough to emerge from the background static.

Damn. He hadn't been paying proper attention. For two weeks *Ohio* had been racing through the ocean depths at such a high speed that broadband sonar was all but useless. During the last three watch periods, though, the skipper had slowed them to twelve knots— slow enough that the rush of water past the hydrophones didn't drown out nearly everything else.

"Control, Sonar," he said. He glanced at his log, then made a notation. "New contact, bearing three-three-zero. Designate Sierra Two-five-one."

"Sonar, Con. New contact, Sierra Two-five-one. What's your guess?"

He closed his eyes and listened for a moment. He could hear the contact over the headphones now, a very, very faint churning of the water.

Dobbs, who was manning the narrowband towed array, tapped in some commands on his console, trying to tune in on the contact. The narrowband rig let him submit a little more data. "Sir, I make it twin screws. Probable civilian target. It's very faint. I think we're getting a CZ contact here."

"Very well."

Sommersby had been out of the control room for several moments. He returned now, the trademark mug of coffee in his hand, and picked up a set of headphones for a listen. "Sounds like a supertanker," he said. He glanced at Caswell's waterfall. "We're close enough to the Gulf of Oman proper here . . . ninety miles, close enough, which would put them within the third CZ. Sounds like she's coming out of the Gulf of Oman."

CZs, or convergence zones, were a useful phenomenon in the science of sonar detection. Under certain conditions, sound from a distant target reflected off the surface toward the depths, then was bent back toward the surface by the extreme pressure of the deep ocean, or by a thermocline, a sound-reflecting layer of deep, cold water. Convergence zones were the points where a listening submarine could detect sounds focused from far beyond their normal range of hearing; CZs occurred at roughly thirty-mile intervals, which was how Sommersby had deduced that Sierra Two-five-one was emerging from the Gulf of Oman, ninety miles ahead.

Ohio's passage of the Indian Ocean had been uneventful, with few contacts. Now that they were nearing the Gulf, however, they could expect commercial traffic to pick up.

They could also expect to begin picking up Iranian

patrols. The word had been passed to *Ohio* via satellite radio traffic some time ago that the American SSN operating in the area—the *Pittsburgh*—had been tracking the new Iranian diesel boats in and around the Straits of Hormuz. There'd been intense speculation among the crew ever since they'd left the Straits of Juan de Fuca about that attack on the *Ohio*. If the Iranians knew about *Ohio* and her mission, or even if they'd simply guessed, they could expect to encounter the enemy's outlying pickets any time now. *Ohio* had just crossed the Tropic of Cancer; a hundred miles to the north was the border between Pakistan and Iran. A hundred fifty miles to the southeast lay Ra's al Hadd, the westernmost point of Oman.

The Gulf of Oman, while it had no hard-lined demarcation, could be said to begin in another ninety or one hundred miles. Here, an arm of the Arabian Sea stretched for 250 miles northwest to the Straits of Hormuz. At the southeastern end, the Gulf of Oman was two hundred miles wide. At the northwest, it narrowed sharply and twisted north into the straits, which at their narrowest were only about twenty-five miles wide.

The Gulf of Oman, then, offered a taste of what *Ohio* could expect on the far side of the Straits of Hormuz—shoaling water, rapidly narrowing to a tightly constricted bottleneck, with no room for maneuver and no room for mistakes.

If the Iranians were hoping to ambush the *Ohio* before she reached Iran, they would try it *here*, in the Gulf of Oman, or within the straits themselves.

And Caswell had let himself be distracted as they entered the danger zone. He was furious with himself, and determined to do better.

But all of the determination in the world wasn't enough to remove Nina, or the pain, from his thoughts.

Communications Center,
Office of the Ministry of Defense
Tehran, Iran
1425 hours local time

Admiral Mehdi Baba-Janzadeh was called by some the father of the new Iranian navy. It was a role he cherished, and in which he took tremendous pride, though publicly he was careful to ascribe his success to the mercy and munificence of Allah. Within his inner circle of confidants, he liked to point out that Allah used human assets to achieve His goals, and clearly He was determined to turn the Persian Gulf into an Iranian lake.

Much of the recent growth of Iran's navy was due to his foresight and will. Long the weakest of Iran's military services, the navy had been all but destroyed during the long war with Iraq. Baba-Janzadeh had been appointed commander-in-chief of the Iranian navy just after that war's conclusion, and despite meddling by army and air force elements squabbling for scarce resources, he'd begun a major buildup that had continued for the past nine years.

He'd continued the buildup of long-range missile defenses—including the deployment of Chinese-built Silkworm HY-2 surface-to-surface missiles on Larak Island in the early 1990s. In 1992 he'd helped broker a deal with the People's Republic of China for Iran to purchase a fleet of seventy-ton Chinese patrol boats armed with Styx antiship missiles.

In 1993, at his urging, Iran had purchased the first two of an eventual six Russian Kilo submarines, along with eight minisubmarines from North Korea. Later, they'd purchased fifteen North Korean semisubmersible gunboats designed for commando operations. Following maneuvers in 2001, the Iranian merchant fleet was consolidated with the naval arm to improve overall fleet efficiency. Other additions and improvements swiftly followed, as Iran sought to replace the obsolescent foreign vessels of its regular navy with new and advanced designs produced in Iran. New destroyers, frigates, high-speed patrol boats, and finally the three Ghadir-class submarines. The goal—largely realized—had been to make Iran's navy self-sufficient and independent of foreign sources.

Five years later, in part as a reward for his efforts, Baba-Janzadeh was promoted to full admiral and appointed Minister of Defense, in charge of all of Iran's military forces. While his increased scope of responsibilities required that he relinquish much of the planning and execution of naval strategies to subordinates, he'd been able to have a hand in the selection of those subordinates. Rear Admiral Hamid Vehedi, the current commander of Iran's navy, had been a classmate of his at the naval academy and was a trusted friend. When Iran's supreme leader, the Ayatollah Ali Khamenei, had approached him to begin work on Operation Bold Fire, Vehedi had taken on much of the actual preparation.

Admiral Baba-Janzadeh stood in the Defense Ministry's basement communications center, a computer printout in his hand. The message had been sent by Vehedi, and it was one he'd been waiting for.

American submarine detected in Arabian Sea, the message read in part.

They were coming.

Things should start moving very swiftly now.

Control Room, SSK *Ghadir*
Gulf of Oman
1548 hours local time

They'd found a tanker at last.

"Sonar contact now bearing three-five-five, Captain," the sonar officer said. "It is almost certainly a tanker emerging from the straits."

The weapons officer completed the TMA—the Target Motion Analyses—and turned to the captain. "Target speed six knots, range nine hundred meters, sir."

Captain Majid Damavandi stepped onto the control room dais. "Up periscope."

The periscope slid silently up out of the well, and Damavandi snapped down the handles and pressed his face against the eyepiece as it rose. He could see the green fog of brightly lit water, then the sudden burst of bright blue sky and sea as the head of the periscope broke through the surface. He did a careful three-sixty first, scanning for possible nearby threats that might have been missed by the sonar, before bringing the crosshair reticules onto the target.

Even a kilometer away, the target was huge. Its long, low hull with the far-aft white-painted superstructure was unmistakable, as was the flag hanging at the taffrail.

"Liberian registry," Damavandi said. *"Texan Star."*

"Two hundred seventy-five thousand tons," Commander Reza Tavakkoli, the sub's executive officer reported, reading from the warbook. "Three hundred four meters loa. Despite the registration, it is American owned and operated."

"She will do," Damavandi said. "Maneuvering! Come left to zero-one-zero and increase speed to twelve knots. Engineer!"

"Yes, sir!"

"Prepare for snorkeling."

"Yes, sir!"

He felt, more than heard, the hum of the vessel's electric motor as *Ghadir* increased speed. Most of a submarine's time was spent remaining very, very quiet, and that meant remaining motionless, or idling along at a couple of knots, just enough to maintain steerage way.

There were times, however, when you simply had to make noise. *Ghadir,* like the Kilo-class submarines Iran had purchased from Russia, was not nuclear-powered. She was diesel-electric, which meant that she ran on the surface with noisy, air-breathing diesel engines, but underwater with quiet electric motors. Unfortunately, a sub running off her batteries could only do so for a limited time—in this case about eighteen hours.

Of course, on the surface and running the diesels—which also recharged the batteries—a sub was vulnerable, easily picked off by the enemy's ASW forces. The Germans had solved that problem for their U-boats by inventing the snorkel—essentially a tube sticking up above the surface from a submerged sub that lets it run the diesels while remaining underwater.

The down side of this was the fact that both diesel engines and the act of snorkeling itself are *noisy,* making a throbbing, pounding, hissing-wake racket easily picked up by the enemy's sonar systems.

The nine boats of Iran's submarine fleet all had been deployed to the narrow waters of the Gulf of Oman, just outside of the Straits of Hormuz. Their orders were to wait, remaining undetected, for the inevitable arrival of one or more American submarines. Savama, Iranian Intelligence, had already given the warning: The Americans' new guided-missile submarine *Ohio* had departed from the U.S. west coast three weeks before, almost certainly en route to the Gulf. When she arrived, the net of Iranian hunter-killers would close on her, trailing her closely and silently into Iranian territorial waters. And when that happened, Iran would have the excuse she needed to present to a watching world—the trigger that would launch Operation Bold Fire.

The problem was remaining undetected until *Ohio* arrived. Savama had also reported that at least one American SSN—the *Pittsburgh*—was in the Gulf already, and that others might be en route. Nuclear-powered, those submarines were unimaginably silent and deadly. How could Iran's fleet of diesel-electric boats remain submerged when—even if they didn't run their electric motors at all—they would still drain their batteries within a couple of days?

The answer had come from a Russian naval advisor working with Rear Admiral Vehedi at Bandar Abbas. Mask the noise you make beneath the louder noise of something else . . . in this case the *Texan Star*. Supertankers were *loud*.

Damavandi could hear the monster now, a deep-throated pounding transmitted like multiple hammer blows through *Ghadir*'s hull. The supertanker was now crossing *Ghadir*'s bows almost directly due north. *Ghadir* had adjusted her course and speed to slip into the tanker's wake. There was a zone perhaps a hundred meters long aft of the tanker's two monstrous screws where the snorkel could be raised and the diesels switched on, and the listening Americans would never hear it.

He continued to guide the maneuver from his station at the periscope. The tanker was so close now he had to angle the scope up to see the highest parts of the superstructure. "Maneuvering! Come right fifteen degrees!"

"Coming right fifteen degrees, by the will of Allah!"

Damavandi grimaced at the helmsman's appeal to

God but said nothing. *Ghadir*'s mullah, Hamid Khodaei, was standing close by, wearing an unreadable expression. It wouldn't do to alert Khodaei to his . . . heresy.

Well, not heresy so much as *practicality,* and an alternate point of view. He considered himself to be a good Muslim, but did not share the belief of most of his officers that theirs was a divinely appointed mission, and under the protection of Allah. Claiming that it was God's will and not the captain's, that was bad enough. Using the name of Allah to bless an act of war seemed little short of blasphemous to Damavandi.

Of course, if the mullahs back in Tehran knew his views on the subject, he would find himself relieved of command in short order. If he was lucky, he might retain a desk job in Bandar-e Anzelli, on the coast of the Caspian Sea. If he were not, it might well require the protection of Allah the Merciful just to keep him alive.

Besides, if religion kept the men focused on their duties, kept them sharp and willing to face hardship, overcrowding, and discomfort for the cause, then Damavandi was all in favor of it.

Allah, he thought, would understand.

Through the periscope, the *Texan Star* appeared to be turning away from the *Ghadir*; in fact, the sub was now swinging directly into line with the tanker's stern, about eighty meters back. From this fish-eye vantage point, the sheer bulk of the supertanker was more abundantly clear than ever. The *Texan Star* was 304 meters long at the waterline; *Ghadir* measured just seventy-six meters bow to stern, exactly a quarter of the supertanker's length.

In tonnage, however, the *Texan Star*'s displacement was nearly nine times that of the slender Ghadir-class boat. To Damavandi, it felt as though he were a minnow attempting to slip in behind a whale.

The supertanker was crawling along at a bare six knots—one did not race a vessel of that much sheer bulk and mass through straits as twisting, shallow, and narrow as these—but the wake still throbbed and thundered around them. *Ghadir* shuddered as she plowed through turbulent water, secure, now, in the knowledge that any nearby Americans would not be able to hear her.

"Raise snorkel!" Damavandi ordered. He had to shout to be heard above the thunder.

"Snorkel raised!"

Damavandi walked the scope around one-eighty to check the snorkel, which had emerged from the aft part of the sail and protruded now a meter above the water. Everything appeared correct. The head valve was open, marked by a slender rod extending above the snorkel head. An engineering auxiliary, meanwhile, was draining the tube into *Ghadir*'s bilges.

A moment later Engineering reported the snorkel drained, and the head valve closed. Damavandi ordered the outboard induction valve opened. When this was done, he gave the final order. "Commence snorkeling!"

The control room lights dimmed suddenly, then came back up. Damavandi heard the clatter of *Ghadir*'s diesel engines starting up aft.

"Diesel engines engaged, Captain! Electric motors off-line and charging!"

The operation was hazardous. The snorkel only extended about three meters above the sail, which meant the submarine had to travel at a shallower depth than was usual for periscope operations. Shallower meant she was more badly buffeted by the supertanker's wake, and that, in turn, meant *Ghadir*'s crew needed to stay very sharp, to avoid accidentally surfacing.

Even if they didn't pop to the surface, there was a chance the supertanker's crew would spot her periscope and snorkel. That was unlikely, of course. Both tubes were slender and camouflage-painted, a hundred yards astern, and the wake they drew would be lost in the far greater seething of white water boiling from the tanker's churning twin screws.

These were risks worth taking, however. By trailing the *Texan Star* for the next six hours or so, which would take them well out into the Gulf of Oman, *Ghadir* could safely recharge her batteries, preparing her for another eighteen to forty-eight hours of submerged silent running. Her sister boats were performing the same operation, but in rotation, so that at any given time at least five of the Iranian subs were silent and listening.

There remained one serious concern—and that was the *Pittsburgh* and any of her sister Los Angeles–class subs that might be in the region. Weeks ago *Ghadir* and her two sisters had been repeatedly towed out of Bandar Abbas and back. The hope was to make any watching American sub captains believe the Ghadir boats were not yet operational, and that the display would actually bring the American subs into the open. The Americans had to be curious about the new submarines, and about their capabilities. Apparently, that had not happened. There'd been absolutely no sign that the Americans had penetrated the considerable ASW defenses surrounding Bandar-e Abbas.

In fact, though, Damavandi was personally convinced the Americans had been out there, watching and listening to every move.

The fear was that the American SSNs might *still* be out there, watching. Unlikely—since the Americans probably didn't have one SSN to track each of the nine Iranian submarines separately.

But when it came to American submarine technology, Damavandi was unwilling to make any rash pronouncements about what the enemy could and could not do.

Soon, though, it wouldn't matter. When the American *Ohio* arrived, there would be too many Kilo- and Ghadir-class submarines closing on her for the American SNNs to handle. If the Americans fired first, so much the better. *That* would be the rallying call to Iran and to the entire Islamic world to commence the jihad that would drive the U.S. Navy out of the Gulf once and for all. If they didn't, the *Ohio* would be driven until she *did* fire first, or until she entered Iranian waters.

And when that happened, the *Ohio* would die, and Operation Bold Fire would begin.

Jihad . . .

Control Room, SSN *Pittsburgh*
Gulf of Oman
1555 hours local time

"So what do you make of it?" Captain Creighton asked the young man across the plot table from him.

"Damnedest thing I've ever seen," Lieutenant Commander Harold Chisolm replied, rubbing his bald scalp. He was *Pittsburgh*'s executive officer, but submarine tactics—at which he'd excelled at New London—were his specialty. "It could be an exercise, tracking tankers coming in and out of the Gulf."

"But you don't think so."

"No, sir, I don't. Kilos—and I assume the new Iranian-built boats as well—pack Type 53 torpedoes: 533mm, range fifteen to twenty kilometers, with active/passive sonar and wake-homing variants. There is absolutely no reason to get that close to a tanker you're about to kill."

"So what are they doing?"

"Two possibilities, sir. They're deliberately sending us a message—'We have submarines out here and we're tracking your supertankers'—or . . ."

"Or?"

"Or they're using the tankers for cover while they snorkel."

Creighton nodded. "That was my thought as well."

For several days *Pittsburgh* had been moving in and out of the Straits of Hormuz, tracking different Iranian submarines. Weeks ago the Iranians had seemed intent on parading the new Ghadir-class boats for all to see, but within the past few days they'd begun making themselves hard to find.

But that had not meant *Pittsburgh* could not find them. She had to get close, and Ridgeway, the sonar chief, declared it was like listening to a hole in the water. But they had picked them up, either waiting quietly on the bottom or creeping along at a barely noticeable three knots.

They'd been tracking one lurking submarine twenty minutes ago, when sonar reported their contact moving, then merging with another contact, a noisy commercial target. By moving in close and using narrowband sonar, they'd been able to pick up key tonals from the target sub, all but masked by the tanker's prop wash.

The Iranian sub was moving at periscope depth just astern of a supertanker.

Three times previously over the past two days, *Pittsburgh* had picked up what sounded like snorkeling diesel-electric boats, but always masked by the racket made by a large commercial surface vessel entering or leaving the straits. This, however, was the first time they'd actually caught the target in the act.

"It's a strange way to deliver a message," Chisolm

admitted, "since they're still playing it quiet and cagey. If I had to guess, I'd say they're setting a trap."

"Using the tankers to cover their battery recharge runs. Yeah. Lets 'em stay quiet and undetected until . . ."

"Until what, sir?"

"That's the question, isn't it? They *may* just be practicing, to see if they can hide their whole submarine force for a week at a time. Or they may be planning on springing the trap."

"Yes, sir. But what's the target?"

Creighton shrugged. "Could be us, if a war starts. Tensions have been going up like hemlines on a Paris fashion-show ramp. You heard Mad-in-a-jar's latest."

"Mad-in-a-jar" was the slang name *Pittsburgh*'s crew had adopted for Iran's president, Mahmoud Ahmadinejad. Fifth Fleet HQ had rebroadcast the translation of his speech of two days before over Armed Forces Radio. In it, Ahmadinejad had predictably followed the hard-nosed line of the Council of Twelve and the Supreme Leader—Iran *would* become a nuclear power, no matter what the American president said; Iran *would* resist the efforts of "foreign colonial powers," meaning the United States, to establish a permanent presence in the Gulf; and Iran *would* take steps to defend its borders, both against foreign powers and against any and all illegal incursions by hostile neighbors.

That last was an ominous statement. The first two declarations had been the standard party line out of Tehran for decades, but defending against incursions by neighbors was something new. The foreign powers part was easy to understand—a not-so-veiled reference to the sinking of the American patrol boat off the Iranian coast a few weeks ago. "Neighbors," however, could mean a number of things, none of them good. Iran still had border disputes with Iraq left over from the 1980–88 war, and no love for the current democratic and U.S.-supported government in Baghdad. In the east, Iran continued to engage in cross-border skirmishing with Afghan bandits, drug runners, and military forces, and resented Afghanistan's damming of the Helmand River . . . again territorial disputes with an American-supported regime.

And Iran still had a long list of ongoing territorial disputes with other nations in the Gulf—especially with the United Arab Emirates and with Oman, just across the narrow Straits of Hormuz. In 1992, Iran had seized three islands claimed by the UAE, including the strategically placed Abu Musa. Iran now claimed that both the UAE and Oman were nothing but American puppets, and that they gave the Americans control of what should be a joint Arab and Iranian resource— access to the Persian Gulf.

It was possible that Tehran was looking for an excuse to cross the Gulf and seize the eastern tip of Oman, the Musand'am peninsula, on the opposite side of the Straits of Hormuz.

Ahmadinejad had promised that Iran would lead the Islamic world to victory over the hated imperialists, the minions of Satan, and that the time of victory was near.

The speech had done nothing to quiet tensions that already had been running high. War already seemed all but inevitable.

"You think maybe the Iranians are looking for an excuse to attack us?" the XO asked.

"Hell, I know they're looking for an excuse. The question is when we're going to give them one. I know this much: If those subs are out there running ovals up and down the Gulf of Oman, it can't be for very long. That means either it's an exercise, just for practice, or . . ."

Chisolm nodded. "Or they expect things to turn hot within the next couple of days, at the latest."

Creighton glanced at the control room clock on the forward bulkhead. *Pittsburgh* wasn't scheduled to come up to periscope depth and broadcast a status report for another three and a half hours yet.

"I think this warrants a priority flash, Harry."

"I concur, Skipper."

"Maneuvering! Come to periscope depth!"

"Maneuvering, come to periscope depth, aye aye!"

Gently, the deck tilted as *Pittsburgh* began rising from the depths.

Tuesday, 24 June 2008

Sonar Room, SSGN *Ohio*
Gulf of Oman
1625 hours local time

"Caswell?" the Chief of the Boat said from the doorway to the sonar room. "How you doing?"

"I'm okay, COB," Caswell replied. It was a lie.

Dobbs chuckled. "He's pining away for his lost love, COB."

"You'd damned well better snap out of it, kid," O'Day said. "No dame is worth it! Anyway, I have a job for you two. Show this zoomie your station, give him a rundown."

Caswell turned in his chair to study the newcomer. It was the aviator, Lieutenant Commander Hawking.

"Dobbs and Cassie'll take good care of you, Commander," the COB said cheerily. "I'll check back with you at the end of your watch."

"I think COB's trying to cheer you up," Dobbs said with a wry grin. "You've been sulking and moping for days now . . . and see what it got you?"

Caswell ignored the dig. "Pull up a seat, Commander. Grab a set of headphones and have a listen."

"I'm told you're the guy I owe an apology to," Hawking said, taking a seat.

"Beg pardon, sir?"

"You were on watch when I did the musical fly-by?"

"Oh, yeah."

"So I apologize. Didn't know I'd be blasting your ears."

"Maybe that's why they want you listening for a while, sir," Dobbs suggested.

"So . . . what am I listening for?"

Caswell began to run Hawking through the broadband sonar procedures. Actually teaching him anything was pretty much hopeless; that was why the Navy sent you to sonar school. However, he could give him a very general introduction.

"That's passive broadband you're listening to, sir. It's kind of like you have a radio that's set to receive all channels at once."

Hawking listened for a moment. "All I hear is static."

"White noise, yes, sir. That's waves breaking on beaches and water moving past the sub and wind blowing and everything else you can imagine. The idea is to try to pick out what sounds . . . different."

"Okay . . ."

"Up in the bow of the sub, there's this big fiberglass sphere twelve feet in diameter, with hydrophones all over it. The chamber's filled with water, so it listens in on everything going on in the sea around us." He pointed at the waterfall display. "We get a visual readout here. Loud noises make a brighter point of light . . . like that one." He pointed to a slanting line across the screen.

"So what's that?"

"Sierra Two-seven-niner. A skimmer."

"Skimmer?"

"To a submariner, everything on the surface is a skimmer. Two-seven-niner is a supertanker leaving the Gulf. Bearing . . . zero-five-eight."

"Yeah? What's the range?"

Caswell made a face. "That's Hollywood. With sonar, you can get an accurate bearing on the target, but not the range. It's not like radar."

"Oh, yeah. They went over that when I had my indoctrination. To get range, you have to move the sub around."

"Right. That lets you triangulate on the target. The chief of the sonar watch can even request that the captain change course, just so we can get a better look at the target."

"So . . . how do you know it's a tanker?"

"That's my job," Dobbs said. "I'm using narrowband here. Right now we're towing a narrowband sonar array behind the *Ohio,*" Dobbs explained. "The BQR-15. It picks up the same sound the broadband does, but feeds it through a computer, our narrowband processor. That sorts through the hash and zeroes in on what we call tonals."

"Tonals?"

"Yessir. Every ship and sub is filled with machinery, and most of it is making noise, one way or another. The screws. Seawater pumps. Turbines. Diesel engines. Every piece of machinery that rotates puts tonals into the water. And the processor can pick 'em out and match 'em to known sounds." He pointed at his display, which showed an oscilloscopelike line of light with a sharp spike in it. "When there's machinery in the area, that's what it shows us."

"That's the tanker again?"

"Yup. Her screws, actually."

Caswell had fallen silent. He was listening now, very, very intently. "Hey, Dobbs?" he said. "You might want to try fifty Hertz."

"Yeah? Whatcha got?"

"I'm not sure. I just thought for a moment . . ."

Dobbs turned a dial on his console. "Jesus!"

"What is it?" Hawking asked.

"I think we have a bandit." Dobbs hit the intercom switch. "Con, Sonar! New contact, Sierra Two-eight-one! Bearing zero-four-five! Fifty Hertz tonals! I think it's a sub!"

"So what's all the fuss about fifty Hertz?"

"*Quiet,* sir!" Caswell said, his voice a harsh whisper. *"Please!"*

"Western electrical systems run on an AC frequency of sixty Hertz, Commander," Dobbs said quietly. "Russians run their equipment on a frequency of fifty Hertz."

"That's a *Russian* sub out there?"

"Russian . . . or a boat purchased from them by one of their clients. Or maybe built to Russian specs. I do know one thing."

"What's that?"

"It ain't one of ours."

Chief Sommersby, the senior sonar tech, entered the room. "Let me have a listen," he said, putting on headphones. For a long moment he was silent. Then, "Control Room, Sonar. Recommend change of course to clear our baffles."

"Sonar, Control Room. Very well."

"Clearing out baffles?" Hawking asked. He sounded bewildered.

"I think we have several potential hostiles out there," Sommersby said. "We're getting lots of tonals, and they're consistent with Kilo-class submarines . . . and those new Iranian Ghadir-class boats. Trouble is, they're real, real quiet. Getting a fix on them is going to be tough. The big danger is that we have one trailing us astern. Can't hear for shit back there, because of the disturbance from our own wake. I just asked the skipper to bring us around in a big circle, which lets us listen to what's going on behind us."

"Contact!" Caswell said after several more minutes. "New contact, Sierra Two-eight-two, bearing one-one-two!"

"Ah-ha!" Sommersby said. "*Nailed* the bastard!"

"I've got him," Dobbs said. "Ghadir-class. He had his nose up our ass!"

"How do you know it's a Ghadir?" Hawking asked, staring at the new electronic spike that had just appeared on Dobbs' screen. The young aviator was clearly becoming more and more bewildered.

"Several weeks ago one of our L.A.–class boats spent some time following Iranian subs in and out of port," Sommersby explained. "Got some great beneath-the-hull photos through the periscope, and also recorded every sound they made. They picked up the tonals from the screw, both the diesel and electric motors, seawater pumps, toilets in the head, even an ice cream maker in the galley. Then they beamed all the data back to Washington by satellite, and they, in turn, beamed it out to us." Swiveling in his chair, he patted a console behind him. "Now our narrowband processor knows *exactly* what to listen for when there's an Iranian sub in the area."

Caswell heard the conversation with some part of his brain, but his full attention was focused on what he was hearing over his headset, and what he was seeing on the waterfall. Two Iranian subs were out there, obviously stalking the *Ohio,* and he hadn't heard a damned thing.

As he adjusted the broadband controls, sweeping the areas where the two subs were lurking, he could hear a difference—faint, but there. Holes in the water . . .

And he'd missed them both.

Control Room, SSGN *Ohio*
Mouth of the Straits of Hormuz
1715 hours local time

Captain Stewart studied the plot board, a remarkably low-tech device for such a high-tech vessel where every few moments a rating marked the position of the *Ohio* with a wipe-erase pen. The exact positions of the Iranian submarines were not known, of course, but their bearings were indicated by straight lines. As *Ohio* completed her baffle-clearing turn, however, additional bearings allowed more precise positions to be pinpointed through triangulation.

Ohio had just swung north in order to enter the Straits of Hormuz, running at a depth of just one hundred feet as the bottom shoaled rapidly beneath her keel. Two—at least—Iranian subs were following her, both now astern, but maintaining their positions relative to the *Ohio,* probably between three and eight thousand yards to the south and the southeast.

"Looks like the trap's been sprung, Skipper," the XO said.

"Well, at least they haven't fired at us," Stewart

replied. "Damn, Sierra Two-eight-two could've taken us any time he wanted."

"What are they waiting for? Are they just playing with us?"

"*Might* be an exercise," Stewart conceded. "But I doubt it. My guess is their orders are to stick close . . . maybe trail us into Iranian waters."

"Yeah. They could hit us there, and claim self-defense."

"At the very least, they'd screw our mission."

"How'd they find us, though?"

Stewart shrugged. "Wasn't hard, I suspect. With this new configuration, we're not as quiet as we once were."

It was true. Ohio-class boomers were extremely quiet—the better to hide from Soviet hunter-killers during the Cold War. However, *Ohio* now carried the ASDS on her afterdeck, which went a long way toward ruining her sleek streamlining. Besides, *Ohio* had been moving at better than twelve knots as she moved up through the Arabian Sea. With some luck, even the relatively poorly trained technicians on board the Iranian boats would have been able to pick her up easily enough.

And this trap had been carefully planned—deploying a number of subs, keeping them submerged and quiet by using oil tankers as cover . . .

What were they planning?

"So what do we do about them, Skipper?"

"Nothing, for now. There's not much we *can* do. However, we're going to have to scrape them off when it comes time to deploy. Put your talent in strategy and tactics to *that* problem, Mr. Shea."

"Aye aye, sir." Shea cocked his head to the side. "One thing to consider, sir."

"Yes?"

"We've spotted two bogies. There might be more, especially now that we're entering the straits."

"I'm well aware of that."

"If we go active, we'll spot them all. It's not like our presence is secret any longer."

Stewart considered this. So far, all of *Ohio*'s sonar contacts were passive, meaning she'd picked up the noises they were making on her hydrophones. Her powerful BQS-15 passive/active sonar had the capability, however, of sending out a powerful pulse of sound, one that would bounce back from every target in the *Ohio*'s vicinity. During the Cold War, Soviet SSNs had used that technique a lot, knowing their boats were noisier than American subs, and therefore easier to detect anyway. American skippers tended not to use the active sonar, since it both pinpointed the U.S. sub's position and let the enemy sub know that his presence—and location—were known.

On the other hand, *Ohio* was entering a tangle of shallow water, islands, and shoals. Passive tracking was going to become more difficult within the Straits of Hormuz. There might be alternatives. . . .

"Later, maybe," he said. "For now, we pretend we don't know they're there. But we watch 'em."

"Yes, sir."

"Skipper?" Master Chief O'Day said, approaching the plot table.

"What is it, COB? We're kind of busy."

"Beg your pardon, sir. It's one of the sonar techs."

"What about him? Who is it?"

"ST2 Caswell, sir. The kid whose girlfriend dumped him?"

"I remember."

"He's just asked me to be relieved."

"Eh? Why?"

"He told me he'd screwed up, that he hadn't been paying attention and he missed the Iranian bogie when it dropped into our wake."

Stewart looked up from the plot, meeting O'Day's eyes. "COB, this is not the time. Tell him to . . . no." He moved back from the plot table. "Have him report to me. Now."

"Aye aye, sir."

A few minutes later O'Day reappeared, a skinny young kid with glasses in tow. Stewart remembered him. "Caswell? What's this I hear about you wanting to quit?"

"Sir, uh . . . it's not that I want to quit. I just . . . I mean . . ."

"Spit it out, son."

"Sir, I really screwed up a few minutes ago! I've been . . . well, things've been a little crazy, and—"

"Caswell, we'll discuss your personal problems later . . . or you can take them up with Mr. Shea or Master Chief O'Day. Right now I'm not interested in them. I need you at your station."

"But, sir . . ."

"I said I *need* you, Caswell. You've got two of the best ears on this boat, and I need both of them listening for the bad guys!"

Caswell looked startled. "But I . . . Sir, I wasn't paying attention. . . ."

"You made a mistake? I'll spot you one. *One.* But you think I'll just let you off the hook when things get tough? Like hell I will!" Stewart raised his forefinger and thumped it, hard, against Caswell's chest. "You, son, are one of my most important assets on this boat, and I will not lose you! You've been trained to do a job and do it well, and by God you *will* do what you've been trained to do, no matter what you happen to be feeling like! Do I make myself clear?"

"Y-Yessir!"

"I want you to be especially sharp. You hear anything like a torpedo door opening, and you sing out. Understand?"

"Yes, sir!"

"If one of those characters astern decides he wants to wind up and take a shot at us, I want you to hear that Iranian captain *thinking* about it before he makes the first move!"

The kid swallowed hard, his Adam's apple bobbing against his skinny throat. "Yes, sir."

"Now get back to your station and tell me where the bad guys are. I'm counting on you. The whole damned *boat's* counting on you!"

"Aye aye, sir!" It was almost a squeak. Turning, Caswell hurried back toward the sonar room.

"I think you just put the fear of God into him, Skipper," Shea said. "You just *ordered* him to use psychic powers? Jeeze. That was pretty harsh."

"You can apologize on my behalf later, Mr. Shea," Stewart replied. "The men are *your* responsibility. The mission and the boat are mine. We can't mollycoddle them."

"No, sir. We can't. It's just . . ."

"What?"

"The stress levels are pretty high already, sir. Most of these kids . . . hell, they *are* just kids. Nineteen, twenty, twenty-one years old. Two-thirds of 'em, this is their first sea duty." The clear implication was that if he pushed them too hard, they would break.

"No, Mr. Shea. They're not kids. They're submariners. There's a difference."

"Yes, sir."

"And as for stress . . . believe me, Mr. Shea, they've not seen *anything* yet."

Control Room, SSK *Ghadir*
Gulf of Oman
1735 hours local time

Captain Majid Damavandi didn't like this sort of situation. Most of his training, both in Iran and at the special sub school for officers presented in Russia five years ago, had emphasized detecting an enemy, closing on it, and destroying it with torpedoes. Simply trailing the enemy vessel had been discussed, but there'd been precious little practical experience to go with the lectures.

The problem was that he couldn't *see*. Somewhere up ahead, perhaps less than a thousand meters, was the giant American submarine, but the only way to track the behemoth was by the sound the vessel made as it slid through the water. Lieutenant Fardin Shirazi, *Ghadir*'s sonar officer, was good, *very* good . . . but the task assigned him was extraordinarily difficult. The American submarine, according to Savama, was carrying an ungainly structure mounted on its deck just aft of the sail, and it disturbed the water in a peculiar way as the vessel moved. The sound was faint, however, and extraordinarily subtle. And the surrounding waters were filled with the noise of commercial shipping.

The real problem, though, was not knowing the precise range to the target. For all Damavandi knew, the American was not a thousand meters ahead . . . but less than a hundred. If it suddenly slowed, or went into a turn, the *Ghadir* could easily smash straight into the enemy vessel's stern.

And *that*, Damavandi thought, might well solve everybody's problem. The American submarine crippled, and its mission, whatever it was, ended.

Unfortunately, a collision would also effectively end

his career as well, assuming the *Ghadir* even survived the encounter.

He longed to order the sonar officer to send out an active pulse. His Russian teachers had stressed the importance of knowing the precise range to the target, had stressed that American sonar technology was the best in the world, and that in most cases the captain hoping to track an American submarine would be better off revealing his own position in order to have a definite fix on his target.

Unfortunately, this was a tactical situation that clearly precluded revealing his own position—or his presence. As far as could be determined from the American's movements, he didn't yet know that he had a growing flotilla of hunters stalking him. Twice, now, in the past several hours, the American vessel had abruptly turned, completing a full 360-degree swing in order to check to see if he was being followed. Each time, *Ghadir* had gone completely quiet—even switching off her already quiet electric motor—and drifted in complete silence, waiting until the American resumed his original course.

Such tactics were to be expected; they did not prove the enemy knew the Iranian subs were there. Damavandi suspected that if the American *did* spot them, he would be off and running at high speed. An Ohio-class sub could easily outpace a Kilo or a Ghadir-class boat. All he needed to do was move at high speed, then go silent once more.

But instead the American continued moving slowly north into the straits.

"Captain!" the sonar officer called.

"Go ahead."

"Target vessel is increasing revolutions! He appears to be increasing speed to ten knots."

What now? "Maneuvering! Increase speed to ten knots."

Control Room, SSGN *Ohio*
Mouth of the Straits of Hormuz
1738 hours local time

The newest sonar contact, Sierra Two-nine-five, was another tanker, this one moving north, deeper into the straits. Stewart had just given the order to fall into the vessel's wake, moving close enough that they could feel the pounding of the screws and the rough shuddering of the turbulent water just ahead.

Two could play this game . . . using the passage of a large, twin-screwed tanker to mask the far quieter creeping of a submarine just astern.

"Control Room, Sonar," Chief Sommersby called. "We've lost everything but Sierra Two-nine-five. Estimated range to target . . . one hundred yards."

"Very well. Maneuvering! Slow to six knots!"

"Maneuvering, slow to six knots, aye aye!"

The Straits of Hormuz were a tough playground for submarines in any case, with shallow bottom and narrow sea lanes always crowded with shipping. Even in the best of circumstances, sound echoed weirdly from rocks, shoals, and obstructions.

Stewart looked up toward the overhead. "Catch us if you can," he said.

Control Room, SSK *Ghadir*
Gulf of Oman
1749 hours local time

"We have lost them, sir," Lieutenant Shirazi reported. "They used the noise from the tanker to mask themselves."

Damavandi looked up from the plot table and bit off a sharp curse. Mullah Hamid Khodaei was at his side, studying the tangle of red and blue lines showing the relative movements of *Ghadir* and the American intruder. Turning to the cleric, he shrugged and said, "As God wills."

"Perhaps," the cleric said, "God wills a more aggressive approach."

"Indeed? And what would God, the Almighty, suggest that we do? *He* may be able to suspend the laws of physics, but I cannot."

"Be careful, Captain," Khodaei snapped. "Remember who it is with whom you are speaking!"

Damavandi glanced at Commander Tavakkoli, who carefully looked away. The rest of the personnel in *Ghadir*'s control room appeared to be very still, very intent, and very careful not to appear to take notice of the sudden confrontation at the plot table.

"And what do you propose that we do, Mullah Khodaei?"

"Use our active sonar, of course."

"To do so would reveal our presence, Mullah."

"So? The enemy clearly knows our submarines are in these waters already. And we *must* know where he is, and what he is doing."

Damavandi considered this. He also considered Hamid Khodaei.

Mullahs were Islamic clergy, men who had devoted

their lives to the study of the Qu'ran and the Hadith, doctors of the law of *sharia* who were considered to be experts on all religious matters.

Religious matters. Unfortunately, within the Shi'ite fundamentalist worldview of the current Iranian government, *everything* was a religious matter, from the way a man dressed and spoke and acted, to the zeal with which he carried out his duties to the state. The Guardian Council, in its infinite wisdom, had seen fit to install civilian mullahs on board each vessel of the Iranian navy, ostensibly to safeguard the spiritual lives of the crew.

However, at the same time they were in an excellent position to report on the loyalty and the religious zeal of the men in command of those ships.

It was an idea rooted in Soviet doctrine. As far back as the Second World War, or earlier, perhaps—the Russian Civil War—Russian military units had gone into battle with commissars actually sharing command with military officers. It had been, Damavandi reflected, a bad idea. The commissars were supposed to guarantee the political reliability of both the officers and the men, in an atmosphere steeped in mistrust and paranoia. In fact, all too often command decisions did not fall into clearly separate domains—the military and the political. The effect, he believed, had been to weaken the Soviet army, if only because its commanders were unwilling to take risks that might result in their arrest and court-martial.

The mullahs of the Guardian Council had applied the concept to military units within the Iranian military, especially the elite Pasdaran. They'd avoided the inherent problems of divided command, technically, by not giving the unit clerics rank or official military status, but officers *were* expected to pay careful attention to their advice, and to disregard that advice at the peril to their own careers.

Damavandi had three choices now. He could follow Khodaei's advice. If things went wrong, he at least would be able to demonstrate that he'd done God's will. Or he could use his better judgment, his *military* judgment, which was to remain hidden and to continue to draw close the net already spread about the American intruder. If his strategy worked, his rejection of Khodaei's advice would be ignored. If it failed, however, he would have to answer for it at his court-martial.

The third option was the one most often adopted by Soviet commanders saddled with a militarily incompetent commissar. He could buck the whole problem up the chain of command.

"Maneuvering!" he snapped. "Bring us to periscope depth!"

"What are your intentions, Captain?" Khodaei asked.

"We are all very small parts of a much larger plan, Mullah," he replied. "A misstep on our part could cause that plan to unravel. We will ask headquarters how to proceed."

"By the time they make up their minds, Captain, the American will have eluded us!"

"I think not," Damavandi replied. He gestured at the chart on the light table between them. "It's not as though he has many places in which to hide."

Wednesday, 25 June 2008

Control Room, SSGN *Ohio*
South of Hormoz Island
Straits of Hormuz
0015 hours local time

"Up periscope."

Stewart waited as the scope slid up out of its well, took hold of the handles when they reached his chest, and rode it the rest of the way up, circling to make sure there weren't any skimmer surprises close by.

It was night on the surface, but the Type 18 scope, switched to low-light mode, revealed the surroundings in eerie swatches of black and green, punctuated by the bright white stars of lights.

According to the plotting tables behind him, *Ohio* rested now just a mile south of the island of Hormoz, one of the twin guardians to the port city of Bandar Abbas.

Bandar Abbas is nestled into a bight in the southern Iranian coast just at the point where the Straits of Hormuz take a sharp elbow turn to the southwest and the entrance to the Persian Gulf proper. The bight is sheltered by the island of Qeshm, sixty-eight miles long, which at one point is separated from the coast by a shallow strait less than two miles wide. The easternmost tip of Qeshm, however, is some fifteen miles south of Bandar Abbas; just to the east of that, two small and roughly circular islands form the gateway to the sheltered waters of Iran's largest and busiest port. To the southwest is Larak, and ten miles to the northeast is Hormoz.

Through the scope, Stewart could see a scattering of lights along the coast of Hormoz. More lights gleaming south and west were probably ships and boats entering the sheltered area. Bandar Abbas itself was invisible, fifteen miles to the northwest, but the glow from the city's lights turned the sky all the way across the northern horizon a hazy green, backlighting the bulk of Hormoz Island.

This appeared to be a good place to wait out the Iranian search, at least through the night hours. Come sunrise, they would need to be gone. Hormoz was a ruggedly volcanic island just four miles across but over five hundred feet high, its highest peak capped by the ruins of a medieval fortress. Once these shallow waters became sunlit, an observer on that hilltop—and Stewart had no doubt there would be observers up there—might be able to make out the long, dark shadow of the *Ohio* as she lurked offshore. When daylight came, she would need to seek deeper and darker waters.

For the next few hours, however, this was a good hiding place. The shallow water—less than twenty fathoms deep at this point—offered shelter from Iranian sonar. *Ohio* had followed in the tanker's wake for nearly seven hours before dropping astern and creeping off to the north at a bare five knots. With luck, the Iranian subs were still following the tanker, going around the kink in the straits and headed southwest for the Gulf.

They wouldn't go too far, though, before breaking off and returning to this area to begin a careful search. They must know that *Ohio*'s interest was in this stretch of coast—from Bandar-e Charak, 125 miles to the west, through to Bandar Abbas here in the east. They would also guess that *Ohio* had entered Iranian territorial waters.

Their antisubmarine warfare forces, including swarms of ASW aircraft, would be out in major strength.

"Control Room, Sonar. New contact, bearing zero-one-two. Designate Sierra Two-three-seven. Single screw, four blades. Probable commercial traffic."

"Sonar, Control Room. Very well."

He swung the periscope to the indicated bearing. There, against the black loom of Hormoz, he could see a slowly moving pair of lights casting reflections on the still water. The glow cast illumination enough for the low-light optics to distinguish the shape of the craft, with its characteristic high prow and flat stern—a native dhow, of the type known locally as a *ghanjah*.

A fisherman, then, or a local merchant . . . or, even more probable, a smuggler. The authorities in Bandar Abbas, he knew, were plagued by smugglers, carrying everything from drugs and alcohol to illicit human cargo—both refugees from Tehran's religious persecution and the victims of a far darker and more vicious traffic in slaves . . . even if in the enlightened years of the twenty-first century they were no longer called by that name.

Whatever its cargo, this solitary dhow was motoring slowly through the darkness close by the southern coast of Hormoz, possibly on legitimate business, but more likely, like *Ohio* herself, attempting to elude local surveillance.

"Down scope," Stewart ordered. The periscope was coated with RAM—radar-absorbing material—in order to reduce its radar signature and the chance of detection, but American sub skippers still preferred to reduce their exposure above the ceiling to an absolute minimum. There was also the danger of collision in these busy waterways; the sonar gang would do their best to keep him aware of approaching threats, of course, but accidents did happen, and a small, quiet craft like that dhow, its engine noise masked by the noisy waters around it, might hit the scope, and that would end the mission—and quite possibly the life of every man on board.

"So what's the game plan, sir?" Shea asked.

"We wait." He glanced at the clock on the forward bulkhead. A quarter past midnight . . . and in these waters, at this time of year, they could only count on another four to five hours of sheltering darkness. "Two hours. Then we find a deeper hole. And pass the word for Commander Drake, Mr. Mayhew, and Mr. Wolfe to see me."

"Aye aye, sir."

Communications Center,
Office of the Ministry of Defense
Tehran, Iran
0125 hours local time

Admiral Baba-Janzadeh didn't like being awakened from a sound sleep. He had not stood a night watch for more years than he could remember, and at sixty-four he was getting too old for this sort of thing.

Still, Admiral Vehedi's call from naval headquarters had been urgent, and indicated that Bold Fire was in jeopardy, and that news commanded his full attention. He left both of his wives asleep and called a motor pool driver to take him to the Defense Ministry. There, in the basement communications center, he watched the situation unfold in lengths of colored string tacked onto a wall-sized map of the Straits of Hormuz.

Six of Iran's nine submarines were currently in the straits, searching for the giant American submarine that had vanished there during the early evening hours. Given the American's known capabilities, it could be anywhere within the straits now, though the most probable area, bounded by a rectangle of bright red string, was somewhere off Bandar Abbas—possibly close to the harbor entrance, possibly south of Qeshm. The local ASW forces had been alerted as well, and they were beginning a sweep of the harbor's waters, a sweep that would move south to Qeshm and southeast into the straits proper as the early morning hours passed. Admiral Vehedi had also put as many of his airborne ASW assets into the sky as he could. They were busy deploying sonobuoys and mines now, seeding those areas through which the *Ohio* would have to move.

The possibility existed, however, that the *Ohio* had not entered Iranian waters, but had moved south through the straits. She could be sheltering in the relatively deep waters of the international channel south of Iran's coast, or she could be making for the port facilities of the U.S. Fifth Fleet three hundred miles to the west, at Manama, in Bahrain.

Even if the *Ohio* was lurking now in Iranian territorial

waters, the possibility remained that she would elude the search. Admiral Baba-Janzadeh had a great respect for American technology, and in particular for their ability to move submarines silently and invisibly through the tightest of defenses. His Russian teachers, former officers of the Soviet fleet, had spent a lot of time emphasizing American stealth capabilities. During the Cold War, only rarely had Russian hunter-killer subs found and successfully tracked American ballistic missile submarines like the *Ohio* and her sisters, and it was an open secret that their Los Angeles–class subs had repeatedly entered Soviet waters—even slipped inside of Soviet ports—to carry out missions of reconnaissance and espionage.

His Russian teachers had spent so much time on the superiority of American technology that he suspected they were trying to save face; that they were anxious to cover the fact that the Americans had penetrated their most heavily defended bastions.

Face-saving or not, the lectures had impressed Baba-Janzadeh, and he was determined not to underestimate the enemy.

Of one thing he was certain. Unless the American submarine captain had broken off and was going to join the U.S. fleet at Manama, his target almost certainly was the new special weapons complex at Bandar-e Charak. American naval commandos had attempted to penetrate that facility weeks before, and had been repulsed. Washington would be intensely curious about what was really going on there. If what Savama had reported about the capabilities of the Ohio-class SSGN conversions was accurate, the Americans could be close to landing a very large and powerful reconnaissance force in south-central Iran. Admiral Baba-Janzadeh was determined to be ready for them.

And there was one clear way he could be certain of foiling the enemy's plans.

The admiral reached for a telephone with an outside line. *He* wouldn't like being awakened, either, but there was no way of helping that.

Control Room, Iranian SS *Noor*
South of Qeshm Island
Straits of Hormuz
0335 hours local time

"Captain!" the sonar officer called out. "Splashes ahead and to port!"

"Very well." Commander Fareed Asefi was not worried. "They are ours."

Noor was one of Iran's six Tareq-class submarines—what the West called Kilos. *Noor,* hull number 902, had been acquired from a cash-desperate Russia in 1993, the second of an initial purchase of three diesel-electric submersibles. Like other Kilo-class vessels, she was 74.3 meters long, displaced just over three thousand tons, and was operated by a crew of fifty-three—fifty-four if you counted the mullah Reza Sharabiani.

A moment later a sharp, ringing *ping* sounded through *Noor*'s control room. Sharabiani started, looking upward. "What is that?"

Asefi smiled. "Active sonar. One of our aircraft is overhead, dropping sonobuoys. These are devices that float on the surface of the water, sending out active sonar pulses. The pulses are like radar. They reflect off of ships and submarines, are picked up by the buoy, and transmitted back up to the aircraft."

"And you say it is one of ours?"

"Assuredly, Mullah. We are well within Iranian territorial waters here. Our ASW forces are joining in the hunt for the American submarine."

"Active sonar pulses, Captain," the sonar officer announced, confirming Asefi's guess. "Iranian origin. Bearing zero-eight-one."

"Ah." Sharabiani stroked his beard, relaxing. "Then we can be sure the enemy will soon be cornered and brought to the surface. Ah . . . how do our pilots know that the signals picked up by their sonobuoy are from a friendly submarine, and not from the enemy?"

In fact, Asefi had just been considering that point. True, a Tareq-class sub was almost one hundred meters shorter than the *Ohio*. It would take a skilled sonar operator to judge target size from a series of reflected pings. Fortunately, headquarters would have put their best ASW personnel into the air for this operation.

"Captain! Torpedo in the water!"

"What?" Or perhaps not.

"Torpedo in the water, bearing zero-five-five! It has acquired! Torpedo has gone active!"

Which meant an Iranian antisubmarine torpedo was now homing on the *Noor*.

"Range!" With active sonar in the water, from the sonobuoy and from the torpedo itself, it was possible for *Noor*'s sonar officer to calculate the torpedo's range.

"Sir! Twenty-eight hundred meters!"

"Maneuvering! Come hard to starboard! Make course . . . two-three-five! All ahead full!"

Calculations flitted through his mind, relentless and unforgiving. For air-launched ASW work, Iran used Mark 46 light torpedoes, weapons originally acquired decades ago from the United States. The Mk. 46 had a range of eight thousand meters and could travel at 45 knots. At her best, *Noor* could manage seventeen knots.

At 45 knots, the torpedo would cover 2.8 kilometers in just under two minutes. In that same time, *Noor*, running directly away from the incoming weapon, would cover about three-tenths of a nautical mile, or half a kilometer. The Mark 46 would cover that additional distance in another twenty or thirty seconds. *Make it . . . make it . . .*

"Torpedo impact in one minute, twenty seconds!" the sonar officer reported, beating by a hair Asefi's own calculations. Less than he'd been thinking . . . but then, *Noor* would need precious time to accelerate to a full seventeen knots, and more time still to complete her turn away from the torpedo.

"This is madness!" Sharabiani cried. "Raise them on the radio! Tell them they've fired on one of their own!"

"It's not that simple, Mullah." In fact, unlike a wire-guided torpedo from another submarine, the Mk. 46, once fired, could not be recalled or disabled. "I wish it were."

"Torpedo now at twelve hundred meters," Lieutenant Mohammadi, the sonar officer, reported. The man sounded impossibly calm, almost bored. "Time to impact, fifty seconds."

"But they are firing on their own submarine!"

"I know, Mullah. Friendly fire. It is one of the dangers of warfare."

The mullah's face had gone death-white. His beard wagged up and down as he mouthed a fervent, desperate prayer.

Fareed Asefi joined him, silently. *Allah, the merciful and the most wise! If it be your will, save us! . . .* The captain of the *Noor* was absolutely convinced in the rightness of the Shi'ite Islamic cause, and of the power of almighty God. He was realist enough to know, however, that fatal accidents *did* happen in war, no matter how just and holy your cause.

"Diving Officer! What is our depth?"

"Sir! Depth twenty-eight meters!"

Deep, for these waters.

"What is the depth beneath our keel?"

"Sir! Depth beneath keel, fifteen meters!"

There was no hope of finding a thermocline beneath which they could hide from the approaching weapon's sonar. Sometimes you could find a thermocline out in the main channel, where the water was as much as sixty meters deep. But not here, in these shallows.

"Range seven hundred meters," Mohammadi announced. "Time to impact, thirty seconds."

"Release countermeasures!" Asefi snapped. Either God would deliver them in the next few moments, or He would not. There was yet a human trick or two, however, that Asefi knew he could use to improve the chances of divine intervention.

A pair of cylinders dropped from the *Noor*'s flanks, swiftly falling astern. Moments after release they began filling the water around them with a dense cloud of bubbles, created by the interaction of seawater and the chemicals they carried. With luck, the torpedo's active sonar would reflect from the bubbles, breaking its lock on the *Noor*.

"Maneuvering! Come hard right, twenty degrees!" Asefi ordered. It would help if, when the torpedo punched through the decoy bubble cloud, *Noor* were no longer directly ahead of it. Once the torpedo lost its target, it was programmed to begin circling, sending out active pings in quest of a target. The idea was to turn away from it and try to get outside of its reach. After traveling eight kilometers, the torpedo would exhaust its fuel supply.

"I have lost the torpedo, Captain," Mohammadi announced. Several men let loose a cheer.

"*Silence!*" Asefi yelled. "We're not out of this yet!" Sonar had lost the incoming target behind the bubbles, but it would emerge any moment now. . . .

"I have the torpedo again, Captain," Mohammadi reported. "Torpedo is now circling . . . torpedo has reacquired."

Someone in the control room groaned aloud. Asefi did not bother to reprimand him. The countermeasure ploy had failed.

"Range now four hundred meters," Mohammadi said, an emotionlessly recited death sentence. "Time to impact . . . twenty seconds."

Sharabiani let loose a wail of despair, dropped to his knees and began praying aloud.

"Diving Officer!" Asefi yelled. "Blow all ballast! Up planes! Emergency surface! Surface!"

The deck tilted sharply, bow rising, and Asefi heard the sharp and boiling hiss of seawater being blasted from *Noor*'s ballast tanks by high-pressure air.

There was just a chance that the sudden maneuver would outfox the simple-minded torpedo bearing down on them. Besides, if the *Noor* were about to be hit by a warhead consisting of forty-three kilograms of PBXN-103 high explosives, he would buy precious time for the crew if they were hit on the surface, rather than fifty meters down.

"Time to impact, ten seconds! Eight seconds! Five . . . four . . . three . . . two . . ."

Sonar Room, SSGN *Ohio*
South of Qeshm Island
Straits of Hormuz
0339 hours local time

"*Explosion in the water!*" Caswell called, pulling the headset from his ears. The blast, a loud, solid thump like the slamming of a door, had been loud enough to leave his ears ringing. He looked at the bright white line appearing now on the waterfall. "Bearing two-one-five degrees."

"Sonar, Control! Give me a range estimate!"

"Sir . . . About ten thousand yards."

"Confirmed, Captain," Dobbs said at his side. "That matches the track for Sierra Two-four-four."

Caswell stared at the waterfall display, as if to see beyond the moving points of light to the drama unfolding somewhere in the depths up ahead. Twenty minutes ago he'd been yawning. After standing the afternoon watch the day before, he'd been scheduled for the midnight watch this morning, and he was running short on sleep. All tiredness had evaporated, however, when out of the hiss of background static he'd heard the quiet hum of an approaching Kilo—Sierra Two-four-four, approaching steadily from the southwest.

He'd reported the contact, and in seconds the skipper had cut *Ohio*'s forward movement to a couple of knots. Now she was creeping along the seabed, hoping to remain invisible against the bottom. Moments later Dobbs had picked up tonals that he'd interpreted as a helicopter passing overhead . . . and moments after that they'd all heard the sharp if distant ping of the sonobuoy. The Iranians had been scattering the things all along the southeastern coast of Qeshm Island, evidently hoping to spot the *Ohio* as she crept southwest, ten miles off the shoreline.

The launch of a torpedo, though, had caught them all by surprise. From the sound of things, the Iranian ASW helicopter had picked up one of their own submarines, mistaken it for *Ohio,* and popped a fish at it.

That sharp thud echoing through the sea told them all that the Iranians had just scored an own goal.

Ears still ringing, Caswell picked up the headset and pulled it back over his ears. Like any good sonar tech, he could pick up more with his ears than the boat's electronics could sort out and put on the waterfall display.

It took no special effort, though, to hear that curiously high-pitched shriek in the distance, the sound of a woman screaming, overlaid with deeper thumps and popping sounds.

"Control Room, Sonar," he said. "I'm getting breakup noises from Sierra Two-four-four."

"Acknowledged."

Caswell and the others in the sonar room were silent for a long time. Submariners everywhere share a special bond with all other submariners, whatever their nationality or politics, a camaraderie born of shared suffering and danger. What was happening to that other submarine out there could easily happen to *Ohio* and her crew.

He found himself thinking of those other sailors, and hoping that they made it ashore safely.

Weather Bridge, Iranian SS *Noor*
South of Qeshm Island
Straits of Hormuz
0344 hours local time

The torpedo had struck *Noor* on her starboard side
near her stern. The shock had thrown everyone in the
control room to the deck and, as electrical circuits and
generators failed, plunged the entire vessel into darkness.

Emergency lighting had switched on moments later,
just as the vessel broke through the surface. Asefi rose
to his feet, grasping a stanchion to stay upright as the
deck continued to tilt. He could tell from the feel that
Noor was heeling over to starboard and going down by
the stern. The engine rooms must be flooded already.

"Abandon ship!" he yelled. He fumbled for the intercom handset, wondering if internal communications
were still working. "All hands, all hands! Abandon
ship!"

The exodus began in an orderly fashion, but as sea-
men began jamming up against the narrow hatches,
panic set in. Most were choosing to move forward, up
the slanting deck, rather than risk going aft to try to
make it out the escape hatch on the afterdeck, which
was almost certainly submerged.

Men screamed and shouted, punching one another.
Within the struggling tangle he heard the voice of Mul-
lah Sharabiani, ragged with fear, invoking the name of
Allah.

Mohammadi and a few others had elected instead to
climb the ladder straight up out of the control room
and through *Noor*'s sail. Asefi waded into the struggling roadblock, grabbing men, yanking them back.
"*That* way! *That* way!" he shouted. "Go that way!"

A shrill, weird scream echoed through the stricken vessel—steel bending and tearing under unimaginable stress. The flooding of the aft compartments, he thought, was putting so much weight on *Noor*'s spine that it was breaking.

The block evaporated at last, as men crowded forward or clambered up the sharply canted ladder. Asefi was alone in the control room.

He would go down with the vessel. There would be nothing for him within the navy after this. Acrid smoke was beginning to filter through from the aft compartments—gases venting from the batteries, he thought, as seawater flooded them. Turning, he started up the ladder.

It was still dark outside, the night a hot and muffling cloak. There was just enough light from a waning half-moon and the lights along the southern shore of Qeshm for him to make out several knots of men wrestling with inflatable rubber boats on the forward deck. As he watched, he could see that *Noor* was settling deeper, the sea washing across half the forward deck between the rounded prow and the foot of the sail. Someone fired a flare, the red beacon streaking high into the sky, arcing over, then igniting with a raw, sullen light.

Overhead, drawn, perhaps, by the flare, a helicopter clattered out of the night, and an instant later the forward deck and sail were enveloped in a harsh, white glare of light. Holding his hand up to shield his eyes from the searchlight, he could make out the Iranian military markings . . . and the fact that a Mk. 46 ASW torpedo was slung beneath the portside weapon rack, but that the starboard torpedo rack was empty.

It was the helicopter that had fired on them.

Someone on board the helicopter shoved a large package out of the open cargo deck hold. It fell and hit the water nearby, off the port side, and began expanding into another rubber boat.

It occurred to Asefi that the American sub would hear the commotion, and might even be taking advantage of it. The crew of that helo, obviously, weren't listening to their sonobuoy transponders now.

"Captain! Captain! Down here!"

It was Mohammadi, standing on the *Noor*'s forward deck, waving his arms. Asefi waved back.

"Save yourself, Captain! Quickly!"

Asefi considered this, then shook his head. Standing at attention, he saluted his officers and men. In another few moments the last of the men on the forward deck were swept into the sea by an incoming wave. *Noor* gave a shudder, then heeled even farther to starboard. He could hear the repeated thuds of bulkheads giving way below, and the shrill hiss and gurgle of water flooding every compartment.

Fear gripped him then . . . and a new thought. If he died . . . what would be the point? There would be a court of inquiry, certainly. And the testimony of *Noor*'s captain might keep unjust charges or recriminations from landing on the men.

Scrambling onto the lip of the weather bridge, he leaped as far out over the water as he could . . . falling . . . falling, then landing in the sea with a splash. The water, after the stifling heat belowdecks, was surprisingly cold.

Then he was swimming, hard, struggling to outrace the suction of the *Noor* as she went down.

And when at last he reached a rubber boat and willing hands had pulled him on board, he turned to look back at his command.

But the *Noor* was gone.

Wednesday, 25 June 2008

Communications Center,
Office of the Ministry of Defense
Tehran, Iran
0425 hours local time

"The Supreme Leader," the bearded cleric told him, "has agreed to launch Operation Bold Fire. How long will it take to implement?"

Admiral Baba-Janzadeh had expected the question and was ready with an answer. "Twenty-four hours, Mullah Zeydvand. We will need that much time to transmit written orders to all of the field commanders. I suggest that we name five o'clock tomorrow morning as H-hour."

"So long?"

The admiral nodded. "The American CIA can intercept all radio communications through their satellites, and we cannot overlook the possibility that they have managed to tap our land lines as well. The only way to ensure surprise is to deliver orders by courier."

Baba-Janzadeh had never heard of a retired Marine named Van Riper, or of his fictitious sinking of the entire U.S. Fifth Fleet in an exercise six years before. Rather, Van Riper had anticipated the admiral's planning, step by methodical step. Surprise was essential to Bold Fire, and the enemy's ability to eavesdrop was, in Baba-Janzadeh's experience, nothing short of magical.

It only made sense to be carefully conservative, and to avoid the enemy's strengths.

One hurdle, at least, had been passed. The admiral's call to Iran's Supreme Leader three hours ago had produced the desired result. The Ayatollah Khameini could have reacted in anger at the presumption of his Defense minister calling with the request that Operation Bold Fire be launched immediately. Instead, after a few questions—the first few angry, the last few concerned—Khameini had agreed that the escape of the enemy submarine necessitated drastic and immediate action.

Originally, Bold Fire was to have been launched by the interception of the American submarine inside of Iranian waters. Subsequent Iranian actions could then be presented to an understanding world as purely self-defense.

But the escape of the enemy vessel—from under the very noses of the Iranian submarine armada—necessitated a change of strategy. To relocate the *Ohio,* the entire military southern command would have to be fully mobilized, and that, in turn, would put the American Fifth Fleet on its highest alert.

Instead, Tehran would launch Operation Bold Fire immediately, using the enemy's incursion as an excuse. The *Ohio* would be tracked down and destroyed as part of the larger operation.

A telephone rang, and a moment later a junior officer handed it to him. "Admiral? It's Admiral Vehedi."

He took the handset. "Baba-Janzadeh," he said. He listened. The man on the other end was excited, almost hysterically so.

"Gently, old friend," he said after a moment. "You're sure of your facts?" He listened a moment more. "Very well. New orders will be coming within the next few hours." He handed the phone back to the officer, and turned to Zeydvand. "A new development, Mullah," he said. "An important one. One of our submarines has been sunk."

"No! Where?"

"A few miles south of Qeshm. *Inside* our territorial waters."

"The Americans have sunk one of our warships?"

"As it happens, no. An hour ago the submarine *Noor* was sunk by one of our antisubmarine helicopters. An accident."

"No . . ."

"A fortunate accident, however."

"How is that?"

"We may know differently, but so far as the world is concerned, an American submarine has entered Iranian waters and torpedoed one of our vessels. We could not have planned such a stroke of luck!"

In fact, during the planning for Bold Fire, the possibility of sacrificing an Iranian warship had been discussed. The possibility of the truth getting out, however, had been deemed too great. It had been decided instead to attempt to trap the American submarine in a clear violation of Iranian sovereignty.

Operation Bold Fire—the invasion of Oman and the United Arab Emirates *and* the destruction of the

American Fifth Fleet—could be launched now without fear of negative political consequences.

The Americans would be seen as the clear aggressors, the Iranians as the holy defenders of Islam and the Gulf.

And no matter what the outcome of the battle itself, victory, *political* victory, would be assured.

Control Room, SSGN *Ohio*
Waypoint Alpha, South of Qeshm Island
Straits of Hormuz
0515 hours local time

"Up scope."

Stewart took his time studying the horizon. It was fast growing light, and there was no need for the low-light optics. North, twelve miles away, was the western tip of Qeshm Island, though only the hilltops showed above the horizon. One mountain, to the northeast, stood well above all of the others—Kuh-e Bukhow, its almost perfectly dome-shaped summit glowing gold in the light of a sunrise that had not yet reached sea level.

South, only four miles distant, was another of the small and circular islands that dotted this stretch of the straits. Two and a half miles across at its widest, it carried the ungainly name of Tonb-e Bozorg on the charts. Its highest elevation was only about seventy feet above sea level, but it was large enough to possess an airstrip and a few straggling villages. The waters nearby were clear, however. Not even any local dhows. And this region offered reasonably deep water for the next part of the operation.

The key word was *reasonably*. In fact, the entire west end of Qeshm Island was surrounded by extremely shallow water. Satellite photographs showed the shallows as a horseshoe of pale aqua encircling the narrow island's western tip . . . coral reefs and shoals barely covered by seawater a meter or less in depth.

South of the shoals, however, and close to little Tonb-e Bozorg, the bottom dropped off sharply. The major Gulf shipping lanes entered the Straits of Hormuz from the Gulf proper just a few miles more to the south, and there the channel reached its greatest depth—sixty meters.

Here, the steeply sloping bottom passed the forty meter line—just over 130 feet deep. *Ohio* had been creeping along this undersea ridge, literally feeling her way using her depth finder sonar—highly directional transponders sending out extremely weak pulses of sound that would not be picked up by an enemy unless they were literally right on her tail.

And that, of course, was still a possibility, but Stewart was pretty sure they'd eluded the fleet of Iranian subs that had been following them the night before. After waiting out the search in their hide southeast of Bandar Abbas, they'd spent the rest of the night slipping west ten miles south of the coast of Qeshm Island.

And that had brought them . . . here.

"Down scope." He turned to face the three SEALs standing by the plot tables. He pointed to a spot the quartermaster had just marked on the chart—their current location, designated Waypoint Alpha. "We're on station, gentlemen," he told them. "You'll have to take it the rest of the way yourselves."

Commander Drake nodded. "We're squared away and ready to book, Captain." He looked at his watch. "We'll lay low and begin loading the ASDS in six more hours. She'll be ready to detach one hour after that . . . say . . . 1200 hours."

"High noon. And you're certain daylight won't be a problem?"

"Negative, sir." The SEAL gave him a wintry grin. "Unlike your vessel, Captain, the ASDS doesn't have much of a footprint."

"They've got sixty nautical miles to cover, Captain," Lieutenant Wolfe explained. "At eight knots, that's seven and a half hours. They'll be hitting the beach at just about an hour before dark. That last bit of daylight will give them some recon time, and let them pick where they'll be coming ashore."

Stewart nodded. This was the SEALs' show, and they knew what they were doing. *Ohio* had gotten them to their drop-off point. Now the ASDS would take them the rest of the way in.

Actually, the minisub would only be carrying sixteen SEALs, under the command of Drake's exec, Mayhew. Drake would remain on board *Ohio* with the remaining fifty SEALs, ready to take them in as a reserve, or for what was euphemistically referred to as "special action," if needed. Lieutenant Wolfe would also remain aboard. He'd already been ashore on that barren coastline; he was along now strictly as an advisor.

The question, though, was whether *any* advice, experience, or preparation would be enough to get the SEALs through what was coming.

Or, for that matter, the *Ohio* herself.

Enlisted berthing, SSGN *Ohio*
Waypoint Alpha
Persian Gulf
1025 hours local time

Caswell lay in the narrow confines of his rack, trying to sleep, yearning for sleep, and unable to find it. He was so tired . . . exhausted physically, but more, exhausted emotionally, wrung out, drained, and limp.

Some part of his mind kept telling him that it was mid-morning, *not* the middle of the night. With his curtain drawn, the inside of his rack area was dark, but enough of a glow spilled through from the fluorescents outside; and men, as always, kept moving back and forth, getting up for their watch, going or coming from the head, getting dressed, quietly talking or bantering. . . .

He wanted to scream at them all to shut the fuck up and let him sleep.

But he knew that even in perfect silence and darkness, sleep would still elude him.

He'd made it through the last several watches, but ever since *Ohio* had entered the Gulf of Oman, played her cat-and-mouse games with Iranian submarines in the Straits of Hormuz, and was now quietly entering the Persian Gulf itself, he'd been stretched to the very limit of emotional endurance, and, he thought, well beyond. He'd almost gotten the entire crew killed by missing those Iranian subs on sonar. He'd been following his training since, but, like the old joke about the rabbit from that battery commercial, the crises simply kept coming and coming and coming.

He felt stretched so thin. Nina. He missed her so much. Why hadn't she stood by him? Why had she sided with . . . them?

ASDS, SSGN *Ohio*
Waypoint Alpha
Persian Gulf
1145 hours local time

Hospitalman Chief Tangretti clambered up the steel ladder within the long, narrow, and vertical cylinder, squeezed up through the double hatch above, and emerged inside a dark spherical chamber. It had four hatches—the one in the deck he'd just climbed through, another overhead, leading up onto the upper deck, and two more, one going forward, one aft. Squatting, he called down to Hutchinson, who was peering up along the ladder at him, his square face framed by the hatchway.

"Okay, Hutch. Pass 'em up."

"Here y'go, Doc."

A bundle squeezed its way up through the deck hatch—a backpack and gear satchel. Pulling it the rest of the way, he turned and pushed it through the afterhatch, into the cargo deck of the ASDS, where TM1 Avery was waiting to receive it.

"Weapon coming up. Safe is on," Hutchinson called.

"Got it."

An M-4 rifle with collapsible stock and M-2 Aim-point laser targeting scope came up through the hatch. He took it, checked the safety, and passed it through to Avery.

More gear came up and he passed it on, before finally joining Avery on the cargo deck. Hutchinson replaced him in the lockout chamber and began accepting his gear from Lambardini.

It was going to be a close fit, and the ASDS had to be loaded step by step, both with men and with their equipment, in a precise order. The routine had been practiced many times before, until it was all but automatic for them, but they still proceeded with meticulous attention to each step.

The idea was to make it work the first time, with no false starts, no retries, no delays.

At last they all were on board—fifteen SEALs and all of their gear for an anticipated two nights and one day ashore—food, water, ammo, targeting gear, communications equipment, all of the matériel, high-tech and low-tech both, necessary for the modern covert op deployment.

It took the better part of an hour to load it all. The only way on board was through the lockout chamber. With *Ohio*'s refitting as an SSGN rigged for covert operations, her first two ICBM tubes had been transformed into lockouts for divers, or, as they were configured now, as access ways to either Dry Deck Shelters or the ASDS minisub mounted on the submarine's aft deck.

The Advanced SEAL Delivery System—ASDS—was a blunt torpedo sixty-five feet long, divided into three sections. Aft was the cargo deck, with Tangretti and his fourteen teammates, designated Delta One and Two. Forward was the spherical lockout chamber, an airlock, actually, that currently was sealed with the special DDS-adaptor on the hatchway, which had once been the outer hatch on one of *Ohio*'s ballistic missile tubes. Forward of that was the cockpit, just big enough for two men—the SEAL detachment commander and the ASDS commander.

Lieutenant Mayhew was the last SEAL to come aboard, just ahead of Lieutenant Commander Jason Taggart, the minisub's skipper. He stuck his head in through the cargo deck hatch. "Everything secure?"

"Everything secure, sir," Tangretti told him. "We're squared away and set to roll."

"Yeah!" MN2 Hobarth called out. "Let's *do* it, man!"

"Let's go kill us some Eye-ranian tangos, Wheel!" That was RM1 Gresham's booming voice.

"Fuckin' A, Wheel!" BM1 Olivetti added, and several other SEALs chorused their agreement.

"Outstanding," Mayhew said, grinning. "Chief, looks like you have your hands full."

"If they give me any trouble, sir, I'll have 'em running laps."

That raised some laughs. With fifteen men and all of their gear crammed into a tube not quite big enough to stand up in, the SEALs were wedged in side by side so tightly they could barely move. The thought of *breathing* in these sardine-can confines for the next seven-plus hours was daunting, to say nothing of calisthenics.

"Good man."

Mayhew turned and vanished, moving into the cockpit forward. Taggart came on board a few minutes later; by ancient nautical custom, the commander of a vessel was always the last on board a small boat or launch, and the first off. The ASDS, serving purely as transport from the *Ohio* to the beach, qualified.

The deck hatch in the lockout chamber clanged shut, and the SEALs could hear other thumps and clangs from below as *Ohio*'s crew sealed their side of the hatches.

"Delta Sierra Delta ready to detach," sounded over the intercom. Delta Sierra Delta was the designation for the ASDS. A moment later a final thump echoed through the cargo deck, the SEALs felt the cylinder roll slightly to port, then stabilize.

They were under way.

Tangretti looked at his watch. It was five past noon. The journey—about sixty nautical miles—was expected to take between seven and a half and eight hours. The ASDS could make better than eight knots; how *much* better was classified. However, they wouldn't be able to run the little vessel full throttle continuously. The silver-zinc battery array that drove the minisub's sixty-seven-horsepower electric motor needed to be nursed carefully on this long a haul. According to the manuals, the ASDS had a total range of over 125 miles—again, how much more was secret—but the run, sixty miles in and sixty out, was pushing the vessel's envelope pretty ruthlessly.

Still, the wonder was that the ASDS was operational at all. A long and at times vicious battle had followed the project from its very inception.

Until the 1990s, SEAL delivery vehicles, like the workhorse Mk. XIII Mod 1 SDV, were all wet submarines, meaning the SEALs were fully suited up and exposed to the ocean for the entire run. The Mk. XIII was twenty-two feet long and rated to carry six SEALs—two operators and four passengers. It had a maximum speed of six knots and a range of about seventy nautical miles . . . but that was a polite and usually overlooked fiction. Seventy miles at six knots meant almost twelve hours in a wet suit, unable to move, and in water that ranged from chilly to frigid.

SEAL training—the BUD/S course at Coronado—emphasized building the would-be SEAL's endurance to the point where he could tolerate severe discomfort and hypothermia. But twelve hours in freezing water without being able to move or stretch, followed by swimming ashore to carry out an operation that might involve long marches, hours of motionless surveillance, or the supreme rigors of combat? Forget it. Even SEALs had their limits.

For decades the SEAL community had tried to get a dry delivery vehicle, one that would allow them to ride all the way to their drop-off point underwater, but warm and in relative comfort. It was an important distinction. Even in a wet suit and even in relatively warm water, hypothermia sets in fast, and few things are as debilitating.

Hypothermia. SEAL recruits are deliberately exposed to it during BUD/S, especially during the sadistic rite of passage involving sleeplessness, torture, and exhaustion known fondly as Hell Week. Tangretti could still remember his last hours of Hell Week, sitting in a water-filled clay pit with a dozen other anonymous tadpoles, coated with black and slimy mud, teeth chattering, body shivering so violently he thought he was going to rattle himself to death. He would have stood up and rung the bell, signaling his decision to drop out of the program, except that he'd been too tired to move. To have even considered engaging in a firefight after that would have been sheer fantasy.

He'd also completed numerous training operations with the Mk. XIII, as well as two other SEAL wet SDVs, the Mk. VIII and the Mk. IX. In all of them, the range limitation had not been battery life, but the endurance of the SEALs on board.

The Navy Special Warfare community had fought long and hard for dry submarines, a seemingly reasonable request that repeatedly had been refused. The reason, irrational as it might have seemed, was simply that the line Navy insisted that dry submarines belonged to the submarine service, *not* to NAVSPECWAR. For the SEALs to get their own submarines would be an intolerable trespass of the line Navy's turf.

At long last, though, Navy Special Warfare had gotten their dry submarine, the ASDS. But the victory had come with a price. Until then, SEAL vehicles had been operated by SDV platoons attached to the SEAL Teams, with SEALs as their drivers. The Navy Department would permit the ASDS project to go forward only if the minisub were commanded, not by a SEAL, but by a line Navy officer.

It was an uncomfortable compromise. SEAL training emphasized complete reliance on your fellow SEALs. You *knew* you could rely on your teammates, because each and every one of them, including the officers—*especially* the officers—had been through the same training you had, including Hell Week. Once they exited the ASDS, Delta One and Two would be under the command of Lieutenant Mayhew, a SEAL. Until then, however, they were under the command of Lieutenant Commander Taggart, a submariner, and an unknown quantity.

It wasn't that they didn't trust Taggart, exactly. They simply . . . didn't, well, *trust* him. Not like another SEAL.

Tangretti leaned back on his bench, elbows propped on knapsacks to either side. Seven and a half hours. Back when he was stationed in Coronado, when he had liberty he sometimes drove up the coast to visit a friend in San Francisco—four hundred and some miles. The way *he* drove, that was about seven and a half or eight hours.

He would try to enjoy the ride, or at least endure it.

Control Room, SSN *Pittsburgh*
Off Abu Musa Island
West entrance to the Straits of Hormuz
Persian Gulf
1427 hours local time

"*Jesus*, Skipper! Lookit this!"
"Is *that* any way to deliver a message, sailor?"

Lieutenant Commander Chisolm said, his voice stern and sharp-edged.

The sailor, a twenty-year-old radioman second class, stopped in his tracks, ashen-faced. "Uh, sorry, sir."

"That's okay, sailor," Creighton said. "What do you got?"

"This just came through, sir!" He handed a translated message flimsy to Creighton.

TIME: 25JUN08/1415HR
TO: CO PITTSBURGH, SSN 720
FROM: HQNAVCENT, JUFFAIR, BAHRAIN
PRIORITY: MOST URGENT

SPEECH BY KHAMEINI ON AL JAZEERA TV JUST ANNOUNCED CLOSING OF STRAITS OF HORMUZ BY IRAN. LARGE SCALE MILITARY ACTION BY IRAN PROBABLE WITHIN 12 TO 24 HOURS, BUT ACTIONS AGAINST GULF SHIPPING POSSIBLE AT ANY TIME. KHAMEINI HAS THREATENED US FORCES, SAYING THEY WILL BE DESTROYED IF US DOES NOT EVACUATE GULF.

SSN 720 IS HEREBY DIRECTED TO ASSUME DEFENSE POSTURE BRAVO AND AWAIT FURTHER INSTRUCTIONS. DO NOT REPEAT DO NOT INITIATE HOSTILE ACTIONS.

SIGNED
RUSSELL SCOTT, ADM
CONAVCENTCOM

"Christ on a crutch," Creighton said slowly, almost reverently, when he finished reading the flimsy. He glanced at the sailor. "Comm has acknowledged this?"

"Yes, sir!"

"Very well. Go back to your station."

"Aye aye, sir!"

Trust the *Pittsburgh*'s internal communications grapevine. Every man aboard would know about this within thirty minutes.

Pittsburgh, at the moment, was at a depth of 150 feet, in the main shipping channel just north of tiny Abu Musa Island. Abu Musa was a point of contention in this region, seized, along with two other flyspecks, the Greater and Lesser Tunbs, back in 1971 by Iran and from the United Arab Emirates. Even before the Shah had been deposed and the clerics seized power, Iran had coveted control of the straits between the Gulf and the open ocean. Seizing those islands had been a vital step toward gaining control. All three had had Iranian military forces posted on them ever since their takeover. Abu Musa, in particular, was rumored to have a Chinese-made Silkworm battery, one capable of taking out tanker traffic in the main shipping channel. *Pittsburgh* had been trying to get close enough for a look-see when the message arrived.

Iran's complete control, however, would be accomplished only by two things—the seizure of the Musand'am peninsula, on the south side of the straits, from Oman and the UAE . . . and the neutralization of the U.S. Fifth Fleet.

Until now, neither possibility had seemed likely. But if Iran's Supreme Leader had just announced the closing of the straits, that might very well change.

"Defense Posture Bravo." That was one of a number of alternate battle plans laid up against the possibility of open hostilities in the Gulf. Creighton would go break the orders out of his safe shortly, but he already knew what they entailed, in general.

Remain undetected.

Wait and watch.

Return fire if fired upon, but take care not to initiate hostile action.

Return fire if friendly vessels are fired upon but, again, do not initiate hostile action.

"Mr. Chisolm, sound general quarters," he said.

The Ayatollah's pronouncement didn't mean all-out war—not yet—but it was the next thing to it.

Wednesday, 25 June 2008

Control Room, SSK *Ghadir*
Northeast of Abu Musa,
West entrance to the Straits of Hormuz
1710 hours local time

Most of a submarine's patrol time is spent waiting.

"New sonar contact bearing two-nine-five, Captain," the sonar officer said. "It sounds like another tanker, trying to enter the straits."

The weapons officer completed the TMA moments later. "Target speed eight knots, range thirteen hundred meters, sir."

Captain Damavandi stepped onto the control room dais. "Up periscope." Taking the periscope handles, he rode it to the surface. Harsh afternoon daylight glared off the water to the west, where a giant loomed against the horizon. He completed the requisite full circle, checking for other nearby vessels, then centered the targeting reticule on the contact.

Another huge one . . . larger than the *Texan Star* or any of the others they'd tracked so far. And it was heavily laden, the massive hull low in the water.

"Liberian registry," Damavandi said. He read the name off the bow. "*Escondido Bay.*"

"Three hundred fifteen thousand tons," Commander Tavakkoli reported, reading from the warbook. "Three hundred thirty-one meters loa. American owned and operated."

"Excellent," Damavandi said. "Maneuvering! Come right to two-zero-five and increase speed to fifteen knots. Communications Officer!"

"Yes, sir!"

"Send to Bandar Abbas. 'Holy Mountain.'"

"Yes, sir!"

With *Ghadir's* periscope raised, the submarine's UHF antenna was above water as well. They continued to watch the target's steady approach, waiting for confirmation. Slowly, the angle on the bow increased, until the entire length of the vessel could be seen, spanning the northern horizon. Damavandi gave orders to swing to starboard, bringing her forward tubes to bear.

Less than five minutes after the initial transmission, *Ghadir's* communications officer announced, "Captain! Message from Bandar Abbas Naval Command! The message is 'Fire upon the sea!' It is confirmed, sir!"

Damavandi nodded, smiling. He'd thought this would be the one. Tehran wanted the largest target possible, the better to drive home its message: *The straits are closed!*

"Weapons status."

"Sir!" Lieutenant Taqi Ashkani, the weapons officer,

reported. "Tubes one, three, two, and four are loaded and ready to fire!"

Damavandi took another long look through the periscope, as though to memorize every detail of the huge vessel now passing less than a kilometer off the *Ghadir*'s bow. "Fire number one."

Ashkani's palm slammed against a switch at his fire control console. "Tube one fired electrically!" Damavandi heard the hiss of air expelling the torpedo from the tube forward, felt the slight rocking of the deck in response.

"Fire three."

"Tube three fired electrically," Ashkani reported.

"Fire two."

"Tube two fired electrically."

"Fire four."

"Tube four fired electrically. Allah be praised! All torpedoes running straight and true."

Damavandi glanced at Mullah Hamid Khodaei, seated at his accustomed place by the weapons board, and kept his face impassive. A submarine is no place for religious fervor, he thought, but it was a thought he would keep to himself.

"Torpedo one has acquired its target," the weapons officer announced. A moment passed. "Torpedo one is locked."

"Cut the wire to torpedo number one."

"Wire cut. Torpedo one is running free."

He found himself watching the sweeping second hand on the big clock mounted on the control room's forward bulkhead.

"Torpedo three has acquired its target." *Good.* "Torpedo three is locked."

"Cut the wire to torpedo number three."

"Wire cut. Torpedo three is running free."

Ghadir was equipped with Russian-designed 533mm torpedoes. Wire-guided, they were fired toward their target, but could be controlled by signals sent along the wires that connected them to the submarine. Once close enough to the target that they could pick them up with their own on-board sonar, the wires were cut and the torpedoes free to travel the rest of the way to their target.

Through the periscope, Damavandi saw a sudden geyser of water erupt from beneath the supertanker's stern; moments later they heard the heavy thud of the warhead's detonation, and the men in the control room broke into a frenzy of cheering and shrill cries of *"Allah is great!"* and *"Death to America!"*

"Silence!" Damavandi bellowed, and the clamor subsided almost at once. "Attend to your posts!"

A second geyser of water erupted from the supertanker's starboard side, this one amidships. This time, when the explosion rumbled through the hull, the men didn't cheer, but Damavandi could feel their excitement, their raw joy.

"Torpedo one has missed, Captain," the weapons officer announced. And, when another moment had passed. "Torpedo four has also missed."

"No matter," Damavandi said, watching through the periscope. "I believe they have received our message. Communications Officer!"

"Sir!"

"Send to Bandar Abbas. 'The sea is burning.' "

"*Yes,* Captain! Allah be praised!"

Allah be praised. Fire was engulfing the stern third of the ship, which had already begun to settle visibly deeper into the water. Men were burning to death out there . . . a hideous way to die.

Ghadir, however, had just scored her first kill.

Combat Center, SSGN *Ohio*
Waypoint Alpha
1745 hours local time

The Combat Center had been set up forward of the *Ohio*'s control room, a compartment dedicated to managing operations ashore. When Stewart walked in, Drake and Wolfe both were there, bent over a map table upon which a satellite photo had been blown up into a large map. The resolution was high enough that Stewart could see automobiles, construction equipment, and individual people.

"Have you heard the latest priflash?" he asked.

Drake looked up from the table. "No, Captain. What is it?"

Stewart handed him the translated flimsy that had just been handed to him. "Tehran has just upped the ante," he said as Drake read the message. "They've just torpedoed a supertanker in the straits."

"Christ Almighty . . ."

"HQ-NAVCENT has given all U.S. forces in the Gulf their orders—Defense Posture Bravo. That means we initiate no hostile action, and shoot back only if we or one of our ships is fired upon."

"Does that include that tanker, sir?" Lieutenant Drake asked.

"It means I could have decided to sink the sub that torpedoed her," Stewart replied, "if we'd been in the area. But can I launch Tomahawks now? No. However, this does bring Operation Sea Hammer into question."

Drake scowled, shaking his head. "Call it off? Can't do it, Captain. Not now. Damn it, they're two hours from the coast, and they haven't surfaced for an update. Besides, this isn't a NAVCENT/CENTCOM op. It's NAVSPECWAR, which means J-SOC."

Stewart nodded at the tangle of alphabet soup. "I understand that. But we should keep our options open, in case someone decides to start micromanaging. Don't you agree?"

Ohio's operational status was hazy, at best. She was in the AO—the Area of Operations—under the military jurisdiction of U.S. Central Command, or CENTCOM, headquartered across the Gulf at Manama. Operationally, however, she was following orders given by Naval Special Warfare, which in turn was operating under the authority of the Joint Special Operations Command, headquartered back at Fort Bragg, Stateside. If CENTCOM issued him a direct order, he would clear it with J-SOC first.

Stewart doubted that CENTCOM would attempt to force the issue . . . but it could happen. Even in this age of instantaneous satellite communications, messages went awry and decision makers neglected to talk with one another. The biggest problem was that the situation here had just leaped another level on the crisis meter. With the attack on the *Escondido Bay*, this was now a shooting war.

And the *Ohio* was smack in the middle of it.

ASDS Delta Sierra Delta
Off Bandar-e Charak, Iran
1958 hours local time

The cockpit of the Advanced SEAL Delivery System was more like that of a modern combat aircraft than that of any kind of boat or ship Mayhew was familiar with. The two naval officers were squeezed in side by side in a space less than seven feet wide, like pilot and copilot. Digital readouts, touch-screen controls, and a pair of TV monitors were situated on the forward console instead of traditional periscopes or windows on the outside world. The craft boasted two separate sonar systems—forward-looking sonar for detecting obstacles ahead, including man-made ones, and side-looking sonar for terrain and bottom-mapping, and for mine detection.

It was only right, Mayhew thought. The ASDS was a blunt and ugly looking vehicle on the outside, and as cramped as a trash can aft; the cockpit had better have some damned sexy controls if it was to justify the vessel's $230 million price tag.

"Time to bring her up and get a fix," Taggart said. "Raise the masts."

"Up scopes," Mayhew said, touching his control screen.

The ASDS possessed two masts, mounted side by side. The port mast was an optical periscope, though the image came up on a TV monitor on the console, instead of in an eyepiece. The starboard mast was for satellite communications, and also took an automatic GPS fix on the vessel's location each time it was raised above the surface.

The two men studied the image on the screen for a moment, walking it first through 360 degrees to make sure there weren't any surface craft close by. They appeared to have this stretch of beach to themselves.

"We're about five kilometers from where we want to be," Mayhew observed, studying the GPS readout. His official position, at least until he locked out with his men, was navigator.

"Less than two miles," Taggart said. "Not bad for sixty miles of dead reckoning."

Mayhew shot the older man a glance. Was he being

sarcastic? Mayhew had trained long and hard with the ASDS, and took supreme pride in his ability to navigate. The truth was, a two-mile error *wasn't* bad, considering they hadn't poked the GPS mast above water since leaving the *Ohio*. But there was that whole submariner-SEAL rivalry thing, which could crop up at the damnedest times. Non-SEAL officers tended to see Special Warfare personnel as mavericks, as cowboys—or, worse, as lunatics—and didn't always take them seriously. Mayhew's only strategy throughout the training, both with Taggart and with other fleet officers, was to maintain a strictly professional mien.

But Taggart appeared serious. Maybe he was trying to keep things strictly professional as well.

"Yeah," Mayhew agreed. "Looks like we're just west of the port. We want to be at the river mouth to the east."

The landscape, revealed by an orange sun hot and low in the west, might have been the surface of an alien planet. It was barren, for the most part—sand and rock, salt plain and desert, baking in the summer heat. Several black, dome-shaped massifs rose from otherwise flat pans of sand, salt, and gravel. Inland, rugged mountains—the Shib Kuh coastal range—glowed in the evening sun against the northern sky.

The village of Bandar-e Charak was a clutter of square, single-story buildings for the most part, stretched in an arc along a mile of the coast. A river entered the Gulf on the east side of the town, emerging from behind a long, low sand bar. West were scattered docks, a few petroleum-processing facilities, and a fishery.

Six miles northeast of the port itself, one of those black massifs rose from the surrounding desert floor, a huge, rounded dark backdrop. Their objective—the Darya-ye complex, code-named White Scimitar—was located at the southern edge of that massif, tucked away within a steep-walled valley.

The failed Operation Black Stallion had attempted going in well to the west of Bandar-e Charak, the SEALs moving inland across a beach and a road, then swinging east to come at the site over the flank of the mountain. According to Lieutenant Wolfe, back on the *Ohio*, Pasdaran troops had been waiting for them up in those hills, with a large patrol emerging seemingly from nowhere. Possibly the SEALs had tripped sophisticated sensors going in, or, possibly, mission security had been compromised, most likely by the radar detection of the two SEAL boats. Either way, the Iranian troops had been hunting for intruders, and they'd found them.

Operation Sea Hammer was planned with an alternate approach, moving up the unnamed river and through the salt marshes behind it, swinging behind Bandar-e Charak and up into the massif from the east.

Taggart took the joystick control on the console in front of him and pulled it to the right. Obediently, the little submersible swung to starboard, turning east.

"We've got a priority flash coming through," Mayhew said. "Five gets you ten we're getting recalled."

"That sort of thing happen to SEALs often?"

"It happens often enough." The message was in text rather than voice. He ran it through the decoder and brought it up on-screen. "Well, shit."

"What is it? We going back to the barn?"

"It's a waffle. They're not calling off the mission, but we're not supposed to make the bad guys mad, either." He read Taggart the text.

"Doesn't apply to us," the submariner said. "We're not Fifth Fleet."

"No, but I'll bet that defense wouldn't help much if

we got court-martialed for taking a dump in Fifth Fleet's living room."

"How do you want to handle it, Lieutenant?"

"You're asking me?"

Taggart shrugged. "Way I see it, we're not threatening anybody so long as we're parked out here and safely submerged. Your part of the mission is where it gets dicey—taking fifteen well-armed psychopaths six miles into Injun country. Can you do that without kicking over the hornet's nest?"

"Well, the way SEALs see things," Mayhew replied, "is the successful op is the one where no one sees you going in, no one sees you coming out, and no one ever knows you were there . . . at least until the fireworks go off. Yeah, we can do it."

"Okay, then. Let's get this bus east to your drop-off."

Churning silently through shallow water, the ASDS motored south at eight knots, unseen from the shore.

Sonar Room, SSGN *Ohio*
Waypoint Alpha
Persian Gulf
2105 hours local time

Sonar Tech Second Class Caswell listened to the weirdly echoing chirps and pings coming through the broadband equipment. Charting them—determining accurate distances and ranges—was all but impossible. Echoes off the shoal water to the north confused the picture, and there were a number of enemy transmitters. So far he'd identified at least two submarines in the area that were using active sonar, as well as a surface vessel and several stationary transmitters that were probably sonobuoys.

Master Chief O'Day stepped into the sonar shack. "How ya doin', Cassie?" the older man asked.

Caswell jumped, startled. "Shit, COB!"

"Sorry, kid."

" 'S'okay. Jesus. Give a guy some warning next time."

The Chief of the Boat grinned. "I just wanted to know how you were getting on."

Caswell nodded. "Okay, I guess. Work helps, y'know?"

"Yeah. Y'know, my wife left me after twenty-one years. I came home one day, and found she'd cleaned out her stuff and left. Took the joint account, too. It still hurts."

"How long ago was that, COB?" Dobbs asked.

"About six years."

"Jeeze, doesn't it ever stop hurting?" Caswell asked.

O'Day shrugged. "I dunno. Haven't gotten that far yet. Point is, you get through it. Kind of like kicking the bottle. One day at a time."

Caswell nodded. "I guess that's what I'm learning. I . . . I was kind of close there, for a while. . . ."

"Close to what?"

"I don't know. Doing something stupid."

"Killing yourself?"

Caswell hesitated, then nodded.

"Yeah. I kind of figured."

"You did?"

"Like I say, I been there." O'Day rubbed his jaw. "You in the mood for some advice?"

"I guess so."

"Don't. If you think you're in a world of shit now, just try killing yourself."

"What do you mean? The idea is to make it stop

hurting." The words started coming faster. "I mean . . . it just keeps going on and on and on! I try to forget her, but I can't. I try to sleep, and I can't. I try to pay attention to my work . . . and *she* keeps getting in the way. I don't want to screw everything up for everybody."

"Of course you don't. That's why you're *not* going to kill yourself."

"Huh?"

"Look, on board a submarine, there are only so many ways to off yourself. The doc has all the dangerous drugs locked up. No place to hang yourself. No *privacy*. No, you'd have to get a weapon out of the arms locker and try to blow your brains out.

"And let's say you're able to do that, see? There'd be an inquiry. Jesus, kid, do you hate the skipper that much that you'd put him through that kind of hell? That's assuming he survived, 'cause if you fired off a weapon down here, the Iranians would hear it, and they'd be all over us. You want to take your shipmates with you?"

"N-No, COB."

"But the *real* pain would be if you fucked it up. There was this guy on a sub I was stationed on about fifteen years ago . . . nice kid. Twenty, maybe twenty-one. His brand new wife dumped him, and he went off the bulkhead. Trying for a Section Eight. We had ourselves a nice little stand-off in the torpedo room, him stark naked and raving about Jesus Christ and holding a pistol to his head, while me and the boat's doc tried to talk him down."

"What happened?"

"Damnedest thing I ever saw. The boat's skipper came down, held out his hand like this, and said, 'Give me that weapon, mister. I'm Jesus Christ on this boat, and that's a fucking order!' This kid damned near fainted, but he lowered the gun and handed it over.

Pure force of will, I guess. We had him in handcuffs and sedated before he knew what hit him. Inside of twenty-four hours he was on his way stateside."

"Did he get court-martialed?" Dobbs asked.

"Nah. The skipper recommended a medical discharge. He got it, eventually, but he was in the hospital for quite a while. So, Caswell . . . how bad do you want out of the Navy?"

Caswell shook his head. "Not that bad."

"Good. Because, like the skipper said, we need you. We need your ears. Right?"

"Right, COB."

"What was that? I couldn't hear you."

"I said, 'Right, COB.' "

"That's better. Now listen up. I've been where you are right now, okay? And let me tell you something. It never, ever gets so bad you can't wait one more day. Can you do that? Wait one more day?"

"Y-Yeah. I guess so."

"Know so. I'm not going to make pacts with you, or any of that shit. All I want is that if you get to where you want to kill yourself, you just make a pact with yourself . . . to wait one more day. I think you'll find that you're glad you didn't do it. You hear me?"

"Yes, COB."

"Good. You've got some good people looking out for you. Your department head. The exec. Doc Kettering. Me. We're all watching you to make sure you *don't* do something stupid . . . but we're also here to help you if we can. You can always—"

Caswell held up his hand, a sharp, urgent movement. The pitch of one set of sonar pings had just changed and was growing stronger. He hit the intercom switch. "Control Room, Sonar. An enemy vessel has just changed course and is heading straight toward us. Heavy pinging."

"Acknowledged, Sonar. What can you tell me?"

Caswell closed his eyes, as if to better merge himself with the sound. He could hear the steady throb of the other vessel's screws behind the *chirp-ping* of its sonar.

"Control Room . . . target is a surface vessel. Twin screws. Type 174 hull, sonar bearing two-eight-five. Speed twenty knots. Estimated range . . . two thousand yards." He listened a moment longer. "Captain, I don't think he has a lock. He's moving too fast."

"Acknowledged, Sonar. Keep on him."

The pinging was audible now to unaided ears throughout the *Ohio*. The chirps and their echoes grew louder . . . more insistent . . .

. . . and then they were receding as the pounding of the ASW warship's screws passed overhead.

O'Day let out a long, pent-up breath. "Good call, kid."

"I think the bastard is trying to drive us," Dobbs said. "At twenty knots, though, he's not going to hear very much."

"He's changing course again," Caswell said. "He's turning south, out into the middle of the straits. Still banging away like mad."

"Probably hopes to spook us," O'Day observed. "Maybe get us to pop a fish at him."

"There's something else," Caswell said. Damn! This one was close! "Control Room! Sonar! I have an air contact, directly overhead! Sounds like a helicopter, hovering low over the water."

"Acknowledged."

For a long, achingly tense moment, Caswell listened to the faint sound of a helicopter's rotors, a muffled *whop-whop-whop* transmitted down through the water. He was listening now for the telltale splash of something dropping into the water—sonobuoy, torpedo, depth charge. . . .

And then the sound of the helicopter began fading.

"Control Room, Sonar. Helicopter contact is moving off toward the south."

"Very well."

O'Day sagged, leaning against the sonar room entranceway. "Jesus, kid. Good ears."

"Just doing my job, COB."

"Well . . . keep on doing it. Well done." The Chief of the Boat turned and left the compartment.

Just doing my job.

Caswell was startled to realize just how important that was right now. How very much he didn't want to let down his shipmates.

And even how much he wanted to please the skipper.

A long time later, he was startled again when he realized he hadn't thought about Nina once during that whole encounter.

Thursday, 26 June 2008

SEAL Element Delta One
Five miles north of Bandar-e Charak
0135 hours local time

Delta One had reached their objective.

With the ASDS remaining submerged a mile offshore, eight of the sixteen SEALs had egressed through the upper hatch, inflated a pair of rubber ducks—slang for their CRRCs—with silenced electric motors, and slipped ashore within the dune-choked estuary east of the town. Leaving the CRRCs buried on the beach, the site marked by handheld GPS units, Delta One had made the long passage up the nameless river, slipping silently and unseen past the drowsing fishing village of Bandar-e Charak. For the first mile the stream had been deep and clear; they'd followed it easily, swimming along through the shallows, and at times wading. After that, however, the river branched rapidly, fed by three streams that in turn drained a large and marshy area extending in a broad fan shape another three or four miles inland. For another two miles, the SEALs waded through brackish, knee-deep water, and at times were forced to crawl through the noisome muck of salt marsh and swamp, dragging their satchels of equipment behind them.

By the time they left the streambed, at a point determined by GPS, they'd all acquired camouflage more effective than the combat black utilities they all wore—a heavy coating of viscous mud. It made them effectively invisible.

It was also *heavy,* and slowed them down considerably.

Tangretti was forcibly reminded of his BUD/S training—crawling for hours through mud this thick and this fetid in a field at Coronado until every muscle in his body was one sharp, throbbing ache. At last, however, they emerged from the marsh, crossed a road coming down from the north, and began climbing the flank of Kuh-e Gab, the mountain ridge rising sharply behind the port village of Bandar-e Charak.

Now, four and a half hours after exiting the ASDS, Tangretti lay flat on his belly, studying the objective spread out below him through his night vision goggles. The landscape, shrouded in midnight, was revealed through the NVG in eerie shades of green that presented an image that, if monochromatic, still yielded nearly as much detail as daylight. The Darya-ye complex—the target designated White Scimitar—was huge, much larger than he'd imagined it from the sat photos he'd studied, or even from the images transmitted by Black Stallion's UAVs.

His hide was 750 feet above sea level, on the top of a barren ridge looking down into a valley cleaving the mountain of Kuh-e Gab above Bandar-e Charak. A dirt road wound up the valley from the southeast; when the valley twisted to the southwest, the road continued straight, vanishing into the canyon wall. No fewer than eight tunnel mouths were visible in that cliffside, massively reinforced with concrete. Tangretti had been in Afghanistan, where tunneling into mountains had been a way of life, first to hide from the Soviets, and then to seek shelter from the Americans and their smart bombs.

The excavated area visible in the planning photographs was actually separate from the tunnel complex area, a large, bulldozed area embracing the mouth of the valley about three-tenths of a mile away, on the desert plain between the mountain and the marshes through which the SEALs had come. The area was enclosed by a high steel-mesh fence topped by razor wire. A number of buildings were still under construction there. The trick was to figure out what those buildings were for.

The entire complex, clearly, was a fortress, guarding access to the valley and to the tunnels in the mountain. There were at least a dozen massive bunkers scattered over fifty acres, along with what looked like mounts for antiaircraft guns and surface-to-air missiles. Tangretti counted thirty-seven heavy army trucks, and a number of civilian rigs as well, including five tractor-trailers. There were soldiers everywhere, in front of the main gate, patrolling the fence inside and out, moving about inside the fenced compound, and coming and going up the half-mile canyon road to those enigmatic tunnel entrances into the mountain's interior.

Illumination was provided by several streetlights—dazzlingly bright through his night vision optics—and a searchlight in a tower that swept the sand and gravel outside the fence perimeter. The Iranians even had a tank—an old Russian T-72, squatting in one corner of the compound like some drowsing, prehistoric beast.

Tangretti's experienced eye checked the logistical side of the complex. Water . . . there was a huge, steel water tank rising on three legs above the main compound. At the bottom were a pair of tank trucks. They probably hauled all of their water in from Bandar Abbas, where the closest desalinization plant was located.

Power. That was a tougher question to answer. One or more of those fortresslike bunkers might house generators, and there were a couple of big, squat POL tanks inside the fenced compound. There was no sign of power lines. Those might all be underground, however. Did the tunnel complex get power from generators in the base at the mouth of the valley? Or did they have underground generators up there?

At his side, Lieutenant Mayhew used his own NVGs to scope out the objective. "Well, Chief," he said after a long moment, "it beats the hell out of me. What do *you* think the damned thing is?"

"With that kind of security? There're only four options, and it may be some combination of the four, or it may even be all of the above—N, B, C, or a base to launch them from."

"Agreed. Washington's worst nightmare, all wrapped up in one tidy package."

Nuclear, biological, or chemical warfare. The great equalizers when it came to disparities in conventional military forces.

"But we'll need confirmation," Tangretti said. "And for that, we'll have to go down there."

"Like they say, Chief. The only easy day—"

"Was yesterday," Tangretti said, finishing the old SEAL joke. There was no way around it. The SEALs were going to have to penetrate that fortress.

And from the look of things, getting into the place in

one piece was going to be a hell of a lot easier than getting out.

Straits of Hormuz
0630 hours local time

The Sultanate of Oman is one of the more enlightened of the nations sharing the Arabian peninsula, a desert kingdom with a middle-income economy, possessing considerable oil and gas reserves but without the wildly excessive lifestyle of their Saudi neighbors. Formerly a British colony, the Sultanate has preserved its longstanding good relations with Great Britain, both politically and militarily. Moderate in both politics and religion, the nation has historically attempted to maintain good relations with all of the Islamic states in the region, including the non-Arab Iranians across the narrow straits.

With just twelve-hundredths of one percent of the land arable, the vast majority of Oman is desert. Nor is all of the country's territory contiguous. The northern tip, the Musand'am peninsula, is separated from the rest of Oman by the federation of seven desert principalities known as the United Arab Emirates. The Omani portion measures just fifty-five miles north to south, and less than twenty-five miles east to west at its widest point. In addition, a tiny Omani enclave, Al Madhah, exists midway between the Musand'am peninsula and Oman proper.

This entire peninsula has long been cherished by other nation-states in the region desiring to control the vital straits through to the Persian Gulf, Iran chief among them. It forms the southern coast of the Straits of Hormuz, and so assumes an exaggerated strategic importance, an importance wildly out of proportion to the actual character of this barren and sandstorm-scoured strip of land.

To defend its territory, the Sultanate of Oman possesses a 36,000-man army—the Royal Armed Forces, or RAF—a 3,000-man Royal Omani Navy, with six warships; and a 3,500-man Royal Omani Air Force flying forty-four combat aircraft, including two squadrons of British-made Jaguars. The RAF itself is well-trained and professional, and includes 6,000 household troops; the 4,500-man Royal Guard of Oman; two Special Forces regiments trained by the British SAS, totaling about 700 men; the 20,000-man Royal Omani Land Forces; and about 3,700 foreign troops, including British advisors. Two tank squadrons are outfitted with U.S. M60 tanks and British Chieftains—a total of perhaps 150 tanks. In addition, the Musand'am peninsula is patrolled by a rifle company of tribal militia—the Musand'am Security Force.

The seven emirates of the UAE are also British-trained and equipped, with an army numbering about 46,000 men, with 335 tanks, 800 APCs, 425 pieces of artillery, 55 aircraft, and 22 ships.

Across the straits, Iran possesses two side-by-side military establishments, the regular army and the Iranian Revolutionary Guard Corps, or IRGC—the infamous Pasdaran. Of the two, the regular military is by far the stronger and better equipped, possessing some 400,000 active-duty personnel. The IRGC, however, had assumed a key importance within Tehran's theocracy as guardians of the Revolution and caretakers of the military's Islamic purity. In addition, the IRGC was responsible for selecting and indoctrinating officers for the regular army as well as the Pasdaran.

Both the regular military and the IRGC combined army, navy, and air force units. The IRGC numbered about 120,000 men in all. Its navy included ten brand-new Chinese Huodong fast-attack craft armed with antiship missiles, perhaps a hundred smaller boats, shore-based antiship missiles, and a large combat swimmer force.

The Iran-Iraq War of the 1980s had largely gutted Iran's military. Much of their equipment—in particular combat aircraft and warships—had been provided by the United States during the reign of the Shah, and with Washington's embargo against Revolutionary Iran, most planes and ships were soon rendered useless by the lack of spares and trained personnel. Over the next two decades, Tehran had aggressively sought to rebuild her military through arms purchases from other nations, including 104 T-72 tanks from Poland; 422 T-72s from Russia; 413 BMP-2 Infantry Fighting Vehicles from Russia; SA-2, SA-5, and SDA-6 surface-to-air missiles from Russia and China; 106 artillery pieces from China; MI-17 helicopters, SU-24 strike aircraft, and MiG-29 fighters from Russia; and older F-7 fighters from China. By the early years of the twenty-first century, Iran's combined military arms included 1,500 tanks, 1,500 APCs, 2,000 pieces of artillery, 220 aircraft, and 30 warships.

Although impressive on paper, a side-by-side assessment of Iran's military with those of its neighbors didn't tell the whole story. Most observers agreed that Iran's offensive military capabilities were weak to the point of impotence. Iran could close the straits temporarily, at least—using a combination of antiship missiles, small attack boats, mines, and her submarine force. More to the point, however, was the key question: *why?* Closing the straits would hurt Iran at least as much as it hurt other nations dependent on the flow of petroleum from the Gulf. After two decades of war and international isolation, Iran's economy was all but bankrupt, and she depended on the world oil market for survival. Besides, the United States—in particular the U.S. Fifth Fleet based at Manama—could be counted on to apply whatever force was necessary to reopen the straits. Large as Iran's armed forces were, the country could not stand up to a direct conventional military confrontation with the United States.

And so many observers worldwide had discounted the latest round of posturing and saber-rattling coming out of Tehran. Iran had threatened to close the straits before, and nothing had come of it, and so the simultaneous naval landings at Kumsar, al-Khasab, and Bukha, down the western coast of the Musand'am peninsula, caught the international community totally by surprise.

Iranian strike fighters hit first, screaming across the Straits of Hormuz at wave-skimming altitude from marshaling circles off Bandar Abbas, targeting the tiny Omani military base at al-Khasab, and also swinging out over the Gulf of Oman to hit larger bases within Oman proper, at Suhar, al-Khabura, and the capital at Muscat. Their targets were radar installations, SAM sites, and aircraft parked on the ground.

While the bombs and missiles were still falling, a fleet of Iranian CH-47 Chinook helicopters—relics of days when the Americans had poured military arms and equipment into the Shah's Iran as a bulwark against the Soviets—lifted off from Bandar Abbas and Qeshm Island and turned south, clattering low across the straits. Iranian Special Forces commandos swarmed down the lowered cargo ramps at Kumsar, a tiny fishing port at the very northern tip of the peninsula. The rest touched down at the only airfield on Omani Musand'am, at the principle city of al-Khasab. Farther down the western coast, at Bukha, naval troops emerged from a freighter that had arrived at the dockside late the evening before, seizing the port and holding it until reinforcements could arrive.

The first ultimatum was issued from Tehran an hour later.

Combat Center, SSGN *Ohio*
Waypoint Alpha
0740 hours local time

In *Ohio*'s Combat Center, Stewart and the two SEAL officers were gathered around the electronic plot table that took up much of the compartment's space. At the moment, the plot displayed a highly detailed satellite image of Objective White Scimitar, overlaid by lines and geometric shapes rendered in colored markers that showed the position of Delta One, and of various features of the Iranian military base as relayed back by the SEALs. On the forward bulkhead, a large TV monitor currently showed a low-light-optics view of the tunnel mouths. The SEALs had a camera trained on the tunnel entrance, and were transmitting back to the *Ohio* in real-time.

A radioman entered the Combat Center. "Flash urgent, Captain," he said, handing him the sheet. Stewart read it through twice, as if to wring every possible drop of information from the sparse, almost cryptic words.

TIME: 26JUN08/0705HR
TO: ALL U.S. FORCES, CENTCOM AO
FROM: HQNAVCENT, JUFFAIR, BAHRAIN
PRIORITY: MOST URGENT

IRANIAN ARMED FORCES ENGAGED IN SIGNIFICANT MIL-
ITARY INCURSION ON MUSANDAM PENINSULA, LAUNCH-
ING AIR STRIKES AGAINST OMANI AIR ASSETS ACROSS
STRAITS OF HORMUZ, FOLLOWED BY LANDINGS OF HELI-
BORNE TROOPS AT AL-KHASAB AIRPORT. INITIAL RE-
PORTS OF HEAVY FIREFIGHTS BETWEEN IRANIAN SPECIAL
FORCES AND LOCAL MILITIA. OMANI AIR ASSETS BE-
LIEVED CRIPPLED. FOLLOW-UP FORCES REPORTED LAND-
ING AT THIS TIME AT AL-KHASAB AND OTHER PORTS IN
LARGE NUMBERS. ACTIVITY APPEARS DESIGNED TO SE-
CURE OMANI MUSANDAM AS FOLLOW-ON TO CLOSING
OF STRAITS OF HORMUZ YESTERDAY.

ALERT LEVEL FOR ALL U.S. FORCES IN CENTCOM AO
HEREBY RAISED TO ALERT-2. DEFENSE POSTURE REMAINS
BRAVO, REPEAT, BRAVO. STAND BY FOR FURTHER OR-
DERS.

SIGNED
RUSSELL SCOTT, ADM
CONAVCENTCOM

Stewart passed the sheet to Drake. "Iran has invaded
Oman," he told the others as Drake read. He kept his
voice emotionless, masking the bounding excitement he
felt. "Less than an hour ago. Started with an all-out air
strike. Caught most of the Omani planes on the ground.
Then they sent in their Special Forces on helicopters."

Wolfe's brow creased. "They can't invade the whole
country by helicopter," he said. "They don't have the
logistical base for something that ambitious."

"Apparently, their first target was al-Khasab Airport." He turned to the satellite map displayed on the plot table, keyed in a set of coordinates on the console, and brought up another satellite map, this one showing the Straits of Hormuz and the north-thrusting spike of the Musand'am peninsula. "Here. Apparently there was a sharp firefight with the militia security troops stationed there, but once they had the airstrip, they could start ferrying troops across on C-130s."

The others studied the map. The Musand'am peninsula resembled a left hand with mangled fingers, held palm up. The fingers were represented by a tangle of four smaller peninsulas, all rugged, mountainous desert, twisting north into the Straits of Hormuz from the end of a single, narrow, S-shaped causeway less than a mile wide; the thumb was blunt and straight. The port of al-Khasab was located at the base of the thumb and fingers, with the single-strip, 2,500-yard runway inland.

"There're only two main roads on the whole peninsula," Drake observed. "Along here, down the middle . . . and over here on the coast." He pointed them out, one a twisting, looping line running south from al-Khasab along ridgetops and crests for over thirty miles before turning west to enter the UAE near Ra's al-Khaymah, and the second hugging the coast counterclockwise from al-Khasab, south through Bukha, and on into the United Arab Emirates at Ash Sha'm. "And that's damned rugged terrain in there. It won't be hard to contain the bastards. All the UAE needs to do is block those two roads."

"Works both ways, sir," Wolfe pointed out. "If they secure the main towns along the Musand'am coastline, it'll be easy for them to keep others from coming in."

"Have they hit the UAE yet?" Drake wanted to know.

"Apparently not," Stewart replied. He nodded at the paper in Drake's hand. "That's all we have so far.

Maybe all they want is the Musand'am peninsula. They might figure that if they have that, they have all they need to completely control the straits."

"They've got to know Washington's not just going to let this pass," Drake said. "Fifth Fleet and CENTCOM are going to come down on them like Desert fucking Storm."

"Maybe. For right now, we need to plan for contingencies. We're less than fifty miles from the Iranian naval air base on Qeshm, and a hundred from Bandar Abbas. If we thought the straits were busy over the past couple of days, it's nothing compared to what it's going to be like now. The whole Iranian navy is going to be concentrated in this area—mostly supporting their invasion, but also looking for us."

"What are you proposing?"

"Every submariner's first line of defense, Commander. We go deep, and we hide."

Straits of Hormuz
1000 hours local time

Knowing that they could not hope to achieve a permanent conventional superiority over either the neighboring Gulf states or the hated American military presence in the area, the Tehran regime had for years focused heavily on nonconventional solutions to their problem—the disparity in reach and in destructive potential between Iran's military forces and those of the West. To that end, and for almost two decades now, they'd made their NBC warfare programs their top priority.

Nuclear, biological, and chemical weapons were truly

the great equalizers of modern warfare. Because of their sensitive nature politically, all nonconventional warfare efforts came under the direction of the IRGC—the Revolutionary Guard—and, therefore of the Council of Guardians and the Supreme Leader.

Despite appalling economic conditions, exacerbated by two and a half decades of trade sanctions imposed by the West, Iran had managed to stockpile several hundred tons of chemical weapons, including nerve, blister, choking, and blood agents. Weaponry included artillery rounds and bombs, as well as short- to medium-range missiles capable of striking targets across the Persian Gulf. Iran had signed and ratified the UN's Chemical Weapons Convention of 1992, a pact that obligated Tehran to destroy its chemical weapons stocks within ten years. Signatory to the treaty or not, Tehran was not about to surrender its strategic deterrent when its old enemy, Iraq, had chemical weapons, and in the 1980s had demonstrated their willingness to use them.

Iran also possessed biological weapons—in particular anthrax and botulin toxin. As with other nation-states that had pursued this research, they faced serious problems in disseminating biological agents. Their options, essentially, were through terrorist saboteurs, through sprays directed from ships or aircraft, or in missile warheads. The technical problems in delivering such warheads, however, were considerable, and no one—including the Iranian military—knew how successful such an attack would be. Despite this, some within the Iranian military felt bacteriological warfare was Iran's best hope if things came to war with the West, a cheap and effective means of potentially inflicting the same kind of casualties as a low-yield nuclear strike, and with no means of protecting against it.

The key ingredient in Iran's deterrent stockpile, of course, was her potential nuclear capability, and the promise of acquiring a workable nuclear device. Most observers believed that Iran was within two years of producing such a weapon, once she acquired the necessary fissionable material.

For some time now Iran had attempted to acquire that material, or the means of producing it. Tehran was also signatory to the Nuclear Nonproliferation Treaty, and had repeatedly pledged that its interest in developing nuclear power was solely to support its efforts to generate electricity for its population and civilian industry.

With its civilian nuclear power program still in a rudimentary state, however, Iran had repeatedly attempted to gain access to the technology that would enable them to build power plants, but which would also give them the ability to build nuclear weapons. During the past decade, Iran had diverted enriched uranium from a poorly guarded facility in Kazakhstan; research reactors from Argentina, India, China, and Russia; full-scale nuclear power plants from Russia and China; gas centrifuge equipment and technology from Germany and Switzerland; a gas centrifuge enrichment plant from Russia; uranium conversion plants from Russia and from China; and a laser enrichment plant from Russia.

All of these attempts were discovered by the West, and all were thwarted by a combination of U.S. diplomatic efforts and political pressure ... all *known* attempts, at any rate. Covert efforts had continued worldwide, and most outside observers believed that Iran had managed to acquire at least small amounts of both plutonium and enriched uranium, enough to build a handful of devices, at least. As far back as 1999 an Iranian student in Sweden had been caught trying to smuggle thyratrons to Iran—complex bits of technology that could have applications to civilian research . . . but were also vital in the manufacture of nuclear triggers.

So far, Pakistan was the world's only nuclear Islamic state, and they were ostensibly, if not publicly, in America's pocket. Iran was determined, at any cost, to develop nuclear weapons technology, and they were very, very close.

They were so close, in fact, that they already had five warheads, though no one outside of a handful of military and government leaders and the technicians themselves knew about it. They'd not advertised the fact, nor had they exploded a device to demonstrate their capability, for several important reasons.

First, when the West became convinced that Iran possessed nukes, they would act. On that, Tehran had no doubt. And they might act before Iran had the chance to develop the *other* vital component of a nuclear weapon besides the warhead itself—a means to deliver it.

Iran possessed a number of potential delivery systems. The background of her missile force consisted of some three hundred Shahab-1 and one hundred Shahab-2 missiles purchased from North Korea; about two hundred CSS-8 missiles from China; and a precious handful of Shahab-3 systems, which had been manufactured in Iran. All of these save the last were short-range missiles similar to the infamous Iraqi Scuds. The Shahab-1 had a range of two hundred miles, the Shahab-2 of just over three hundred, just barely enough to reach across the Gulf at most points. The Chinese missiles had a range of less than a hundred miles, which made them useless for anything but attacks against Iraq or the very closest parts of Oman and the UAE; with a sufficiently powerful warhead, though, the CSS-8 could be used to close the Straits of Hormuz, or to destroy concentrations of U.S. warships off the Iranian coast. The Shahab-3 had a more respectable range of eight hundred miles, which put Israel, eastern Turkey, and most of Saudi Arabia within reach.

In 2004, Iran had successfully tested the Shahab-4, a home-grown intermediate-range ballistic missile with a declared range of 1,200 miles, far enough to strike Israel, most of Turkey, or any part of the Arabian peninsula, and with far greater accuracy than the Shahab-3. Reportedly, they were having technical difficulties with the Shahab-5, which was expected to be an intermediate-range missile capable of hitting targets over 6,200 miles distant; if launched from the northernmost portions of Iran, the Shahab-5 might just reach much of the U.S. eastern seaboard, possibly even Washington, D.C. At the very least, the Shahab-5 could strike any city in Europe . . . which might mean that the United States would stand alone in any future confrontation with Iran.

Throughout the past decade, however, Iran remained dependent on foreign technology—from Russia, China, and especially on North Korea, which alone could supply the actual rocket motor assembly for the Shahab series. That made her vulnerable in the event of war: to blockade, and to being unable to replenish her means of delivery.

Both the planners for Operation Bold Fire and the senior officials within the Tehran government had been divided on the question of whether to wait on the invasion of the Musand'am peninsula until the facility at Darya-ye was complete. If they did wait, Defense Minister Admiral Mehdi Baba-Janzadeh and his supporters had argued, Iran would be in an ideal position to hold the Americans at bay simply by the threat of nuclear, chemical, or bacteriological attack. The Ayatollah

Khamenei and his supporters, however, had pointed out—accurately—that Iraq's perceived NBC capabilities had not deterred either Desert Storm or the American invasion in 2003. Iran's nuclear force could not be expected, therefore, to deter an American invasion of Iran.

In fact, the closer Iran got to being able to deploy weapons of mass destruction, the more likely was a pre-emptive strike by either the United States or, conceivably, by Israel. All remembered well Israel's air strike against the Osirak nuclear reactor in Iraq in 1981.

In the end Khamenei and his people had won the argument . . . in large part because of the failed American penetration of the Darya-ye complex just a few weeks before. Clearly, the Americans suspected the nature of the facility beneath Kuh-e Gab, and they would continue to try to learn its secrets. If Iran actually dared use the weapons stored and assembled there, the Americans *would* retaliate in kind—of that there could be no doubt—and that would be an economic and political disaster for the nation, one which the Tehran government knew it would not survive.

Better, they argued, to launch Bold Fire while relying purely on conventional weapons. If America could be goaded into appearing to be the aggressor, Iran would have a political victory without needing to fire another shot; in fact, there was a better-than-even chance that the Americans would back down entirely. It was an election year in the United States, after all, and the voters were wary of another long and bloody engagement, such as the long-running insurrection by Iraqi Sunni fundamentalists. Give them a bloody nose, and they might pull out. If they fought back, Iran could hold out long enough for the Islamic world to rally to her side.

And there *were* those five warheads at Kuh-e Gab, to

use as an absolute last-ditch resort. Constructed of plutonium acquired from former Soviet military personnel in Kazakhstan and Ukraine, using triggers smuggled in from North Korea and from Pakistan, the mere suspicion that they existed served as *some* measure of deterrence against a U.S. invasion, the warning message of Iraq notwithstanding. And attacking before the special weapons facility was completed gave them a measure of surprise. If the Americans suspected what was under Kuh-e Gab, they would expect Iran to hold its plans until the facility was fully operational.

In fact, Darya-ye was functional, though some of the defensive systems were still being assembled; functional enough that the IRGC could begin the final assembly of at least five weapons delivery systems there.

What they didn't know was that the U.S. Navy SEALs were in the hills three hundred feet above the tunnel entrances to the complex, watching with considerable interest, and reporting everything by satellite to the USGN *Ohio* and to Washington.

Things were coming to a head faster than anyone had realized.

Thursday, 26 June 2008

SEAL Detachment Delta One
OP Tamarind
Above Objective White Scimitar
1345 hours local time

The sun had long ago turned the crumpled flanks of the
Kuh-e Gab into a blazing furnace. During the night
hours, the eight SEALs of Delta One had set up their
OP, literally burrowing into the ridgetop above the military base by scraping shallow trenches into the stony
soil, then stretching camouflaged tarps from pegs two
feet above the ground to create a patch of shade.

It was still damned hot, but the shade and the insulat-
ing effects of the walls of the shallow trenches helped.
Had they waited out the day laying in the direct sunlight,
they swiftly would have succumbed to heat exhaustion
or sunstroke. They moved as little as possible, and drank
as freely as possible from their water stores.

Two SEALs at a time, however, were always on watch, laying side by side at the edge of the tarp shelter, in a position that let them look down both on the tunnel openings directly below and onto the fenced-in military compound three-quarters of a mile down the valley.

In the intense heat of the Gulf in late June, activity in the Kuh-e Gab base had slackened off considerably. Most of the sentries remained inside, or stood in patches of shade cast by buildings or vehicles. Even so, at around noon Tangretti and TM1 Avery were watching through powerful binoculars as a flatbed truck arrived at the main base from the north, escorted by a pair of BMP-2 armored personnel carriers and a truck full of soldiers.

Through their binoculars, they could see a large something on the back of the transport, a roughly cylindrical shape strapped down securely and covered by canvas. The convoy was waved through the main gate, and the flatbed and one of the APCs proceeded up the narrow valley to the tunnel entrances. In a brief flurry of activity, the flatbed was backed into the third tunnel from the left, vanishing inside. After a brief wait, the APC returned down the valley to the main base, and activity at the tunnel complex—at least outside in the sun—returned to the slow and languid pace of midday in the tropical summer.

Tangretti and Avery captured the whole operation through the powerful lenses of a digital video camera. Behind them, connected to the camera by a gray cable, was a sixteen-pound AN/PRC-117F satellite communications unit—affectionately called a "prick"—its separate cruciform antenna set up on a small tripod in the glare of the sunlight outside the tarp shelter. A KY-99 crypto device was hooked up to the prick, providing signal security. The antenna was focused on a military geosync satellite high above the southern horizon, which was relaying the image back down to the *Ohio*'s Combat Center, as well as to watchers in the Pentagon basement, 6,500 miles and eight time zones away.

"What do you think?" Avery asked in a whisper. They were too far from the nearest Iranian troops to be overheard, but SEAL training and long habit are powerful conditioners.

"It's something important."

"A warhead, maybe? It was about the right size for a Sahab nose cone."

"Could've been an air conditioner, for all we know." Tangretti shifted the angle of his binoculars slightly. "Still . . ."

"What?"

"I see four more flatbed trucks down there, exactly like the one that just went inside the mountain."

"I see 'em."

"Tarps and chains lying on the backs, but no cargo loads."

"Five air conditioners?"

"Or something."

The upper end of the valley, just beyond the tunnel entrances where the canyon kinked around from northwest to southwest, was fenced off and guarded, effectively turning it into a part of the main base at the canyon mouth. The four empty flatbeds were parked side by side against this westernmost fence.

"I think we're going to want to have a closer look at those vehicles," Tangretti said.

Thunder rolled overhead. The SEALs glanced up, but then ignored a pair of Iranian MiGs streaking through the cloudless sky from northwest to southeast. Aircraft of various types had been in the sky all day, most of them headed east, toward Bandar Abbas, or southeast, toward the south side of the straits.

Ohio had broadcast the news of Iran's invasion of the Musand'am peninsula early that morning, before alerting the SEALs to the fact that they were going deep—and out of touch. The peninsula lay roughly east-southeast of the SEAL OP, and the Iranian flights no doubt were on their way to continue providing air support for their troops.

Tangretti returned his full attention to the tunnels below. The concrete reinforcement suggested bunkers: thick-walled and well-protected. The soldiers guarding them . . . that was the curious part. They weren't regular Iranian army. Their uniforms were more ragged, less like uniforms than a mix-and-match of cast-off army surplus.

Pasdaran, then, which confirmed what Black Stallion had reported. It also confirmed a key part of SEAL Detachment Delta's premission briefing, back in the States. Iran's unconventional warfare assets—their nuclear, biological, and chemical weaponry—were controlled by the IRGC and not by the army regulars.

A new sound gradually imposed itself on Tangretti's awareness . . . a low clatter approaching from the west.

"Uh-oh," Avery said. "Company."

"Alert the others."

Avery slipped away, backing deeper into the shade of the tarp. Some of the other SEALs would be asleep.

The clatter grew louder. West, through his binoculars, Tangretti could see six dark shapes low above the mountain ridge. Helicopters.

MiGs traveled too high and too fast to have any chance of spotting the SEAL OP on the ridgetop below, but helicopters were something else. Behind him, the rest of Delta One came fully awake and alert, grabbing their weapons. Hutchinson swiftly pulled the satellite communications antenna out of the sunlight and under the tarp.

Moments later the shapes resolved themselves into a flight of Iranian CH-46 transports, the same big, twin-rotored aircraft favored by the U.S. Marines. They were flying in a rough V-formation less than two hundred feet above the mountain, and appeared to be on a course that would take them directly over the SEAL hide.

At the last moment, though, they sheared off, swinging south and out over the steel-blue waters of the Gulf. Brilliant sunlight flashed off Plexiglas canopies and windows. It was not a patrol, then, searching for intruders on the Kuh-e Gab, but another load of soldiers en route to the war zone over northern Oman. Their new course was actually more dangerous for the SEALs than their old, since, at a lower angle, the patch of shadow beneath the tarp was more visible, and a bored-soldier looking out one of the aircraft's windows might see them. After a tense moment, though, the helicopters continued on their new course, evidently having been routed away from the mountain base. The SEALs relaxed back into routine. Richardson and Hutch set up the satcom antenna again, realigning it on the coded signal transmitted by the satellite. Tangretti and Avery went back to watching the sleepy base below.

Patience was one of the SEALs' key weapons. They would wait, and watch.

At least until nightfall.

Control Room, SSGN *Ohio*
Persian Gulf
1420 hours local time

"Periscope depth, Captain," Lieutenant Hanson, the Diving Officer of the Watch, reported.

"Very well. Up scope."

He rode the periscope up as it rose, angling the head straight up to check the surface directly overhead before it even pierced the roof, then circling carefully, taking in everything on the horizon, and checking the sky above as well.

They were in the clear, at least for the moment. "Communications," he said. "Transmit our position."

"Aye aye, sir."

With *Ohio*'s Type 18 scope above water, they were again in satellite communications with the outside world, could take a GPS fix on their precise position, and with the ESM receiver affixed to the mast—the acronym stood for Electronic Support Measures—they could sample the flood of radio and radar signals passing through the air above the waters of the Gulf.

And there was a lot to listen to. Iranian military radar was thick and constant, and the air was crackling with radio calls on military frequencies. Much of it was short-range FM, signals that didn't go beyond the horizon and therefore weren't even encoded. *Ohio*'s communications center quietly recorded everything, uploading it to Washington via satellite as it came through.

Radio waves weren't the only thing coming thick and furious, however. Active sonar pinging was picking up fast, most of it coming from the north. The sonar department had reported heavy search activity all along the Iranian coast, both from submarines and from surface vessels, and the Iranians were making extensive use of air-dropped sonobuoys as well. By plotting all of the active sonar sources on a chart, it became clear that the Iranians were attempting to create a wall of sound all the way from the bight of the Straits of Hormuz to Ra's al Mutaf, halfway up Iran's Gulf coast.

Most of the activity was, of course, focused around

the two points of greatest American interest—Bandar Abbas and the area where the two U.S. patrol boats had been intercepted the previous month, off Bandar-e Charak. Stewart was glad he'd decided to move off into deeper water. There was less search activity out here, and the bottom was deeper, with more room to hide.

Things were going to get dicey, though, when *Ohio* had to move back to the shallows to retrieve the SEALs. Somehow, they were going to have to penetrate that wall of sound without being detected, and that was going to take some doing.

They'd moved thirty miles to the southwest, to a point just north of the island of Abu Musa, a triangular speck of land less than three miles across at its widest point, with scarcely room enough for a single runway and a small port.

This was close to the center of the Gulf's main shipping channel. The water was over two hundred feet deep here—still damned shallow for an Ohio-class boat, but offering better protection than the shallows tucked in close under the lee of Qeshm, where there was barely enough for them to remain submerged.

Bandar-e Charak was over seventy miles to the northwest. Technically, the SEAL ASDS could make it all the way out here for retrieval, but after spending a couple of days close inshore, the minisub's batteries would be running on the electrical equivalent of fumes.

As of the last report, the ASDS had dropped Delta One off near Bandar-e Charak. Those SEALs were at Objective White Scimitar now, carrying out their primary mission. Taggart had then piloted the ASDS farther east along the coast, and put the second SEAL group ashore to check out reports of mobile missile launchers in the vicinity of Bandar-e Lengeh, thirty miles away.

According to the mission track, both SEAL teams

would complete their ops tonight, exfiltrate, and execute retrievals on the ASDS. The SEAL sub would then bring them all back to Waypoint Bravo for pickup, an empty stretch of water fifteen miles off the coast and halfway between Bandar-e Charak and Bandar-e Lengeh.

That pickup point could easily be changed if the tactical situation warranted, but Stewart was determined to get as close to shore for the retrieval as he could. Those SEALs deserved no less, and, if things got hot for them ashore, they were going to need all the help with their travel arrangements he could manage.

He took an extra long time studying Abu Musa through the scope, recording it on 70mm film and giving the electronic warfare boys plenty of eavesdropping time. The Iranians were known to have Chinese Silkworms on the island, and possibly other antishipping assets as well. The island was also a possible flashpoint for a widening of hostilities. So far, all of the fighting appeared to be limited to Iran against the Omanis, but if the United Arab Emirates decided to get involved—or if Iran decided it wanted more than just the tip of the Musand'am peninsula and went after the UAE as well, the UAE might decide to take back the island, which had been snatched from them back in the 1970s.

Still, the bottom dropped off in a steep cliff just north of the island, providing a good hiding area. The only time *Ohio* risked being sighted was, as now, when she had to come to periscope depth to stick her satcom antenna above the surface. Still, those times were few and kept as brief as possible. The chances of their being spotted from the air were—

"Control Room, Sonar."

"Control Room. Go ahead."

"I'm picking up aircraft noises, sir. Close and to the east."

Quickly, Stewart pivoted, bringing the Type 18 around to the left. Nothing on the horizon. He angled the head of the scope up, scanning empty blue sky. . . .

No, *not* empty. Sunlight flashed from a canopy.

"Down scope!" Stewart snapped. "Diving Officer! Take us down! Deep as she'll go!"

He'd only had a glimpse, but he thought it was a Fencer.

And it was damned close . . .

Iranian Su-24
Over the Persian Gulf
1428 hours local time

Sheer luck . . . or, possibly, the munificence of Allah. But that, always, is the way of battle.

Lieutenant Colonel Alireza Tolouei was on his way back to Bandar Abbas, his munitions expended after a long-range strike against the Omani air base at Muscat. His aircraft was a Russian-built Sukhoi-24, a fighter bomber that had carried the NATO designation Fencer since it was first introduced in the early 1970s. Iran had purchased fourteen of the aircraft from the Soviet Union, but this one had come into Iran's inventory by way of Iraq, one of eighteen Su-24s flown across the border by defecting pilots during America's first war with that country. It was a rugged and fairly dependable aircraft with a swing-wing variable geometry similar to that of the U.S. F-111.

A straight-line flight from Oman's capital to Bandar Abbas would have taken him east of the Musand'am peninsula, but Military Air Traffic Control had routed him far to the west, over the Gulf, to avoid heavy helicopter traffic currently operating over the Straits of Hormuz. He was flying north low and slow, a few miles east of Abu Musa, and just happened to be in exactly the right place, with the sun at exactly the right angle.

All he saw was a shadow, a long and very narrow black shape in the water, but he knew instantly what it was—a submarine just beneath the surface.

He also knew it wasn't an Iranian vessel. This thing was a monster, two and a half times longer, at least, than a Kilo attack boat. All Iranian pilots had been briefed to be on the lookout for an American Ohio-class submarine believed to be operating now inside the Straits of Hormuz.

And Tolouei had found it.

His bomb racks were empty, and in any case he'd been carrying munitions designed to crater Omani runways, not sink enemy submarines. Putting the Sukhoi into a sharp left bank, he began to orbit the enemy's position.

"Bandar Abbas Control, Bandar Abbas Control," he called over the radio. "This is Mountain Eagle. I have a sighting. . . ."

Control Room, SSGN *Ohio*
Persian Gulf
1432 hours local time

"Do you think they spotted us?" Shea asked, looking up at the control room overhead as though to see through steel and water and up to a threatening sky.

"I don't know," Stewart replied. "No torpedoes in the water yet."

"They might not have been loaded for ASW work."

"No. Probably wasn't, in fact, if it was a Fencer . . . and I think it was. It was in a tight left bank, and the wings were extended."

"Swing wings," Shea said, nodding.

"Yup. But he was swinging around and heading our way. He might have spotted us, if the sun angle was right. We have to assume he did."

"Right."

"Helm . . . come right to three-zero-zero."

"Helm, come right to three-zero-zero, aye."

"Mr. Kelly, what's the depth beneath our keel?"

"We're scraping barnacles, Captain. The bottom is dropping, but we only have about three fathoms to spare."

"Follow the bottom down. Our friend topside could have an ASW helo overhead inside of five minutes. I want to be lost by that time."

"Aye aye, sir."

"Sonar! This is the captain."

"Sonar, aye aye, sir."

"Stay especially sharp. We may have company any time now."

"Aye aye, sir. Uh . . . you should know, though, that the background pinging is washing everything out."

Stewart understood. The splash of a torpedo or a so-nobuoy hitting the water, the soft beat of a diesel-electric sub in stealth mode, the sound of an aircraft overhead—those were all remarkably subtle sounds, tough to pull from the background clutter under the best conditions. With all of the sonar banging away in the distance, it was like trying to hear a coin drop with the stereo speakers cranked up to the max. It was amazing the sonar boys had picked up that Fencer.

If the Iranians had one of their submarines out there,

there'd be very little chance of hearing it, unless it went active.

And by then it might well be too late.

**Communications Center,
Office of the Ministry of Defense
Tehran, Iran
1450 hours local time**

"Sir!" The naval aide was excited. "We've located the American Ohio submarine, sir."

Admiral Baba-Janzadeh turned, gesturing toward the large chart unrolled on a table nearby. "Show me."

"Yes, sir. One of our fighter-bombers spotted a shadow in the water . . . just here." The aide pointed, indicating a spot five miles north of Abu Musa.

Out in the middle of the shipping channel. Interesting. That was farther out than he'd expected. If the quarry was one of the new ballistic missile submarine conversions, it should have been much closer inshore, the better to drop off and recover naval commandos.

"Does our plane still have the enemy in sight?"

"No, sir. He reported it was already going deeper when he spotted it, but we have a course, and the pilot's report that it was moving very slowly. We have naval ASW aircraft en route now."

General Ramezani, his chief of staff, cleared his throat. "Sir. The *Tareq* is on patrol less than twenty kilometers from this location." He pointed to another spot on the map, to the northeast. "We could have Captain Jalali plot an intercept course. Ring this area with sonobuoys, and we have him."

Tareq was the first of the Kilo submarines purchased

from the Russians: hull number 901. Jalali was experienced, one of the best of Iran's submarine skippers. Baba-Janzadeh nodded agreement. "Transmit the orders."

"Yes, sir."

"Admiral," one of the other staff officers said. "That is in international waters. We were ordered to find and trap the American inside our territorial waters."

"That no longer matters. With Bold Fire now under way, we can claim an accident of war, if necessary. However . . . have you forgotten that Abu Musa is Iranian territory?"

"Uh, no, sir. Of course not."

"Of course not. The lawyers can argue about lines on the map, but the rest of the world—the Islamic world—will know that we discovered and destroyed an American nuclear submarine just a few kilometers off of our coast. The Guardian Council will have their excuse for a full-scale confrontation with the Americans."

"Yes, sir."

"But we must not let them slip through the net again! I want the American found. I want him destroyed. Clear?"

"Clear, Admiral!"

"Good. Make it clear to our people in the operational area as well."

"Yes, sir. At once."

Baba-Janzadeh turned his attention back to the chart, where an aide was marking the position of the sighting, and drawing a straight line toward the northwest, indicating its last known heading.

The fact that the enemy vessel was there, almost fifty miles from the mainland and over seventy from the sensitive area near Bandar-e Charak . . . what did it mean? That the Americans had not been able to get close enough to send in their commandos? Or that they had already done so? Abu Musa was a good point from which an American submarine could conduct electronic surveillance of the air, sea, and land Omani operations. But had they put their special operations commandos ashore? If they had, were the commandos still in Iran, or had they been retrieved already?

And . . . if the Americans knew the key details about the secret beneath Kuh-e Gab, what were they prepared to do about it?

A very great deal was riding on the answers to those questions.

Sonar Room, SSGN *Ohio*
Persian Gulf
1532 hours local time

Caswell was pretty well fried. Emotional stress had taken its toll, and, in some ways, his talk with the COB had made things worse. He was no longer actively contemplating suicide, but with that option slammed shut, he felt more trapped than before. It was as though there was literally no place to go, nothing to do, to escape the intolerable pain.

Ohio's duty schedule was adding to the stress. Six hours on, twelve off . . . except that he'd been standing extra shifts when the boat was under high alert. Then rules said he was supposed to get eight hours sleep, but for days now sleep had been impossible. Doc Kettering had offered him something to help him sleep, but he had refused. He needed a clear head.

Which, of course, he didn't have to begin with. Dobbs had picked up the sound of that approaching aircraft.

Caswell knew he'd screwed up again, and it could have been a bad one.

Damn but the hash was loud outside! He could hear an almost constant barrage of chirps and cheeps, echoing and reechoing across the shallow waters of the Gulf. How the hell was he supposed to hear—

Ping!

The sonar pulse was loud, loud and *close,* coming literally out of nowhere. "Control Room, Sonar!" he yelled, mashing down the intercom switch. "Active sonar transmission, bearing zero-five-five, range . . . range less than two thousand yards!"

"Acknowledged."

Ping! Ping!

The barrage of sound was so loud now you didn't need earphones to hear it ringing against the hull. "Control Room . . . he's locked on to us!"

And, despite the noise, Caswell heard what was just possibly the most ominous sound a submariner could hear and recognize.

It was the grating broadband squeak of the outer doors to the torpedo tubes on another submarine as they slid open.

Thursday, 26 June 2008

Control Room, SSK _Tareq_
Persian Gulf
1533 hours local time

Captain Mehdi Jalali brought his fist down hard on the plot table. "Fire torpedo number one!"

A sharp hiss . . . and the deck lurched as the torpedo was ejected from _Tareq_'s forward tubes by a blast of compressed air, momentarily interfering with the vessel's trim.

"Torpedo one fired electrically, sir!"

"Fire number two!"

"Torpedo two fired electrically, sir!"

"Fire number three!"

"Torpedo three fired electrically, sir!"

Jalali looked at the clock on the bulkhead, noting the position of the sweep second hand. Range to target was 1,800 meters . . . one and a half minutes, close enough.

He would have liked to have gotten in closer before firing, but his first active sonar pulse had returned a target—good, strong, and close. He hadn't expected to find himself with the enemy already squarely in his sights, Allah be praised. He would have been foolish to wait, hoping for a better solution, especially when the American now knew *Tareq* was here, and exactly where she was.

Three torpedoes to sink one submarine was probably excessive, Jalali thought . . . but then, this was an exceptional target. Ohio-class subs were big, and one 533mm torpedo might not be enough.

And he was well aware that he might not get a second chance.

"All torpedoes running normally," the weapons officer announced. "Allah be praised!"

Allah be praised indeed . . . when the warheads found their mark.

Control Room, SSGN *Ohio*
Persian Gulf
1533 hours local time

"Torpedoes in the water, Captain!" came the urgent call from Sonar. "Two . . . no, now *three* torpedoes! Range eighteen hundred yards!"

"Snapshot!" Stewart yelled. "Sierra Three-one-one!"

Ohio never went on patrol with fewer than two of her four tubes loaded and ready to fire at all times, and since entering the Gulf, Stewart had ordered four warshots loaded. Boomers weren't expected to use their torpedoes; their weapons were twenty-four MIRVed Trident ICBMs, and if the boat had to fire a torpedo, it was because an enemy hunter-killer sub had found them, and because their mission—to remain undetected and serve as a deterrent—had failed. In her new role as an SSGN, the *Ohio*'s operational envelope left a lot more leeway. She was still expected to remain undetected, especially when carrying out a clandestine insertion op along an enemy coast. However, the very fact that she did have to approach that coast meant she was a lot more vulnerable. Firing in self-defense was a lot more likely now.

A "snapshot" was just that, a quick, return shot fired without aiming. The idea was to loose one of the ready torpedoes as quickly as the tube could be flooded and the outer door opened, getting it off and running. If the incoming enemy torpedoes destroyed the *Ohio,* at least there was a chance that the American submarine would take her killer down with her.

"Torpedo tube three fired, Captain," the weapons officer announced. "Running hot, straight, and normal." A pause. "Torpedo three has acquired the target, Captain."

"Cut the wire, Lieutenant. Helm! Hard left rudder! Maneuvering, ahead full!"

"Torpedo three is running free, sir."

"Helm, hard left rudder, aye aye!"

"Control Room, Maneuvering. Ahead full, aye!"

Stewart felt the building power trembling through the deck as *Ohio* accelerated into a turn. He grabbed hold of the edge of the plot table to stay upright. The deck was canting beneath his feet.

This was why the helmsman and planesman stations actually had seat belts, though they usually weren't needed on boomers. Normally, submarine maneuvers were gentle enough, but high-speed combat maneuvers were something else entirely. Stewart heard a loud crash from somewhere forward as some piece of unsecured gear flew loose and struck the deck.

The hell of it was that the water here was just too shallow to allow any real maneuvering. With so little third dimension to work with, the *Ohio* might as well have been a skimmer, stuck on the roof. Her single available weapon now was speed, to literally outrun the oncoming torpedoes. Soviet-made 533mm torpedoes could travel at 35 knots, while the *Ohio* could manage 25 or a bit more. That meant that the torpedoes, now 1,500 yards astern, were closing with a relative velocity of ten knots.

Ohio had just extended her remaining time to four and a half minutes.

The problem, though, was that the torpedoes had a range of eight nautical miles, and could travel for twelve minutes.

They would reach *Ohio* a good seven to eight minutes before they ran out of fuel.

Control Room, SSK *Tareq*
Persian Gulf
1534 hours local time

"Captain! One enemy torpedo is running! It has not yet acquired us!"

"Cut the wires," Jalali ordered. All three of *Tareq*'s torpedoes had locks on the American vessel. They no longer needed to be guided by wire. "Helm! Come right to zero-one-zero degrees! Maneuvering! Ahead flank!"

The *Tareq* began picking up speed, turning away from the oncoming American torpedo.

Control Room, SSGN _Ohio_
Persian Gulf
1535 hours local time

"Control Room, Sonar. Range to nearest torpedo . . . seven hundred yards."

Stewart did a fast calculation in his head. Seven hundred yards with a closing rate of ten knots meant a minute and forty-eight seconds.

"Tell me when the range is five hundred yards," he said.

"Aye aye, sir."

Stewart looked at the chart showing _Ohio_'s current position. There was Abu Musa, just five miles to the south.

When you looked at the bottom topography, however, Abu Musa was revealed as the top of a mountain, with a large plateau—the shallows along the Saudi Arabian landmass—extending off to the south. On the north side, directly ahead, the side of that mountain plunged from the highest peak on Abu Musa—a rocky crest called Jabal Halwa, a hundred feet above sea level—to the sea floor some 250 feet below. The slope was fairly steep, more cliffside in places than hill.

And the _Ohio_ was racing directly toward that cliff now at 25 knots. At that speed, they would reach the flank of the underwater mountain at just about the same time the torpedoes caught up with them.

It was going to be damned tight. . . .

The next minute crawled past at an agonizing pace.

The sea floor, as revealed by _Ohio_'s BQR 19 navigation sonar, was rising rapidly to meet the fast-moving submarine's keel. The sub was at a terrible handicap. The shoaling water now was less than 120 feet deep, but the *Ohio* herself was almost eighty feet tall, from keel to the top of her fair-water.

"Captain!" the dive officer shouted. "We're breaching!"

"Can't be helped," he shouted back. If he could make them *fly* to escape those fish, he would. "Control Room, Sonar! Range five hundred yards!"

"Release countermeasures!"

It might buy them another few precious moments. . . .

SSGN *Ohio*
Persian Gulf
1536 hours local time

A pair of cylinders fired from launch tubes in *Ohio*'s flanks slowed, then exploded into clouds of bubbles. In seconds the torpedoes' sonar locks were broken as, from their perspective, their target vanished behind a large and fuzzy wall of sonar returns.

Moments later the first torpedo punched through the bubble wall. *Ohio* was already turning, swinging sharply to the right and pulling clear of the torpedo's cone acquisition zone—the cone-shaped space in front of it in which the torpedo could "see." Lock broken, the torpedo continued chirping, seeking a new target.

Seconds later it found one, closed the range at forty knots, and struck. . . .

Control Room, SSGN *Ohio*
Persian Gulf
1537 hours local time

The thunderous roar of the explosion rang through
the hull. A second later the submarine rolled hard to
the right, tipping farther . . . farther . . . until note-
books, pencils, coffee mugs, and unsecured gear
crashed to the deck . . . and still farther as men
grabbed hold of chairs or consoles or anything else
anchored down to keep from falling into the starboard
bulkhead.

And then *Ohio* rolled back, righting herself. Several
men gave brief, heartfelt cheers, but quieted immediately. One torpedo was down—detonating against an
underwater cliff. But there were two more still coming.

Stewart felt the telltale shift and lurch of a submarine
moving at speed on the surface. Submerged, submarines felt nothing of the wave action on the roof unless
they were very close to surfacing. Once surfaced, they
felt the effects of wind and wave the same as any other
ship.

"Helm! Keep us in the turn," Stewart ordered. "Bring
us around to . . . make it zero-three-zero!"

"Make course zero-three-zero, aye aye!"

"Diving Officer! We're naked! Get us back where we
belong!"

"Yes, *sir!*"

"Make depth one hundred feet!"

"Make depth one-zero-zero feet, aye aye!"

Stewart locked glances with Shea. "We're violating
our first order."

" 'Remain undetected.' I kind of got that, sir."

"Sonar! Where's that next torpedo!"

"The second torpedo has not reacquired, Captain. It's hunting. . . ."

It would have been programmed to begin turning in circles, looking for the target it had lost. The question of the moment was which way it would turn. If it swung right, it might very well reacquire the *Ohio* on its first pass. If it swung left, toward the island . . .

A second massive thud sounded through sea and hull metal, this one more distant.

"Captain, Sonar! Second torpedo has detonated."

"Acknowledged!"

"What about the third?" Shea asked.

"It was trailing the other two," Stewart replied. "It might not have lost us in the decoy."

"Captain, Sonar! Third torpedo is still locked! Range four hundred!"

"Release countermeasures!"

"Countermeasures deployed, sir!"

Ohio had now completed a full half-circle, and was moving to the north-northeast, away from the island and toward the Iranian Kilo.

"Come right to zero-eight-five!"

"Come right to course zero-eight-five, aye aye, sir."

Shea looked at Stewart. "You're trying to get inside his turn."

"Might work."

"Control, Sonar! Range two hundred!"

"Then again," Stewart said.

They could hear the shrill hum of the torpedo as it closed the gap.

Control Room, SSK *Tareq*
Persian Gulf
1537 hours local time

"Countermeasures!" Jalali yelled. "Now!"

"Countermeasures released, Captain!"

"Hard left helm! Bring her around!"

Sweat dripped down Jalali's face and drenched his uniform. *It's just the wet air,* he told himself. These Russian diesel subs were cramped, hot, and wet. There was always condensation everywhere, and the humidity on board often was so high it was impossible *not* to sweat as badly as the pipes, metal surfaces, and bulkheads themselves.

But he looked at the tight, pale faces around him, the wide eyes staring at the aft bulkhead.

No, this time it wasn't just the humidity.

Moments before, the entire crew had erupted in cheers as the rumble of an explosion reached them. A hit! Perhaps a kill!

But then the sonar officer had reported transient noises. It sounded as though the American was surfacing. He was damaged, perhaps, damaged and surfacing to put off the crew.

But the sonar picture was murky, and it was hard to make any sense out of what they were hearing.

But then they heard something they understood only too well—the high-pitched chirp of an enemy torpedo acquiring them and bearing in for the kill.

"What are you doing, Captain?" It was Bavafa, the cleric, a painfully thin, oily man with the look of an ascetic . . . or a fanatic.

"Foxing the American torpedo," he told him. "Or trying to."

"How?"

"By giving it something else to lock onto, at least for a moment. While it chases our decoy, we change course and slip away."

"Captain! Enemy torpedo has lost its lock!"

"Well done!" Bavafa said, face creasing in a smile.

"Don't count your blessings yet, holy man. We're not out of this yet."

The Kilo possessed an important advantage over the huge American vessel in its superior maneuverability. It wasn't as fast as the *Ohio*, but it could easily turn well inside the radius of the much faster torpedo, forcing the torpedo to make a long, wide swing around in a circle to reacquire if it missed.

"The enemy torpedo is circling. It has not reacquired. . . ."

Seconds passed.

"Sonar!" Jalali said. "Go active. I want to know what happened to the American!"

"Captain, the American is destroyed, surely!" Bavafa said. "We heard the explosions!"

"One thing you learn as a submariner, cleric," Jalali told him. "Take *nothing* for granted."

Ping!

"Captain!" the sonar officer cried. "The American! He's directly ahead! Bearing two-zero-four, range one thousand, speed twenty-five knots!"

So . . . not damaged after all, and certainly not destroyed.

"He's passing us off the port bow, Captain! Turning away . . . he's turning away from us!"

A chance to fire another shot, and take him at point-blank range. "Ready torpedo tubes four, five, and six!"

"Tubes four, five, and six are ready to fire, Captain!"

"Captain! Sonar! Incoming torpedo, dead ahead!"

"Idiot! The torpedo is astern of us, not in front!"

"No, sir! It's *our* torpedo, coming back at us!"

The tactical picture dropped into place for Jalali at that instant. The last of his three torpedoes had missed the American, who'd evidently pulled the same inside-turn maneuver he'd been attempting with the *Tareq*. Decoyed a second time, *Tareq*'s torpedo had missed the *Ohio*, begun searching for its lost target, and acquired . . . the *Tareq*.

"*Do something, Captain!*" Bavafa screamed.

"Do?" He could already hear the whine of the torpedo coming closer. "There is nothing to do, cleric, but pray."

The explosion hurled both men across the deck, slamming them into the weapons console as the port side of the control room opened to the sea. For a thunderous instant men shrieked and struggled and died.

And there was only the sound of water flooding *Tareq*'s crew spaces, as the Iranian submarine nosed into the soft bottom.

Control Room, SSGN *Ohio*
Persian Gulf
1538 hours local time

"Captain, Sonar. I'm getting breakup and flooding noises. We got him!"

"Where's our other fish? I don't want to score an own-goal like our friend out there just did."

"It's gone silent, sir. Must've run out of fuel." American torpedoes were set to flood and sink when they ran out of fuel, so as not to pose a hazard to surface ships.

Stewart allowed himself a long, slow, and somewhat shaky breath. Ohio boats simply were not designed to pull off maneuvers like an SSN. And yet, somehow, *Ohio* had pulled it off . . . and in water no deeper than a bathtub.

"Okay, gentlemen," he said, speaking into an utterly silent compartment. "It's not over. Not by a long shot. Diving Officer, take us as deep as we've got. Maneuvering, slow to one-third."

"Maneuvering, slow to one-third, aye, sir."

"Making depth one-zero-five feet, sir."

"Very well." He looked at Shea. "You can breathe again, Wayne," he told his XO.

"My God, Captain. You handled her like an attack boat!"

"And for our next trick," Stewart said, "we go north. We have some SEALs up there who are counting on us."

"Yes, sir!"

SEAL Detachment Delta One
OP Tamarind
Above Objective White Scimitar
2212 hours local time

They would conduct the recon in two groups of four. Tangretti, Hutchinson, Avery, and Hobarth would carry out the actual descent and infiltration; Mayhew, Richardson, Olivetti, and Wilson would remain at the top of the cliff as the tactical reserve, and maintain the satellite link with the ASDS and with Washington.

They'd found a stretch of canyon wall around the bend in the valley above the tunnel entrances, a steeply descending slope with one vertical descent, a forty-foot drop. After carefully scoping the area out through their

NVGs, they secured four rappelling lines at the top of the cliff, checked climbing gloves, harnesses, and equipment, then backed over the edge, bouncing lightly down the face of the canyon wall in long, easy bounds.

At the bottom, Tangretti let Mayhew know they were all down safely over his M-biter. That was SEAL slang for the AN/PRC-148 (V) Maritime MultiBand Inter/Intra Team Radio—or MBITR for short—a 2.7 pound tactical radio each man wore attached to his combat harness.

"Delta One-one, One-two," he whispered into the needle mike beside his lips. "Down, set, and good to go."

"Copy, One-two. Good luck."

The descent lines were drawn up the cliff face by the men waiting above. There was no sense in risking having them discovered by a passing Iranian patrol.

They'd actually given thought to making their descent *inside* the complex fence. The Iranians had fenced off both ends of the valley, but not bothered with the sheer rock walls to either side. During the daylight hours, the SEALs had watched as several patrols went past along the canyon rim, several on foot and one by helicopter. None had noticed, however, the small and carefully camouflaged SEAL hide.

In any case, the canyon walls inside the base perimeter were sure to be more carefully watched than those outside, possibly by men using infrared or low-light goggles, or by electronic surveillance through cameras or more subtle technological means.

And so Tangretti's One-two descended to the canyon floor two hundred yards west of the fence, then made their way back along the canyon wall, moving slowly, quietly, and remaining blended with the shadows.

The pole lights inside the fence provided more than

enough of a glow for them to navigate using their NVGs. Those lights also guaranteed a bonus; sentries inside the fence or close by it outside would not be dark-adapted. It would be that much harder to see four night-black shadows moving silently through the darkness.

When they reached the fence, they moved north along the outside, crossing the valley until they were about twenty yards from the four flatbed trucks parked inside the wire. After checking to be sure the chain-link fence itself wasn't wired, Hutch used a set of wire cutters to carefully snip open an entryway, a triangle-shaped flap that he left connected along one side. With the improvised gate open, the four SEALs crawled inside, and Avery wired the flap shut behind them, using short lengths of silver wire.

"One-one, One-two," Tangretti whispered. "We're in."

"Copy."

They crawled flat on their bellies, two at a time, across a patch of open but deeply shadowed ground. As Tangretti and Avery neared the trucks, however, he froze, raising a fist to signal a halt. He could hear boots crunching gravel just ahead.

The Pasdaran sentry rounded the back of the nearest flatbed, an AK-47 slung carelessly over his shoulder. He walked past the SEALs within ten feet of them, stopped, looked around, and then began fishing inside the front of his trousers. In another moment he was urinating against a slab of rock leaning against the north wall of the canyon, whistling tunelessly.

Tangretti and Avery lay motionless, flat on the ground; in the dark, the human eye sees movement before it can make out shapes, and so far the Iranian soldier hadn't seen them. In another moment the man refastened his trousers, turned, and walked back toward the nearest tunnel entrance, about fifteen yards away.

Gradually, Tangretti made himself relax, then continue crawling. The two SEALs reached the flatbed, crouching in the shadows, as Hutch and Richardson joined them.

Avery pulled a Geiger counter from an equipment pouch and swept the wand along the side of the truck. The instrument had been designed for covert ops such as this one—in this business, you never knew when you were going to be surreptitiously searching for traces of nuclear material—and it was silent, without the irritating clacking sound made popular by the movies.

"Okay, guys," Avery whispered over the tactical channel. "I've got a positive."

"Copy that," Mayhew said over the SEALs' headset receivers. "How strong?"

"Just a trace. But they've been moving *something* nasty around on this truck."

After carefully recording the readings taken from a complete sweep of the back of the truck, Avery and Hutch moved on to the next vehicle. Tangretti and Richardson used strips of duct tape, pressing them down at different points on the back of the truck, then lifting them, rolling them up, and transferring them to small, watertight plastic tubes. The nature of the trace radioactivity could be determined in a radiation lab stateside. Traces of plutonium dust, for example, would adhere to the tape and be detectable later, as would alpha particles; beta or gamma radiation would leave no source particles, however, but might contaminate dirt or specks of metal lying on the flatbed. By analyzing the strips of tape in the lab, looking for types of radiation and the nature of any particles adhering to them, the NEST birds—the

Nuclear Emergency Search Team scientists—would be able to make a very good guess at just what those trucks had been transporting, and when.

The fact that there was radiation was a lucky break, Tangretti thought as he sealed his first specimen container and stowed it in a pouch. If the Iranians had been more careful, they'd have stowed the material securely in a lead container, and no amount of duct tape in the world would have picked anything up. The likeliest scenario was that they'd assembled nuclear warheads somewhere else, then shipped the warheads here on the trucks. With a bit of sloppy technique, traces of radioactive material might have been smeared on the outside of the warheads, then transferred to the trucks during the ride.

Tangretti and the others had been assured during their briefing stateside that any radiation they encountered on this op would be very low level—as much, perhaps, as they would get in a chest X ray—and would not be hazardous. He tried not to think about the fact that exactly how much radioactivity was lingering on the outside of the warheads depended almost entirely on how careful the Iranian missile technicians had been in assembling them. There was a good chance that the warheads weren't actually atomic bombs, but were instead "dirty bombs" using conventional explosives to scatter a cloud of plutonium dust. Such a bomb could contaminate much of a city and cause thousands of deaths through cancer—a true terror weapon. If that was what they were dealing with here, all bets were off. Plutonium was the single most toxic substance known to man, and a microgram could kill you.

Tangretti was very careful in how he handled the tape, and he planned to dispose of his black combat gloves just as soon as he had the chance.

For the next hour the four SEALs continued their covert reconnaissance. They took samples and readings off all of the trucks, as well as from a couple of jeeps and a covered four-by-four parked nearby. They examined several of the tunnel entrances, verifying the thickness of the steel doors—and the fact that the Iranians tended to leave those doors open. They took photographs with a digital camera, transmitting each image as they snapped it back to Mayhew, who routed them on up to the satellite and back to Washington. And they took careful GPS readings at the tunnel entrances, relaying that data back as well.

Three more times they froze in position as Iranians wandered past, including one with a large, black German shepherd on a leash. The dog caught their scent and barked; its handler cuffed the animal and forced it to keep going.

So much for high security in a top-secret nuclear storage facility.

Finally, the four SEALs made their way back to the opening in the fence, unwired it, slipped through, and wired it tightly shut behind them once more. Half an hour later they were climbing the lines lowered by their teammates at the top of the canyon rim.

This, Tangretti thought, was the ideal SEAL mission. Somehow, the Hollywood version always seemed to end in gunfire and mayhem, but a totally successful sneak-and-peek like this one had the operators slipping into the objective, doing their job, and slipping out again, all without being detected by the enemy. Even quietly killing a sentry would have compromised the mission, since the chances were good that the man's body would be found, and the Iranians would know *someone* had been inside their base.

All that remained now was for the team to exfiltrate

the area, link up with the ASDS offshore, and then get back to the relative security of the *Ohio*. According to the last report they'd had, *Ohio* had given ASW forces the slip and would be at Waypoint Bravo as planned.

As planned. Tangretti felt an unpleasant twinge at that, a foreboding, more superstitious than anything else. So far the op had gone perfectly. They'd gotten where they were supposed to be and done what they were supposed to do.

But there was still that old military maxim about no plan surviving contact with the enemy.

There was still plenty of room for something to go terribly, terribly wrong.

Friday, 27 June 2008

Combat Center, SSGN *Ohio*
Persian Gulf
0120 hours local time

"Good morning, Commander," Stewart said as Lieutenant Commander Hawking entered the Combat Center.

"Thank you, sir. Is that what it is?" He looked at his watch. "Morning?"

"It is indeed. Did we get you up?"

"I was racked out, yes, sir. You know, this six on, twelve off, shit sucks. Sir." He looked at Stewart, then at the two SEAL officers with him. "On the other hand, you guys look like you don't sleep. Ever."

"It seems that way sometimes, Commander. How are you doing?"

"I'm still a nonqual puke, sir, if that's what you're asking." He shook his head with a wry and lopsided

314

grin. "I had no idea there was this much to driving a sewer pipe underwater."

"Not what I meant. How would you feel about driving your *Manta*?"

Stewart saw the flash of excitement in the young man's eyes.

"Sir! Ready, willing, and able, *sir*!"

"Have a look at this." He gestured, inviting Hawking to examine the chart now on the plot table. A blue line running south to north marked *Ohio*'s movement during the past several hours, and her current position—eighteen miles southwest of the island of Jazireh-ye Forur, and forty due south of Bander-e Charak.

Two islands guarded the approaches to Charak Bay. The larger one, to the northwest, was Jazireh-ye Qeys, nine miles wide, east to west, and crowded with military bases, missile batteries, and an airstrip. The smaller, Jazireh-ye Forur, measured less than five miles wide, north to south, and appeared uninhabited—a barren, volcanic lump of rock. The opening between the two measured about thirty miles.

Marked across the northern half of the chart were dozens of symbols and notations in red—small diamonds marking sonobuoys, and lines, circles, and rectangles indicating the probable positions and courses of ships or submarines using active sonar. The red symbols formed a curved wall all the way from Ras-e Nay Band, a cape 112 miles west of Bandar-e Charak, to Hormoz Island, 160 miles east of the port. Another heavy area of active sonar activity was the north-south corridor between Qeshm Island, outside of Bandar Abbas, and the Musand'am peninsula.

"This," Stewart said, sweeping his hand along the curved forest of red symbols, "is our problem. We have to get here." His forefinger came down on a patch of sea a few miles east of Jazireh-ye Qeys. "Waypoint Bravo, where we're supposed to pick up the ASDS later this morning. The Iranians have this whole stretch of coast—and *especially* Charak Bay, here—covered with active sonar. There's no way we can sneak in there without being spotted."

"What is it you want me to do? I can't pick them up."

"No, but you can clear the way for us a bit. We can put that speed of yours to good use. This contact—Sierra Three-six-one—and this one—Sierra Three-seven-three—are, we believe, Iranian submarines put there specifically to run us down once we're spotted. These here are probably sonobuoys. This one in close to the beach, we think, is an Iranian ASW patrol boat. I'm wondering if it's possible for you to zigzag in ahead of the *Ohio*. Make a lot of noise . . . over here, say . . . and then get the hell out before they get too close. They're expecting an ex-boomer with a top speed of twenty-five knots, not an underwater speedboat going at a hundred. I'm thinking, when they hear you on their passive receivers, they're going to try to close with you. If you pull them out of position, we can exploit the holes they leave in their defensive perimeter, slip in, and grab our SEALs. What do you think?"

"My God," Hawking said. "That's beautiful! Yeah, I can do that. One problem, though . . ."

"Yes?"

"There's going to be a lot of active sonar banging away in here, even after their ships and subs move. They'll still see you, no matter what I do."

"Probably. We're counting on the fact that when they hear you and that wonder sub of yours, they're going to be so confused they won't be coordinating real well."

"I see."

"There *is* a risk," Stewart went on. "If I was their fleet admiral, I'd hold some assets back, maybe in the lee of one of these islands here, active sonar off, or ASW aircraft, but patched in on this sonobuoy line, as a second line of defense. Let the noisy ones go chasing shadows. They're still in place, locked and loaded, if the shadows turn out to be a decoy."

Hawking grinned. "I doubt you have to worry about that, Captain. These boys don't seem to be all that bright."

"Mister, if there's anything I've learned as a sub driver, it's to not underestimate the enemy. We damned near got nailed yesterday afternoon by a Sukhoi and a Kilo working in tandem. You assume the other guy is at *least* as smart as you are and plan accordingly. If you don't, your loved ones are going to be getting a very unhappy telegram in the near future. You read me?"

"Yes, Captain. Loud and clear."

"Good. How long before you can launch?"

"By the book, prelaunch is a couple of hours. But I can give you a special deal."

"How special?"

"One hour from when you give the word."

"You've got it. And now . . . the specifics . . ."

They began making detailed plans, seeking to anticipate each possible contingency.

But anticipating every possible problem, Stewart thought, was impossible. War, by its nature, was so chaotic, there was no way to foresee every detail.

But they had to try.

XSSF-1 *Manta*
Persian Gulf
0310 hours local time

Lieutenant Commander Hawking kept his speed down to about thirty knots as he pulled away from the *Ohio*. He didn't want to make so much racket in *Ohio*'s immediate vicinity that he attracted the attention of Iranian sonar operators to the American vessel. That wouldn't do at all.

But once he was a mile away, he began easing the throttle open, accelerating through black water at sixty knots . . . then seventy. Punching a hole through the water at that speed made noise, a lot of it, no matter how streamlined the vessel. There could be no doubt that the Iranians were hearing him . . . and probably scratching their heads as they wondered just what the hell he was.

The water around him was completely black, a light-less void surrendering no information. He had to rely on the *Manta*'s on-board sonar . . . but there was a problem with that, too. As with larger submarines, when the fighter sub was moving at speeds much above twelve knots or so, passive sonar was largely useless. The rush of water past the hydrophones drowned out every other sound in the vicinity.

His *Manta*'s hydrophones were picking up the loud-est of the active sonar pings, however. Sierra Three-seven-three was chirping away madly at a bearing of three-zero-one degrees.

Accelerating, he eased his control stick over and headed toward the Iranian sub.

SEAL Detachment Delta One
Beach east of Bandar-e Charak
0335 hours local time

The eastern sky, beyond the low, rocky hills, was showing the first faint, faint trace of a promise of dawn as the SEALs splashed wearily down the stream flowing into the Gulf close by the village of Bandar-e Charak. There were no lights on in the town, but Tangretti could see the running lights of a small ship—a patrol boat, possibly—on the south horizon.

Their exfil so far had gone without incident. Twice during the withdrawal—once up in the Kuh-e Gab, and again on the desert plain between Bandar-e Charak and the main Pasdaran base—they'd gone to ground to wait out Iranian patrols sweeping through the night. Neither enemy group appeared to be equipped with NVGs, which gave the SEALs a tremendous advantage. They remained motionless and silent as the patrols passed . . . once within a scant four feet of Tangretti's position.

The SEALs clambered out of the muck and across the low sand spit that had built up along the mouth of the stream where it entered the sea. A careful check showed the beach empty, so they began moving east along the spit, making for a clump of low, scraggly date palms that marked the hiding place of their CRRCs.

They found them, apparently undiscovered and undisturbed. As Avery and Hutch began pulling them out of their hide, the other SEALs took up perimeter defense positions, watching the surrounding night. Mayhew squatted on top of the sand dune, looking out to sea.

"Sierra Delta, this is Delta One. Sierra Delta, Delta One. Do you copy, over?"

"Delta One, this is Sierra Delta," Taggart's welcome voice responded in their headsets. "I read you."

Tangretti was startled by the quickness of the response. Taggart was supposed to be waiting with his radio mast above water, listening for the Team's arrival on the beach, but the presence of Iranian forces could easily have driven him back into deeper water. Had that been the case, he would have moved back to the surface every half hour.

Evidently, Taggart had decided not to let a little thing like an Iranian patrol boat keep him underwater.

"Sierra Delta, we're on the beach and moving to pickup. Three-zero mikes. Over."

"Copy that, Delta One. Three-zero minutes. We'll be there."

Hobarth and Wilson held their position as rear security element while the two rubber ducks were manhandled into the water. The other SEALs helped drag them off the shelf, then held them against the lap of the waves as the last two SEALs splashed off the beach and clambered aboard. The electric outboards were fired up, and the two SEAL CRRCs began quietly moving out to sea.

Tangretti gave the beach a last worried scrutiny. Things had gone so well, he more than half expected to see a Pasdaran patrol trotting across the sand spit after them.

But the night remained empty.

"I think we got away with it, Chief," Mayhew said.

"Seems that way, sir. Let's not jinx it."

"Roger that."

They still had a long way to go.

Control Room, SSK *Ghadir*
North of Jazireh-ye Forur
0410 hours local time

Captain Majid Damavandi was a patient man. He knew how to wait. The Mullah Hamid Khodaei, however, was not.

"Captain! Allah uses us all as His tools, as His weapons, if need be . . . but we must act in order to be used! I must insist that you get this vessel under way!"

"Indeed, Mullah Khodaei?" he replied, keeping his voice pleasantly noncommittal. "And what would you have us do?"

"I don't know! You're the submarine captain! But something other than sitting here on the bottom as the hunt proceeds without us!"

Damavandi cocked his head slightly, listening to the background noise ringing against the hull. Even without headphones, the confusion in the surrounding waters was evident. Half of Iran's navy must be banging away out there now, determined to find the American intruder.

He reached for the intercom mike and switched it on. "Lieutenant Shirazi. This is the captain. Report, please."

"The new contact is still bearing toward the northwest, sir. High speed . . . and erratic, as though it's zigzagging. I still cannot identify it."

"Keep on it, Lieutenant. If it approaches us, sing out."

"Yes, Captain."

He replaced the mike. "Mullah, we are doing something. We are acting as a strategic reserve."

"What is that supposed to mean?"

"Consider this, Mullah. Right now we have a *very*

large number of ships and sonobuoys scattered all throughout this part of the Gulf, making a very great deal of noise. Either that noise will keep the American away, or we will be able to spot him as he enters these waters, and we begin picking up active sonar returns. Do you understand?"

"Yes . . ."

"With all of those ships, submarines, and air-dropped buoys already taking part, this vessel could not add anything to the search."

"But . . . but we have detected an intruder! The high-speed contact!"

"Yes. And I find that contact extremely suspicious."

"Huh? What do you mean?"

"Mullah Khodaei, submarines by their nature are secretive beasts. They survive by remaining undetected. They are quiet. And American submarines are the quietest in the world. They are very, very good at what they do."

"So I've heard you say on numerous occasions, Captain."

"Do *not* take that tone with me! Do you wish to understand or not?"

"My . . . apologies, sir. Continue."

"If the American submarines are so silent, then what is the nature of that high speed contact? Lieutenant Shirazi has not heard anything like it, ever before. It is as fast as a torpedo—faster, in fact. Sonar returns suggest that it is fairly large, much larger than a torpedo. Certainly, it has a much greater endurance. And, because it is so fast, it is noisy. What is it?"

"Some sort of American submersible device," Khodaei said. "They do love their toys."

"Indeed. And some of their toys are quite dangerous." Damavandi sighed. "I'll tell you what I believe it

to be, Mullah. The Americans have been experiment-
ing lately with a number of unmanned vehicles. Their
UAV technology is superb."

" 'UAV'?"

"It stands for Unmanned Aerial Vehicle," Damavandi
said, giving the Farsi words. "Our intelligence agencies
report that they are working on underwater drones as
well, Unmanned Underwater Vehicles.

"I believe we are hearing one of those. An unmanned
submersible drone would be of great use. Guided from
a manned submarine, it could penetrate minefields, locate opposing submarines, scout out shallow approaches
and harbor entrances, and—significant in this case—
act as decoys."

"Decoys!"

"Exactly. Why make so much noise unless you *want*
the other side to hear?"

Khodaei looked pale. "We should . . . we should alert
the other ships of the fleet! Let them know that they are
chasing a drone!"

"No, Mullah. We should do exactly what we are doing. We are under the lee of Forur Island. If the American is approaching Charak Bay we will be able to detect
him from the backscatter of our sonar long before he
can detect us. If we pick him up, we will alert the fleet
at that time, and then move in for the kill."

"You . . . you believe the American is coming here,
then?"

Damavandi grinned. "You must admit that they have
been most interested in this area lately. They tried to
penetrate the bay with their patrol boats last month.
Now they are doing so by submarine."

"You placed *Ghadir* here deliberately, then. An ambush!"

"An ambush, yes. And I am not going to spring that

ambush prematurely by chasing around after shadows . . . or decoys."

"I understand, Captain. You are right, of course. I . . . I was wrong to question you. I just have trouble sitting and doing nothing."

"Yes. I've noticed." Khodaei looked stricken, and Damavandi laughed. "Don't worry. Submarine combat, for those not used to it, is extraordinarily wearing. Hours upon hours of doing nothing, remaining silent, sneaking about like mice . . . and then a few minutes of stark and brain-numbing terror. It's not a life for everyone."

"I am beginning to understand that, Captain Damavandi."

He glanced at the clock on the bulkhead. "It is nearly time for morning prayer," he said. "I will permit the ship's company to pray, but in three shifts. Understand?"

"Yes, Captain."

"And *quietly*. Whispers only."

"Allah will hear us nonetheless."

"I will leave the spiritual well-being of this ship to you, then."

Damavandi watched the retreating back of the cleric. What had possessed the government to saddle their officers with such nonsense? The men knew their jobs and were well-trained. They didn't need a cleric watching over their faith.

No matter. The men would do their jobs when the time came.

And he was certain that that time would be very soon now.

Control Room, SSGN *Ohio*
Waypoint Bravo,
Off Jazireh-ye Qeys
0425 hours local time

"Coming up on the sixteen-fathom line, Captain," the enlisted rating at the plot table announced.

Sixteen fathoms. One hundred feet. Close enough. Waypoint Bravo was tucked into an indent in the seabed topography, a short ravine east of Qeys Island. They should be pretty close by now.

"Water is shoaling, Captain," Connors, the Dive Officer of the Watch, added. "Three fathoms beneath the keel forward."

Eighteen feet. Scraping barnacles again. "Maneuvering, ahead slow."

"Maneuvering, ahead slow, aye aye."

He stepped over to the periscope. There was no need to order the boat brought to periscope depth. They were already there. "Up scope."

He rode the scope to the roof, checking above, then swinging through a 360 pan of the horizon.

"Nav. You got our GPS fix?"

"It's coming through, sir. Waypoint Bravo . . . within forty meters, give or take."

"Damn, you're good," Shea said.

"Damn *we're* good," Stewart corrected him, continuing to study the horizon. There was the coast along Charak Bay. He couldn't see the beach—the scope was too low in the water to see that far—but he could take a laser sighting off the top of a large, rounded hill that he knew was right on the coast—Jabal Yarid, according to the charts. The sighting confirmed what the GPS was telling them. They had reached the pickup point, sixteen miles south of Bandar-e Charak. Fourteen miles to the west was the eastern tip of Qeys Island. Seventeen miles to the southeast was barren little Forur.

They'd made it, and without being detected. The sonar crew had been following Lieutenant Hawking's escapades off to the southwest, where, to judge from the volume of active pinging, the whole damned Iranian navy was chasing him like hounds after a fox, leading them farther south into the Gulf shipping channels.

They were still moving slowly forward, at about three knots.

"Two fathoms beneath the bow," the diving officer announced. "One fathom beneath the bow . . ."

The bottom was coming up fast. "Maneuvering! All stop!"

"All stop, aye."

But eighteen-thousand-tons-plus did not stop on the proverbial dime. Stewart felt a gentle, grating shudder through the deck, heard the scrape of mud beneath the bow.

"Maneuvering! Back slow!"

"Maneuvering, back slow, aye aye!"

Ohio's screw reversed. Every man in the control room was death-silent, listening, straining to hear, to *feel*, if *Ohio* was going to go aground. There was another slight scraping sound, and then an empty silence, a feeling of drifting free.

"All stop."

"All stop, aye aye, sir."

"Nicely done, Skipper," Shea said.

"Bullshit. I kissed the beach."

"Kissing the beach and making a lifetime commitment to the beach are two different things, Captain. With these damned tides, it's a wonder we can get in this close."

True enough. The tidal picture inside the Persian

Gulf was enormously complex, so much so that extensive computer modeling was used to make tide predictions here for naval operations, and even those weren't always of much use, but sheer guesswork rather than hard information. Each of *Ohio*'s incursions close to shore had been planned to take place during high-tide periods, to give the submarine some extra maneuvering room. In water this shallow, even a few feet could make a difference. Some parts of the Gulf coastline saw no more than a couple of feet difference between high and low tide . . . but the spring tides near Bushahir could reach eight to ten feet. In general, narrow passages like the Straits of Hormuz tended to amplify rising tides, and the difference between high and low water could be enormous, unpredictable, and, therefore, dangerous.

Tidal currents could be complex, too, especially inshore, and strong enough to sweep even a vessel as large as the *Ohio* into shoal waters or the side of one of these damned little islands scattered along this part of the coast as thickly as mines in a minefield.

"Okay, maneuvering, I want back dead slow. Very, very gently now."

"Maneuvering back slow, aye."

"Helm, come hard right. We're going to parallel-park this beast."

With the helm right and the screw reversed, *Ohio* began slowly turning to the left, her bow swinging away from the dangerously shoal water ahead. He wanted to be pointed south, ready to cut and run the moment Mayhew and his people were back on board.

Damn these shallow waters. And damn armchair admirals who would send 140 men into waters too shallow to provide decent cover. It was still dark on the roof, but should rapidly be growing light. When the sun came up, *Ohio* would be starkly visible from the air, even fully submerged.

Stewart checked the bulkhead clock—0448 hours.

"Our retrieval window for the ASDS is set from 0500 through 0600," he said. "High tide is at 0510 hours this morning; sunrise at 0507. If our SEAL friends are late, we're going to be facing ebb tide and full daylight in water that's already shallower than in my bathtub at home." He raised his hand and rubbed his eyes.

"Skipper?" Shea asked. "How long has it been since you had any rack time?"

"Damfino. Eighteen hours?"

"I don't think so, sir."

"Thirty-six, then. Don't remind me."

"You need rest, sir. We made it to Waypoint Bravo. It'll be another hour before the SEALs are here, at least. You could catch that much sleep."

"Negative, Mr. Shea." He nodded at the overhead, indicating the search under way in the distance. "Not with all *that* going on. With luck, we'll get the SEALs on board, slip back out to the channel, retrieve Mr. Hawking and his infernal machine, and then get the hell out of Dodge. Two more hours. Max."

"Yes, sir." Shea didn't sound convinced.

Stewart grinned. "Don't worry. I've only run us aground once this morning. And I don't intend to do that again."

"I wasn't worried about *that,* sir. But you're dead on your feet."

"Better than dead in my—"

"Control Room, Sonar!"

"Control Room. Go ahead."

"Sir! We have a new contact! Sierra Three-three-nine, bearing one-one-five . . . and, sir! She's *close!*"

"What is she, Chief?" He recognized Chief Sommersby's voice.

"Submarine, Captain. We're getting tonals off her even without the towed array. Sounds like it might be our friend from the Gulf of Oman."

"Has she spotted us?"

"Don't know, sir. I'd have to guess yes, though. There's a lot of backscatter in the water."

All of the active pinging in the distance was sending sonar pulses throughout this part of the Gulf. Like stray light illuminating a visual target, scattered sound waves reflecting off surface and bottom could "illuminate" a submarine target, make her visible to the passive sonar of another boat.

All question, however, vanished as a sharp, ringing *ping* sounded through the *Ohio*. The Iranian sub had just gone active with his sonar.

"Captain!" Sommersby shouted over the intercom. "He's opening his outer doors!"

"Maneuvering!" Stewart called. "Ahead two-thirds!" He looked at Shea. "Hang on, Wayne. This is going to get rough!"

Friday, 27 June 2008

Control Room, SSK *Ghadir*
West of Jazireh-ye Forur
0449 hours local time

"Range to target . . . sixteen hundred meters!" the weapons officer shouted. "Outer torpedo tube doors open!"

"Fire torpedo one!" Captain Damavandi ordered.

A sharp hiss, and a lurch, as the torpedo erupted from *Ghadir*'s bow.

"Tube one fired electrically!"

"Fire two!"

"Tube two fired electrically."

Damavandi turned to Tavakkoli, his exec. "We have him."

"Thanks be to Allah!"

Damavandi glanced at Khodaei, who was standing nearby. "Yes."

"Torpedo one has acquired the target, Captain," the

330

weapons officer announced. A moment later, "Torpedo two has also acquired!"

"Cut the wires," Damavandi ordered. "Helm! Bring us left to course one-eight-five. Maneuvering, ahead full!"

By using every stealthy trick he'd learned from his Russian teachers, by virture of the *Ghadir*'s superb battery-driven silence—and, yes, by the grace of Allah the Mighty in Battle—they'd been able to sneak up on the American giant. The moment they'd sent out that ranging ping, however, the enemy captain had heard them and become aware of his danger. If he had a torpedo ready and loaded, he might execute what the Americans called a snapshot, in an effort to kill the *Ghadir*. By turning south and accelerating to full speed, Damavandi hoped to preserve *Ghadir*'s tactical freedom, giving the Iranian sub space and depth within which to maneuver.

The American didn't have that freedom. He was close up against shallow water—Lieutenant Shirazi had reported sounds of the enemy vessel scraping bottom moments ago—and he was at a dead stop. If he bolted, if he ran for open water, he risked running solidly aground, and then the Iranian navy would have the ultimate prize, an American nuclear submarine as hostage, as bargaining chip, as propaganda victory . . . even as a source for a working nuclear reactor. Iranian nuclear research would be bootstrapped forward by years.

That possibility, Damavandi knew, had been endlessly discussed by the higher-ups within the Iranian Ministry of Defense. For a time, Operation Bold Fire had included a scenario—wishful thinking, so far as he was concerned—of using Iranian submarines to drive an intruder American submarine aground, capturing it instead of destroying it. Ultimately, that scenario had

been dropped as something too uncertain, too dependent on too many variables, to work. Surely, the Americans would not be so stupid as to risk one of their
nuclear vessels so close in to shore.

But it appeared that chance—or Allah—had just delivered precisely that opportunity squarely into Damavandi's hands.

For a time, as he'd quietly followed the slow-moving
enemy vessel north, he'd considered approaching the enemy with active sonar blasting away, hoping to startle
him into a rash movement that would put him aground.
He'd decided against that, however. The American submarine forces were well-trained and, while incredibly
bold—if some of the tales told by their Russian col-
leagues were true—were not given to rashness or to
panic. An all-out charge by the *Ghadir* would be as
likely to elicit a torpedo as flight.

Damavandi had chosen, therefore, to raise his radio
mast and transmit a coded message to Bandar Abbas
and to all Iranian ASW forces in the area, alerting them
to the American's presence between Forur and Qeys
Islands, and then to prepare to fire torpedoes.

The American submarine had been fully submerged
at the time; it should not have heard the radio call.
Luck—or just possibly divine providence—was most
assuredly working to the advantage of Iran this day.

By firing two torpedoes at the enemy, he'd done his
best to cover all eventualities. If the enemy sub ran,
the torpedoes might sink him, would almost certainly
cripple him, possibly in water so shallow that salvage
of the secrets of the American nuclear reactor would
be easy. If anything could make the American captain
act in a hasty or rash way, it was word that two
Russian-made torpedoes were bearing down on him.

There was an excellent chance that he would run aground after all.

Either way, the rest of the ASW forces in the Charak Bay region were heading this way at flank speed.

"Torpedo one is closing with the enemy, Captain!" the weapons officer called. "He's still moving slowly. Impact in thirty seconds!"

For this American submarine captain, there was no escape now. . . .

Control Room, SSGN *Ohio*
Waypoint Bravo,
Off Jazireh-ye Qeys
0450 hours local time

"Torpedo impact in thirty seconds, Captain! Range six hundred!"

"Release countermeasures!"

"Countermeasures released."

Stewart watched the bulkhead clock, as sweat beaded on his forehead and upper lip. He'd already ordered ahead flank; the trouble was that just as it took time to stop eighteen thousand tons already moving forward, it took time to get eighteen thousand tons moving from a dead stop.

Thank God, however, he'd already ordered the *Ohio* to swing around with her screw toward the beach, to save time once they'd picked up the SEALs. By accelerating straight out the way they'd come in, they shouldn't run aground.

But those torpedoes had been fired almost at point-blank range, for submarine combat, and *Ohio* wouldn't cover much ground before they arrived. Unless divine providence came through with another miracle, they were going to be in trouble a lot deeper than the water around them very shortly now.

"Control Room, Sonar! Torpedo one appears to have lost its lock! I think it's going for the decoy!"

"Please, God, make it so," Shea said at his side.

They waited. There was nothing else to do.

Iranian Torpedo One
Waypoint Bravo,
Off Jazireh-ye Qeys
0451 hours local time

Russian ASW torpedoes could be set to travel at one of two speeds—slow, for long chases in order to conserve fuel, and fast, for short ranges. This one was running at better than forty knots—high speed—and its simple-minded on-board processor had focused on the expanding cloud of bubbles.

Traveling northwest, it streaked through the bubble cloud, losing its targeting lock. According to programming, it began to go into a turn, entering a search pattern to reacquire its lost target.

At forty-plus knots, though, it could not turn within a tight radius. Seconds after passing the decoy cloud, it entered rapidly shoaling water and, as it began turning, it entered shallower water still.

Northeast of Qeys Island was a sandbar and coral reef that very nearly reached the surface. . . .

SEAL Detachment Delta One
Approaching Waypoint Bravo
0451 hours local time

Tangretti sat in the near darkness of the ASDS, exhausted, cold, aching in every bone and joint of his body. It was always this way at the end of an op. As the adrenaline began to leave his system, he began feeling the stress and strain of the exertion.

It had taken twenty minutes to motor out to the waiting ASDS, which had come up until its upper deck was awash. They'd transferred their gear down the upper hatch in a pitching sea, knifed the empty CRRCs to send them to the bottom, and clambered aboard.

The second platoon, Delta Two, was already on board. They'd completed their missile-launcher hunt on the headland south of Bandar-e Charak yesterday, and returned to the ASDS early that evening. For the next hour and half, or a bit more, the ASDS had made its slow way south across Charak Bay. They should now be within a mile or so of their rendezvous with the *Ohio*. If anything was going to go wrong on this op, now was the time. . . .

The sudden boom transmitted through the water and the minisub's hull brought all of the SEALs up short. "What the hell was that?" Avery cried.

"Depth charges!" Wilson said. He looked scared.

"Whatever it is, it's not depth charges," Tangretti told them. "And *we're* not the target."

"If not us, who? Olivetti asked. "Maybe they're shooting at our ride!"

"*Ohio* can take care of herself," Tangretti said.

He wondered, though, how true that was in shallow water, surrounded by half the Iranian navy.

Control Room, SSGN *Ohio*
Waypoint Bravo,
Off Jazireh-ye Qeys
0451 hours local time

The crack of an underwater explosion close astern thundered through the *Ohio,* and sent the long vessel surging ahead like a surfboard riding a wave. Overpressure caused pipes to burst in several compartments. In the control room an overhead pipe suddenly gave way, sending a white stream of high-pressure water blasting across the compartment.

Two enlisted men, well-trained, thoroughly drilled, and with many hours experience in the submarine casualty simulator at New London, Connecticut, with exactly this sort of event—a "casualty," in submariner terminology—leaped for the broken pipe, wrestling a clamp into place against the torrent and tightening it shut. In seconds the water had stopped.

"Good job!" Stewart commended the soaking wet men. "Mr. Jarrett! What do you have for me?"

"Reports still coming in," *Ohio*'s damage control officer reported. "No injuries so far. A few busted pipes. Nothing major."

"Keep on it. Sonar! Where's that second fish?"

"Locked onto us again, Captain! Seven hundred yards . . . closing fast! Forty seconds to impact!"

"Maneuvering! What's our speed?

"Now passing twenty knots, Captain. We're at all ahead flank, making revs for twenty-five."

"Control, Sonar. Incoming torpedo now at four hundred . . . three-five-zero. . . ."

"Release countermeasures."

"Countermeasures released."

"Helm! Come left four-five degrees!"

"Helm, come left four-five degrees, aye aye, sir!"

"Torpedo at two-zero-zero yards . . ."

"Release countermeasures."

"Countermeasures released."

"Torpedo still tracking us, Captain," Sonar reported.

"Sonar, this is the Captain. Which side is it coming in on?"

"S-Sir?"

"Is that you, Caswell?"

"Yes, Captain!"

"Caswell, which side of the boat is that torpedo homing on? Port or starboard? Or is coming straight up our ass, dead center?"

There was a moment's hesitation. "Sir! It's slightly to port!"

That made sense. Their last maneuver, turning to port forty-five degrees, would have put the Iranian torpedo off *Ohio*'s port stern quarter.

"Torpedo range, one hundred yards!"

Fifteen seconds, a hair less . . . allowing for *Ohio*'s forward velocity.

Silently, he began counting. . . .

SEAL Detachment Delta One
Approaching Waypoint Bravo
0451 hours local time

"You guys okay back there?" Mayhew asked, ducking his head in through the aft lockout chamber hatch.

"Sure thing, Wheel," Tangretti replied. "What's all the racket up there?"

"Don't know yet. We've been picking up a lot of active sonar. I think the bad guys have been hunting for the *Ohio.* That explosion . . . well, that might be what it was."

"Hey, Wheel?"

"What is it, Olivetti?"

"If the bad guys got the *Ohio,* how are we supposed to get back?"

"We'll swim back if we have to. What do you think?"

"Sure," Tangretti added. "Manama and the Fifth Fleet are just 230 miles *that* way, as the SEAL swims."

"If anything happens to our ride," Mayhew added, "they'll come get us. Patrol boats. Rescue helos. Something. They're not going to leave us out here. Okay? They're not going to forget us."

"Okay, Wheel."

Mayhew pulled back through the hatch, dogging it behind them—a precaution in case the ASDS found itself in battle and one or another of its compartments started to flood. The SEALs aft were left alone with uneasy thoughts.

Of *course* the Navy wasn't going to forget them. Still, from the fragmentary reports they'd heard while ashore at OP Tamarind, it sounded like a major shooting war had broken out, and if the Iranians were taking shots at the *Ohio,* that war had just escalated, big-time. The safest bet, probably, would be to turn the ASDS around and get back to shore . . . the Iranian shore. The ASDS had a maximum range limited by its battery life, and must be running close to empty already. Ashore, they could dig in, call for help, and wait.

Here, in the Gulf, they were helpless. Sitting ducks when their air ran out and they had to surface.

Of course, the *real* sitting ducks at the moment were the officers and crew of the *Ohio,* a mile or so to the south. . . .

Control Room, SSGN *Ohio*
Waypoint Bravo,
Off Jazireh-ye Qeys
0451 hours local time

"Fifty yards! Sir, it's on top of us!"

"Helm! Come right forty-five degrees!"

He could hear it now, a faint, high-pitched whine, approaching from astern and to port. A second later and they all heard a loud thump, followed by a grating sound, like something heavy and metallic dragging along the port side, moving forward. The sound stopped . . . and then there was a second thump, and a third.

The torpedo was scraping along the *Ohio*'s left side.

It wouldn't have worked if the Iranians had fired a wake-homing torpedo at them, or if they had used a proximity fuse on the warhead. In either case, the torpedo would have detonated by now, and *Ohio* would be sinking, or, at the very least, would be seriously damaged.

And it would not have worked had Stewart not been able to rely on his sonar crew's sharp ears and sharper interpretation of their data. Caswell's ears had let him time the maneuvers perfectly: turning left, first, to bring the incoming torpedo toward that side of the sub, then turning away at the very last moment, so that when the torpedo hit, it did so at such an oblique angle that the impact trigger in the nose didn't fire.

For several long seconds the men on *Ohio*'s control room deck strained to hear the silence.

"Sonar. What's happened to the torpedo?"

"It's gone silent, sir. I heard one sharp clank, like maybe the screw fouled on a steering vane. Its homing sonar is dead, too. I don't hear a thing."

"Keep listening. Helm, continue the turn to starboard. Come to course two-nine-zero."

"Continue hard right to course two-nine-zero, aye aye."

At his side, Shea let out a long, pent-up breath. "My God, Skipper. You know how to time 'em tight! Did I just hear a 533mm torpedo bounce off our side?"

"Thank Caswell. That kid deserves a medal after this."

"Control Room, Sonar! I have Sierra Three-three-nine on passive. Passing us to starboard at seventeen knots!"

Good.

"Helm, come right to new course one-eight-zero!"

"Come right to new course one-eight-zero, aye aye, sir!"

"Maneuvering, make revs for one-zero knots!"

"Maneuvering, making revolutions for one-zero knots, aye, Captain."

A Kilo had a top speed underwater of seventeen knots, and Stewart was willing to bet that the new Iranian Ghadir-class, based on the same design, could do no better. By continuing the turn, he would put *Ohio* on the Iranian sub's tail, in his baffles, and at ten knots, *Ohio*'s sonar would be able to hear the other vessel.

"Weapons Officer! Lock onto Sierra Three-three-nine. Prepare to fire tubes one and three."

"Lock onto Sierra Three-three-nine, aye, Captain. Tubes one and three are loaded and ready to fire."

"Control Room! Sonar! I have aircraft close overhead! Splash to starboard!"

That splash could be sonobuoys, dropped to pinpoint *Ohio*'s position . . . or it could be antisubmarine torpedoes. There was no time to prosecute the attack against the Iranian sub. Time was critical, and he acted without hesitation.

"Maneuvering! Ahead flank!"

Maneuvering repeated and acknowledged, and *Ohio* sped forward, accelerating to 25 knots.

Ping! Ping!

A sonobuoy, then. But a torpedo might follow at any moment.

"Snapshot, tube one, Sierra Three-three-nine!" He could at least send a fish streaking after the Iranian sub, just to return the favor. "Helm! Come left to one-five-zero!" That was to avoid slamming into the Iranian boat from behind.

No plan survives contact with the enemy, Stewart thought.

And in this case, with the plan to pick up the SEALs in their ASDS, that was quite literally true.

XSSF-1 *Manta*
Persian Gulf
0452 hours local time

Lieutenant Commander Hawking, too, had heard the explosion, though it was muffled and far off. At that moment he was nearly forty miles southeast of *Ohio*'s position, leading several Iranian surface vessels on a high-speed chase that they could not possibly win. When he heard the distant rumble, however, and checked the bearing on his sonar, he knew that either *Ohio* had just taken a shot at someone . . . or that someone else had taken a shot at the *Ohio*.

Either way meant serious trouble.

Easing back on the control stick, he let the *Manta* rise toward the surface. A moment later the canopy broke through the water, giving him a brief glimpse of the world above.

The sky was quite light now, with sunrise just minutes away. He could easily see the nearest Iranian vessel, an Alvand-class light patrol frigate, a thousand yards away.

Splashes geysered out of the sea nearby as the frigate opened fire with its 37mm twin antiaircraft mount. Alvands mounted surface-to-surface Sea Killer missiles and an ASW mortar, too, and Hawking didn't want to be the one providing the Iranian sailors marksmanship practice. Pushing the stick forward and accelerating, he slipped back beneath the surface, as rounds continued to pop and hiss nearby. Within thirty seconds, however, he was rocketing through the black depths at eighty knots, easily twice the frigate's top speed, leaving the confused Iranians far behind.

He didn't want to push the speed higher than that. His fuel cells were already weakening, requiring a recharge, and the faster he went, the faster he drained them. But at eighty knots he would be back at the *Ohio* within thirty minutes.

"Hang on, boys," he said aloud. "It's the cavalry to the rescue!"

The question was whether he would get there in time . . . or if *Ohio* had already been sent to the bottom.

Communications Center,
Office of the Ministry of Defense
Tehran, Iran
0459 hours local time

An aide held out the telephone receiver, and Admiral Mehdi Baba-Janzadeh took it and held it to his ear. What, he wondered, would bring the Supreme Leader onto the phone in person? "Yes, sir. Admiral Baba-Janzadeh speaking."

"Yes, Admiral," Khamenei said on the other end. "We have been receiving disturbing reports here from Bandar Abbas."

"Yes, sir." Of course they had. Baba-Janzadeh himself had ordered the reports forwarded directly to the Supreme Leader's bunker.

"Explosions. One of our submarines sunk. American submarines off our coast . . . and the *Alvand* has just reported an . . . an unidentified underwater object. Something traveling at impossible speeds. What do you know of this?"

"Sir, we believe the Americans may be using a small, high-speed submarine drone. We're not sure what its capabilities are, but they may be using it to decoy our forces."

"To what end?"

"They remain interested in the special weapons facility at Bandar-e Charak. That, at any rate, is where most of the activity has been centered. We believe the large American submarine may be trying to put naval commandos ashore."

"Indeed. What have you done about this?"

"I have ordered the Twenty-third Regiment to seal off that entire stretch of beach, to either side of the town. And I have ordered helicopter patrols stepped up over the beaches and above the bay itself."

"That seems adequate. This . . . this unidentified object worries us, however. *Alvand*'s captain was convinced that there were no fewer than three of the things operating in his area."

"Yes, sir. I've seen the report." *Alvand*'s captain, in fact, was prone to exaggeration. It was a wonder he hadn't reported seeing little green aliens driving the thing. "I would not put too much stock in it. In combat conditions, men become excitable. Confused. And eye-witness reports become unreliable."

"I agree." There was a pause. "Except for this . . . excitement off Bandar-e Charak, Bold Fire appears to be going well. And, as you predicted, we have definite evidence of American submarines operating inside our territorial waters."

"Yes, sir." It would have been better if they had the submarine itself, either run aground and captured, or sunken at the bottom of the Gulf. But the plan had succeeded, at least, to the extent of having provided Tehran with the *causus bellum* it sought.

"We are giving the order to initiate Phase Three."

That took Baba-Janzadeh aback, unprepared. "Sir . . . is that wise? We may still defeat the Americans without—"

"Do not question your orders, Admiral."

"No, sir." He hesitated. To press the issue might put his career at risk. "It's just that this seems an unwarranted escalation so early in the process."

"Unwarranted? American submarines have entered our territorial waters, conducted missions obviously related to espionage or sabotage, and sunk *two* of our submarines! They are engaged in combat with our forces as we speak!"

"Yes, sir. But I must point out that, so far, there is evidence of only a single American submarine in the region, and there is an excellent chance that we will have it trapped within the next thirty minutes."

"Admiral, you know as well as I do that the American Fifth Fleet is the object of our exercise in the Gulf, do you not?"

"Yes, sir."

"Good. I was afraid you had lost sight of our principle

objective! The latest reports show that the American fleet has begun preparations to leave Manama. It is putting to sea . . . and it may well be heading for our coast to support this lone submarine of which you speak."

Or it could be preparing to leave the Gulf. He doubted that . . . but it was a possibility. There clearly was no arguing with the Supreme Leader, however, not when he'd worked himself into such a state.

"It is vital, *vital,* that the Islamic world see us taking on the American Satan and delivering a telling blow! For that reason, I am giving the order to execute Phase Three immediately. You should alert your own commands so that they can be ready for any American reaction . . . and in order to follow up on the advantage once the strike takes place."

"Yes, sir. I will alert my people immediately."

"Good. I know we can count on you, Admiral." There was a click, and the line was dead.

He handed the phone to the aide, who'd been standing by impassively, without expression.

No, no, he thought. This is premature. We are not ready for this. . . .

Operationally, Phase Three was a direct strike against the American Fifth Fleet stationed at Bahrain. The original concept had actually been far more complex, involving not only Iran's fleet of Chinese Hudong missile boats, but some hundreds of small craft, pleasure boats, even fishing boats outfitted with Sea Eagle missiles, Exocets, and anything else that could be hurled against the enemy giant to bring him down.

As planning had progressed, however, the plan had been changed. Khamenei and the people closest to him were fixated on Iran's new intermediate range missile force, the Shahabs. In tests, they'd proven themselves far more accurate and deadly than the unlamented Saddam

Hussein's Scud attacks on Saudi Arabia and Israel sixteen years before.

But Baba-Janzadeh did not have the trust in the new technology others did. The Scuds had failed Saddam badly, not only in their performance overall, but in the backlash of public opinion worldwide against him.

At least Khamenei and his sycophants hadn't insisted on making this a *nuclear* strike. Baba-Janzadeh had argued long and hard that the special weapons at Bandar-e Charak should be held back, that simply the *idea* of them made them a deterrent.

Phase Three as originally conceived would have been more sure of success, he thought. Hundreds of missiles flying at the American fleet from all directions, instead of a few dozen. And there was such powerful symbology in the death blow to the enemy being delivered by small and relatively low-tech forces.

But missiles were the ultimate symbols of modern warfare. Technology against technology.

All he could do was alert the other commands to Khamenei's intent. The special weapons, controlled entirely by the IRGC fanatics, were not under his operational control anyway. After that he would focus all of his attention on the battle unfolding outside of Charak Bay, as Iranian naval forces closed in at last on the American intruder.

He reached again for the phone.

Friday, 27 June 2008

Control Room, SSGN *Ohio*
Waypoint Bravo,
Off Jazireh-ye Qeys
0507 hours local time

"Snapshot has missed, Captain."

"Very well." It had been an awkward angle, with *Ohio* already well into a sharp turn. The chance of a kill had been a slim one.

Now, though, Stewart needed to find a way to lower the Iranians' chances of scoring a kill on the *Ohio*. According to the sonar crew, at least five enemy vessels were converging on Waypoint Bravo, all banging away with active sonar. They were still a good distance away—forty minutes to an hour, perhaps, but he thought they must know exactly where *Ohio* was.

And that Iranian Ghadir was out there somewhere as well, still keeping quiet.

Too many to engage. *Ohio* only had four tubes, and one was now empty; it would take about ten minutes to reload.

He consulted the chart on the plot board, checking depths. The tide would be turning in just another few minutes, and he wanted to get away from these shallow waters.

He also needed to locate the ASDS. It must be close to the pickup by now. But *Ohio* would be a very large, very stationary target while taking them on board.

And the first problem would be just finding them.

"Helm! Come left to zero-zero-seven."

"Helm, come left to zero-zero-seven, aye aye."

They would have to go back into the shallows to find the SEALs and complete their mission.

SEAL Detachment Delta One
Waypoint Bravo
0515 hours local time

"Twenty-six degrees, thirty minutes, twenty-six point three seven seconds North," Mayhew said, reading the numbers off the GPS screen. "Fifty-four degrees, ten minutes, five point two-eight seconds East. We're bang on-target, sir. Waypoint Bravo."

"So where do you think they are?" Taggart asked, peering at the television monitor currently transmitting the view from the ASDS periscope. They were wallowing in choppy water, deck awash, at the exact point—within a few yards, anyway, where they were supposed to meet their ride home.

"I don't know. But they'll be here. Our pickup window ruins through 0600 hours."

"Unless the Iranians got them," Taggart said, voice grim. "They won't make pickup if they're sunk."

"They're not sunk," Mayhew replied. "We heard one explosion . . . but nothing else. No breakup noise, nothing like that."

Taggart shot him a hard glance. "Just how much experience with sonar have you had, Lieutenant?"

"Not that much," Mayhew admitted. "ASDS training."

"Uh-huh. Well . . . I'll say this much: If they did get hit, there should be more crap floating on the surface. There's oil, yeah, but there's *always* oil in the Gulf. And it's just a skim, y'know? Not like a ship sank."

"Nothing on side-scanning sonar, either," Mayhew pointed out. "The water's not that deep here, a hundred feet or less. If the *Ohio* sank, we ought to be able to see the wreck."

"Well, they may have gotten clobbered miles from here . . . but I tend to agree with you." Reaching across to Mayhew's console, he flipped a switch. Instantly, the cockpit was filled with an eerie cacophony of chirps and pings, echoing and reechoing through the sea. "Hear that?"

"Yeah . . ."

"Search sonars. A lot of 'em. And headed this way. If they nailed the *Ohio*, I don't think they'd still be looking for her, do you?"

"No." Realization set in, and Mayhew grinned. "No, by God. They wouldn't!"

"So . . . how long do you want to wait?"

"Until 0600, at least."

"Okay, if the Iranians give us that much. It's starting

to get light pretty fast out there. And that sounds like a lot of ships bearing down on us."

"If they're coming toward us, I'll bet that means *Ohio* is closer than they are."

"Right. But just to be on the safe side . . . open that storage compartment there under your console."

"What's in here?"

"Procedure checklist. In case we have to scuttle."

"Ah."

The two men began going through the checklist. The ASDS was a highly sensitive vessel, with numerous secrets about her . . . from the operation of her side-looking sonar, to the sonar equipment itself, to the communications frequencies used for satellite communications, to the very fact that the minisub was here within Iranian waters, carrying out a black op. All sensitive equipment and code books would have to be destroyed if the SEALs had to abandon the little vessel and swim for shore.

And that meant an explosion. A rather large one.

The charges were already set; the two men began arming them . . . just in case.

Less than five minutes later, however, a loud and ringing *ping* sounded through the cockpit. Mayhew looked at the sonar screen. "Jesus!"

"What is it?"

"Look at that! He's almost on top of us!"

"*Ohio?* Or the competition?"

"*Ohio!* Gotta be! No Iranian is that big!"

On the periscope view screen they could see *Ohio*'s periscope now, camouflage painted and extending above the surface. "Sierra Delta, Sierra Delta," crackled over the radio. "This is the *Ohio*. You looking for a ride?"

Mayhew let out a whoop.

"*Ohio,* Sierra Delta," Taggart replied. "That's a big roger. You have no idea how glad we are to see you!"

"Copy that, Sierra Delta. Stand by to be taken aboard!"

As Taggart talked to the *Ohio,* Mayhew scrambled from his seat, undogged the fore and aft hatches to the lockout chamber, and stepped through into the aft compartment to let the men know.

They deserved that much, at least, after two hours of sitting cooped up and motionless in the rocking darkness.

"Hoo-ya!" one of the SEALs—he thought it was Olivetti—yelled, punching the air with his fist, and the other men joined in.

The cheers, he thought, must have carried through the water as far as the Iranian fleet, and caused quite a bit of head scratching.

No matter. They were going home now.

Assuming *Ohio* could evade the trap that was rapidly closing on her.

Control Room, SSGN *Ohio*
Waypoint Bravo,
Off Jazireh-ye Qeys
0536 hours local time

"ASDS reports they're docked and locked," Lieutenant Shea said. "They're starting to come down the ladder now."

"Very good, Mr. Shea. Let's get the hell out of this pocket."

"I concur, sir."

"Helm, bring us to new course . . . one-zero-five."

"Helm, coming to new course one-zero-five, aye, sir."

Shea raised an eyebrow. "East?"

Stewart turned and pointed at the plot table chart. "Yeah. Most of the pinging is to the south, on this arc between Qeys and Forur. If we head a bit south of east, we'll slip just north of Forur Island—about here—then we can swing south past the east side of the island and run for the shipping lanes."

"That means staying in shallow water longer. This stretch north of Forur is *damned* shallow, according to the chart."

"I know. But if we go straight south now, we run smack into the arms of that armada. No, we need to pull an end run here. With a bit of luck, we can get into deep water before the ebb tide strands us on a mud flat somewhere."

"Hope you're right, Captain." Shea didn't sound convinced. "How about Commander Hawking?"

"He can keep up. I'm just hoping his *Manta* is the only vessel in the Gulf that can. Otherwise . . . we have one hell of a big tactical problem."

XSSF-1 *Manta*
South of Jazireh-ye Qeys
Persian Gulf
0540 hours local time

Hawking eyed the warning lights with the same blend of annoyance and concern that a driver might muster for the low-gas light on his dashboard. Clearly, he'd overdone it a bit, pushing the *Manta* too fast, too hard.

The engine was overheating and the power levels were falling a lot faster than they should.

The reason, he thought, almost certainly lay with how dirty the water was in the Gulf. The constant tanker traffic—not to mention the large number of wells and oil production facilities up and down the coast—meant that the Persian Gulf was perpetually blessed by the mother of all bathtub rings, and the surface carried a constant scum of oil and filth. Each time he surfaced, or moved within a few feet of it, his water intakes gulped down more of the stuff, which was fouling his compression and pressurization chambers, reducing engine efficiency and increasing power usage.

His engine temp was hovering just shy of 550 now, definitely red-lining it. At 600 or 650, he might face shutdown.

He cut back his speed to fifty knots. At least he was now entering the general area where *Ohio* had been operating. He wasn't getting a transponder signal, however. Where the hell was she?

He slowed sharply, letting the *Manta* drift slowly downward at ten knots while he took a careful listen to the sonar. His screen was showing a hash outside from a dozen sources. The bad guys were definitely stirred up and searching. He didn't see anything on the screen, though, or hear anything over his headset that might be a submarine.

Hold it. There *was* something. An active sonar source that his computer suggested was ten miles ahead. A sonobuoy? Or a submarine going active?

He increased power and pulled the stick right, angling to move in for a closer look.

Control Room, SSK *Ghadir*
South of Jazireh-ye Forur
0545 hours local time

Damavandi spent a long time studying the chart. This
American submarine captain . . . he was a clever one.
Unpredictable. After somehow avoiding *Ghadir*'s attack, he'd fired a single torpedo, maneuvered as though
to drop onto *Ghadir*'s stern, then suddenly broken off
and turned east.

The amazing thing was how maneuverable the enemy
submarine was, for such a titanic vessel. However, the
American was rapidly running out of options. The tide
now was in full ebb, and the regions inshore of the two
guardians of Charak Bay—Forur and Qeys—were going to rapidly become both shallower and more tricky
to navigate as the currents picked up. Damavandi knew
these waters. His father had been a fisherman, as had
his father before him, and as a boy Damavandi had
worked on his father's boat, learning these waters and
the ways of the Gulf.

These were his waters, his ground.

East . . .

The American, he decided, must be attempting to cut
north of Forur, before turning south toward the relative
safety of the central Gulf. That made sense in terms of
avoiding the Iranian fleet now moving to intercept him
from the south. It put his ship in serious jeopardy, however.

Especially now that Damavandi had a very good idea
of where he was trying to go.

"Helm," he ordered. "Come left to zero-nine-zero."

He would take *Ghadir* south of Forur Island, then
swing north to meet the American as he came south.

And he would be waiting for him.

But . . . he needed to be sure the American didn't double back on his track, and pass between Qeys and Forur after all.

"Raise the radio mast," he said. "Communications, this is the captain. See if you can contact the *Yunes*."

Yunes was another of Iran's Kilo submarines, hull number 903, purchased from the Soviet Union in 1997. Her captain, Commander Massoud Dadashi, was a friend and classmate of Damavandi's, and a good man.

During his last radio contact with Bandar Abbas, Damavandi had learned that *Yunes* was entering the Charak Bay area and was currently on station just south of Qeys. She should have her radio mast up and be able to receive a transmission from the *Ghadir*. If Dadashi headed straight east, following the American intruder, and if he did so with active sonar blasting away, that should drive the American to continue around the north of Forur . . . and straight into *Ghadir*'s waiting trap.

Sonar Room, SSGN *Ohio*
North of Jazireh-ye Forur
0610 hours local time

Ping!
Caswell looked at the sharp, almost vertical line of white blips on the waterfall display. Each dot was a ping. The fact that they were in a vertical line meant the transmitter was not changing course relative to the *Ohio*. He was in *Ohio*'s baffles, almost directly astern, but blasting with his active sonar loudly enough that the SSGN's passive sensors could pick up his pinging even above disturbance of her own wake.

"Sonar, this is the captain. Caswell . . . what's our friend doing?"

"Sir, he's still on our six. Range . . . about twelve thousand. He doesn't seem to care whether we hear him or not."

"Very well. Stay with him. And keep an ear out for anything waiting for us, okay?"

"Will do, Captain."

Dobbs, sitting next to Caswell, shook his head. "The Old Man thinks we have eyes out there."

Caswell patted his console. "This is just as good. Better, maybe."

"What I can't figure," Dobbs said, "is . . . if they got us, why haven't they popped a fish at us? They're in range."

"Simple," Sommersby said. "We've outmaneuvered a couple of torpedoes already, which suggests that our antitorpedo tactics are very, very good . . . or their torpedoes aren't so good. If they shoot and miss, we run, they might lose us."

"They also might not be sure it's us," Caswell added. "From that far back, they know they have a target . . . but they don't want to score another own goal. Maybe they're waiting to be sure."

"Yeah. Or maybe they're still processing." Dobbs shook his head. "There is so fucking much crap out there . . . background noise, sonobuoys . . . And their equipment isn't as good as ours, either."

"Just so you don't start depending on that, Dobbs," Sommersby warned. "We can hear their active sonar from dead astern okay, but if he sends a fish up our ass, we might not hear it until it's too fucking late. So stay sharp, both of you!"

"Right, Chief," Caswell said.

"In any case," Sommersby continued, "if I was the Old Man, right now I'd be thinking the bad guys might be trying to *drive* us. Herd us into a trap."

"That," Dobbs said, "doesn't sound good."

"No, it isn't. But you know what?"

"What?"

"I'd be willing to bet that the Iranians've never had to contend with anyone like the skipper." He chuckled. "Anyone who can take a school bus and handle it like a sports car has *got* to be a guy to be reckoned with! So just keep your ears screwed on tight, stay sharp, and don't let the Old Man down. He'll get us through this. Copy?"

"Copy that," Caswell said.

He closed his eyes, trying to focus on what he knew must be an Iranian diesel submarine stalking them eight miles astern. He could *see* the other vessel in his mind's eye, her teardrop body, her outsized fair-water. No match at all for a U.S. Navy nuclear boat . . . but seeking to take advantage of these shoal waters and strengthening tidal flow.

Ping!

Control Room, SSK *Yunes*
North of Jazireh-ye Forur
0612 hours local time

"Captain, we have a firing solution."

"Very well." Massoud Dadashi considered the tactical situation for a moment. Damavandi, his old friend, had suggested he drive the American submarine north of Forur Island and into Damavandi's trap . . . but that

didn't preclude the possibility of taking a shot himself if
the situation warranted it. *Yunes'* active sonar showed
the enemy to be within twelve kilometers' range—a long-
range shot, but possible. With the American's speed, he
was pulling away from the *Yunes,* which was already
moving at seventeen knots, her best speed.

If Dadashi fired now, he would urge the American to
keep moving forward. North it was too shallow, and the
south was blocked by Forur Island. A torpedo would
encourage the American captain to keep to his current
course.

And . . . anything was possible. Even such a long-
range shot as this might hit the enemy vessel.

And Dadashi found that he *wanted* that kill.

He would take the chance. "Ready torpedo tube
one!"

"Sir! Tube one is loaded and ready to fire!"

"Fire one!"

XSSF-1 *Manta*
North of Jazireh-ye Forur
Persian Gulf
0612 hours local time

The other submarine, Hawking had decided, was Iranian. As he closed the range, his on-board computer,
processing the sounds coming from the other vessel, had
identified the active sonar as a low-frequency MGK-400
Rubikon, a Russian export design designated as "Shark
Teeth" by the West.

He was tracking one of the Iranian Kilos.

His engine warning light was flashing again, and he

cut back slightly on the speed. The enemy vessel was less than a mile ahead now. He ought to be able to see it soon.

In his ears he heard only the rush of water outside and the pulsing throb of the *Manta*'s engine. It was a trade-off. If he used the *Manta*'s single serious tactical advantage—its speed—he lost the ability to hear the enemy.

Above the water, the sun had been up for a good hour now, and the water was fast growing light. Visibility was hampered somewhat by particles of debris suspended in the water, but Hawking found he had fairly good visibility out to about eighty feet. That wasn't the same as being able to hear the enemy eight or ten miles away, but it was something. It made things less claustrophobic . . . and more like sitting in the cockpit of a fighter plane at twelve thousand feet.

Ping!

The Kilo up ahead was still pinging away, and that provided Hawking with a perfect homing beacon. He wondered if the guy was tracking the *Ohio* or just randomly probing the depths ahead.

He leaned forward, trying to see through the murk. There was something. . . . Yes! The Kilo emerged out of the gloom, a huge, elongated shadow, still almost invisible in the murk, but he could make out the T-shaped control surfaces on the tail and the outsized sail amidships. He switched on the *Manta*'s external lights, the better to see.

At sixty knots he streaked down the Kilo's starboard side.

Control Room, SSK *Yunes*
North of Jazireh-ye Forur
0612 hours local time

"Torpedo one fired electrically!"

Yunes lurched and rolled slightly with the launch. But there was something else, too . . . a shrill fluttering sound that appeared to be coming from aft, but that was moving rapidly along the submarine's right side, from back to front. For a moment Dadashi thought something had gone awry with the torpedo launch, but he could not imagine what might have happened. Had something torn loose on *Yunes'* hull?

"Captain! Sonar! Unidentified contact close aboard to starboard!"

"Sonar, this is the captain. What is the contact?"

There was a hesitation on the part of the sonar officer, and Dadashi shoved aside a flash of irritation with himself. *If the man knew what it was, he wouldn't have called it "unidentified."*

"Sir, I don't know. But it's fast! Sixty knots! It's cutting across our bow!"

Dadashi felt a surge through the deck beneath his feet. The object, whatever it was, must be throwing out a tremendous wake.

"It must be the American drone," he said. "Track it!"

He wondered how he could kill an enemy vessel that was capable of traveling at sixty knots, with a torpedo that, at best, could manage forty.

XSSF-1 *Manta*
North of Jazireh-ye Forur
Persian Gulf
0612 hours local time

Hawking saw the torpedo leave the Kilo, sliding out of an open door on the port side just abaft the huge, rounded nose in a sudden cloud of bubbles. He was already past the Kilo and banking left to come back around, but he could see the long, pencil-slender black shape of the torpedo vanishing into darkness.

He wasn't entirely sure whether the Kilo was shooting at him or at the *Ohio* somewhere up ahead. Either way, however, his own orders were clear. The bad guys had just taken a shot at the good guys . . . and now the good guys could shoot back.

Circling around to the rear of the Kilo, he brought the *Manta* into line with its tail, about two hundred feet astern and a bit high, looking down on her afterdeck. He touched three spots on his touch screen, arming one of the fighter sub's torpedoes.

On the joystick, his thumb came down on the firing trigger.

"Fire one!"

It seemed appropriate.

Friday, 27 June 2008

XSSF-1 *Manta*
North of Jazireh-ye Forur
Persian Gulf
0613 hours local time

Just as revolutionary new technologies had opened a whole new world for submarines in high-speed heavier-than-water "flying" craft like the *Manta*, they had opened a new world in underwater weaponry as well. The perfect example was the rocket torpedo.

A Russian invention named "Shkval," for "squall," the rocket torpedo had a range of 7,500 yards and could travel at an unheard-of 200 knots—about 230 miles per hour. Western intelligence had been following the Russian development program for a long time. In 1998, China had purchased forty of the weapons, and there were reports that a Chinese naval officer had been aboard the ill-fated *Kursk* to observe Shkval test firings.

The western press first learned of the device in April 2000, when an American businessman named Edward Pope was arrested by the Russian FSB and charged with espionage. Pope, it seemed, had acquired detailed plans for a revolutionary, high-speed rocket torpedo.

The weapon, in both its original Russian version and, now, in the American copy, was a solid-fuel rocket that lubricated its passage through the water by releasing a high-pressure stream of bubbles from its nose, coating its entire body in a thin layer of gas. The process, called "supercavitation," essentially allowed the torpedo to travel at high speed inside an envelope of gas, which tremendously reduced drag from the surrounding water.

The original Shkval had been a three-ton monster designed to carry a tactical nuclear warhead fired by a simple timer, and was intended to take out U.S. aircraft carriers or other big-ticket items. Later versions had carried conventional warheads, and one application had been to use the high-speed capability to quickly put a warhead in the general area of an enemy ship, then slow to conventional speeds in order to conduct a search and home on the target.

The new American Stormwind Supercavitating Torpedo (Rocket), or STR, was considerably smaller, and had been designed with the *Manta* and various drone weapons platforms in mind. It carried only a small H.E. warhead—euphemistically referred to as a "lethality enhancer"—relying for most of its punch on mass and speed to achieve a kinetic kill. When a half ton of rocket hit the hull of a submarine at 230 miles per hour, it didn't need much in the way of high explosives to finish the job.

The *Manta* carried two of the weapons, nestled within an internal bay. When Hawking keyed the touch screen, the bay had opened and one of the STRs was lowered into the water. Its bubble jet switched on, and when Hawking pressed the trigger, it released, the rocket engine firing several seconds later.

A simple-minded active sonar guided the weapon in. Hawking felt a jolting lurch as the weapon fired, then watched a white streak of bubbles instantly appear, stretching from beneath the *Manta* to a point on the Kilo's hull on the upper deck just abaft of the sail.

For a longtime science fiction fan who'd been raised on *Star Trek,* the effect was remarkably similar to firing phasers. A large hole magically appeared in the Kilo's aft deck; an instant later an enormous, silvery blob of air exploded from the hole, rising.

The warhead possessed a slight time delay. As the air bubble expanded upward, the entire submarine shuddered, the hull visibly crinkling in places with the stress. More bubbles appeared from a dozen spots on the hull, and the sail appeared to wrench to port and crumple.

The shockwave hit Hawking almost immediately, and he found himself struggling to keep the *Manta* upright and in control. At fifty knots, he hit the expanding pressure wave, and the effect was much like flying into a solid wall. For several moments he had no attention at all to spend on the stricken Kilo; it was all he could do to keep the *Manta* from stalling out as the shockwave not only reduced his forward speed to zero, but actually swept him backward like a leaf caught in a gale.

Gradually, the stubborn little vehicle responded to his commands. He put the *Manta* into a dive to pick up speed, then reengaged the engine. "Note to R and D," he said aloud, as if addressing an invisible audience. "Next time, don't shoot the damn thing from point-blank range!"

Gently, he pulled up, leveling off at a depth of fifty

feet and a speed of fifteen knots. Warning lights flashed; he ignored them. He was transfixed by the scene below.

"Whoa," he said.

The Kilo had already hit the seabed, at a depth of less than a hundred feet here. Under *Manta*'s powerful forward lights, he could see large chunks of hull plating and debris that had broken off and fallen to either side, and the entire fair-water had torn free, ripping a huge gash through the upper deck just about where the control room had been. Bubbles continued to boil from the wreckage, and the water was filled with swirling bits of flotsam—sheets of paper, a tennis shoe, something that might be a bedsheet.

And a body . . . a man in uniform falling up toward the surface, an expression of shock and horror etched into his face that Hawking knew would be branded in his memory for the rest of his life.

Accelerating again, he began racing east, in the direction the Iranian torpedo had been traveling. He used his broadband sonar, listening for the homing ping of the weapon. The torpedo would have been wire guided, but the connection with the Kilo had been broken moments after launch; he didn't know if the torpedo had been dragged down with the sinking Kilo or if it had gone free and was now tracking the *Ohio*.

He began sending out his own sonar pings, searching for a small, fast, relatively nearby target. He increased his speed. For a long-range shot they would have had the weapon set for a fuel-conserving 35 knots; by now it would have covered a good half mile or more.

Damn it, where could it be?

Control Room, SSGN *Ohio*
Waypoint Bravo,
East of Jazireh-ye Forur
0614 hours local time

"You heard *what*?"

"Yes, sir! I'm definitely picking up the *Manta* somewhere astern. High-speed jet and active pinging. And . . . and breakup noises, sir. There was an explosion, and then the sound of a sub breaking up and sinking. There's no mistaking it, sir." The kid sounded shaken.

"Very well."

"Sounds like the Kilo following us had an accident," Shea commented.

"Yeah. An accident called Lieutenant Commander Hawking. Maneuvering! Slow to one-third!"

"Maneuvering, slow to one-third, aye, sir."

Stewart caught Shea's quizzical expression. "Just letting our fly-boy catch up. . . . Helm, come left fifteen degrees." He wanted the sonar crew to be better able to hear what was going on back there.

"Helm, come left, one-five degrees, aye."

"Torpedo!" came the sudden call over the intercom. "Torpedo in the water! Coming in dead astern!"

Shit! "Maneuvering! All ahead flank!"

"Maneuvering, all ahead flank, aye, sir!"

As soon as *Ohio*'s speed had dropped to less than twelve knots and turned slightly, the broadband sonar was able to detect the telltale whine of a torpedo.

The Kilo, Stewart thought, must have popped a fish moments before it died.

XSSF-1 *Manta*
Northeast of Jazireh-ye Forur
Persian Gulf
0615 hours local time

There it was. Homing on its sonar return, Hawking had finally spotted the Kilo's torpedo, still on course. He could also "see," in the sonar sense, the *Ohio* several miles ahead.

The torpedo had acquired the *Ohio,* and was closing now for the kill.

Hawking wrestled for a moment with a dilemma. How was he supposed to stop a torpedo traveling at 35 knots without setting the thing off and blowing himself in the process? When he began the chase, he'd been toying with the vague idea, in the back of his mind, that he could match speed with the thing and possibly give it a tap with one of the *Manta*'s extended wings, or bump it from behind. A light nudge might knock it into the seabed, damage its sensitive sonar electronics, or knock out its screw.

But now that he could actually *see* the torpedo, he was having second thoughts. Some of those weapons had proximity fuses, and he might set it off just by getting too close. He also didn't know how sensitive the impact fuse was. If he bumped the torpedo too hard . . . would that detonate the warhead?

Okay, what other options did he have?

He had one STR left, but he didn't know if the rocket torp's homer could pick up such a small target, or if the guidance system was good enough to hit it. The shot would have to be perfect to destroy the Iranian weapon, and there was no third round for a second shot.

There might be a safer, surer way. Easing back on the throttle, he let the torpedo draw ahead of him, and at the same time he angled up, gaining altitude on it. When he was in position, he rammed the throttle forward, giving the *Manta* every bit of power he could.

His speed rocketed upward . . . sixty knots . . . seventy. . . . When he'd brought the *Manta* up, he lost sight of the torpedo, so he now had to guess at its position. When he thought he'd passed it, he shoved the joystick forward, going into a steep dive.

The seabed appeared, brilliantly marked by a fast-expanding circle of light from the *Manta*'s headlights. He pulled back on the stick, bringing the nose up. For an agonizing second or two the craft didn't want to respond; then the nose was coming up, but slowly . . . slowly . . .

. . . and then the nose pulled high, the sea floor dropping away behind him as he started climbing again. The torpedo . . . where was it?

The explosion caught the *Manta* from behind, flinging the craft end for end and slamming Hawking forward against his seat harness. White water exploded around him, and he found himself in the open air, flying, really flying, for just a second or two before he hit the water again and began to sink.

It had worked. By streaking down in front of the torpedo, he'd created a powerful wake that had sucked the torpedo forward and down, dragging it into a dive that sent it slamming into the sea floor. The explosion, though, had been way too close. Hawking studied the Christmas tree of flashing warning lights and raucous alarms. His engine was dead. Could he restart?

The *Manta* was sinking now . . . passing thirty feet. The water here, he noticed, was 110 feet deep; at least he wasn't going to be crushed by the depths, which was the big danger out in the open ocean. All he needed to do was hit the cockpit eject, and he would bob to the surface.

Of course, that would mean capture by the Iranians, who would not be real pleased that he'd just single-handedly sunk one-ninth of their total submarine force. They would also be able to recover the *Manta* easily enough, and there was quite a bit of classified equipment on board.

No, he was going to ride this out if there was any possible way to do it.

He cleared the compression chamber, powered up the start fan, and hit the ignition. Nothing. Sixty feet. He tried again. Seventy-five feet . . .

On his third attempt the engine fired, sucking in seawater, compressing it, expelling it astern. He nudged the throttle forward, feeding it more power. The engine temperature was still high, but the momentary shutdown had let the seawater cool it slightly.

There! The familiar pulse and throb caught hold. He pulled back on the stick and accelerated, reaching the critical flight speed of fifteen knots, and started climbing once more.

Okay . . . now where was the *Ohio?* He sent out another sonar ping, spotted her echo five miles ahead to the southeast, and started picking up speed.

Control Room, SSGN *Ohio*
Waypoint Bravo,
East of Jazireh-ye Forur
0618 hours local time

The crew cheered when they heard the explosion astern.

"Silence on the deck!" Shea barked, and the cheers stopped.

"Sonar, Control Room," Stewart called. "Do you have anything on the *Manta*?" He was wondering if Hawking had done something valiant and stupid, like diving into the torpedo to detonate it.

"Yes, sir!" came back Caswell's excited reply. "I lost him for a minute, there . . . but I hear him now. *Manta* is approaching from astern at three-five knots."

"Very well." Inwardly, Stewart sagged with relief. For hours now the lives of every man on board the *Ohio* had been riding on his decisions, one after the next, under insane stress and the knowledge that one mistake would kill them all. He also knew that his orders had sent Hawking out in an unproven prototype under combat conditions, another decision that could easily have fatal consequences for the *Manta*'s pilot.

For a few seconds he'd been convinced that he'd ordered the man's death.

"Control Room, Sonar! Torpedo in the water! Bearing one-eight-five, closing fast!"

From *ahead!*

"Helm! Hard left rudder!" They were already moving at flank speed. "Come to zero-nine-zero!"

"Helm, hard left rudder, aye! New course zero-nine-zero, aye aye!"

Stewart caught Shea's eye. "The trap closes," he said. "They were waiting for us."

Stewart listened for a moment. He could still hear the background chorus of active pinging. How many ships were out there looking for them? Too many to fight. The *Ohio* wasn't a hunter-killer like an L.A.-class boat. She was designed to take on targets ashore, not at sea.

"Control Room, Sonar. Torpedo has gone active, Captain. Range three thousand and closing!"

"Here we go again," Shea said. "How are you getting us out of this one?"

Stewart was touched that his exec seemed to still have faith in his ability to pull a rabbit out of his tactical ball cap. The truth was, however, that he felt like he was fast running out of ideas . . . and out of options. If they continued the turn to outrun the torpedo, they would be heading back toward the north, and toward the headland near Bandar-e Lengeh. Northwest, the way they'd come, lay the shallows of Charak Bay. Northeast, the shoal waters and coral reefs west of Qeshm Island.

And the entire southern horizon was ringed in by sonobuoys and approaching Iranian ships.

All he could do was wait until the torpedo was close enough to try another decoy, then turn south, hoping to slip past the enemy's ASW net.

"Torpedo range now at two thousand yards, Captain, and closing."

"We're also getting tonals, bearing one-nine-two. They match with that Ghadir-class sub we've been playing tag with. It's not active."

"The trap springs shut," Stewart said. "He must have guessed what we were up to and snuck around the south side of Forur Island so he could be waiting for us."

They needed help, fast, or the Iranians were moments from having them pinned.

XSSF-1 *Manta*
East of Jazireh-ye Forur
Persian Gulf
0620 hours local time

"Come on, baby, come on," Hawking coaxed his battered submarine fighter. "Hold together!"

The engine was cutting on and off erratically. It had

tried to perform an automatic shutdown three times in as many minutes, but each time Hawking had been able to override. He wasn't sure how much longer he could keep it going, however. He figured he had just about enough power left to get back to the barn.

And there she was! He could see the *Ohio* looming out of the murk ahead and below, a true leviathan, black above, dark red below, her fair-water so close to the rippling ceiling overhead it seemed to scrape it.

She was heading due east, and at full throttle, too. Why? Turning, he began sending out more sonar pings. In another moment he'd identified the trouble—another torpedo homing on *Ohio*'s wake.

And in the distance . . . more ships than he could number. His sonar picked up another submarine relatively close by . . . fourteen thousand yards to the southwest. The torp must have come from there.

Well, he knew how to deal with the torpedo now. He just needed to allow himself some more room.

Lining up on the weapon, he accelerated, ignoring the warning chirps from his console.

Control Room, SSGN *Ohio*
Waypoint Bravo,
Off Jazireh-ye Qeys
0621 hours local time

An explosion thundered from astern.

"What the hell was that?" Shea asked.

"Our guardian angel," Stewart replied.

"Hawking?"

"Hawking. I think he's found a way to bounce torpedoes off his wake."

"That son of a bitch. That *wonderful* son of a bitch!"

"Helm! Come right to one-eight-zero!

"Helm, come right to one-eight-zero, aye aye, sir!"

He looked at Shea. "It's time to run the gauntlet, Wayne."

XSSF-1 *Manta*
East of Jazireh-ye Forur
Persian Gulf
0624 hours local time

This time, he'd been well clear of the blast, using his wake to redirect the torpedo, but at a shallower angle. The concussion rocked him, but at least this time he wasn't flung out of the water.

Pulling the stick to the left, he adjusted his course to approach *Ohio* from the port stern quarter. She was turning, he saw, swinging around to the south once more. Passing above her aft deck, crossing port to starboard, he could only imagine what kind of reaction his fly-by would get from those on board.

Pulling right again, he slowed as he flew down the SSGN's vast side, which rose above him like a curving, smooth-faced cliff.

He noted that the ASDS was mounted in its accustomed spot on *Ohio*'s aft deck. Good. The SEALs had returned, had managed to dock with mother. That meant all they needed to do to get out of this mess was to find a way for the *Ohio* to sneak past the Iranian ASW forces.

From the sound of things, they didn't have much time.

He flashed past the huge, bulbous nose housing the

Ohio's delicate broadband sonar. "Sorry, guys," he said. "Hold your ears!" He passed across *Ohio*'s bow.

He was tempted to signal and attempt a docking. His *Manta* was fast failing, the engine overheating again, and alarms flashing warning of a dozen system failures.

The enemy was definitely closing on the *Ohio* now, coming in from all across the southern horizon, sonar blasting. They must have a very good idea by now of exactly where the huge submarine was. The ASW torpedoes would be flying fast and furious at any moment.

The *Manta* would not be able to deal with more than one of them . . . if that.

If only there was a way to jam the enemy sonar, he thought, the way fighter pilots could jam enemy radar. As with sonar, there were two modes in radar, active and passive—sending out signals, and simply collecting signals sent to you by others. Active jamming, he reasoned, generally involved beaming powerful radar signals back at an enemy transmitter, overwhelming it with radio noise.

It was too bad you couldn't overpower the enemy's active sonar transmissions the same way an EA-6B, the Navy's primary Electronic Warfare aircraft, jammed enemy radar.

And then the idea arose, clear, crisp, and perfect. Maybe there was a way after all.

He checked a compartment on his console. *Yes . . . still there.*

"O-kay, then," he said to no one in particular. "Let's get it on!"

Accelerating, he touched a control. . . .

Control Room, SSGN *Ohio*
East of Jazireh-ye Forur
Persian Gulf
0625 hours local time

"Control Room, Sonar." It was Chief Sommersby. "Sir . . . we're getting really screwy noises from out there."

"What kind of screwy noises?"

"I don't know. It's . . . well . . ."

"Pipe it through, Chief."

A harsh static of sound filled the control room. It was strange, like static, but with garbled bits and pieces of what almost sounded like music. Or a voice. And an insistent, driving *thumping*.

Stewart listened to the hash of sound for a long moment. He could almost hear words, choppy, broken, and fragmentary . . . nothing that he could make out. But that beat, that rhythm. Hard. Demanding. Compelling.

"My God!"

"You know what it is, Captain?" Shea asked.

"Yes, Wayne, I think I do. . . ."

Torpedo Room, SSGN *Ohio*
North of Jazireh-ye Forur
0625 hours local time

And in *Ohio*'s torpedo room, forward and two decks down, TM1 Rodney Moone looked at MM2 Jakowiac, a big grin spreading across his face. "Hey, dig it! That's our boy out there!"

"You mean? . . ."

"That, my man, is the Hammer goin' down! M.C. Hammer!"

" 'You can't touch this!' "

"Indeed you cannot! That is freakin' *righteous,* man!"

Accelerating, he touched a control. . . .

Control Room, SSGN *Ohio*
Waypoint Bravo,
Off Jazireh-ye Qeys
0625 hours local time

"Our flyboy friend," Shea said wonderingly, "is playing M.C. Hammer?"

"I think he is, Mr. Shea. You hear the beat?"

"I, ah, don't listen to rap all that much, sir."

"I think we are hearing the ultimate in driving by with the music cranked up too loud. He's drowning out the Iranians' active sonar!"

"He's also drowning out *our* sonar, sir."

"Doesn't matter. We'll stay on this course until we work our way into deep water. Maneuvering! Ahead full! Make revolutions for twenty-five knots!"

"Maneuvering, ahead full. Make revs for twenty-five knots, aye aye, sir!"

Control Room, SSK *Ghadir*
Southeast of Jazireh-ye Forur
0626 hours local time

Captain Damavandi was concerned. The Americans were showing unexpected resilience in this encounter, and were introducing unknown but sophisticated technology. Damavandi did not know what it was he was facing, and that made him nervous.

He refused to back off, however. He was still in the best possible position from which to launch an attack on the American submarine. He still had four tubes ready to go, while the fifth was being reloaded. He would fire four torpedoes, holding the fifth in reserve, just in case.

"Captain, Sonar."

Now what? "Go ahead."

"Sir . . . I'm getting a funny noise."

"From the target?" Perhaps they'd damaged the American after all.

"I . . . don't think so, sir."

Damavandi frowned. They'd all heard the explosion moments before, an explosion too soon to be a successful hit on the American submarine. Lieutenant Shirazi had also reported a loud throbbing noise, an underwater vehicle of unknown design, traveling as fast as a torpedo. An unmanned drone, perhaps?

And now this . . . "funny noise." What was going on?

"Let me hear!"

The sound began thumping from an overhead speaker. Damavandi listened, puzzled. It almost sounded like . . . music, of a sort. Muffled, broken and fragmentary . . . but he could almost swear he was hearing words.

But he couldn't understand them.

In any case, he didn't speak English, and he was sure that was what he was hearing.

"Captain, Sonar. Sir, I can't range on the target! I can't even track it!"

"What? Why not?"

"That . . . sound, sir. It's swamping all of our hydrophones. We're being jammed!"

Damavandi groaned.

The American had escaped once again.

Friday, 27 June 2008

Persian Gulf
0715 hours local time

It had taken time for the orders to reach their respective
destinations, time to prepare the weapons, to fuel them,
to double-check their navigational programming. At
0715 hours, however, the first Iranian missile, a Shahab-
2, rose along its vertical launch rail at the back of a
Russian-made GAZ truck hidden in a ravine in the Kuh-
e Namak, on the coast southeast of Bandar-e Charak,
and climbed steadily and with rapidly increasing speed
into the brilliant early morning light. The second missile
launched seconds later from a trailer outside of Khonz,
deep in the fastnesses of the Zagros Mountains.

The launches were duly noted by a U.S. military reconnaissance satellite some 350 miles above the Indian
Ocean, and the information flashed back to a processing center in northern Virginia, then to the Pentagon.

The launches were also detected by U.S. assets in the Persian Gulf theater of operations, by two Aegis missile cruisers in the Gulf, and by an Air Force AWACS orbiting above it on sentry duty. Before the missiles reached apogee above the Gulf, the alert had been flashed to commands throughout the Fifth Fleet.

And throughout the region, personnel already on high alert scrambled for their stations.

Control Room, SSGN *Ohio*
Persian Gulf
0719 hours local time

"I think, gentlemen, that we've made it."

This time, he let them cheer. When Shea started to say something, he touched his exec's shoulder. "Let them."

"Yes, sir."

For almost an hour they'd crept southward, hugging the sea bottom as Hawking and his infernal device— the nickname had caught hold and spread among *Ohio*'s crew—had zigzagged back and forth between *Ohio* and her pursuers, blasting away with M.C. Hammer's nineties hit at full volume. *Ohio*'s sonar department could no longer pick out individual Iranian ships . . . but if that was so, the Iranians could no longer pick up the *Ohio*.

You can't touch this!

XSSF-1 *Manta*
Thirty miles southeast of Jazireh-ye Forur
Persian Gulf
0722 hours local time

For the past thirty minutes the *Manta* had been moving more and more sluggishly, its power almost completely depleted. Hawking had managed to switch off most of the alarms—there was nothing more he could do about any of them—and reconciled himself to the fact that he was not going to be able to get back on board the *Ohio*. He did not have the power, nor did he have the control. It would be like trying to bring an F/A-18 Hornet in for a trap on a carrier, engine gone and hydraulics frozen—a sure recipe for disaster on the flight deck.

> *"I told you homeboy can't touch this! . . .*
> *Yeah that's how we're livin' and you know can't*
> *touch this. . . ."*

God he was sick of that song! His ears were ringing, and he was beginning to think that if he got out of this, he was going to have permanent hearing damage. But he would keep it going, cranked up to full, for as long as he could.

It seemed to be working. The Iranians hadn't closed with them, apparently hadn't been able to fire at them. The blaring noise from "You Can't Touch This" had created a huge dead zone within which Iranian sonar simply couldn't get a lock.

With a dwindling whine behind the thumping beat of the music, the *Manta*'s engine dead, the fighter sub began drifting toward the sea floor.

It was time to punch out. Lifting a safety cap, he pressed the button beneath, arming the cockpit jettison.

Then he grabbed the red-and-white-striped ejection le-
ver on the deck between his feet—a fair analogue for
the eject handle in a fighter cockpit, and pulled.

Nothing happened.

"So move out of your seat . . .
And get a fly girl and catch this beat . . ."

He pulled again, worried now. And still no response.
Hawking checked the constellation of warning lights
on his console, hit a reset, and checked again. Damn it,
what was the problem with this thing?

There it was. He hadn't noticed it with all the other
damage and malfunction warnings. The cockpit jettison failure light was lit. Somehow—probably during
that first near-miss north of Forur Island—the mecha-
nism had been jammed.

He was stuck.

He settled to the sea bed relatively gently. It was
dark—the depth here was 135 feet—but he could make
out mud swirling up from the bottom.

For a long moment Hawking tried to control the
pounding in his chest, the rasp of his breathing. Panic
hammered at him from some dark corner of his mind—
terror of close spaces, of being helpless, of being in the
dark.

The last thing to go was electrical power for his cockpit. The lights faded away and M.C. Hammer's voice
drawled to an uncertain halt. In silence and in darkness, the *Manta* rested on the sea bottom, its pilot now
encased in a water-shrouded tomb.

Trapped.

Persian Gulf
0722 hours local time

Over the past five minutes three more Shahab-2 ballistic missiles had roared into the early morning skies above Iran, rising to a height of several miles, then pitching over on trajectories ranging from south to almost due west, depending on their launch point. There were now five missiles in the air, and more were nearing readiness on the ground.

Target analyses conducted both in Washington and in the Gulf all drew conclusions based on the evidence of the contrails now scratching their way across the sky over the Gulf. The incoming missiles all were targeting a relatively small area within the Gulf of Bahrain.

The local missile defenses were already on full alert.

For some time now the United States and Israel had worked on joint exercises against just this sort of attack. Code-named Juniper Arrow, they were designed to train personnel and test equipment in antimissile defenses against an adversary to the east that, though identified only as "Red," just happened to speak Farsi. Those exercises had linked Israel's Arrow-2 system, which was designed to intercept incoming missiles at high altitudes in order to reduce the fallout danger from nuclear warheads, and U.S. Patriot missile batteries, designed to intercept missiles at lower altitudes, a second line of defense. Coordination was handled by a U.S. Aegis missile cruiser in the Gulf, which also possessed antimissile systems.

Juniper Arrow had also served as a political weapon, a means of announcing to other nations in the region the fact that America and Israel possessed antiballistic missile capability, and that attacks using such weapons, even missiles carrying nuclear warheads, were by no means assured of success.

That uncertainty was, itself, an important weapon in modern warfare; if the other fellow might be able to survive the initial attack, that fact in itself was a strong deterrent.

And in warfare *nothing* is certain.

Unfortunately, people being people, deterrence at times breaks down. As the missiles streaked toward Bahrain, members of Iran's religious leadership were on live television, announcing the fact that America's unwanted presence was now being cleansed from the Persian Gulf, that Iran was standing against the Great Satan, that Shi'ite Iran was prepared to carry the green banner of Islam in the name of *all* who honored the Prophet.

Control Room, SSGN *Ohio*
Persian Gulf
0722 hours local time

"We've lost all contact with Commander Hawking, sir," Caswell reported. "He's stopped transmitting, and we're not getting anything on active."

"Can you pinpoint where you lost him?"

"Approximately, sir. But only *very* approximately."

"Keep on it. I want him found."

"Aye, sir."

"What do you think happened?" Shea asked.

"I don't know. We're clear of Iranian ASW activity. But I suppose a helicopter or something could have spotted him."

"No explosions."

"No." Stewart thought for a moment. "He might have

suffered damage earlier. Or just pushed the sub-fighter beyond its limits. This was its first use in combat. Combat, real combat, always pushes new systems to their absolute limits . . . and beyond."

"People, too."

"Yes. People, too."

"Doesn't that thing have an escape pod, or something?"

"It's designed to release the cockpit module and let it float to the surface. It has an automatic distress beacon. We'll find it. Diving Officer! Bring us to periscope depth."

"Come to periscope depth, aye aye."

Stewart walked to the periscope dais. "We'll stick our mast up for a quick listen, see if we can pick up his beacon. He can't be more than a mile or so away."

Persian Gulf
0723 hours local time

During the first Gulf War, Iraq, under Saddam Hussein, fired seventy-seven ballistic missiles at Saudi Arabia and at Israel during the space of fifty-six days. The weapon he used was a modification of the Russian Scud, renamed the al-Hussein, which despite design changes remained a primitive device little changed from the V-2 terror weapons launched by the Nazis against Great Britain during WWII.

During that conflict, a great deal of notoriety descended on the U.S. Patriot missile system. Initially, that notoriety was positive in tone, and the system was hailed as "the defender of U.S. troops in the Gulf." Later, however, that image changed.

The Patriot missile had originally been designed in the 1970s strictly as an antiaircraft weapon. In the 1980s it was modified to also provide limited defense against short-range ballistic missiles, such as the Scud. It was not actually tested in combat until the first Gulf War in 1991.

A Patriot missile is 7.4 feet long and propelled by a single-stage solid fuel motor that accelerates it to speeds of around Mach 3 and out to a range of forty-three miles. The missile itself weighs 2,200 pounds, which includes a two-hundred-pound high-explosive warhead triggered by a proximity fuse. When the warhead detonates, shrapnel tears through the target like a blast from a shotgun, shredding guidance and other delicate systems. Guidance was carried out entirely from the ground, through a system called TVM, or Track Via Missile. Radar and high-speed computers tracked the missile and redirected it in flight to intercept the target.

Initially, the U.S. Army claimed a success rate against Saddam's missiles of eighty percent over Saudi Arabia and fifty percent over Israel. Later, however, as data from the conflict was reviewed, those claims were scaled back to seventy and forty percent.

In fact, the system probably didn't even perform that well.

Much of the problem was due to the fact that Iraq's redesign of the original Russian Scud design, which had increased the weapon's speed, had also weakened its structure. Al-Hussein missiles tended to break up as they reentered the atmosphere in the descent phase of their trajectory, which provided Patriot tracking radars with not a single target, but many, tumbling out of control. In some cases the detonation of Patriot warheads had helped break up the Iraqi missiles and push the fragments off-course.

Scuds, however, were already extremely limited in terms of their precise targeting ability. Guided by a primitive gyroscopic navigation system, they had a CEP of three kilometers. The CEP defined the radius of the area within which an incoming missile had a fifty-percent chance of striking. This made them effective as terror weapons aimed at cities, but virtually useless against small targets such as airfields or ships. Being blown off-course by a Patriot missile had little effect on whether they hit a specific target, since their fall was almost totally random in the first place. Some critics claimed that the Patriot defenses actually made the damage inflicted against Israel *worse*.

By the beginning of the new millennium, however, things were changing rapidly in the field. Iran's missile program, aided by technology provided by China, North Korea, and Russia, had reduced the CEP of the Shahab series of ballistic missiles to something less than one kilometer. This was still too large an area to allow pinpoint targeting of something like an individual ship, but it did encourage Iran's military planners to think in terms of a barrage of such missiles, all falling within a single, small area. One missile had a fifty-fifty chance of hitting a target a mile across. With ten missiles falling in that area, or twenty, or a hundred, the odds were that *something* important was going to be hit.

But Patriot technology had improved in the past decade as well. Stung by criticism of the Patriot's performance in 1991, the Army and its two Patriot subcontractors, Raytheon and Lockheed Martin, began working to improve the system's accuracy and its reliability.

The PAC-2, the acronym standing for Patriot Advanced Capability, was a far more accurate missile, with a flight speed of Mach 5 and much greater range.

By 2001, however, PAC-3 was beginning to come on-line. PAC-3 was a much smaller missile—a canister containing four could be loaded into the launch tube of a single PAC-2—weighing about seven hundred pounds. It had a velocity of Mach 5, and a special attitude-control maneuvering system allowing in-flight guidance, coupled with an on-board inertial/active millimeter-wave radar for its terminal homing phase. Unlike earlier Patriots, the PAC-3 was designed with hit-to-kill capability, though it also possessed proximity fusing in case it missed. The warhead consisted of 160 pounds of high explosives as a "lethality enhancer," but the kinetic energy of a missile hitting the target directly at Mach 5 would, it was hoped, detonate the incoming missile or, at the least, so completely fragment it that its warhead would be neutralized.

As five Iranian missiles descended on the northern end of the island of Bahrain, PAC-3 batteries surrounding the grounds of the U.S. CENTCOM headquarters at Juffair, five miles southeast of the Bahrain capital of Manama, came to life, the launch tubes swiveling automatically to face the incoming threat.

A dozen missiles streaked into the sky.

Control Room, SSGN *Ohio*
Persian Gulf
0725 hours local time

"Control Room, Comm."

"Control Room," Stewart said, pulling his face back from the periscope eyepiece. "Go ahead."

"Sir, we're not picking up Commander Hawking's beacon. There's nothing on the emergency frequencies."

Damn . . .

"But a priority flash is coming in by satellite. Urgent, and it's flagged 'new orders.' There's a live visual component, sir."

"Patch it through."

"Aye aye, sir."

The main bridge television monitor was showing the view through *Ohio*'s periscope, but it changed now to show the craggy face of Captain Thomas Garrett.

"Good evening, Captain," Garrett said. "Or . . . I guess for you, it's good morning."

"Good morning, sir."

"We've been receiving your intel packages. Good work . . . and congratulations on a mission well done."

"Thank you, sir." But Stewart knew that Garrett wouldn't be using satellite communications for a real-time conversation just to congratulate him.

"Captain, you are being assigned an urgent new mission, one of the absolute highest priority. Several minutes ago one of our satellites and an AWACS over the Gulf detected a mass launch of ballistic missiles from southern Iran. Those missiles are falling on Fifth Fleet headquarters as we speak."

"Jesus . . ."

"Our Patriot batteries are engaging them. We don't yet know how that will go.

"Your orders are to launch an immediate retaliation against Iran. Your principle targets will be identified missile batteries and mobile launchers . . . including, I might add, the mobile launchers some of your SEALs observed last night.

"Your targets also include Iranian radar and air defense assets along the coast, their port facilities in Bandar Abbas, several other military targets in the Bandar

Abbas region, and certain other targets of strategic importance.

"However, your *primary* target, with absolute top priority, is the facility code-named White Scimitar, near Bandar-e Charak, which your SEALs also investigated last night.

"We've been going over all of the data, from satellites and from your SEAL reconnaissance. We are uploading GPS coordinates and targeting data to your weapons system computer now, along with all necessary launch codes and authorizations. Do you understand?"

"Yes, sir."

"We will be putting together an appropriate military response using other assets in the region, but for now, *you*, Captain, are the sharp end of the sword. Our anti-missile capabilities are limited simply in the number of PAC-3 assets we've been able to deploy to Bahrain. The more Iranian missile launchers you can knock out in the next few minutes, the more of our forces will survive in order to retaliate."

"Sir . . . is there any evidence that the Iranians have initiated NBC warfare?"

"Not yet." Garrett's voice was grim. "We won't know for a while. But . . . that's why you must knock out White Scimitar as well. Before they move the weapons stored there. Before they decide to use them. Understood?"

"Yes, sir."

"Captain, carry out your orders."

"Aye aye, sir."

The control room remained silent for a long moment. Every man there had heard the orders and knew what was at stake.

"Weapons Officer," Stewart ordered. "Prepare T-LAMs for launch."

"Prepare T-LAMs for launch. Aye aye, sir."

Commander Hawking, if he was still alive, would have to wait.

The SSGN *Ohio* had a war to fight.

XSSF-1 *Manta*
East of Jazireh-ye Forur
Persian Gulf
0730 hours local time

Hawking had determined that he had about an hour left to live. He had that much air left in his reserve tank, which he was already breathing through his mask.

Damn it, *Ohio* should have realized he'd fallen behind. They'd made it past the Iranian ASW cordon. Why hadn't *Ohio* swung back to find him and pick him up?

One reason, he concluded, was the fact that he wasn't bobbing around on the surface right now in his cockpit module, broadcasting an emergency distress signal. And the *Manta*'s designers had not included a sonar transponder to pinpoint the sunken fighter sub's position.

Well, he could remedy that. Reaching down, he pulled his survival knife from its sheath. With the rounded end of the handle, he began pounding on the canopy above his head. *Thumpthumpthump. Thump-thump-thump. Thumpthumpthump.*

Three fast, three slow, three fast. SOS.

He hoped someone was out there listening.

Control Room, SSGN *Ohio*
Persian Gulf
0735 hours local time

It had taken several minutes to download the targeting data from the TMPC, or Theater Mission Planning Center, at Norfolk, Virginia. Now, however, the missile tube hatches, aligned in two long rows behind the ASDS on *Ohio*'s aft deck, were swinging open, two by two.

"Weapons Officer," Stewart said quietly. "Prosecute the attack."

"Prosecute attack, aye aye, sir."

The W.O. pressed a button on the BSY-1 Weapons System console.

The Tomahawk Land Attack Missile—TLAM—was *Ohio*'s primary weapon, replacing the Trident nukes she'd originally been designed to carry. The first missile burst upward out of the water, rocket engine firing; Stewart and the entire control room crew watched through the periscope's link with the TV monitor.

For the first few seconds of flight the missile rose swiftly on its rocket booster. Then the booster fell away, the wings and tail deployed, the turbofan intake opened, and the weapon was converted in mid-flight into an air-breathing cruise missile. Skimming the wave tops at an altitude of just a hundred feet, the Tomahawk flew north at 500 knots.

Thirty seconds later the second missile left *Ohio*'s number three launch tube.

Ohio's war against Iran had now truly begun.

Persian Gulf
0735 to 0805 hours local time

Normally, a Tomahawk strike of this scale against a hostile country would have been carefully timed so that all missiles arrived over their respective targets at about the same time. The missiles would also be deployed in at least two successive waves, the first to destroy radars and communications centers, the second to hit the targets defended by those systems.

In this case, however, the coordination of the strike was less important than its urgency. Bahrain was under sustained ballistic missile attack. The Shahab launchers—and White Scimitar—had the highest attack priority.

Following Terrain Contour Mapping programming, or Tercom, the first T-LAM went feet-dry over the Iranian coast near Kuh-e Namak, homing on a cluster of GAZ launchers identified by the SEALs of Delta Two. The terminal phase of its flight was controlled by a relatively new guidance system called Digital Scene Matching, or DSMAC, matching elements of the terrain as viewed through a camera in the T-LAM's nose with images stored in memory. Missile launchers, their launch rails already elevated to the vertical, surrounded by fueling and logistical vehicles, were relatively easy to find and identify.

The first T-LAM was of the variant known as T-LAM-D. Rather than the half-ton high explosive warhead of the conventional T-LAM-C, it carried a dispenser holding 166 BLU-97/B submunitions. Panels on either side of the Tomahawk blew out, and as it streaked low across the valley sheltering the Iranian missile launchers, it released a cloud of high-explosive bomblets. These had been designed to take out aircraft on runways by shredding their thin skins and vulnerable fuel tanks with clouds of shrapnel blasting down out of the air overhead, but they worked equally well against ground vehicles, personnel, and other soft targets.

Ballistic missiles, with their need to keep structural weight low in favor of higher fuel and payload weights, have no armor to speak of and were particularly vulnerable to this type of attack. Fuel and liquid oxygen tanks ruptured, as did the tanks of nearby fuel trucks. Delicate electronics and navigational systems were damaged, and guidance stabilizers punctured. It took remarkably little to damage a missile enough to prevent its launch.

More and more submarine-launched T-LAMs were now in the air. Two minutes after the first strike over Kuh-e Narak, a second T-LAM arrived, and then a third. Radar vans parked on a nearby hilltop were destroyed, as was a convoy of fuel trucks.

And still the cruise missiles kept coming.

At White Scimitar, in the valley above Bandar-e Charak, a T-LAM flew up the valley from the east, bypassing the main base and zeroing in on the leftmost of the eight tunnel entrances. The first missile was carrying special penetrator munitions to rip open the steel doors. The second T-LAM, arriving thirty seconds after the penetrator round, flew through the smoking hole and into the garage-sized tunnel standing open beyond. Half a ton of conventional high explosives lifted a portion of the mountain from inside and brought it smashing down in a fury of destruction.

The main base was taken out later by a T-LAM-D. For thirty minutes, however, missile after missile slammed into the tunnel complex higher up the valley, first opening, then sealing, the tunnels into the face of the cliff.

Somewhere beneath the crumbled face of a mountain lay Iran's first five nuclear warheads.

For her first strike, *Ohio* launched eighty-two T-LAMs

in various configurations, following the operational profile downloaded from the TMPC. Six of these failed in one way or another; two remained in their launch tubes, three lost guidance en route to their targets, and one was shot down by antiaircraft batteries outside of Bandar Abbas.

Within thirty minutes Iran's ballistic missile launch infrastructure throughout the southern district had been crippled, and much of their conventional military had been badly hurt as well.

As for Iran's attack on the Fifth Fleet, by the time the T-LAMs began falling on the launch vehicles, twelve more Shahab-2 missiles were airborne and heading south. The attack would have been more successful had the Iranians been able to launch a larger number of missiles simultaneously, but schedules were still dependent on too many variables—including both luck and simple delays in communications—and so Iran's missile salvo was somewhat ragged.

Of seventeen missiles put into the air, twelve were intercepted by PAC-3 counterstrikes and destroyed several miles out at sea. Another was hit by a salvo of Standard Missile launches from the Aegis Cruiser *Antietam,* operating off Manama.

Of the remaining four, three missed their CEP of six hundred yards by a wide—in two cases a *very* wide—margin, two coming down in the sea, and the third in the Saudi desert fifty miles to the southwest.

The final Shahab missile survived a near miss by two Patriot PAC-3s, breaking into pieces that sprayed down across northern Bahrain. The warhead, as it happened, remained intact, striking a dock in Juffair. The detonation of a ton of high explosives leveled three warehouses and a number of smaller buildings. Fragments struck the USS *Carl Vinson,* a U.S. Navy aircraft carrier in the process of getting under way several hundred yards from the blast. Damage to the carrier was light, and there were no casualties.

Luck—or perhaps the divine protection of Allah— were riding this time with the U.S. Navy.

XSSF-1 *Manta*
Thirty miles southeast of Jazireh-ye Forur
Persian Gulf
0815 hours local time

His arm was beyond tired, but Hawking kept hammering out his SOS. He was very nearly out of air anyway. It wouldn't be much longer now.

He was startled, then, when he heard a loud and urgent thumping on the *Manta*'s canopy. Opening his eyes and looking up, he saw the face of a diver, encased in a swim mask, looking down at him.

Saved . . .

Using emergency manual controls on the exterior of the *Manta,* the two SEALs cracked his canopy, allowing the cockpit to flood. Hawking gulped down a last, thin breath and held it, fighting against panic as the water swiftly rose. Seconds later the canopy opened wide and one of the SEALs pressed a mask against his face. He gulped down a sweet lungful of air. The SEALs helped him unhook his harness and swim free, an emergency air bottle clutched at his side.

On the last of his air, and with the SEALs on either side, he swam twenty yards, not to the *Ohio,* as he'd expected, but the ASDS, hovering a few feet off the muddy bottom. Hawking wouldn't learn until later that Captain Stewart, during a pause in the T-LAM launch series, had dispatched Mayhew and Tangretti on board the ASDS, using the craft's side-looking sonar to locate the sunken *Manta.*

What the media would later dub the War of the Missiles, meanwhile, continued.

Iran and the Persian Gulf
0805 to 0840 hours local time

The pause in the launch process had been to allow satellite reconnaissance of the various targets, and to give *Ohio* a chance to update the targeting data through her Command and Control System—CCS Tac Mark 2. Initial imaging showed a high degree of success in the first strikes, and also revealed new possible targets.

The second wave of launches began at just past 0815 hours, with *Ohio* releasing the rest of her T-LAM missiles. She was joined in the attack by the USS *Pittsburgh,* then on station in the Gulf of Oman outside the Straits of Hormuz. The *Pittsburgh,* a Flight II boat, carried fifteen T-LAMs in her VLS—Vertical Launch System—tubes, and twelve more that could be fired through her torpedo tubes. Where *Ohio*'s targets were predominantly the launch platforms for the Shahab-2 missiles, *Pittsburgh*'s attentions were directed primarily against naval facilities around Bandar Abbas, and to opening several keyholes within the peirmeter of Iran's air defense radar network. This last was important because U.S. military aircraft were already on the way with their own weapons, including F-117 strike fighters based in Kuwait and Saudi Arabia, and B-2 long-range bombers en route from Whitman Air Force Base in Missouri.

By the time the first U.S. aircraft arrived in Iranian airspace, there would be little left of her air defense radar or SAM systems.

Four of the first-wave Tomahawks launched from the *Ohio* remained in the air, en route to their targets. The T-LAM-C had a range of over seven hundred nautical miles. Flying complex paths designed to avoid the Iranian radar net, and hugging the rugged terrain as they crossed the Zagros Mountains, they were aimed at two different targets, which, by a straight-line path, lay 470 and 650 miles to the north. The nearer was an underground site at Esfahan, known to be a center for uranium enrichment.

The farther of the two was a site in downtown Tehran. . . .

Communications Center,
Office of the Ministry of Defense
Tehran, Iran
0912 hours local time

Admiral Mehdi Baba-Janzadeh was thinking about messages.

He was sitting in his office on the sixth floor of the Defense Ministry building in downtown Tehran, leaning back in his padded chair and sipping strong tea. What messages, he wondered, had this debacle delivered to the world?

Operation Bold Fire had been intended to deliver a very specific message to the Islamic world in particular. *Iran is strong. Iran can defy the hated West. Iran is the new leader of militant world Islam. Iran carries the banner that will unite Islam and bring the West to its knees.*

Reports from Bandar Abbas were fragmentary at best, but the mere fact that almost all communications with the south had been interrupted alone delivered a message to Tehran. The strike against the Fifth Fleet had not gone according to plan . . . and the Americans were striking back. Hard.

Minutes before, Baba-Janzadeh had completed a difficult phone conversation with the Supreme Leader. *Surrender now. Minimize the damage, and save what you can. Perhaps you can still head off this nightmare. . . .*

The Americans had a longer reach than any of Iran's military leadership had been willing to credit.

The first of the last two T-LAMs, its fuel nearly spent, smashed into the Defense Ministry's eighth floor. The half-ton warhead detonated an instant later, blowing out the entire floor and bringing down the upper half of the structure in a shower of debris.

The second T-LAM struck thirty seconds later, as the avalanche continued, plunging into the crumbling structure at street level and completing the destruction.

Message delivered . . .

EPILOGUE

Friday, 8 August 2008

TGI Friday's Restaurant
Bremerton, Washington
2115 hours local time

ST2 Roger Caswell walked into the TGI Friday's, an attractive young woman on his arm. "Kettering party?" he asked the hostess.

"Ah!" she said. "The noisy ones! This way, please."

It was Doc Kettering's birthday, and a number of the members of *Ohio*'s crew had gotten together to take him out to dinner. Plans included dinner here, followed by the requisite bar-crawling afterward into the wee hours.

Ohio had returned from her Gulf deployment three weeks earlier, her missile stores expended, to a tumultuous welcome at Bremerton Navy Yard. Over the next week, crew transition had taken place. It had been decided that the old Blue and Gold submarine crew system employed on board U.S. boomers would be retained in *Ohio*'s new incarnation. Caswell and his shipmates were part of the Blue Crew. Gold Crew had now taken over, and was busily outfitting her for her next deployment.

Which didn't mean Blue Crew was off the hook, of course. As always for submarine crews, there was training. And practice. And more training. And more practice.

But the five of them—Caswell, Kettering, Moone, Jakowiac, and Dobbs—had weekend liberty, beginning at 1700 hours that afternoon. There would be no studies tonight.

A big table had been set aside for the Kettering party. Moonie and Jak both had girlfriends along, and Dobbs had brought his wife. A special guest had come along as well, his officer's rank set aside for the evening. Everyone was in civilian clothing, so what did it matter? Gary Hawking—honorary submariner—had been enthusiastically welcomed when he'd asked if he could join them.

"Hey, Cassie!" Moone called, waving. "Get your ass over here!"

"And who is this young lady?" Kettering said as they walked up to the table. "I don't believe I've had the pleasure? . . ."

"Doc, guys . . . this is Kelly Martin. She's a . . . friend."

"Good to meet you, Kelly," Kettering said, rising. He looked puzzled. "But come to think of it, I do believe I've met you before somewhere."

Caswell grinned as he held a chair for Kelly. "Sure you have, Doc. Her stage name is Crystal. Crystal Light. She's a dancer over at BJ's."

"*That's* where I've seen her!" Jakowiac said, delighted.

"Ah," Kettering said, grinning. "*That* explains it. I didn't recognize you with your clothes on, Kelly."

"I thought you gals didn't date the customers," Moone said.

She smiled. "We're not supposed to. But . . . well, Roger was so sweet. He came to the club last week and we started talking and, well . . . we found a way."

"Love always finds a way!" Moone exclaimed. "So, Cassie, I guess this means you've forgotten all about Nina?"

"Nina who?" Caswell asked, his voice carefully neutral. The others laughed.

"Way to go, Cassie!" Dobbs said.

"I'm glad to see you getting out some, Cass," Kettering said. "Seeing people. Best medicine in the world."

"It's not like that, fellas," Caswell said. "We're just friends."

Hawking lifted a glass of beer. "To new friends!" he toasted.

In fact, he knew it would be a long time before he was over Nina. *Nina who?* was a little game he was playing, something to keep the bad thoughts at bay.

He'd had some long talks with Doc during the voyage back to the World. According to him, depression and suicide were *the* major risks to submarine crewmen. Medical personnel assigned to subs went through special classes to keep up on the psychological end of things. Even a sub as big as the *Ohio,* when you came down to it, was a tiny tin can stuffed full of people—an explosion waiting to happen.

This time, though, the explosion inboard had not happened, though Caswell still caught his breath when he thought about how close he'd come. It had been a near thing.

Possibly as near-run a race as *Ohio*'s surviving the Iranian ASW gauntlet. If it hadn't been for Hawking and his weird little craft straight out of the pages of science fiction . . .

A television set high up on a wall was giving the news, the sound turned down but the captions appearing in print at the bottom. The news tonight was all about soaring gasoline prices and the latest crisis in the Middle East . . . this one in Syria. Iran had already faded into the back pages of the world press.

The short, sharp missile exchange with Iran had lasted exactly eighty-five minutes. At that time, the Ayatollah Khamenei had issued a statement calling for an immediate cessation of hostilities, and offered to negotiate a lasting peace. Those talks were now scheduled for mid-September. No one knew what the outcome would be, but for now, at least, the shooting was over. Iran had pulled its forces out of Oman, and things in the region had gone back to their uneasy status quo. Radical Islamic voices denounced American aggression, equating it with terrorism, while moderate Islamic groups kept their heads down and their voices quiet.

If it was peace, it was an ominous and unsettled one.

But for *Ohio,* and the *Ohio*'s crew, there'd been a testing, and a kind of rite of passage. They'd faced combat, survived, and emerged victorious. *Ohio,* in her SSGN incarnation, had proven herself *the* premier system for littoral combat for the twenty-first century, a proven defense against state-sponsored terrorism, and a means of striking a decisive blow against any enemy that might threaten the United States for the foreseeable future.

And *Ohio*'s crew had proven themselves as survivors, and as victors, as well.

"Let me have a Coke," Caswell told the waitress

when she came by to take his and Kelly's drink orders a few minutes later. When she brought the drinks, he raised his high. "To new friends," he said, "but also to old shipmates and submariners."

They all drank to that.

EXPLOSIVE UNDERSEA ACTION
H. JAY RIKER's
THE
SILENT SERVICE

GRAYBACK CLASS
0-380-80466-2 • $6.99 US • $9.99 Can

The year is 1985 and reports have been received of a devastating new Soviet weapon, a prototype attack submarine more advanced than anything in the U.S undersea arsenal.

LOS ANGELES CLASS
0-380-80467-0 • $6.99 US • $9.99 Can

In 1987 a hand-picked team of SEALs will venture into the deadly, Russian-patrolled seas off the coast of the Kamchatka Peninsula to stop an enemy spy from leading a boat full of brave men to their doom.

SEAWOLF CLASS
0-380-80468-9 • $6.99 US • $9.99 Can

In the chaos of the first major conflict of the twenty-first century, the People's Republic of China sets out to "reclaim" by force the territories it considers its own: the Spratly Islands in the South China Sea . . . and Taiwan.

VIRGINIA CLASS
0-06-052438-3 • $6.99 US • $9.99 Can

A rogue Kilo-class submarine built by a shadowy and powerful ally has become the latest weapon in al Qaeda's terrorist arsenal. The sub's brutal strikes have created an explosive hostage situation in the Pacific . . . and have left hundreds dead.

OHIO CLASS
0-06-052439-1 • $7.99 US • $10.99 Can

They served vigilantly during the Cold War. Now an upgraded *Ohio Class* is poised to protect against an even more sinister enemy.

Visit www.AuthorTracker.com for exclusive information on your favorite HarperCollins authors.

SIL 0506

Available wherever books are sold or please call 1-800-331-3761 to order.